D0190443

HAMLET

ILLUSTRATED BY
EMMA VIECELI

Amulet Books, New York

Cataloging-in-Publication Data has been applied for and may be obtained from the Library of Congress.
ISBN 13: 978-0-8109-9324-2
ISBN 10: 0-8109-9324-4

Originally published in the U.K. by SelfMadeHero
(www.selfmadehero.com)

Illustrator: Emma Vieceli
Text Adaptor: Richard Appignanesi
Designer: Andy Huckle
Textual Consultant: Nick de Somogyi
Originating Publisher: Emma Hayley

Published in 2007 by Amulet Books, an imprint of Harry N. Abrams, Inc. All rights reserved. No portion of this book may be reproduced, stored in a retrieval system, or transmitted in any form or by any means, mechanical, electronic, photocopying, recording, or otherwise, without written permission from the publisher.

Printed and bound in China
10 9 8 7 6 5 4 3 2 1

HNA
harry n. abrams, inc.
a subsidiary of La Martinière Groupe

115 West 18th Street
New York, NY 10011
www.hnabooks.com

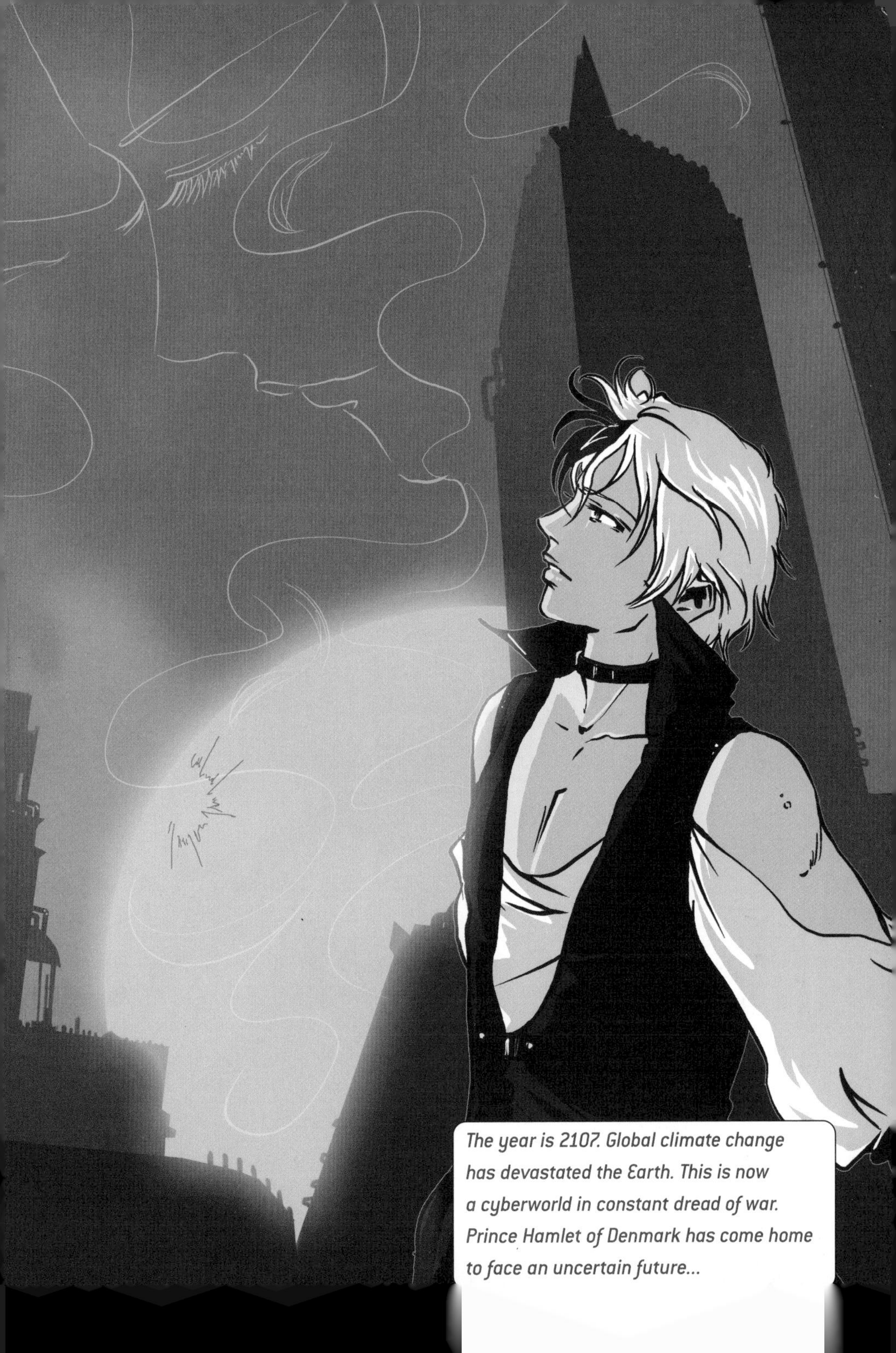
The year is 2107. Global climate change has devastated the Earth. This is now a cyberworld in constant dread of war. Prince Hamlet of Denmark has come home to face an uncertain future...

Hamlet, Prince of Denmark

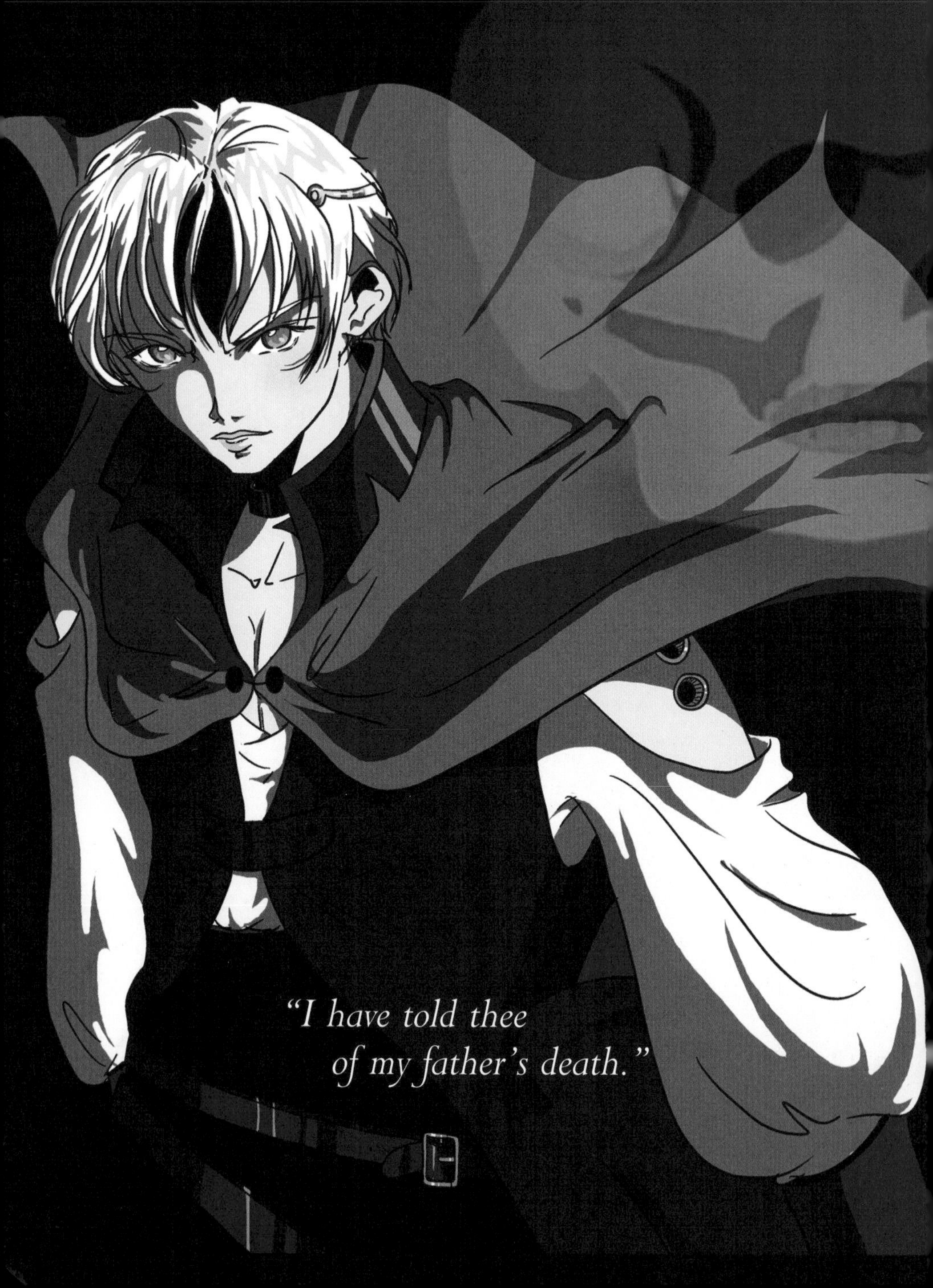
"I have told thee
of my father's death."

loyalty *betrayal*

Rosencrantz *Guildenstern*

Hamlet's so-called friends

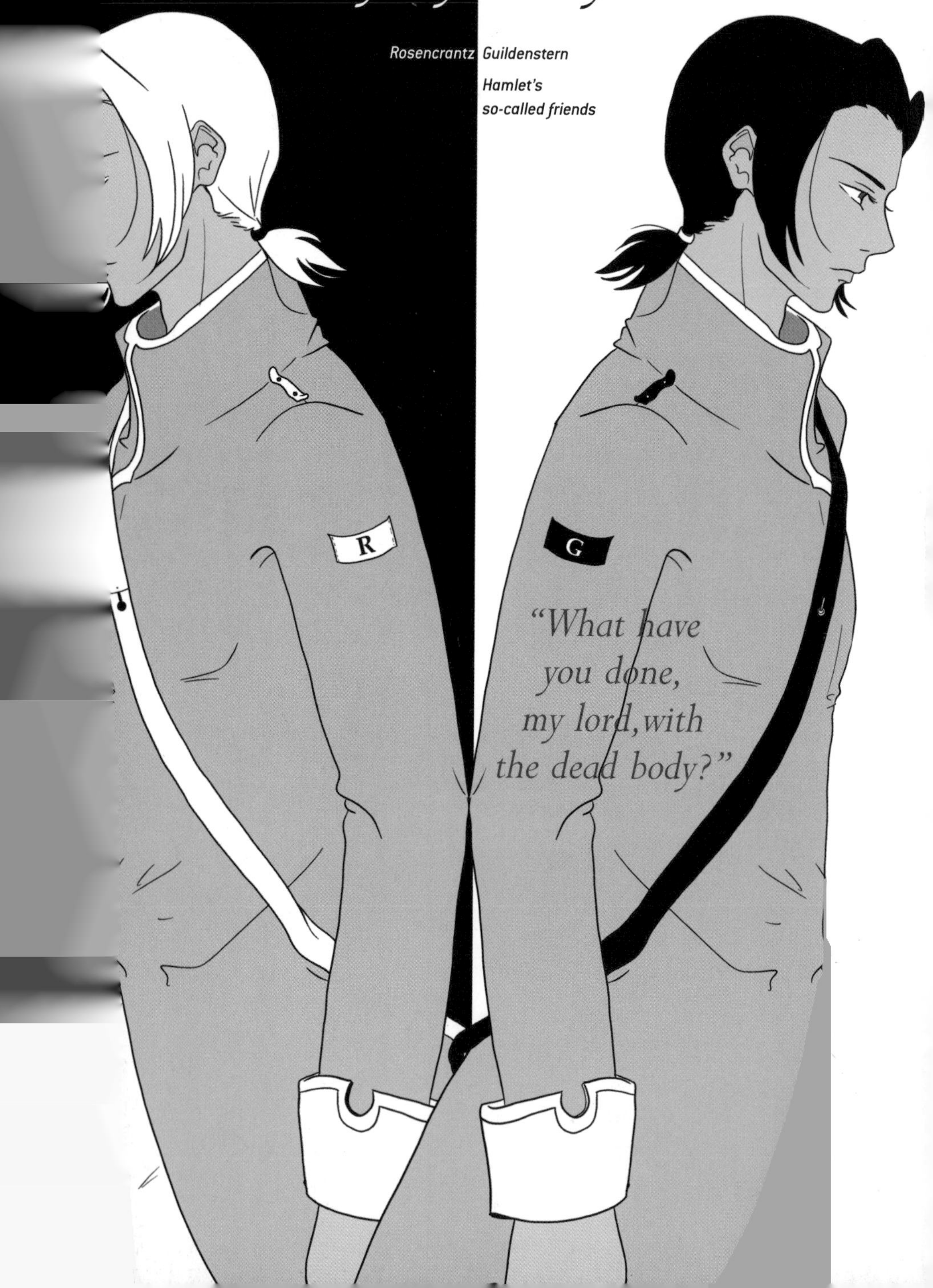
"What have
you done,
my lord, with
the dead body?"

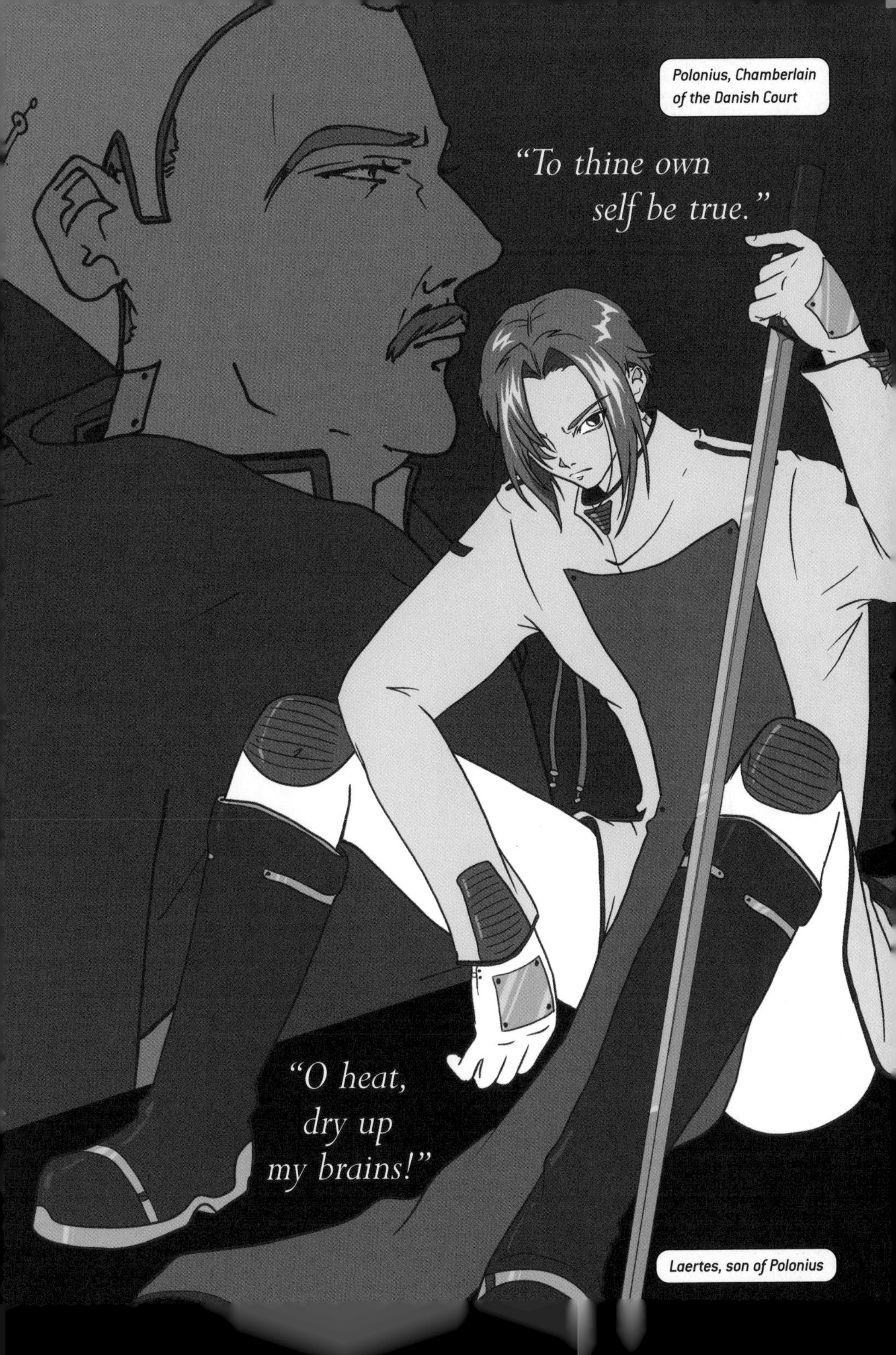
Polonius, Chamberlain of the Danish Court
"To thine own self be true."
"O heat, dry up my brains!"
Laertes, son of Polonius

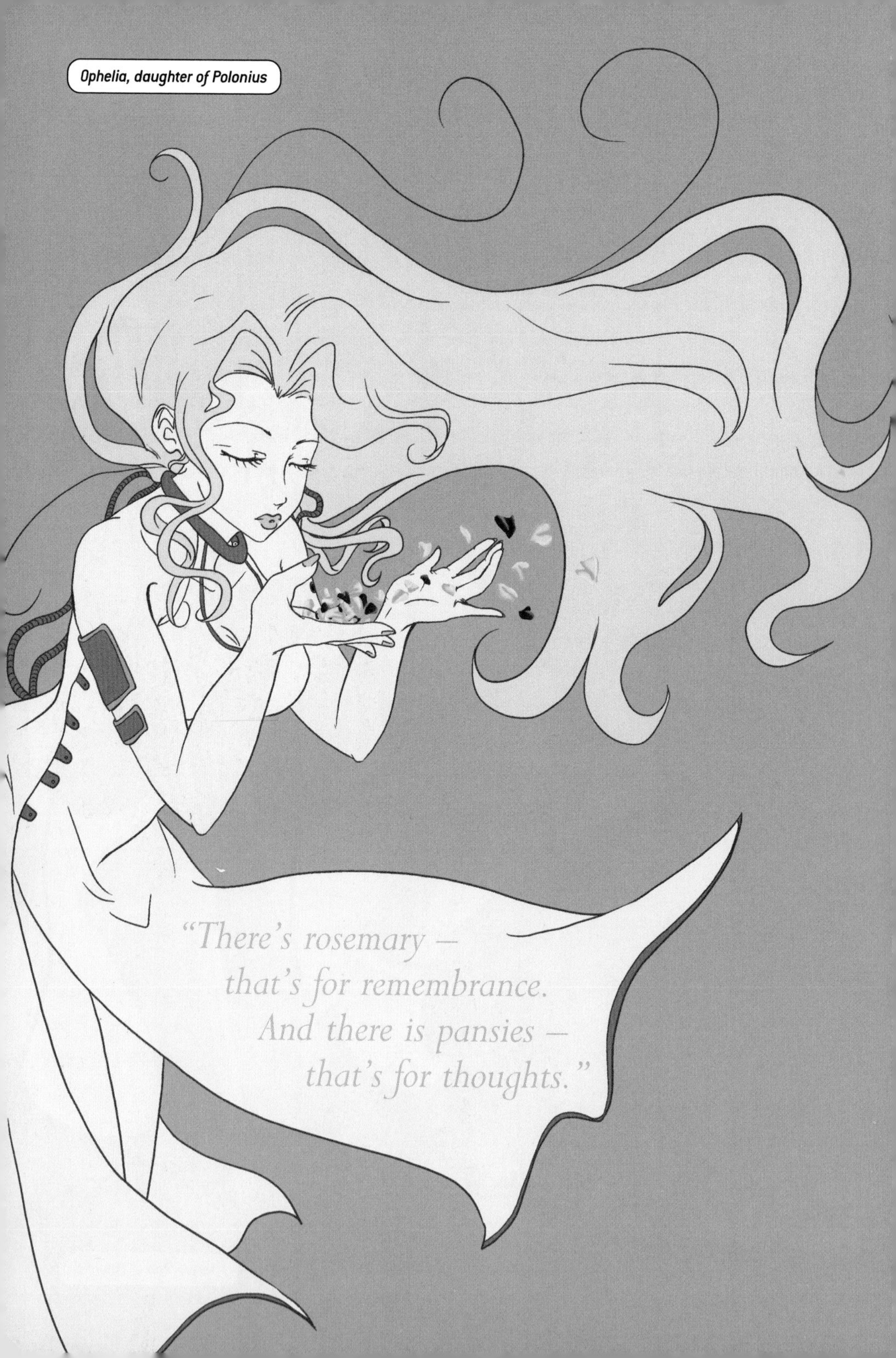
Ophelia, daughter of Polonius
"There's rosemary – that's for remembrance. And there is pansies – that's for thoughts."

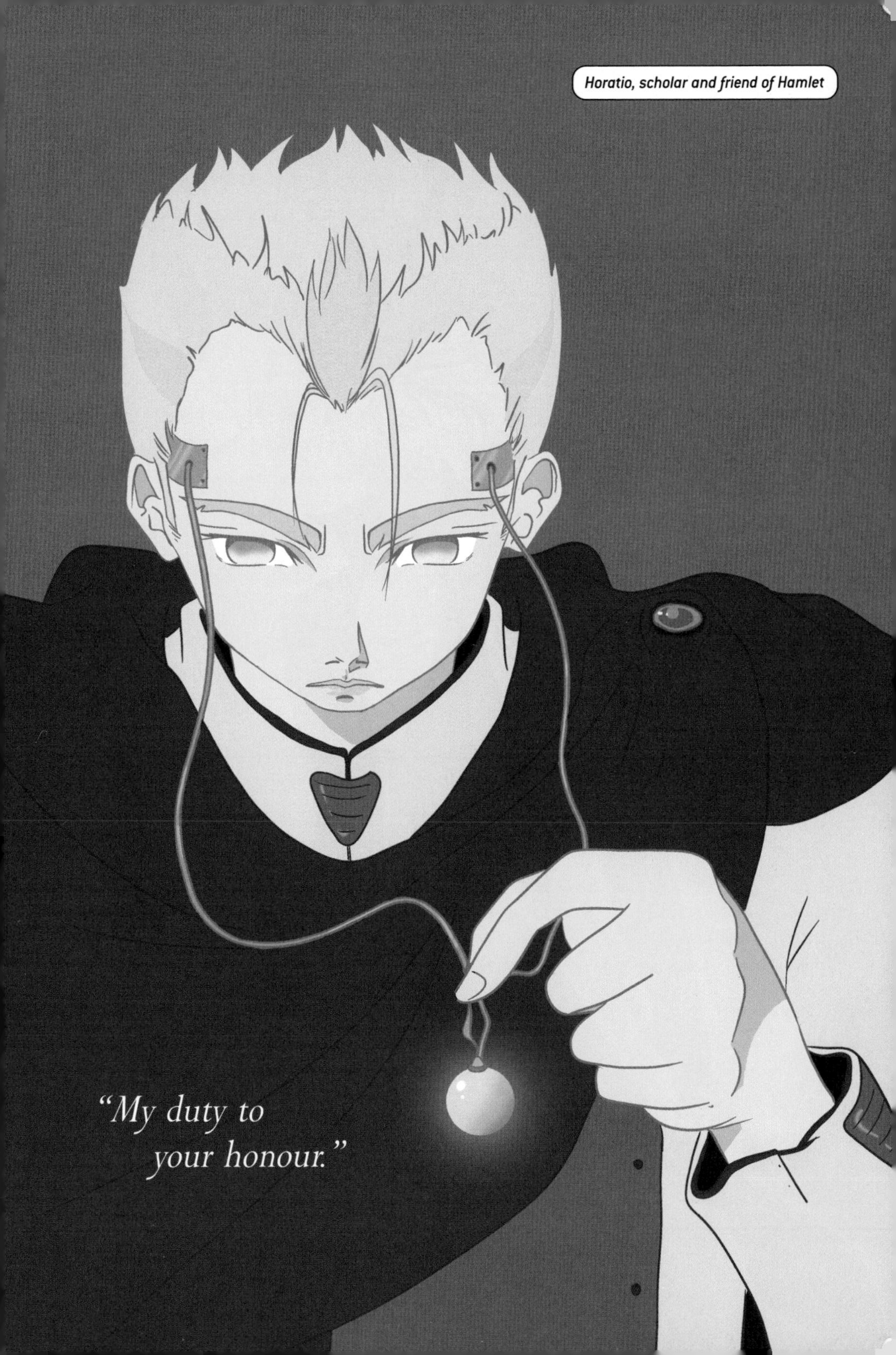
Horatio, scholar and friend of Hamlet
"My duty to your honour."

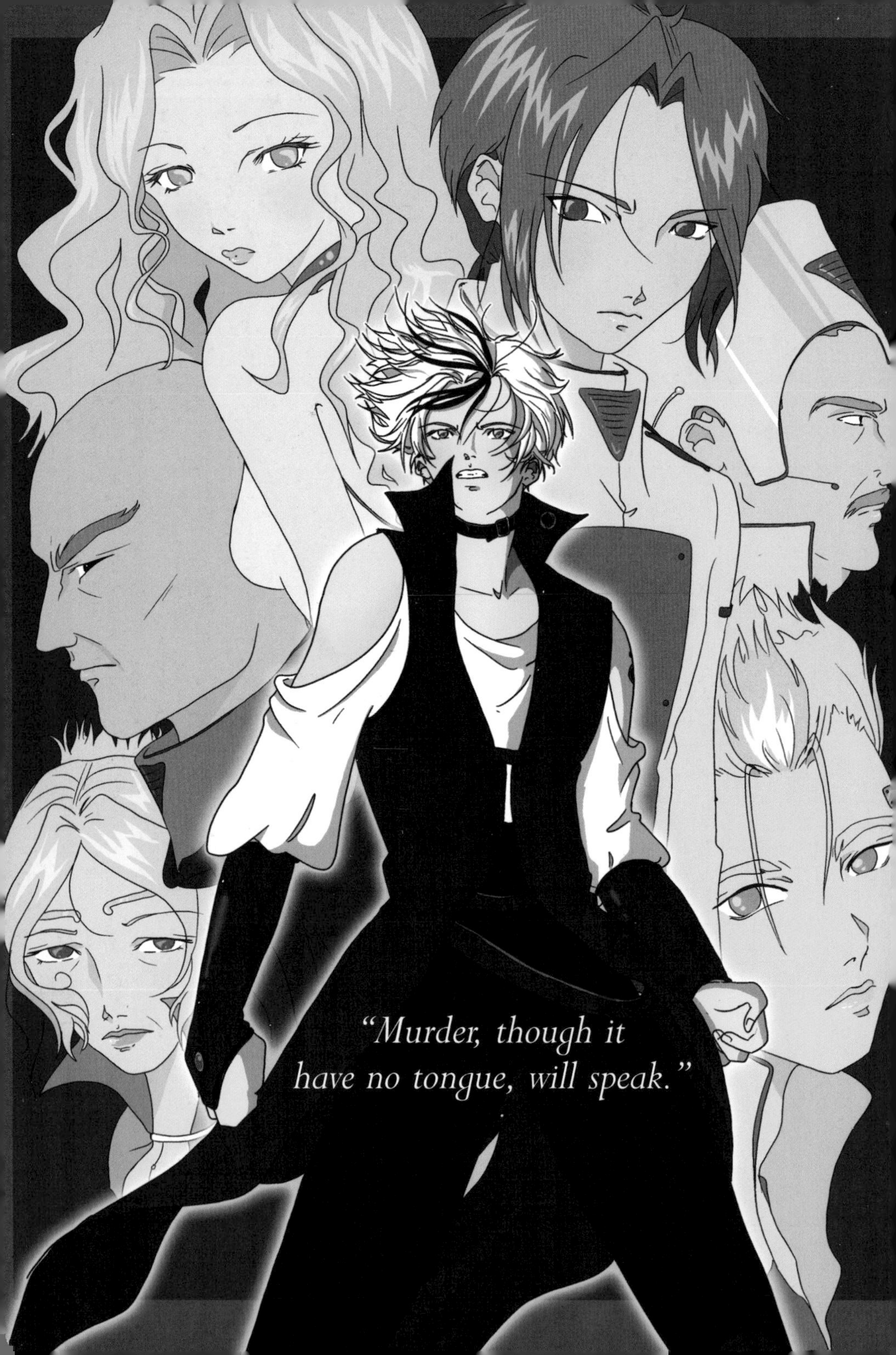
"Murder, though it have no tongue, will speak."

The Tragedy of

HAMLET
Prince of Denmark

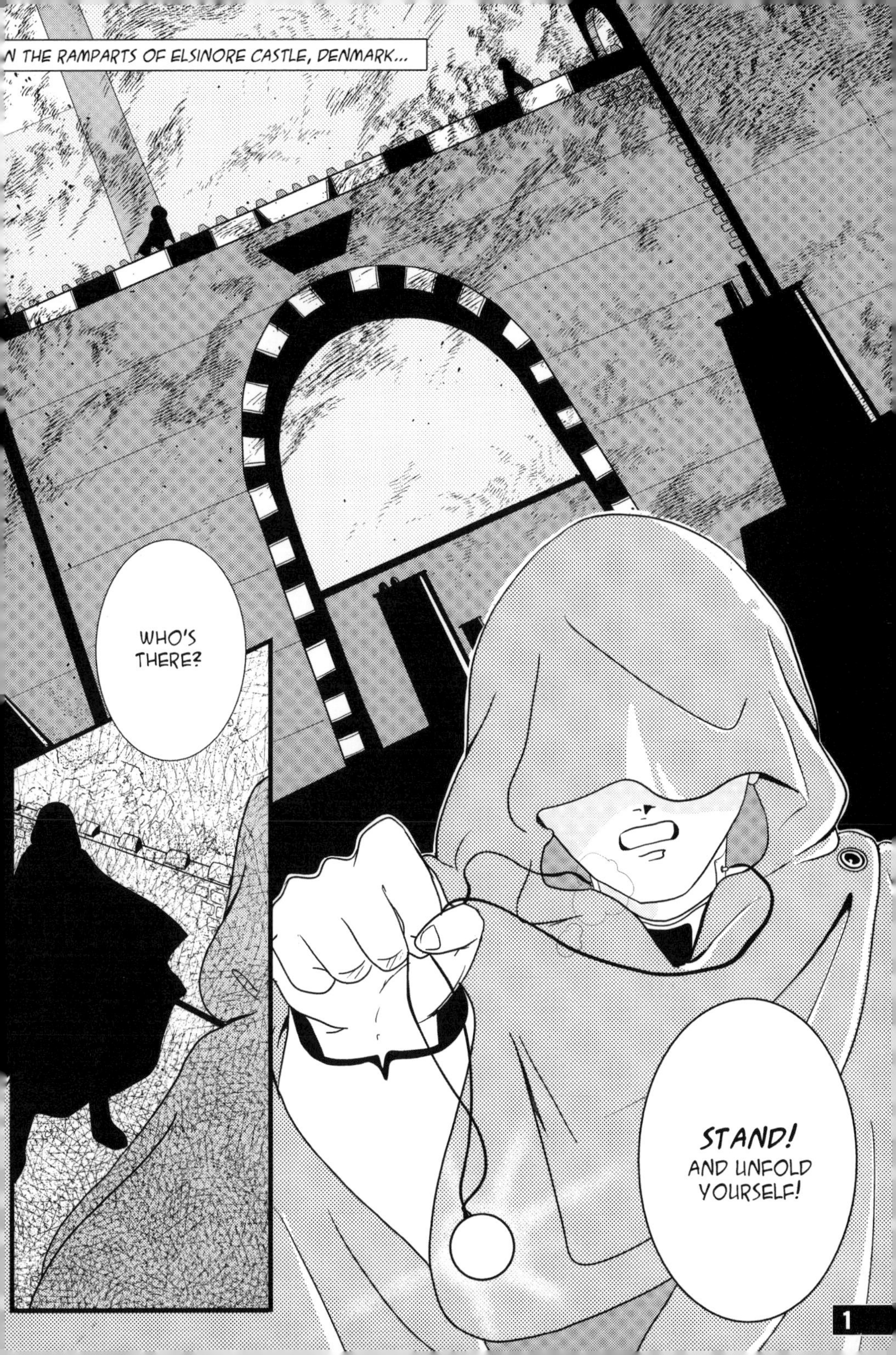
N THE RAMPARTS OF ELSINORE CASTLE, DENMARK...
WHO'S THERE?
STAND! AND UNFOLD YOURSELF!

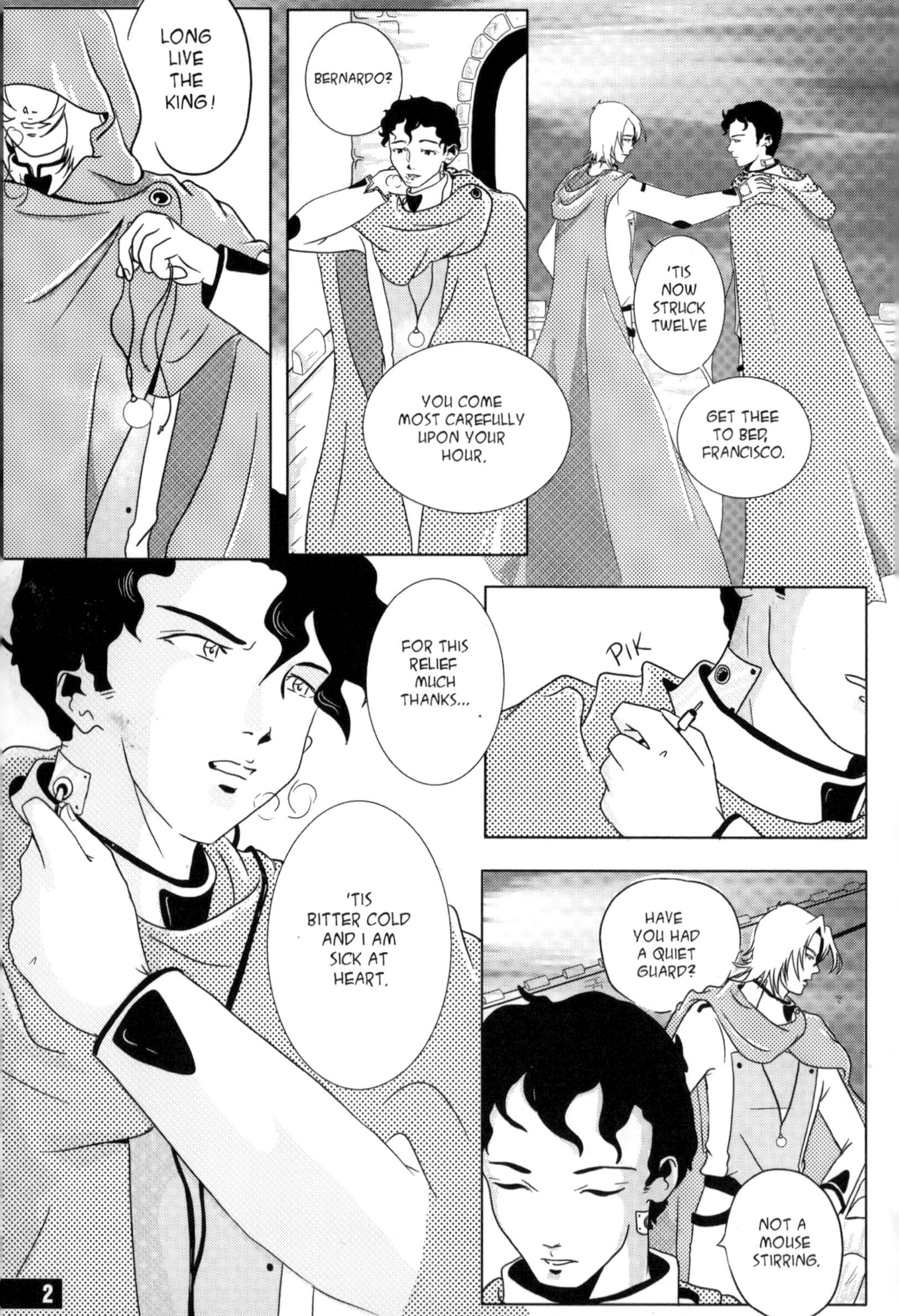
LONG LIVE THE KING!
BERNARDO?
YOU COME MOST CAREFULLY UPON YOUR HOUR.
'TIS NOW STRUCK TWELVE
GET THEE TO BED, FRANCISCO.
FOR THIS RELIEF MUCH THANKS...
'TIS BITTER COLD AND I AM SICK AT HEART.
PIK
HAVE YOU HAD A QUIET GUARD?
NOT A MOUSE STIRRING.

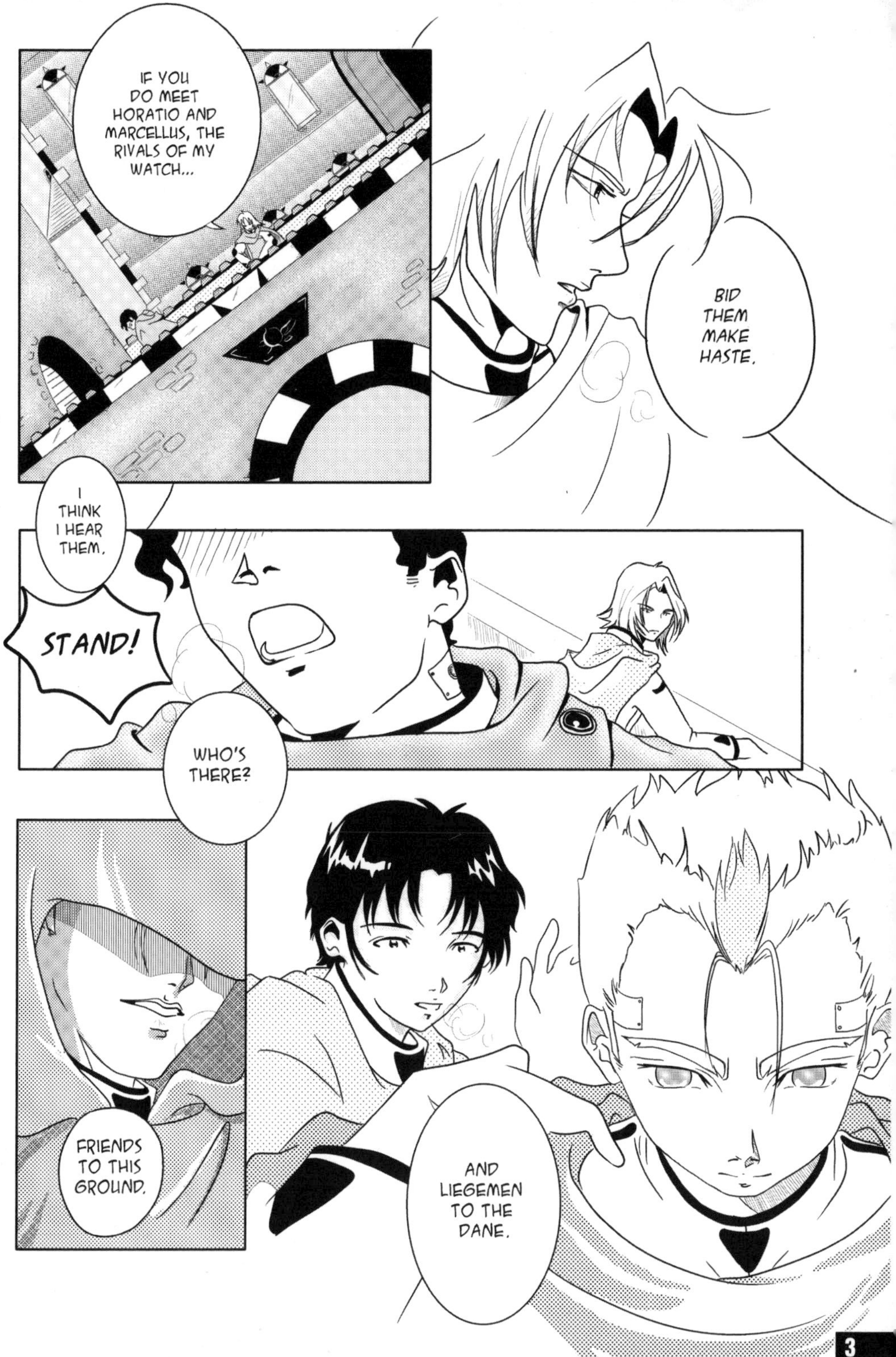

IF YOU DO MEET HORATIO AND MARCELLUS, THE RIVALS OF MY WATCH...
BID THEM MAKE HASTE.
I THINK I HEAR THEM.
STAND!
WHO'S THERE?
FRIENDS TO THIS GROUND.
AND LIEGEMEN TO THE DANE.

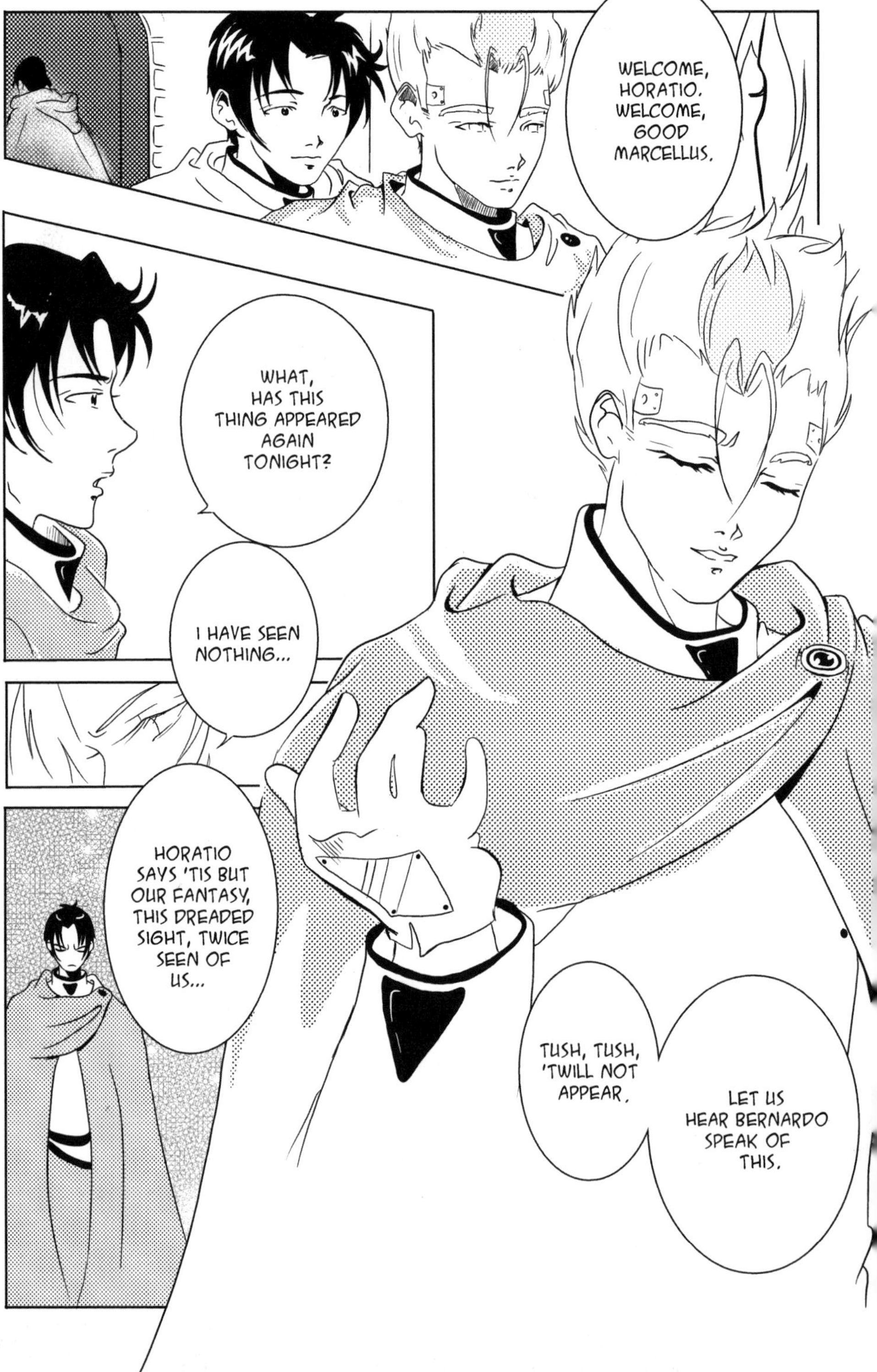
WELCOME, HORATIO. WELCOME, GOOD MARCELLUS.
WHAT, HAS THIS THING APPEARED AGAIN TONIGHT?
I HAVE SEEN NOTHING...
HORATIO SAYS 'TIS BUT OUR FANTASY, THIS DREADED SIGHT, TWICE SEEN OF US...
TUSH, TUSH, 'TWILL NOT APPEAR.
LET US HEAR BERNARDO SPEAK OF THIS.

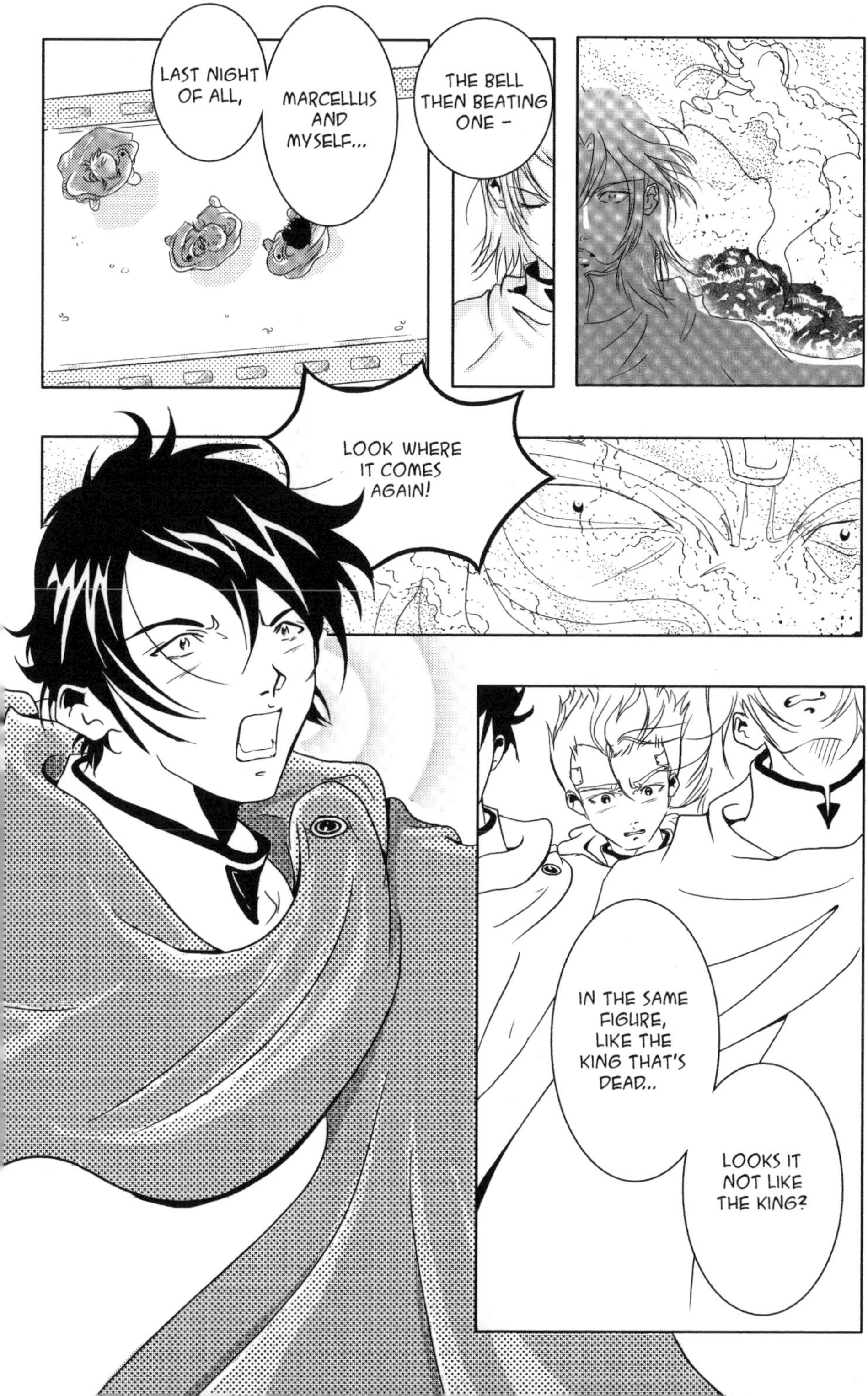
LAST NIGHT OF ALL,
MARCELLUS AND MYSELF...
THE BELL THEN BEATING ONE -
LOOK WHERE IT COMES AGAIN!
IN THE SAME FIGURE, LIKE THE KING THAT'S DEAD...
LOOKS IT NOT LIKE THE KING?

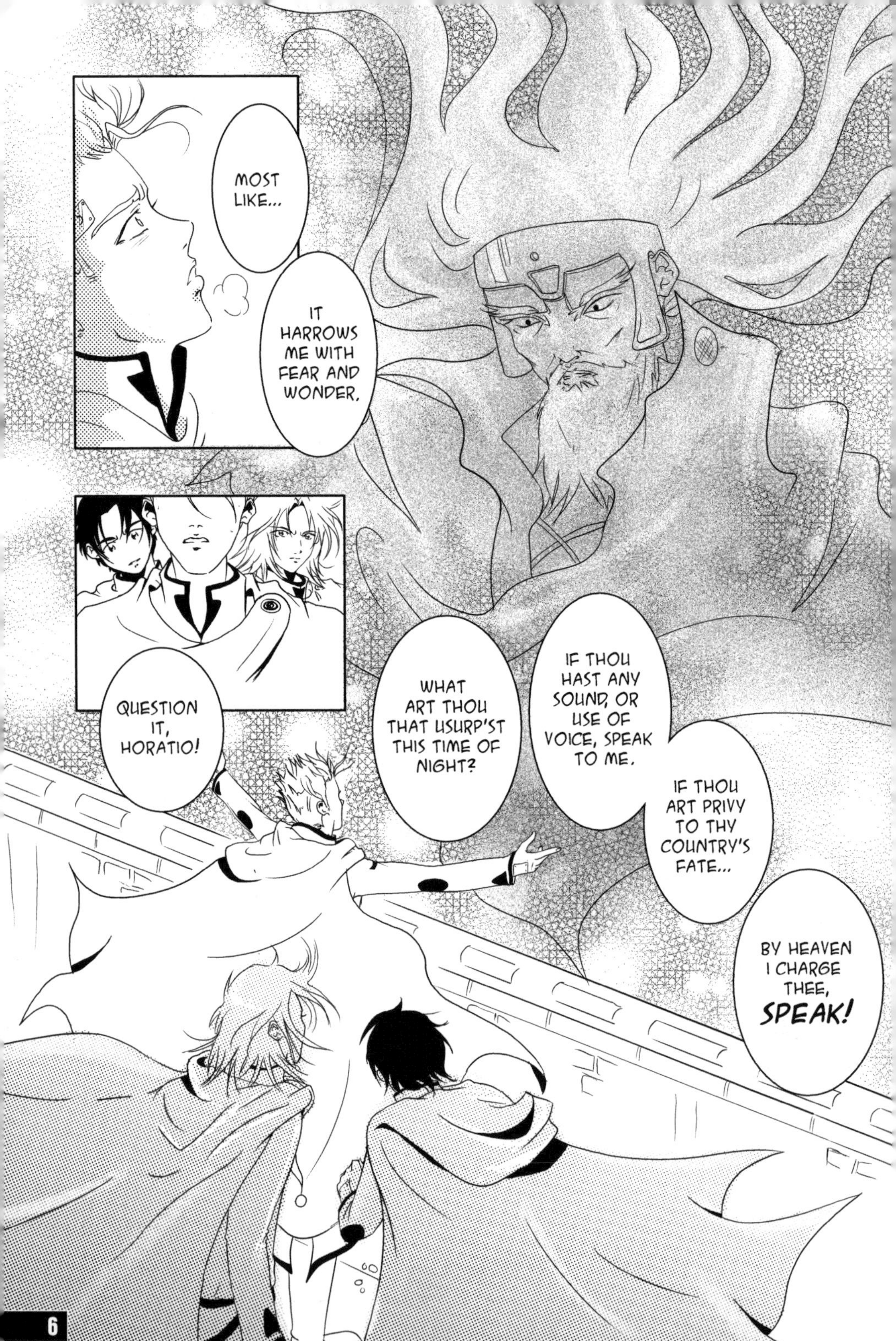
MOST LIKE...
IT HARROWS ME WITH FEAR AND WONDER.
QUESTION IT, HORATIO!
WHAT ART THOU THAT USURP'ST THIS TIME OF NIGHT?
IF THOU HAST ANY SOUND, OR USE OF VOICE, SPEAK TO ME.
IF THOU ART PRIVY TO THY COUNTRY'S FATE...
BY HEAVEN I CHARGE THEE, **SPEAK!**

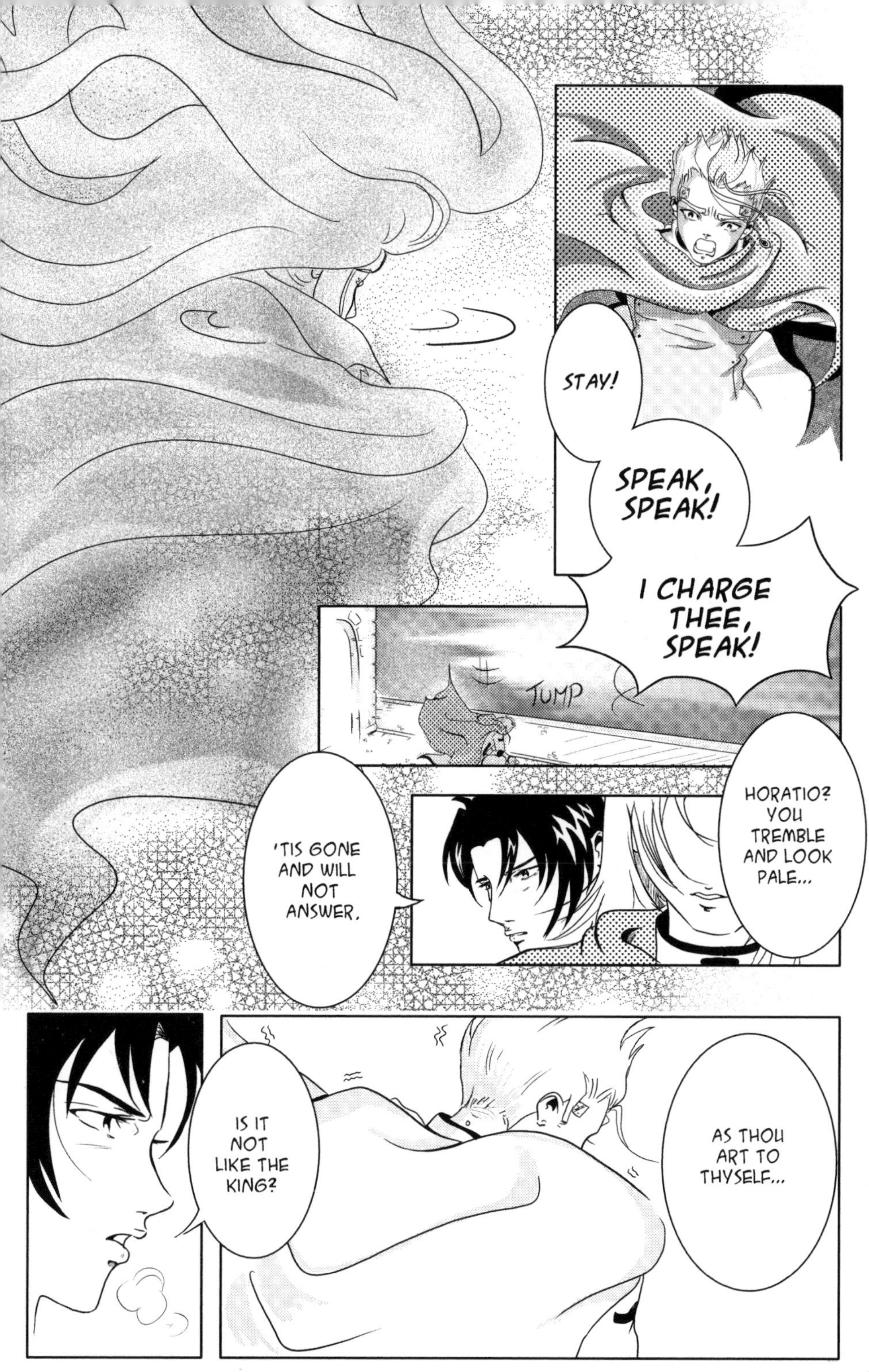
STAY!
SPEAK, SPEAK!
I CHARGE THEE, SPEAK!
JUMP
'TIS GONE AND WILL NOT ANSWER.
HORATIO? YOU TREMBLE AND LOOK PALE...
IS IT NOT LIKE THE KING?
AS THOU ART TO THYSELF...

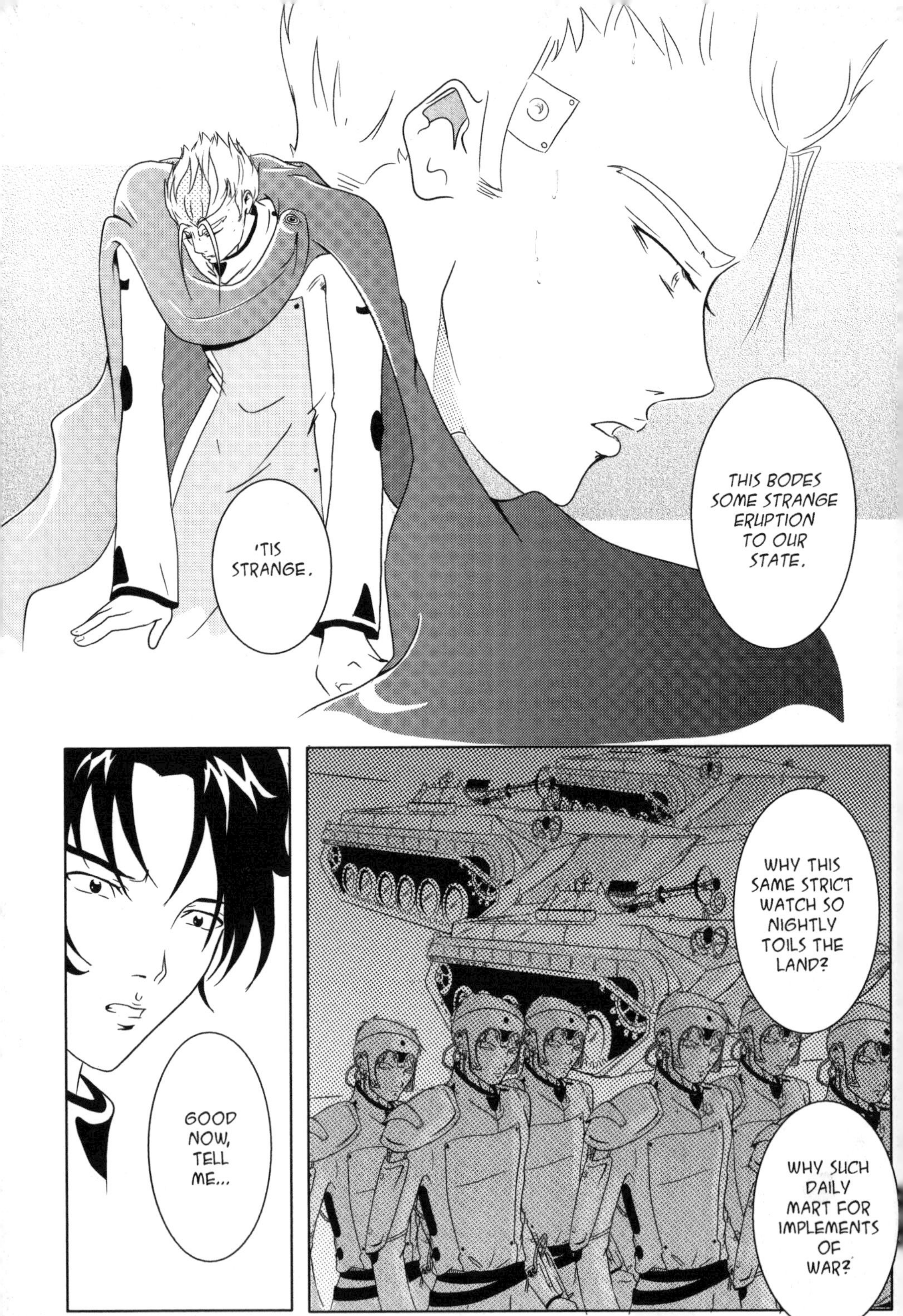
'TIS STRANGE.
THIS BODES SOME STRANGE ERUPTION TO OUR STATE.
GOOD NOW, TELL ME...
WHY THIS SAME STRICT WATCH SO NIGHTLY TOILS THE LAND?
WHY SUCH DAILY MART FOR IMPLEMENTS OF WAR?

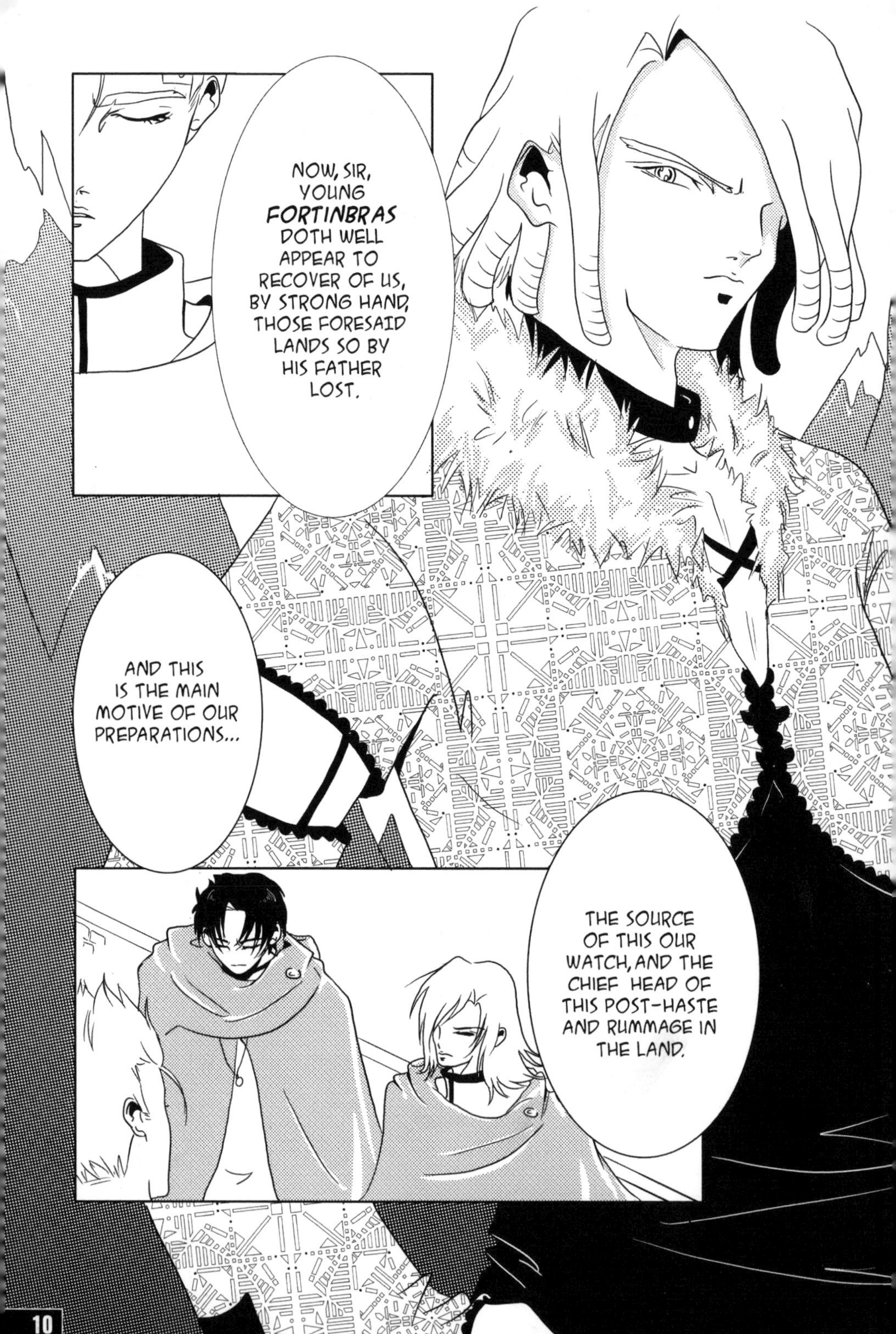
NOW, SIR, YOUNG FORTINBRAS DOTH WELL APPEAR TO RECOVER OF US, BY STRONG HAND, THOSE FORESAID LANDS SO BY HIS FATHER LOST.
AND THIS IS THE MAIN MOTIVE OF OUR PREPARATIONS...
THE SOURCE OF THIS OUR WATCH, AND THE CHIEF HEAD OF THIS POST-HASTE AND RUMMAGE IN THE LAND.

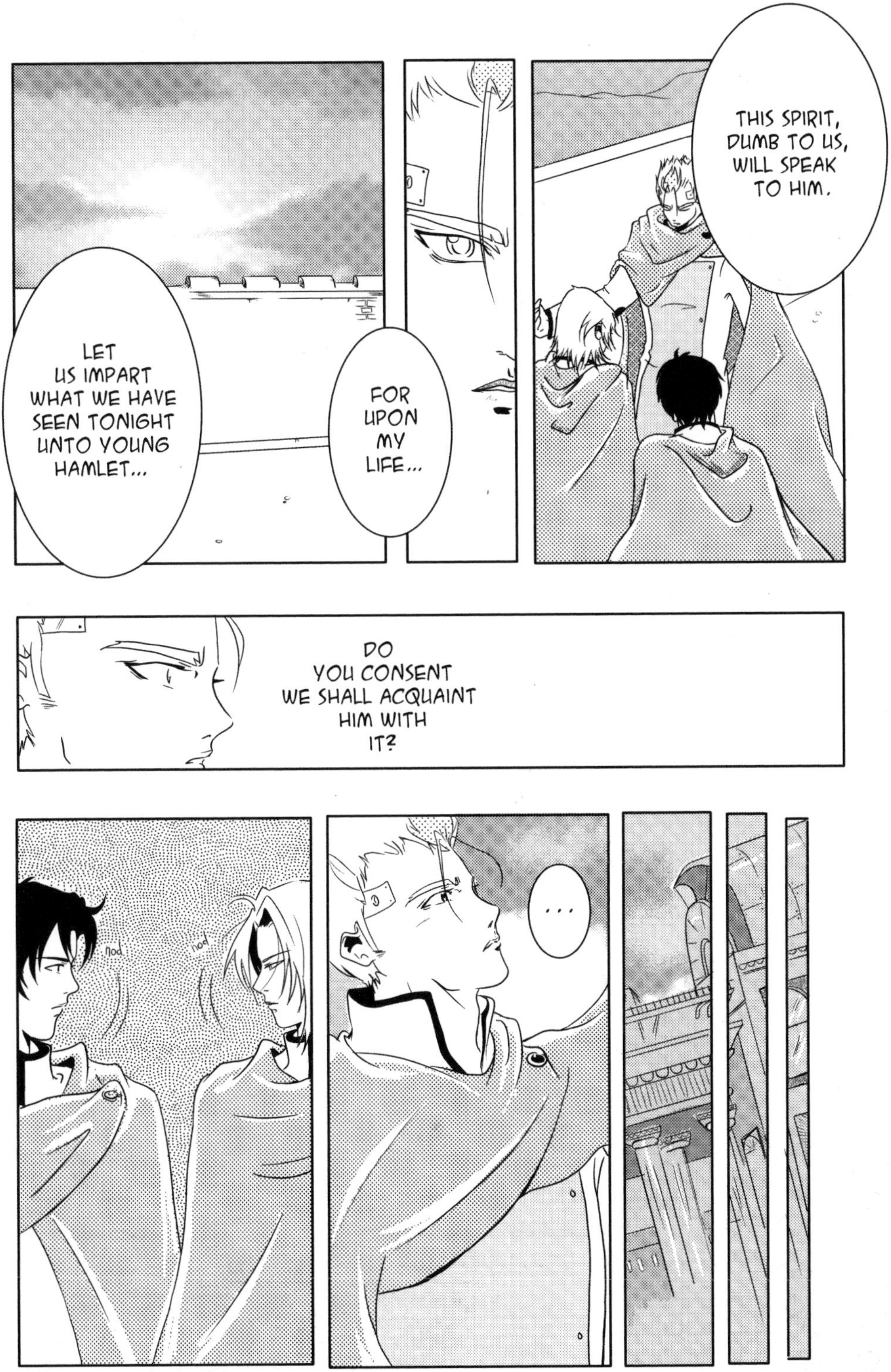
LET US IMPART WHAT WE HAVE SEEN TONIGHT UNTO YOUNG HAMLET...
FOR UPON MY LIFE...
THIS SPIRIT, DUMB TO US, WILL SPEAK TO HIM.
DO YOU CONSENT WE SHALL ACQUAINT HIM WITH IT?
nod
nod
...

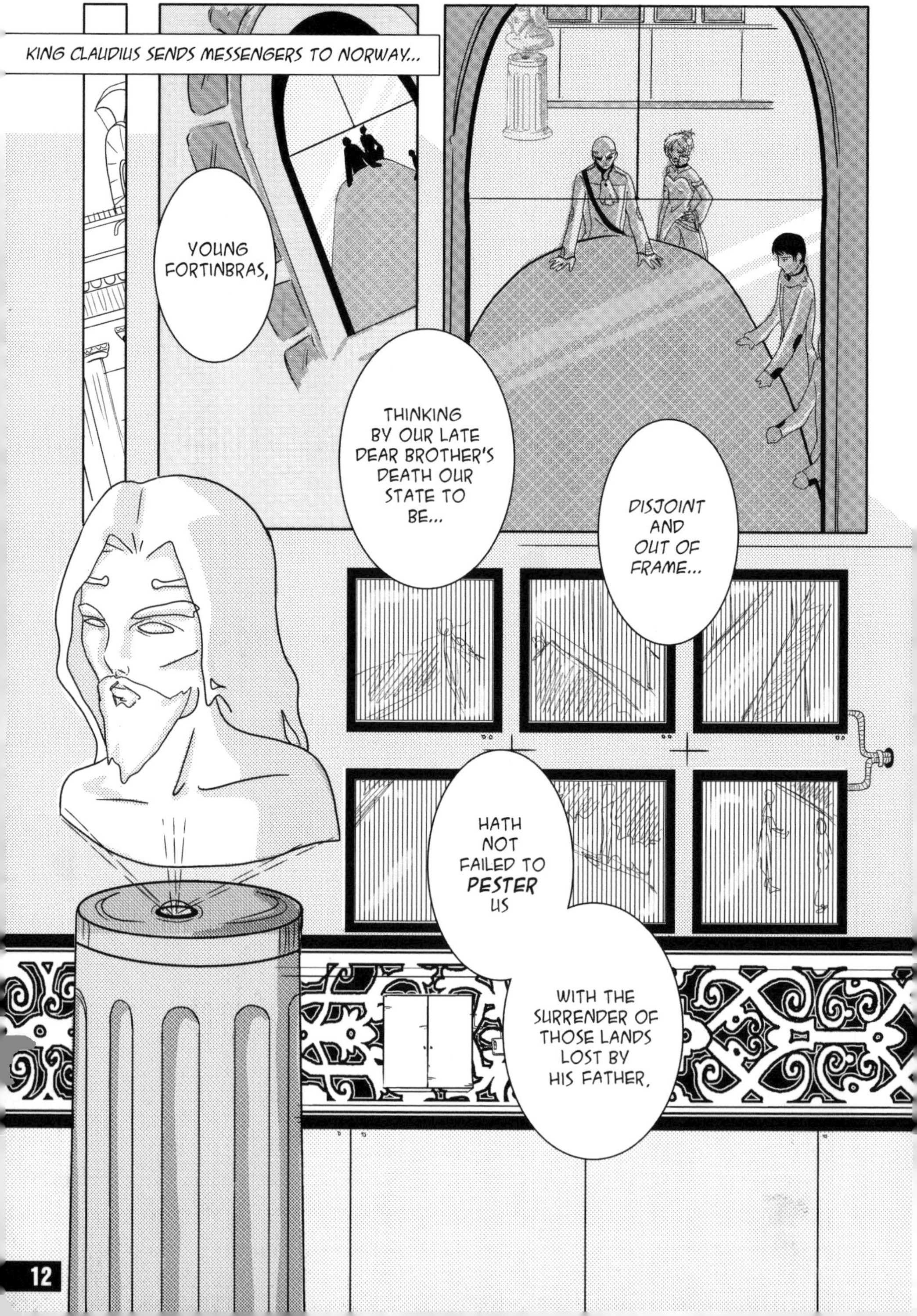
KING CLAUDIUS SENDS MESSENGERS TO NORWAY...
YOUNG FORTINBRAS,
THINKING BY OUR LATE DEAR BROTHER'S DEATH OUR STATE TO BE...
DISJOINT AND OUT OF FRAME...
HATH NOT FAILED TO **PESTER** US
WITH THE SURRENDER OF THOSE LANDS LOST BY HIS FATHER.

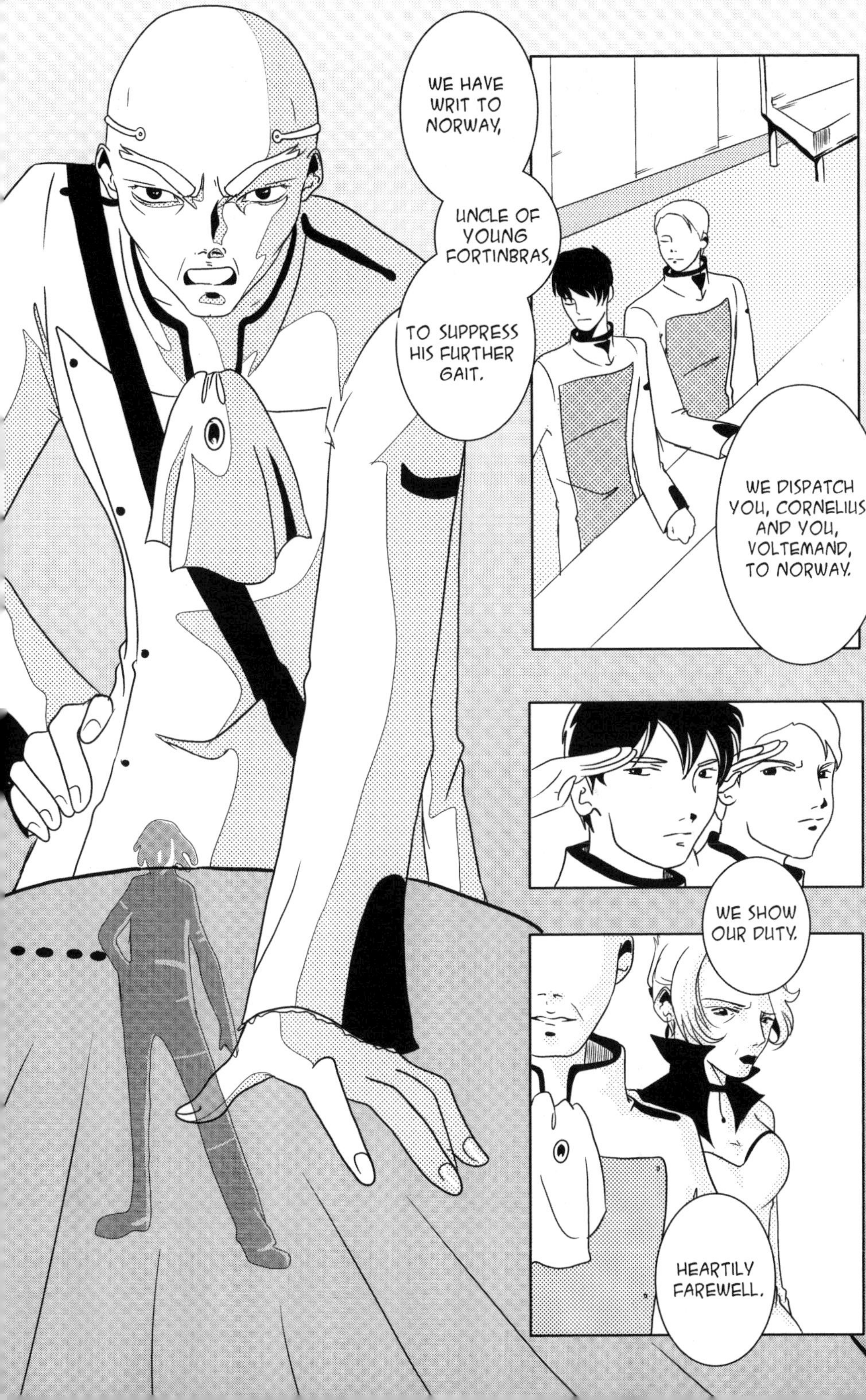
WE HAVE WRIT TO NORWAY,
UNCLE OF YOUNG FORTINBRAS,
TO SUPPRESS HIS FURTHER GAIT.
WE DISPATCH YOU, CORNELIUS, AND YOU, VOLTEMAND, TO NORWAY.
....
WE SHOW OUR DUTY.
HEARTILY FAREWELL.

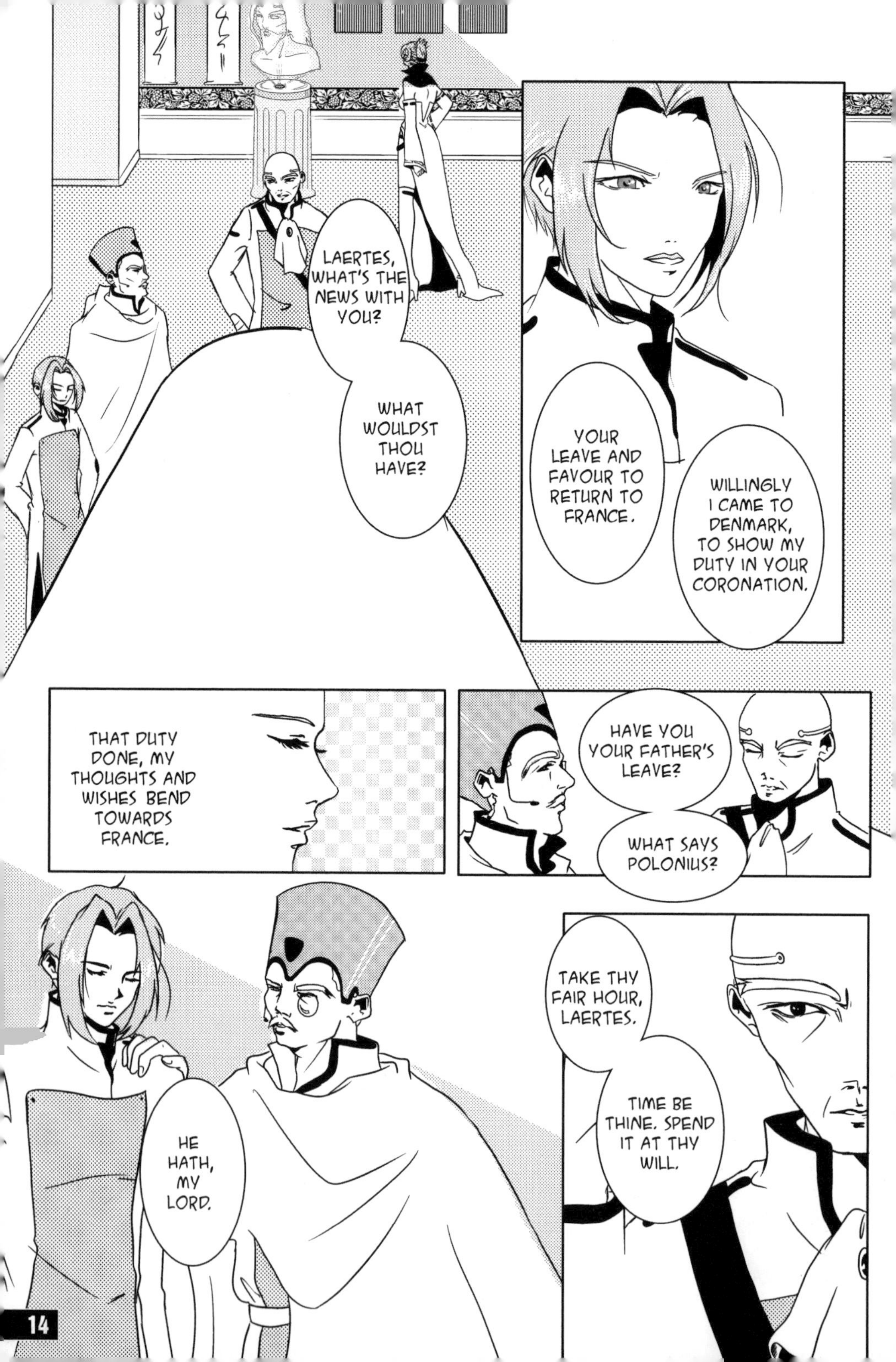
LAERTES, WHAT'S THE NEWS WITH YOU?
WHAT WOULDST THOU HAVE?
YOUR LEAVE AND FAVOUR TO RETURN TO FRANCE.
WILLINGLY I CAME TO DENMARK, TO SHOW MY DUTY IN YOUR CORONATION.
THAT DUTY DONE, MY THOUGHTS AND WISHES BEND TOWARDS FRANCE.
HAVE YOU YOUR FATHER'S LEAVE?
WHAT SAYS POLONIUS?
HE HATH, MY LORD.
TAKE THY FAIR HOUR, LAERTES.
TIME BE THINE. SPEND IT AT THY WILL.

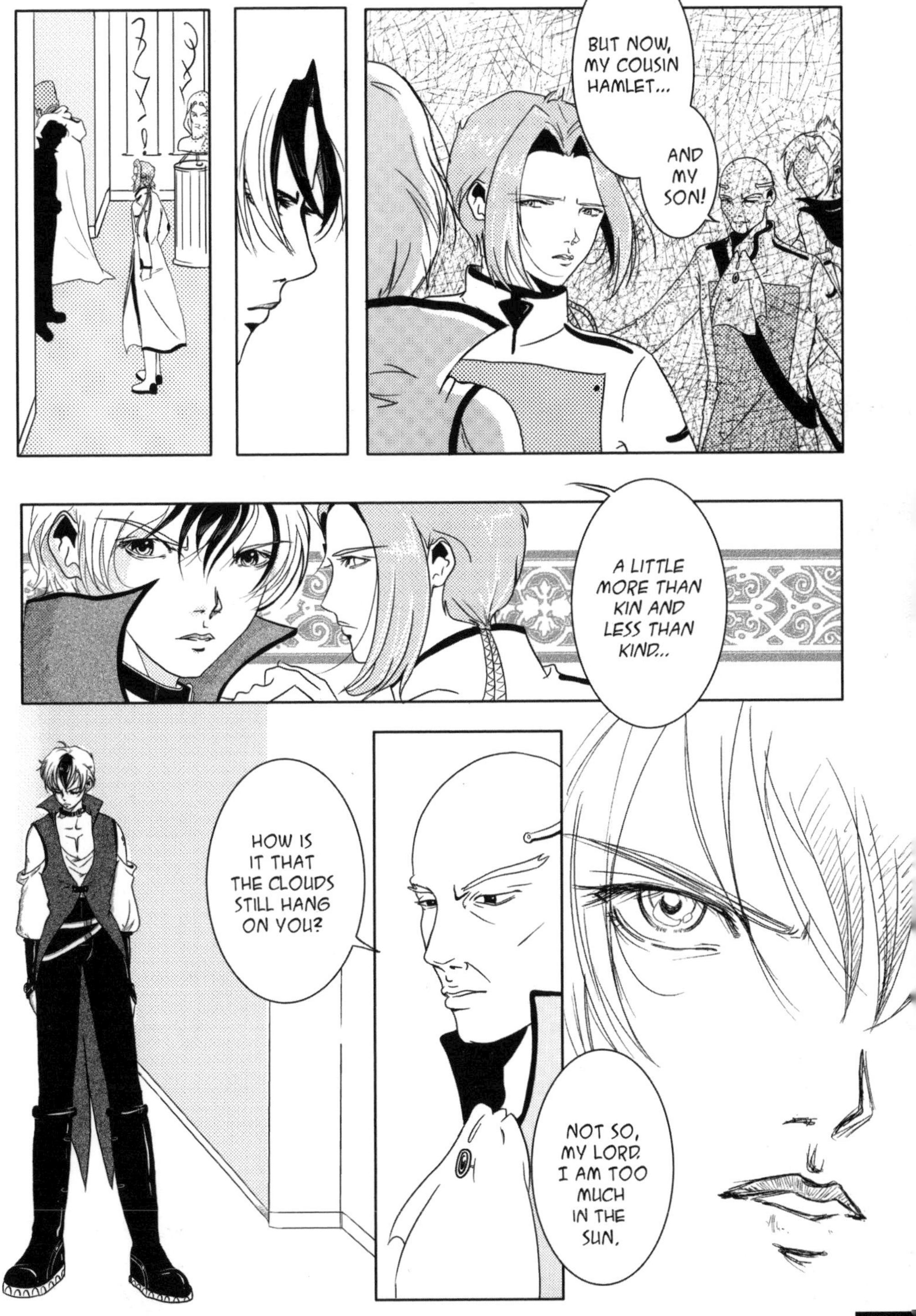
BUT NOW, MY COUSIN HAMLET...
AND MY SON!
A LITTLE MORE THAN KIN AND LESS THAN KIND...
HOW IS IT THAT THE CLOUDS STILL HANG ON YOU?
NOT SO, MY LORD. I AM TOO MUCH IN THE SUN.

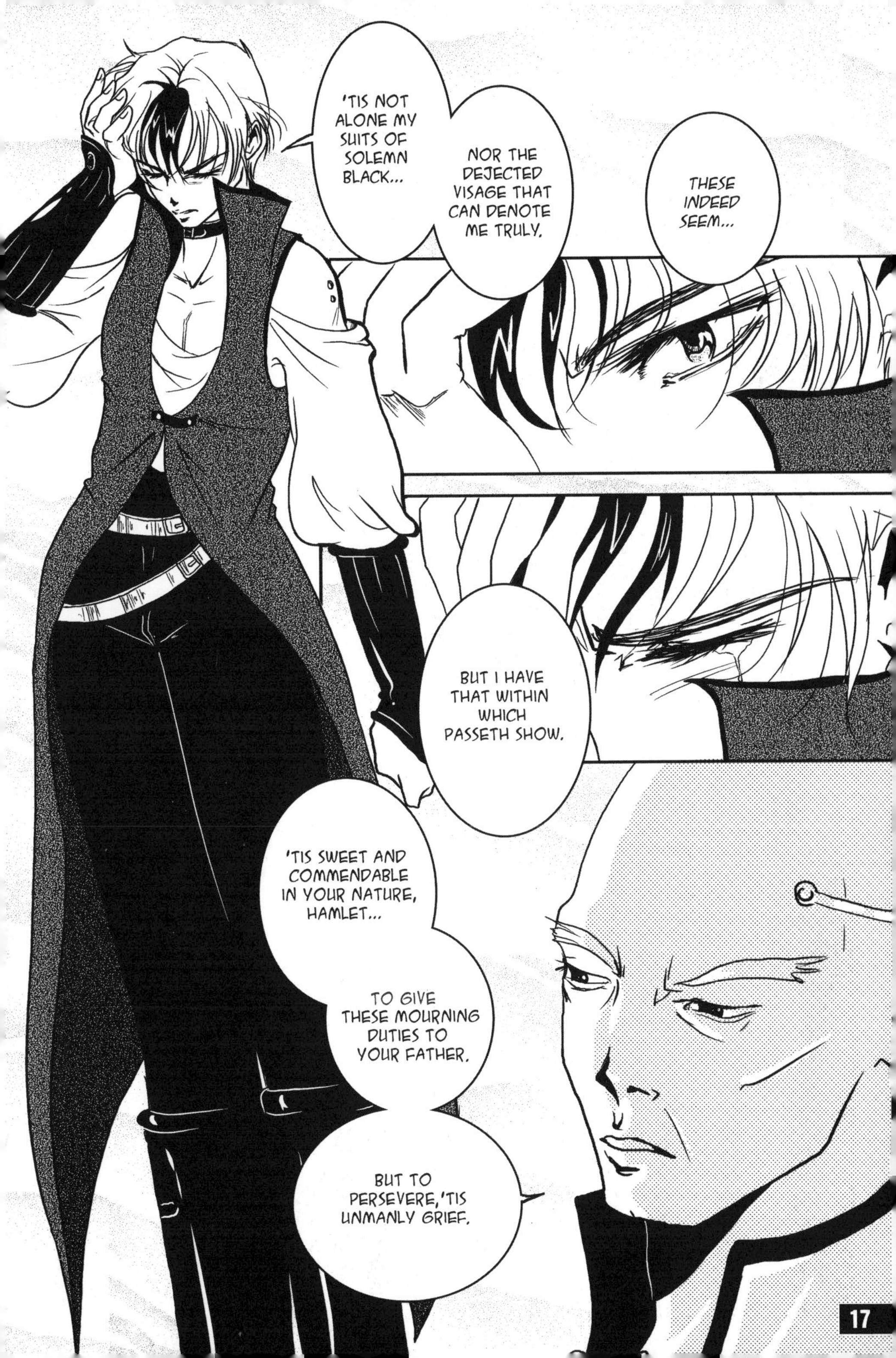
'TIS NOT ALONE MY SUITS OF SOLEMN BLACK...
NOR THE DEJECTED VISAGE THAT CAN DENOTE ME TRULY.
THESE INDEED SEEM...
BUT I HAVE THAT WITHIN WHICH PASSETH SHOW.
'TIS SWEET AND COMMENDABLE IN YOUR NATURE, HAMLET...
TO GIVE THESE MOURNING DUTIES TO YOUR FATHER.
BUT TO PERSEVERE, 'TIS UNMANLY GRIEF.

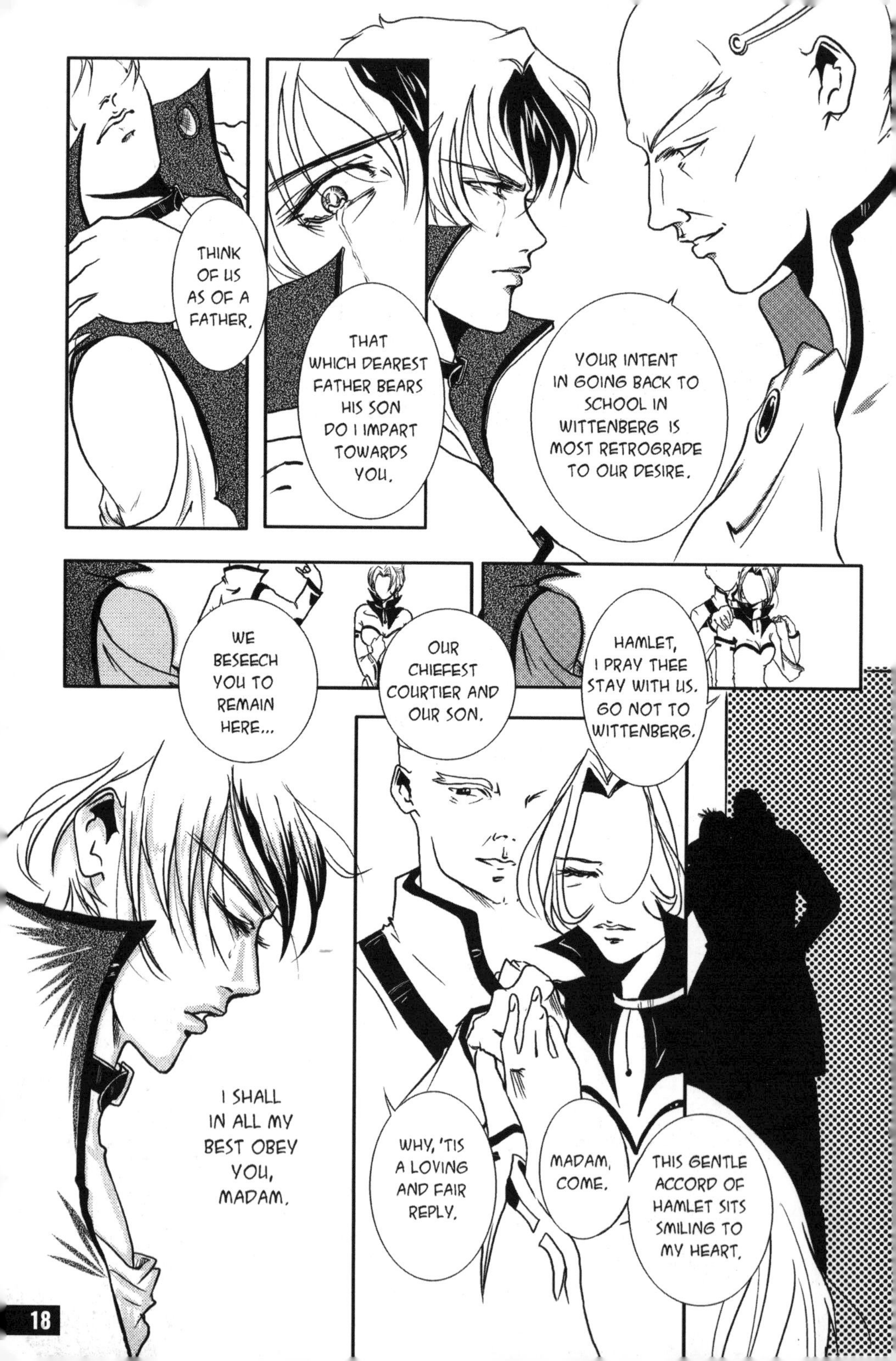
THINK OF US AS OF A FATHER.
THAT WHICH DEAREST FATHER BEARS HIS SON DO I IMPART TOWARDS YOU.
YOUR INTENT IN GOING BACK TO SCHOOL IN WITTENBERG IS MOST RETROGRADE TO OUR DESIRE.
WE BESEECH YOU TO REMAIN HERE...
OUR CHIEFEST COURTIER AND OUR SON.
HAMLET, I PRAY THEE STAY WITH US. GO NOT TO WITTENBERG.
I SHALL IN ALL MY BEST OBEY YOU, MADAM.
WHY, 'TIS A LOVING AND FAIR REPLY.
MADAM, COME.
THIS GENTLE ACCORD OF HAMLET SITS SMILING TO MY HEART.

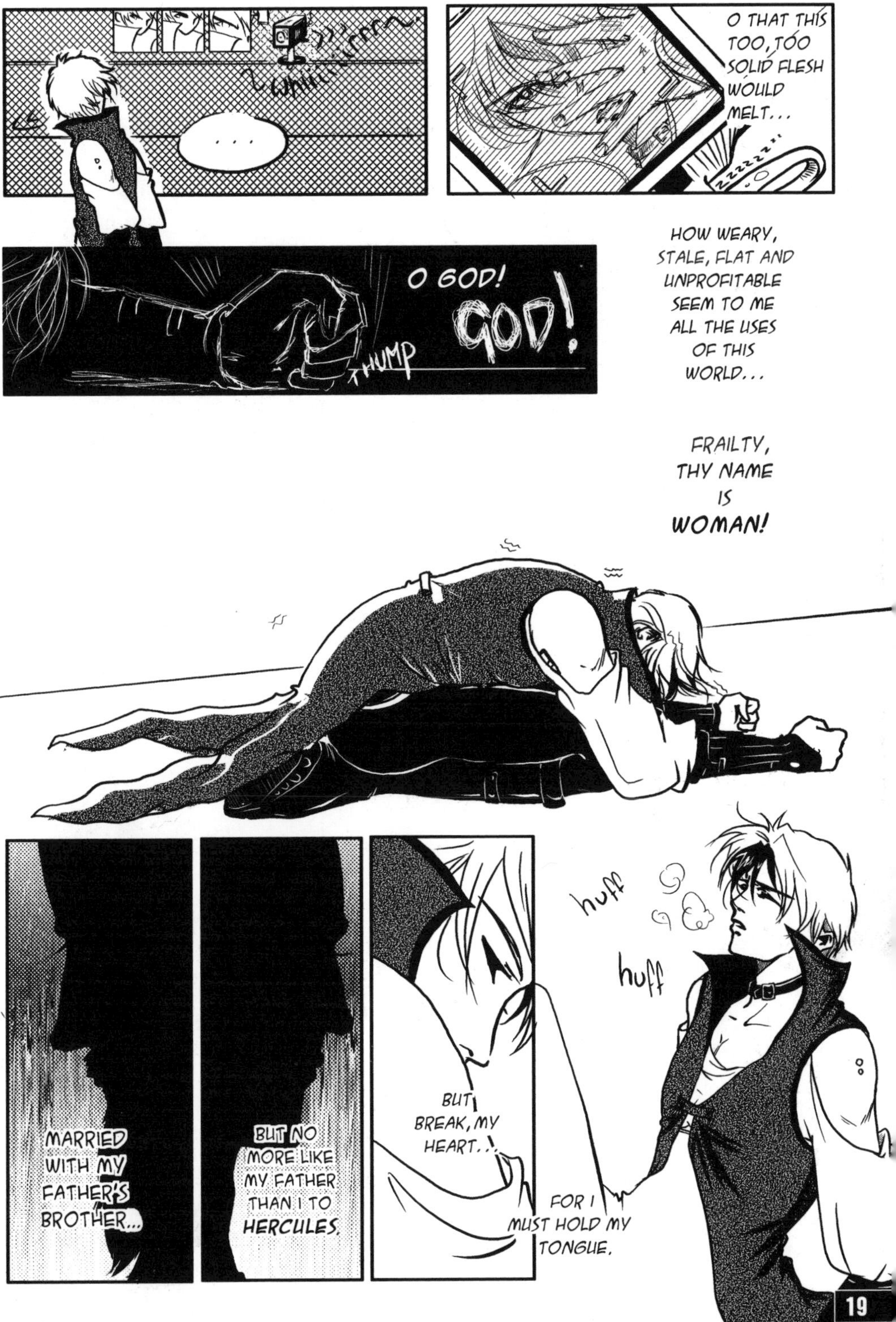

...
O THAT THIS TOO, TOO SOLID FLESH WOULD MELT...
O GOD!
THUMP
GOD!
HOW WEARY, STALE, FLAT AND UNPROFITABLE SEEM TO ME ALL THE USES OF THIS WORLD...
FRAILTY, THY NAME IS **WOMAN!**
MARRIED WITH MY FATHER'S BROTHER...
BUT NO MORE LIKE MY FATHER THAN I TO **HERCULES**.
BUT BREAK, MY HEART...
huff
huff
FOR I MUST HOLD MY TONGUE.

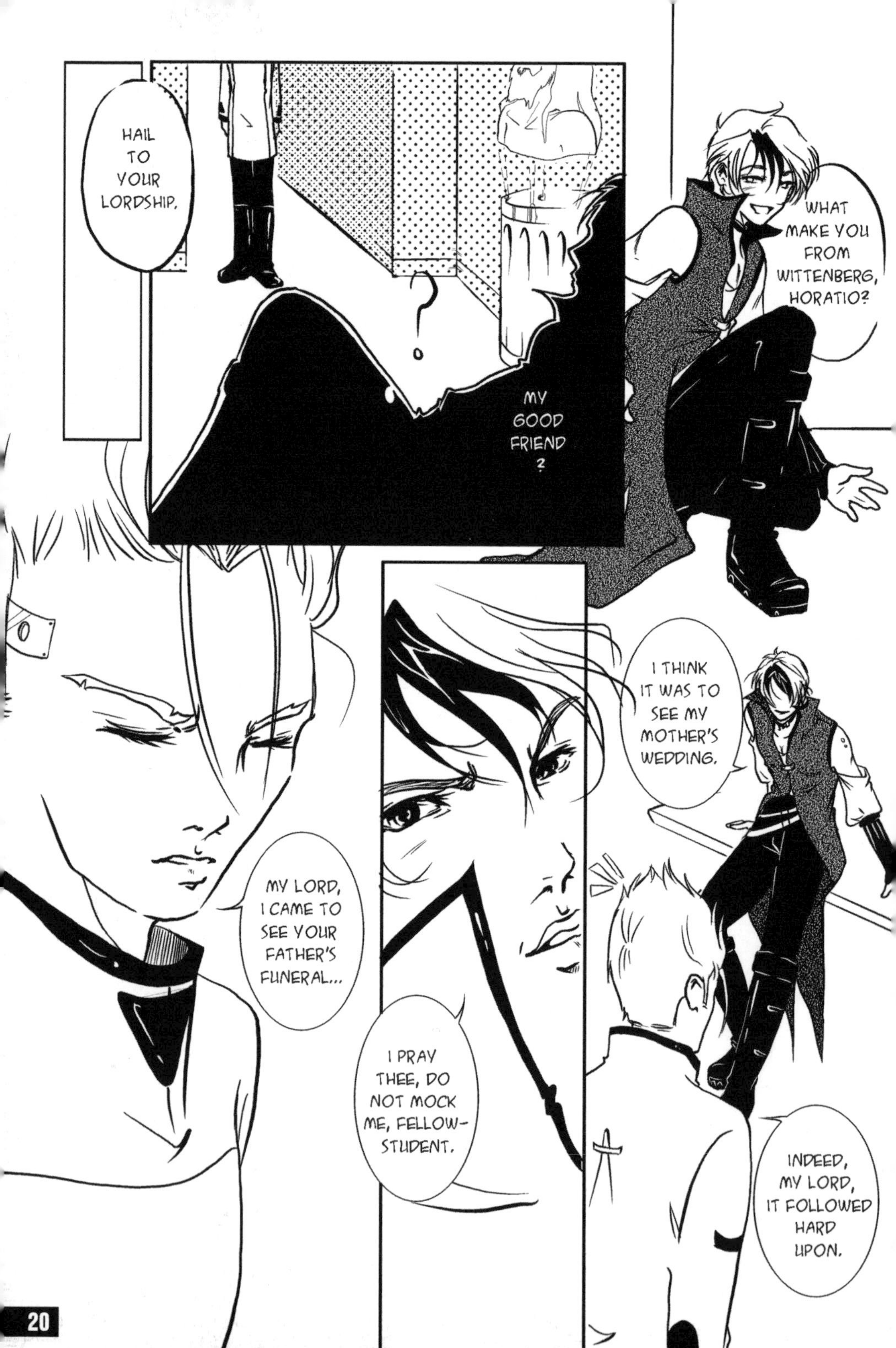
HAIL TO YOUR LORDSHIP.
?
MY GOOD FRIEND?
WHAT MAKE YOU FROM WITTENBERG, HORATIO?
MY LORD, I CAME TO SEE YOUR FATHER'S FUNERAL...
I PRAY THEE, DO NOT MOCK ME, FELLOW-STUDENT.
I THINK IT WAS TO SEE MY MOTHER'S WEDDING.
INDEED, MY LORD, IT FOLLOWED HARD UPON.

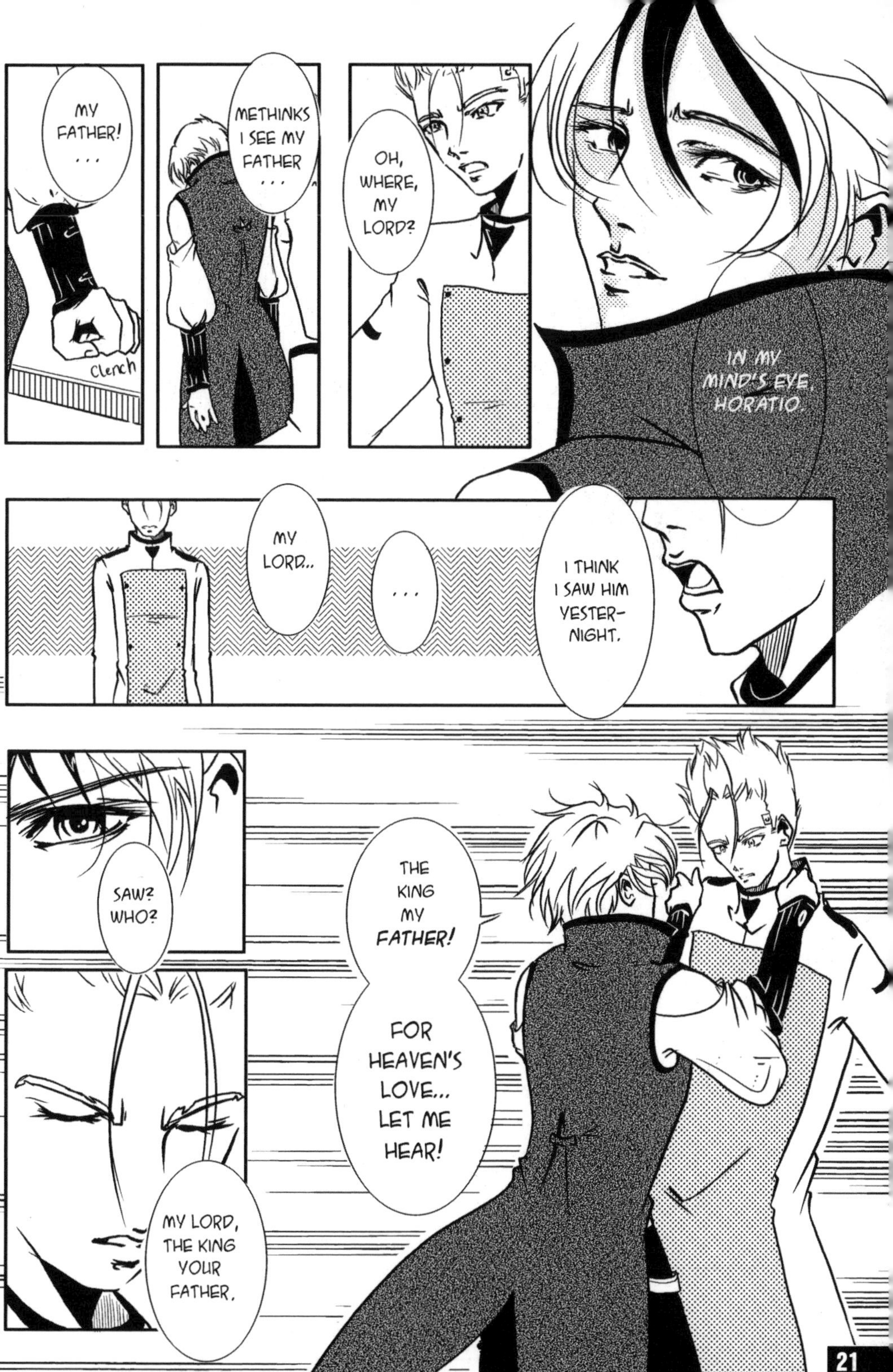
MY FATHER! . . .
Clench
METHINKS I SEE MY FATHER . . .
OH, WHERE, MY LORD?
IN MY MIND'S EYE, HORATIO.
MY LORD...
. . .
I THINK I SAW HIM YESTER-NIGHT.
SAW? WHO?
MY LORD, THE KING YOUR FATHER.
THE KING MY FATHER!
FOR HEAVEN'S LOVE... LET ME HEAR!

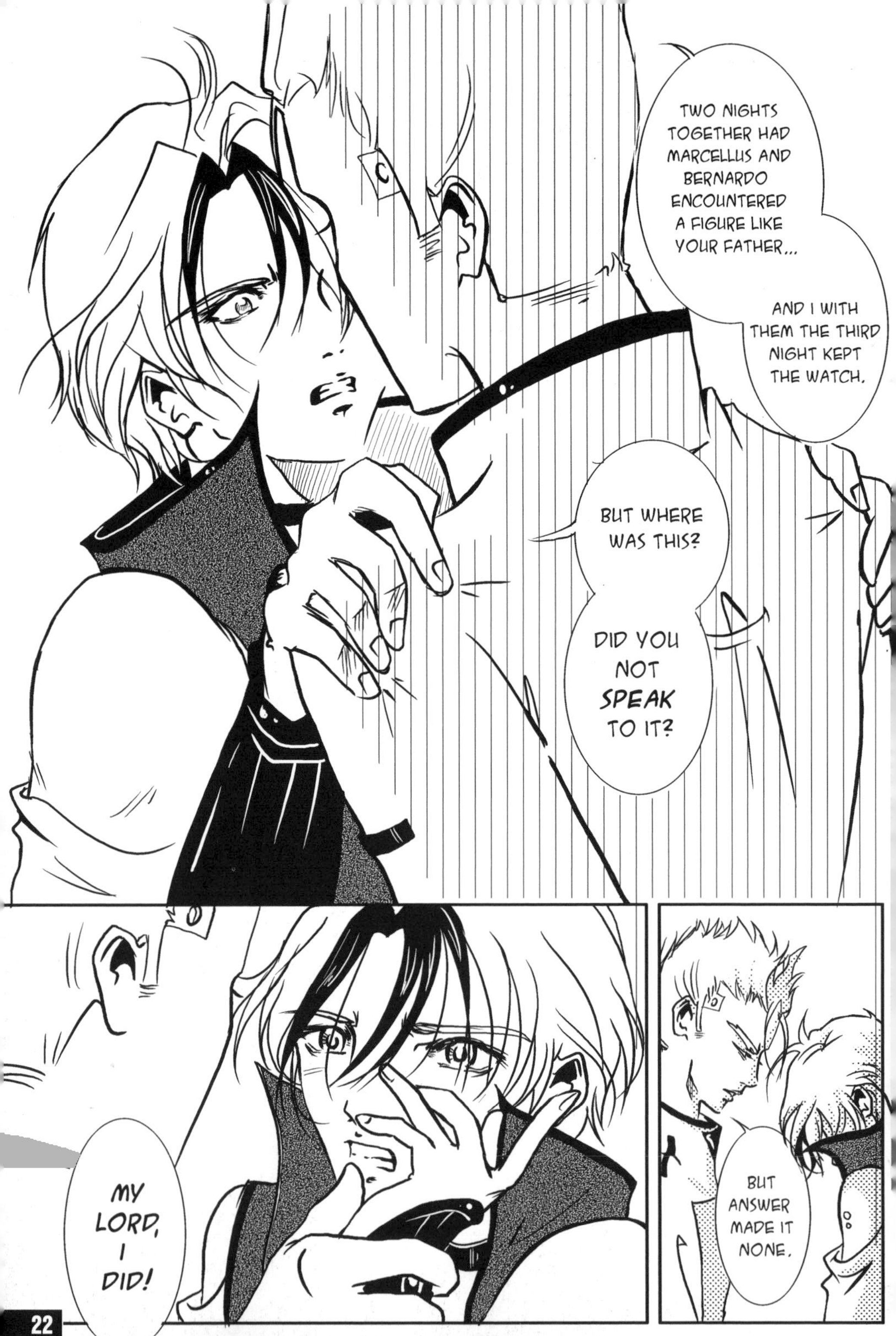
TWO NIGHTS TOGETHER HAD MARCELLUS AND BERNARDO ENCOUNTERED A FIGURE LIKE YOUR FATHER...
AND I WITH THEM THE THIRD NIGHT KEPT THE WATCH.
BUT WHERE WAS THIS?
DID YOU NOT **SPEAK** TO IT?
MY LORD, I DID!
BUT ANSWER MADE IT NONE.

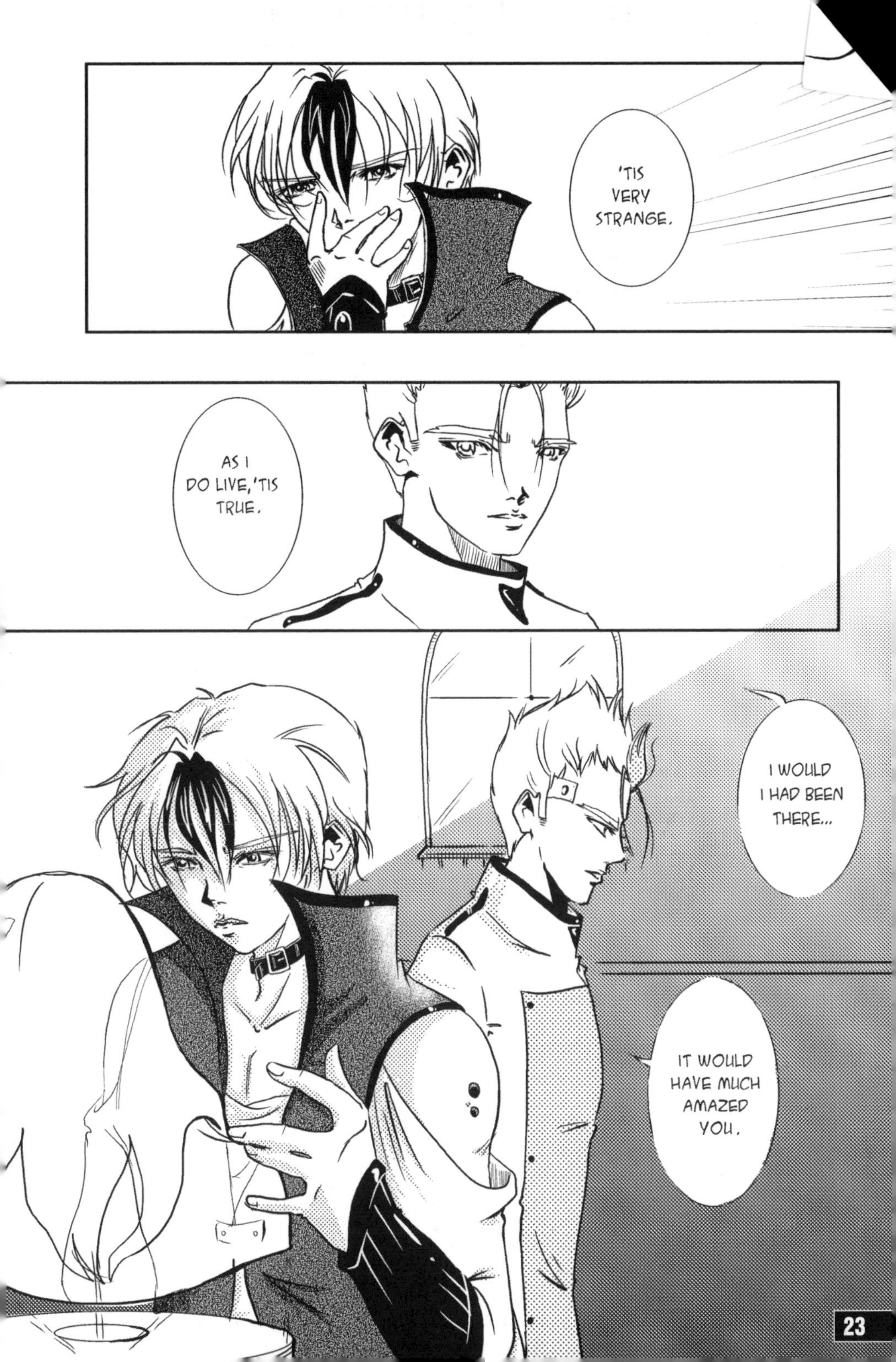
'TIS VERY STRANGE.
AS I DO LIVE, 'TIS TRUE.
I WOULD I HAD BEEN THERE...
IT WOULD HAVE MUCH AMAZED YOU.

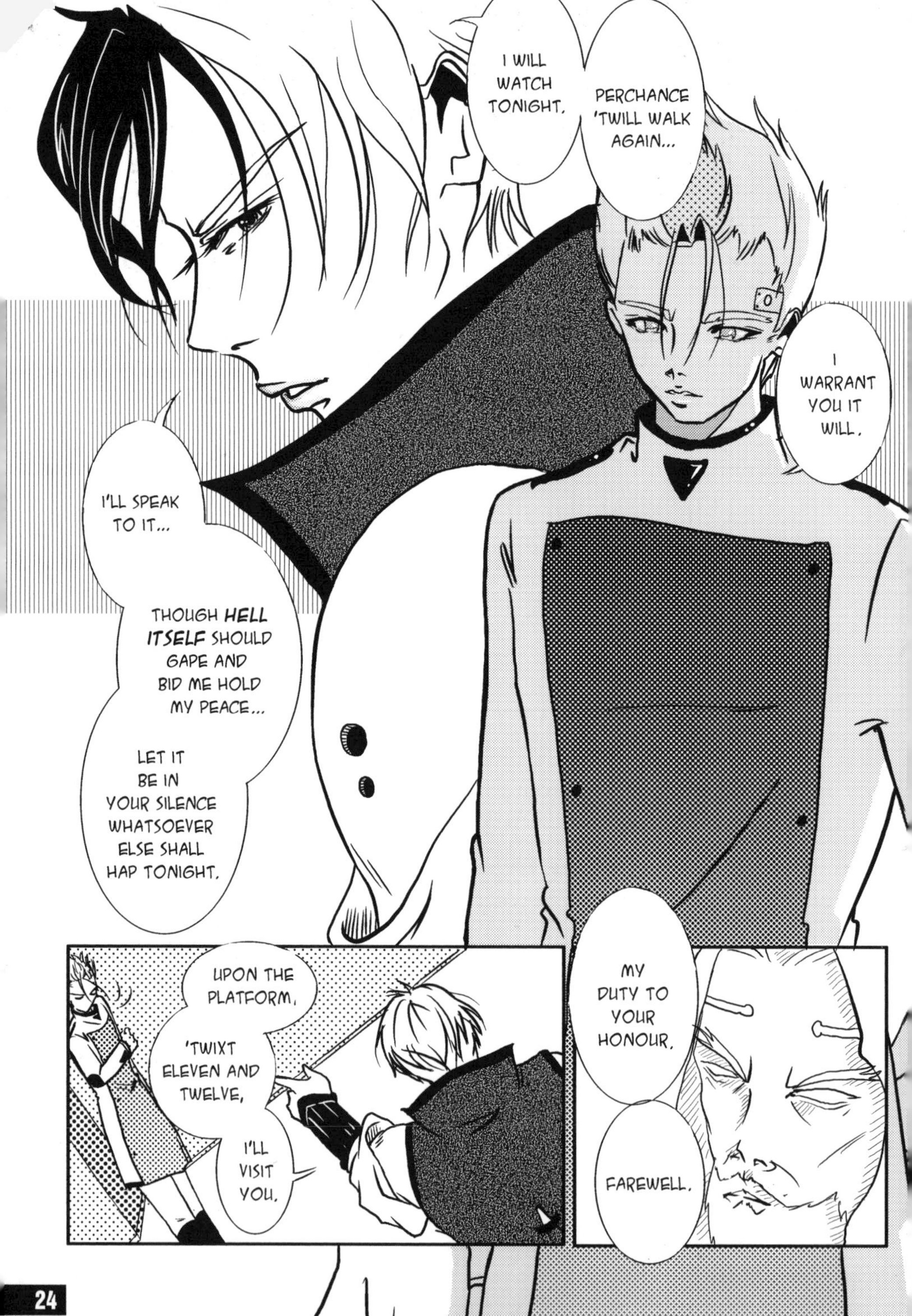
I'LL SPEAK TO IT...
THOUGH **HELL ITSELF** SHOULD GAPE AND BID ME HOLD MY PEACE...
LET IT BE IN YOUR SILENCE WHATSOEVER ELSE SHALL HAP TONIGHT.
I WILL WATCH TONIGHT.
PERCHANCE 'TWILL WALK AGAIN...
I WARRANT YOU IT WILL.
UPON THE PLATFORM,
'TWIXT ELEVEN AND TWELVE,
I'LL VISIT YOU.
MY DUTY TO YOUR HONOUR.
FAREWELL.

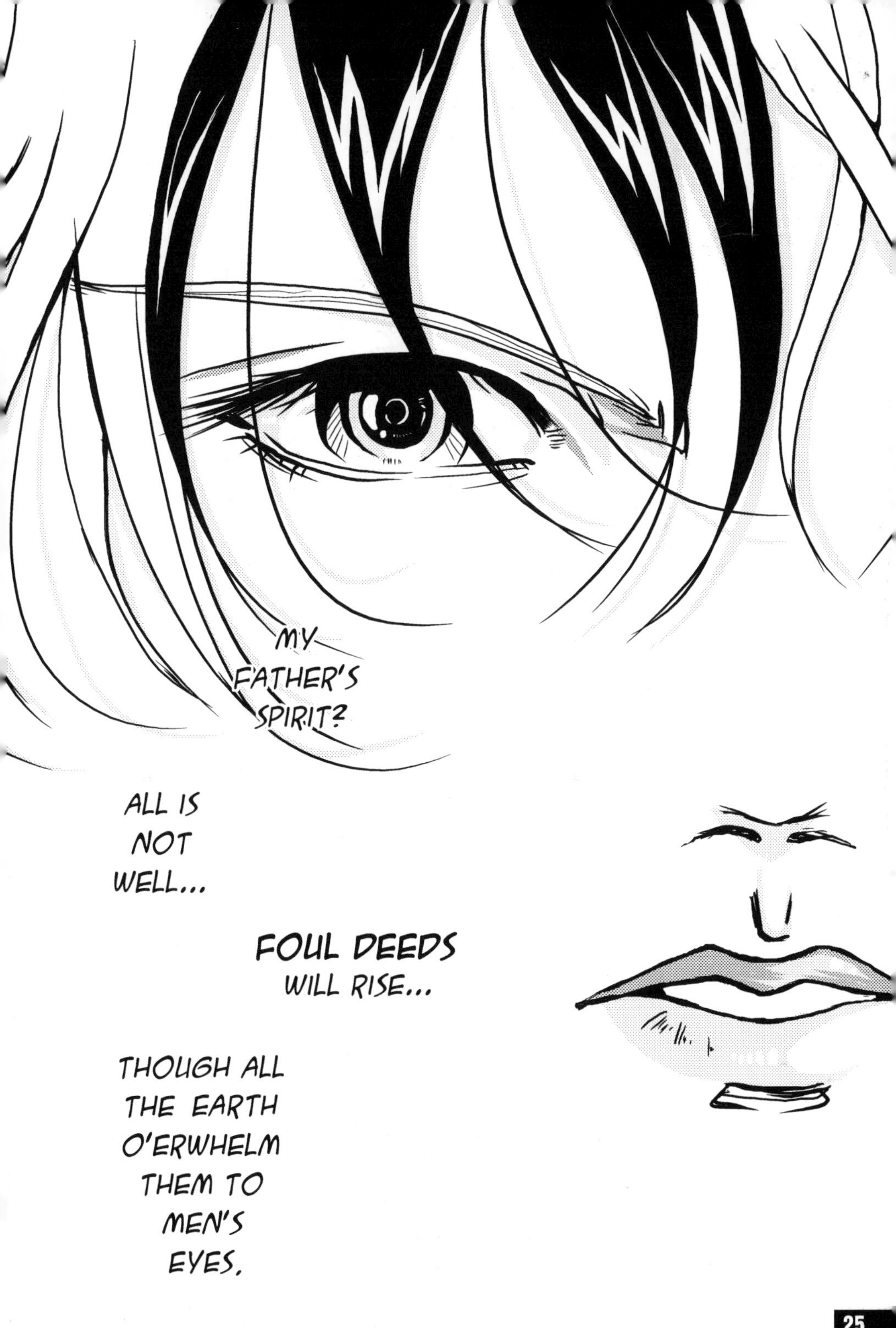
MY FATHER'S SPIRIT?
ALL IS NOT WELL...
FOUL DEEDS WILL RISE...
THOUGH ALL THE EARTH O'ERWHELM THEM TO MEN'S EYES.

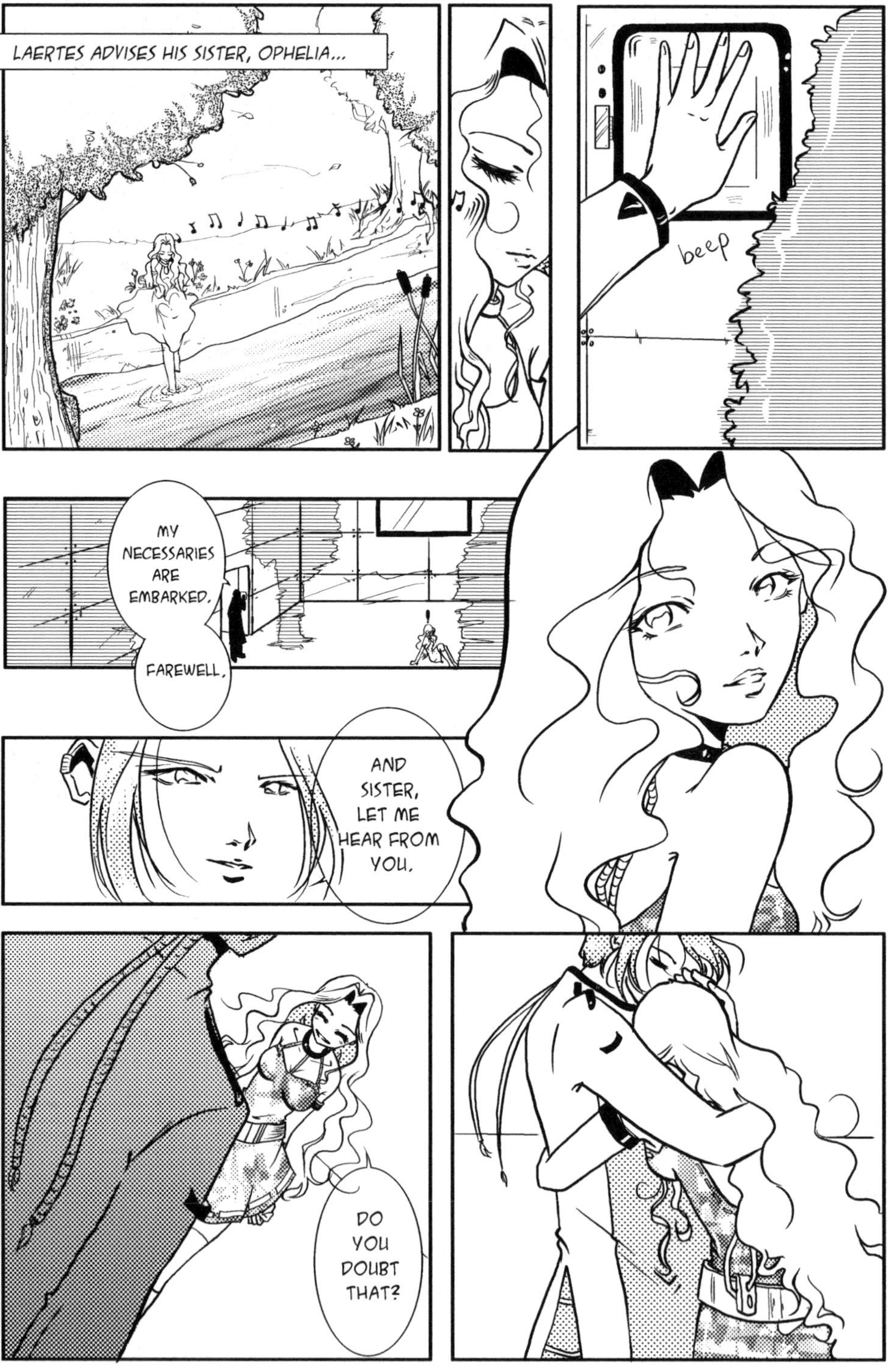

LAERTES ADVISES HIS SISTER, OPHELIA...
beep
MY NECESSARIES ARE EMBARKED.
FAREWELL.
AND SISTER, LET ME HEAR FROM YOU.
DO YOU DOUBT THAT?

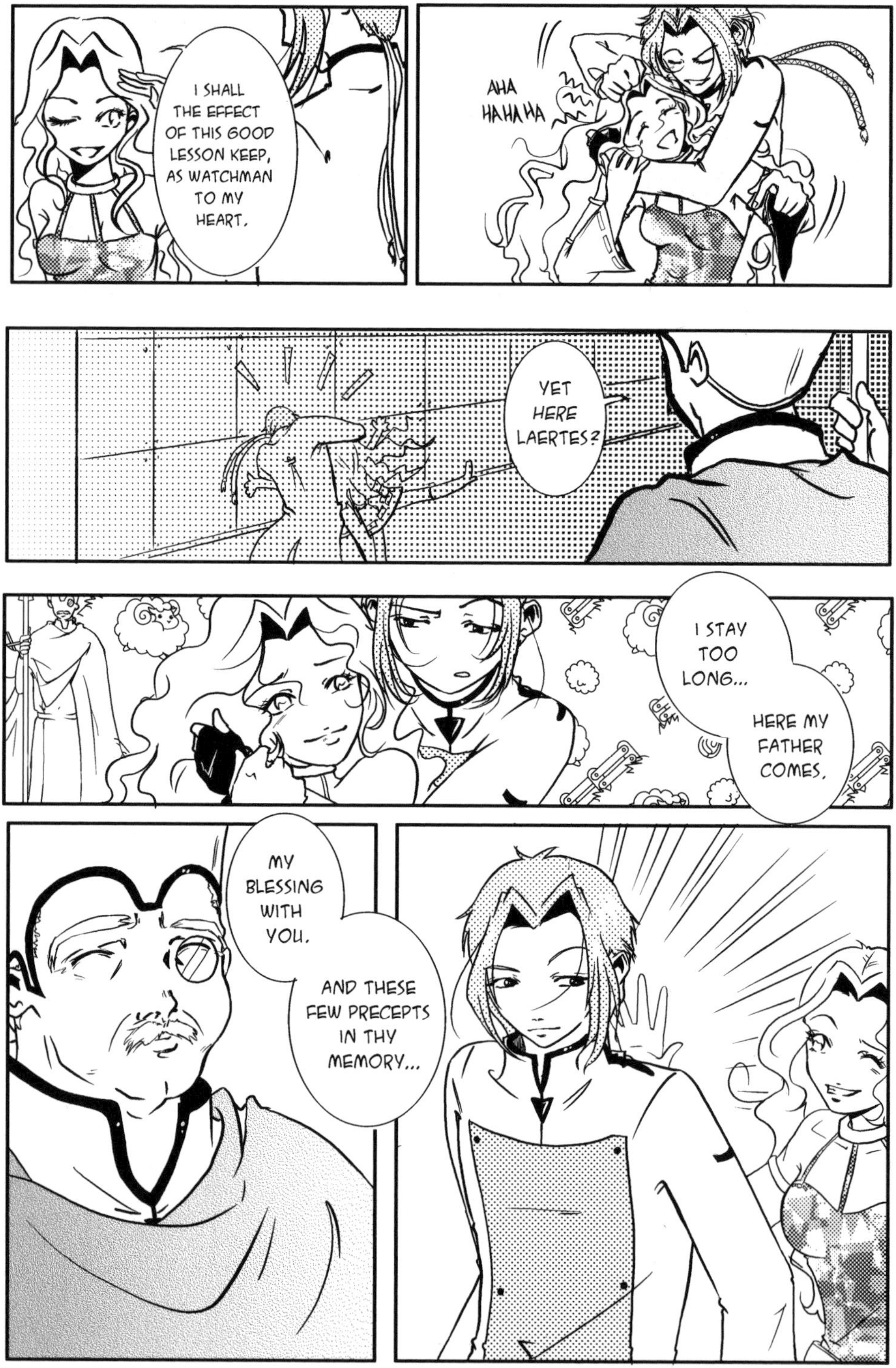
I SHALL THE EFFECT OF THIS GOOD LESSON KEEP, AS WATCHMAN TO MY HEART.
AHA HAHAHA
YET HERE LAERTES?
I STAY TOO LONG...
HERE MY FATHER COMES.
MY BLESSING WITH YOU.
AND THESE FEW PRECEPTS IN THY MEMORY...

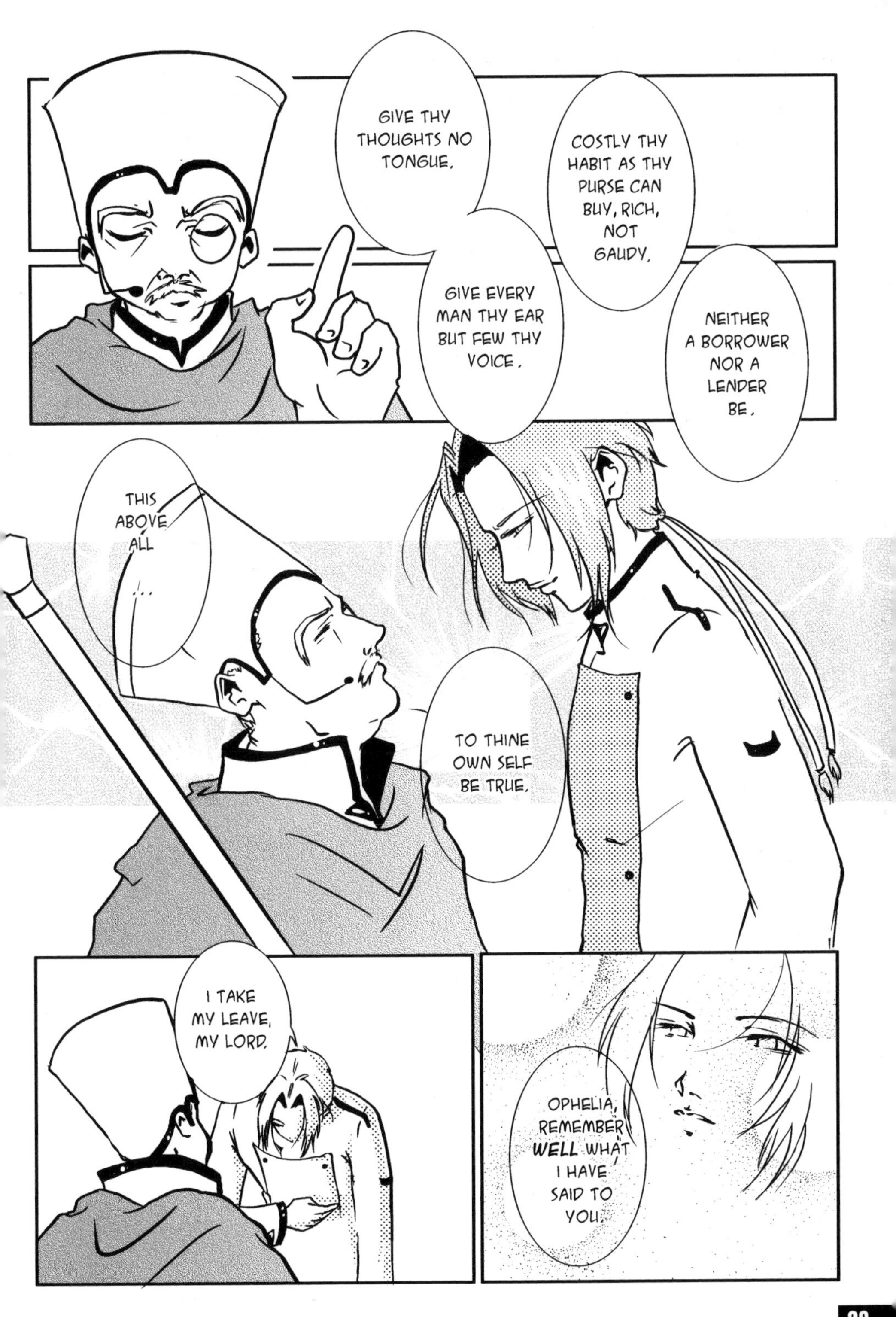
GIVE THY THOUGHTS NO TONGUE.
COSTLY THY HABIT AS THY PURSE CAN BUY, RICH, NOT GAUDY.
GIVE EVERY MAN THY EAR BUT FEW THY VOICE.
NEITHER A BORROWER NOR A LENDER BE.
THIS ABOVE ALL ...
TO THINE OWN SELF BE TRUE.
I TAKE MY LEAVE, MY LORD.
OPHELIA, REMEMBER **WELL** WHAT I HAVE SAID TO YOU.

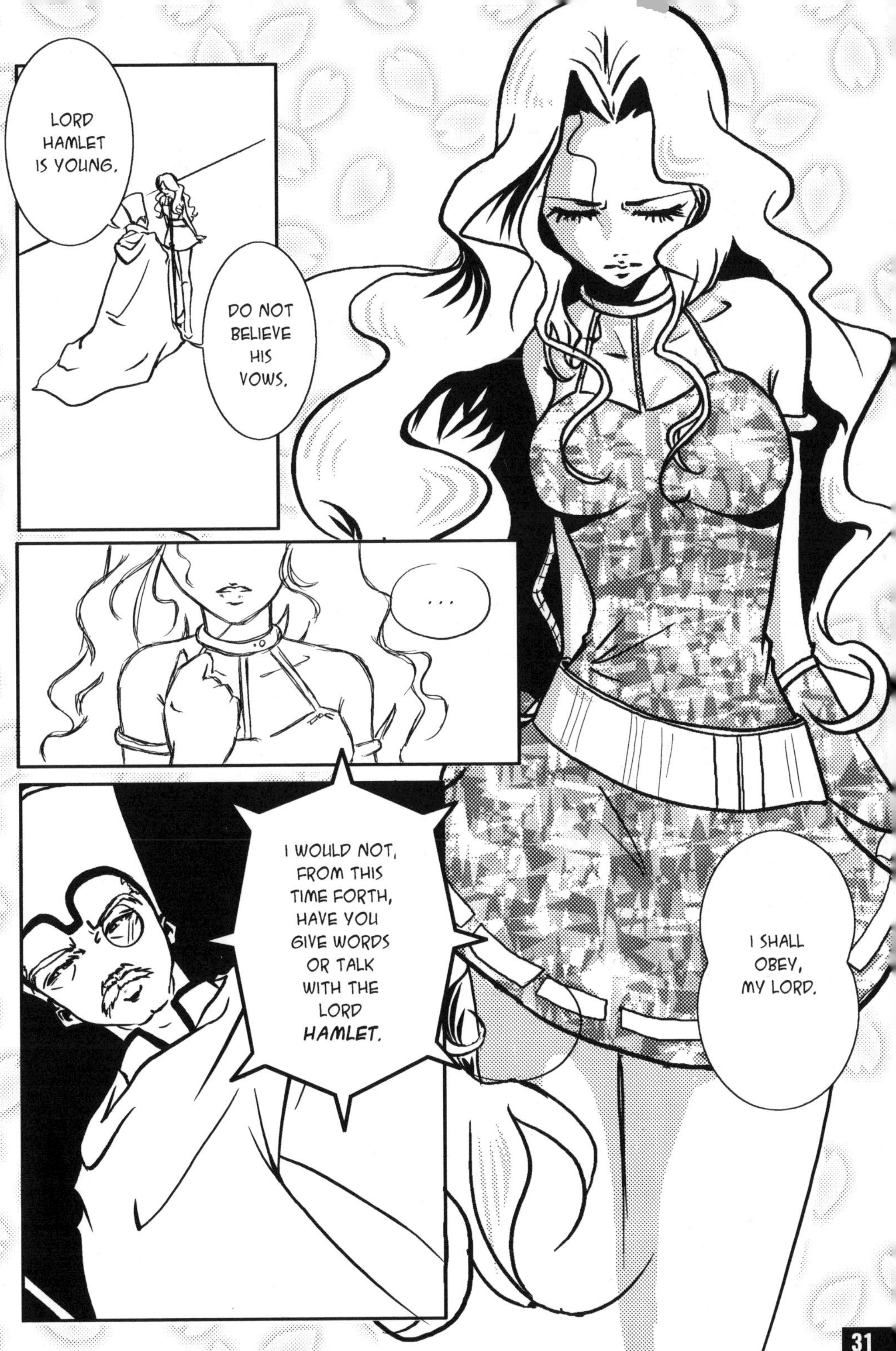
LORD HAMLET IS YOUNG.
DO NOT BELIEVE HIS VOWS.
...
I WOULD NOT, FROM THIS TIME FORTH, HAVE YOU GIVE WORDS OR TALK WITH THE LORD HAMLET.
I SHALL OBEY, MY LORD.

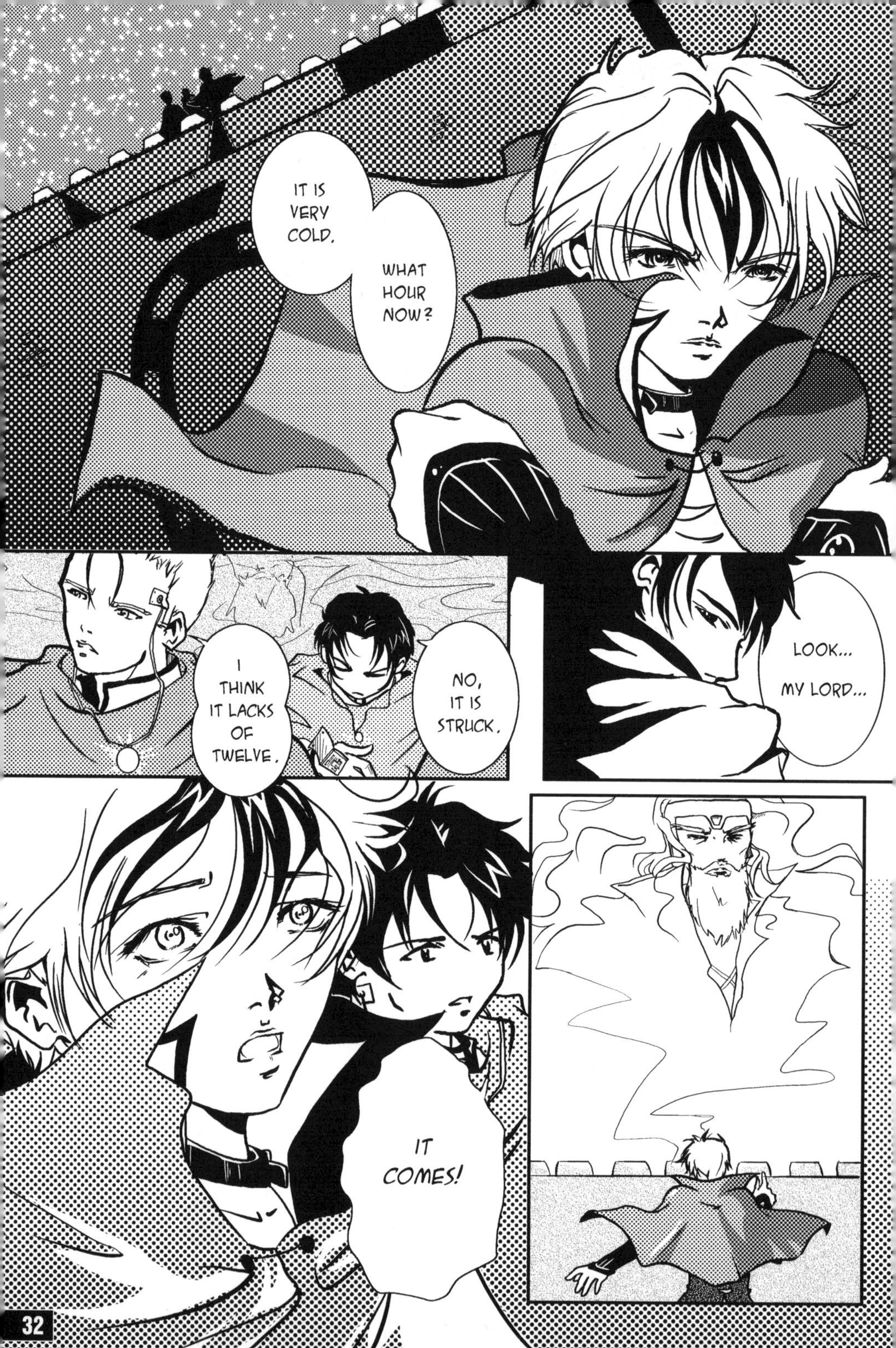

IT IS VERY COLD.
WHAT HOUR NOW?
I THINK IT LACKS OF TWELVE.
NO, IT IS STRUCK.
LOOK... MY LORD...
IT COMES!

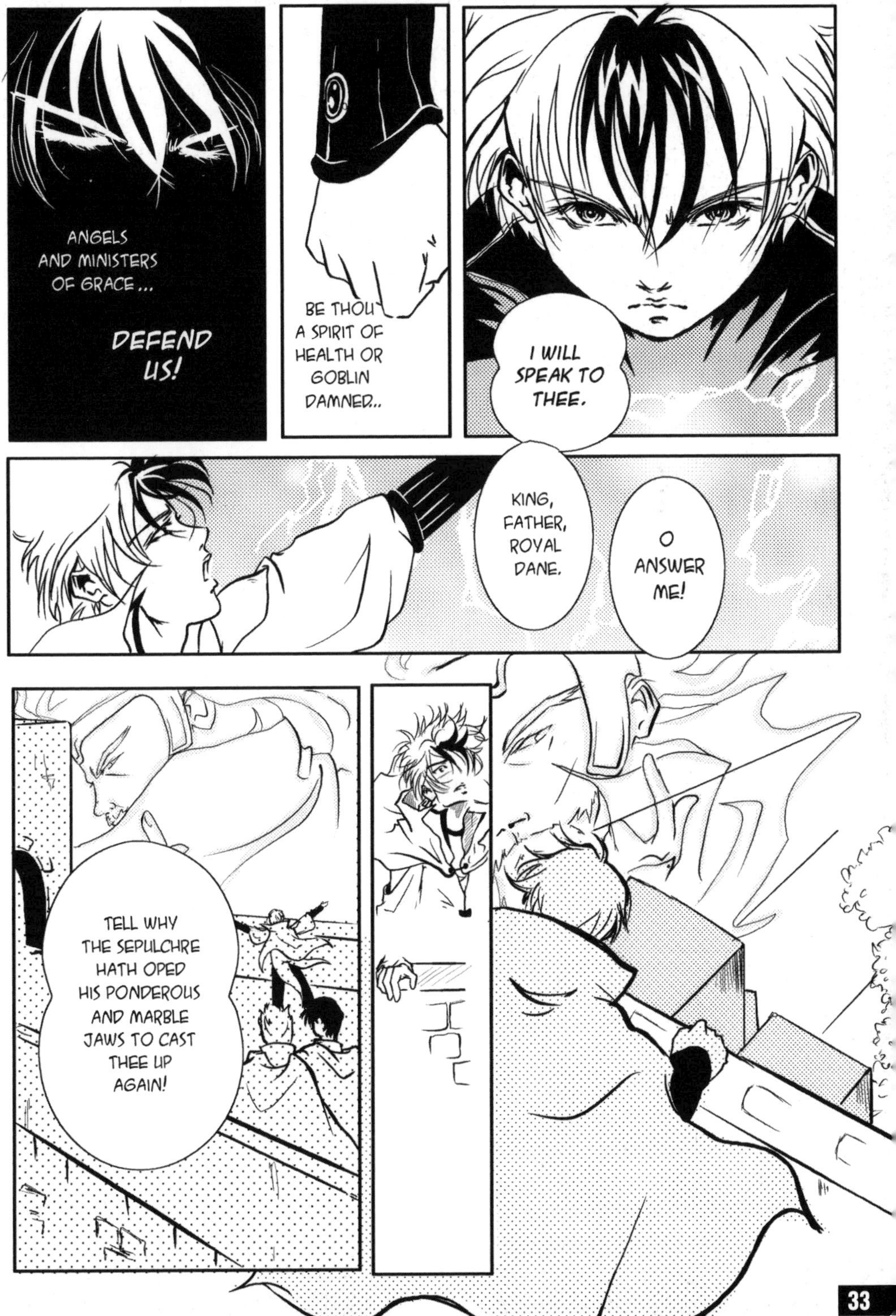
ANGELS AND MINISTERS OF GRACE...
DEFEND US!
BE THOU A SPIRIT OF HEALTH OR GOBLIN DAMNED..
I WILL SPEAK TO THEE.
KING, FATHER, ROYAL DANE.
O ANSWER ME!
TELL WHY THE SEPULCHRE HATH OPED HIS PONDEROUS AND MARBLE JAWS TO CAST THEE UP AGAIN!

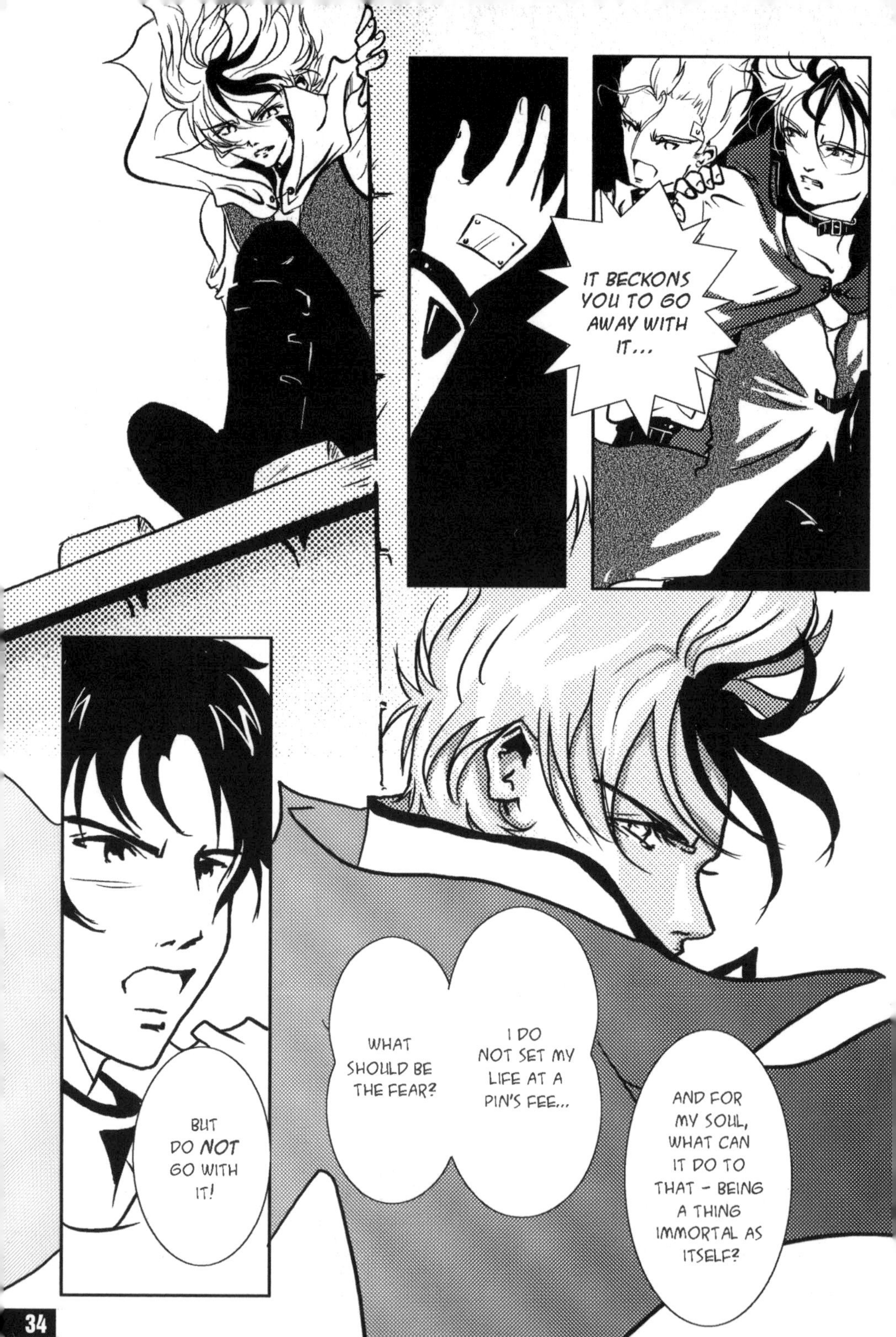
IT BECKONS YOU TO GO AWAY WITH IT...
BUT DO NOT GO WITH IT!
WHAT SHOULD BE THE FEAR?
I DO NOT SET MY LIFE AT A PIN'S FEE...
AND FOR MY SOUL, WHAT CAN IT DO TO THAT - BEING A THING IMMORTAL AS ITSELF?

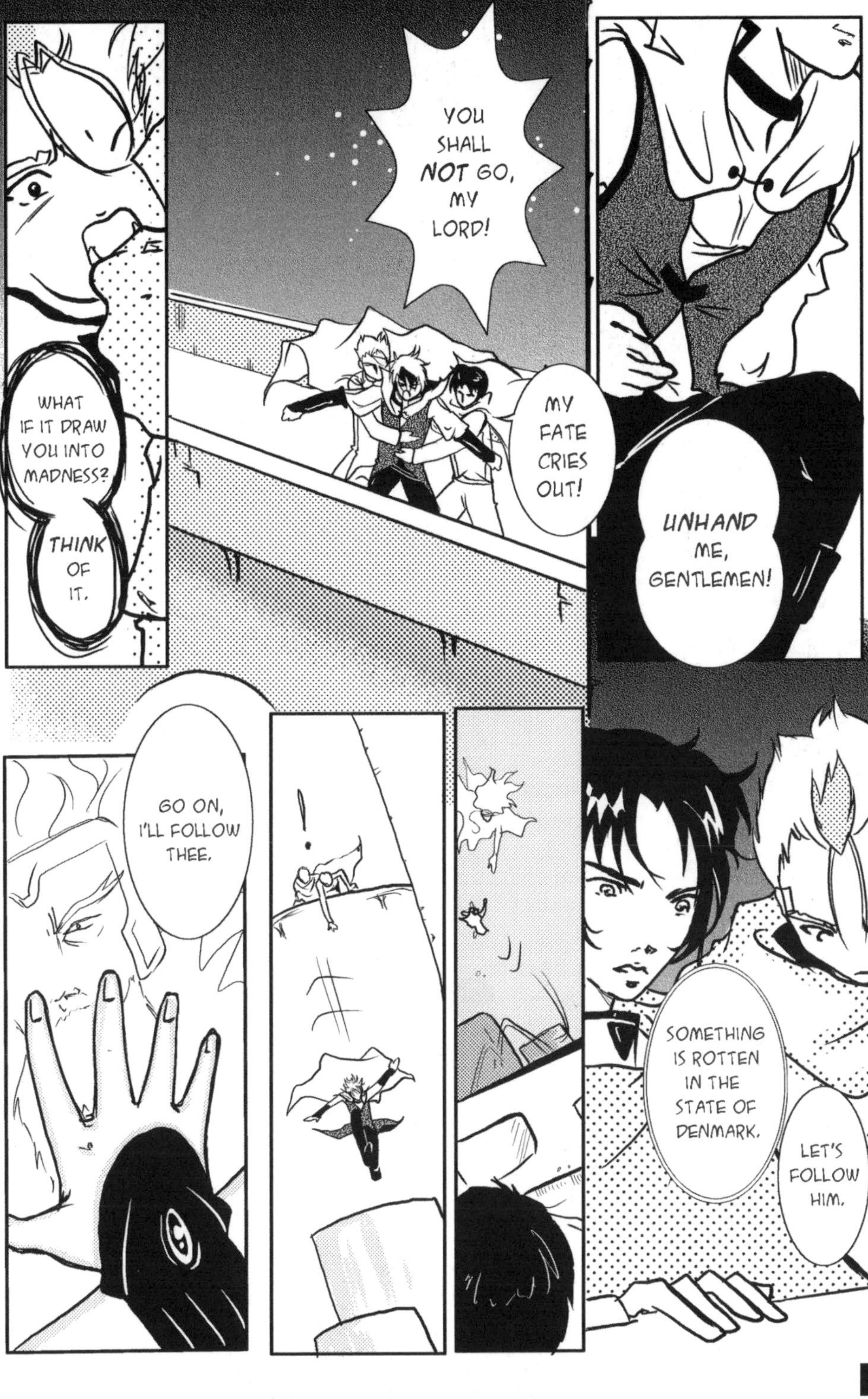
WHAT IF IT DRAW YOU INTO MADNESS?
THINK OF IT.
YOU SHALL NOT GO, MY LORD!
MY FATE CRIES OUT!
UNHAND ME, GENTLEMEN!
GO ON, I'LL FOLLOW THEE.
!
SOMETHING IS ROTTEN IN THE STATE OF DENMARK.
LET'S FOLLOW HIM.

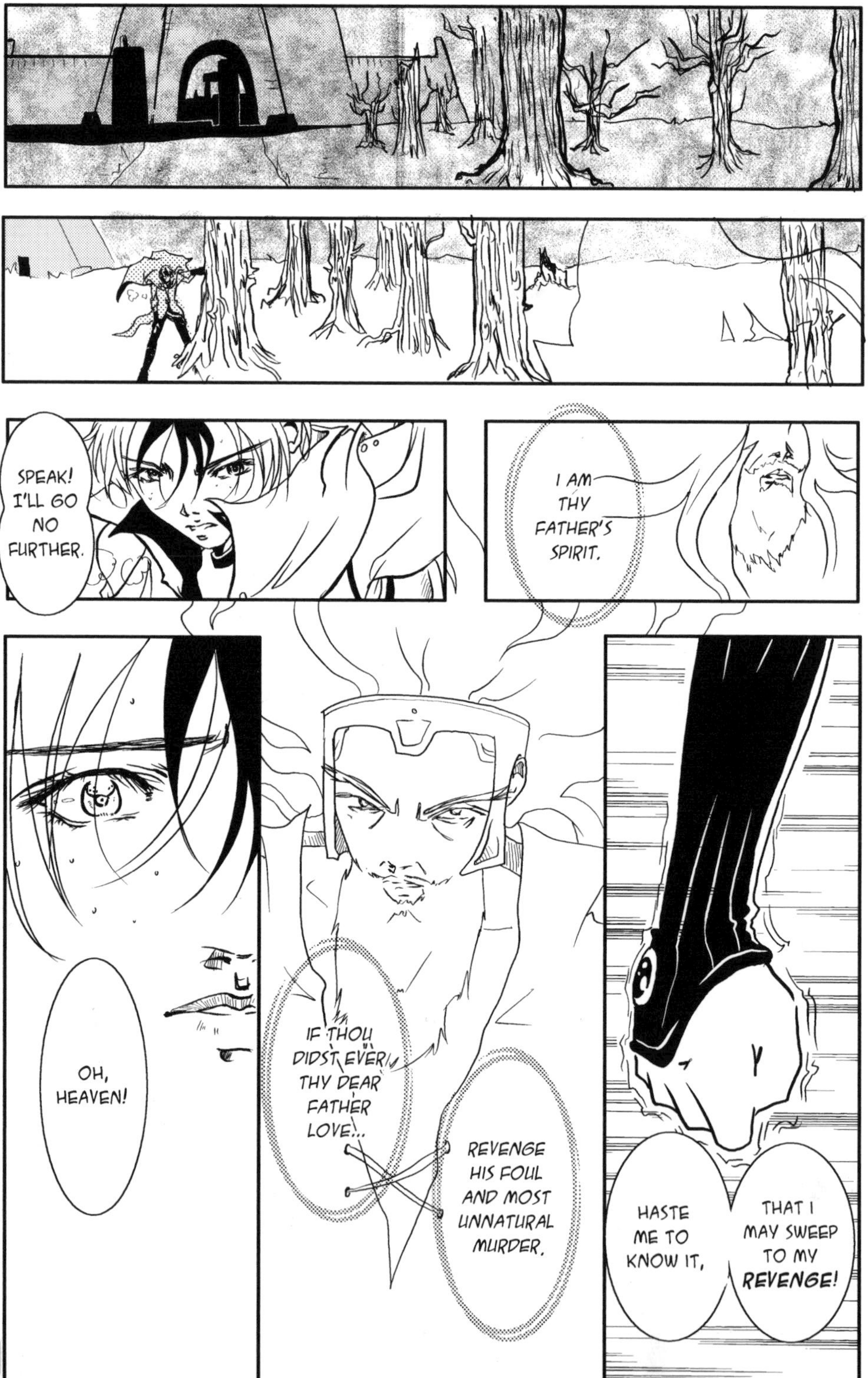
SPEAK! I'LL GO NO FURTHER.
I AM THY FATHER'S SPIRIT.
OH, HEAVEN!
IF THOU DIDST EVER THY DEAR FATHER LOVE...
REVENGE HIS FOUL AND MOST UNNATURAL MURDER.
HASTE ME TO KNOW IT,
THAT I MAY SWEEP TO MY **REVENGE!**

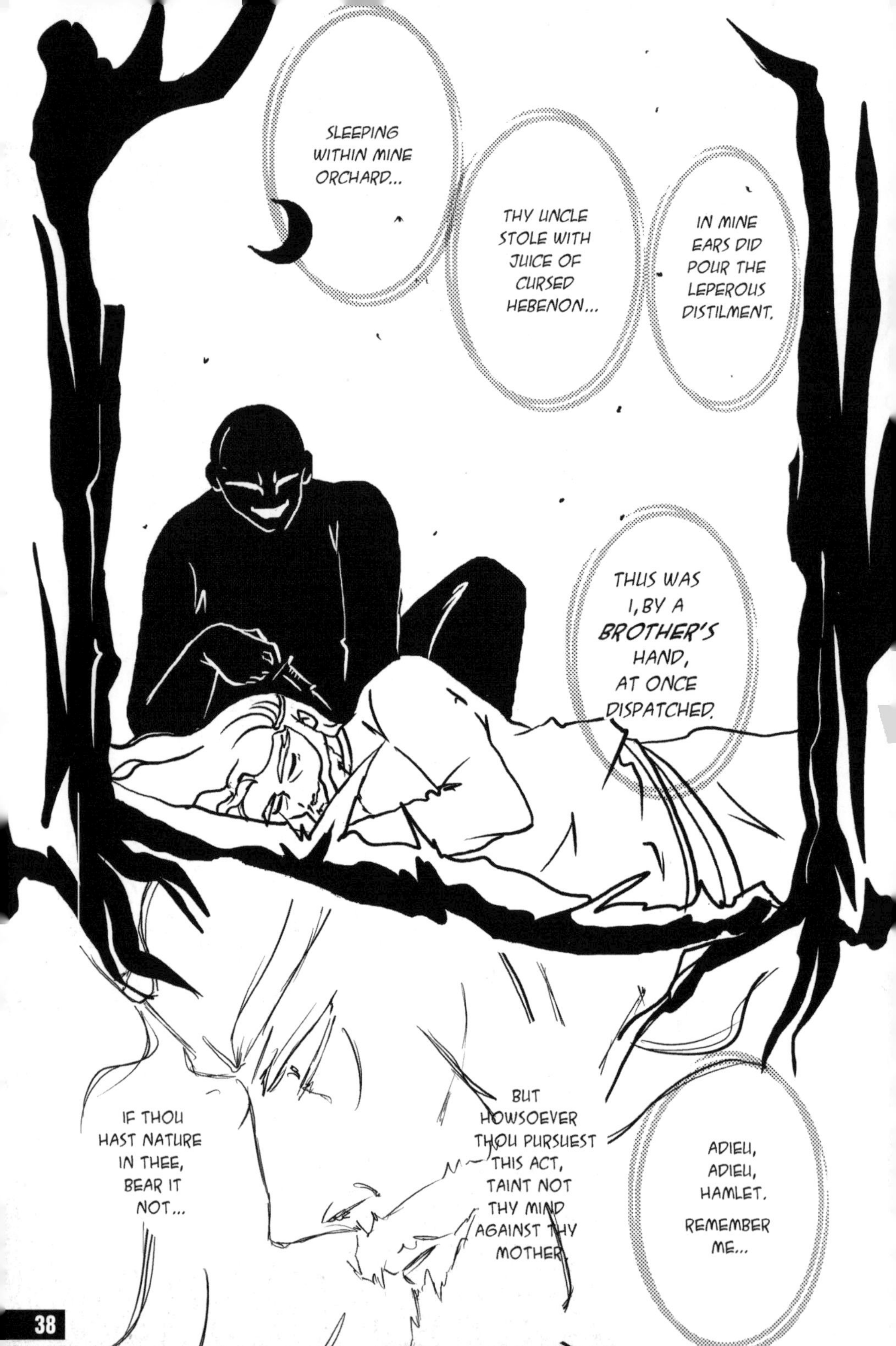
SLEEPING WITHIN MINE ORCHARD...
THY UNCLE STOLE WITH JUICE OF CURSED HEBENON...
IN MINE EARS DID POUR THE LEPEROUS DISTILMENT.
THUS WAS I, BY A BROTHER'S HAND, AT ONCE DISPATCHED.
IF THOU HAST NATURE IN THEE, BEAR IT NOT...
BUT HOWSOEVER THOU PURSUEST THIS ACT, TAINT NOT THY MIND AGAINST THY MOTHER.
ADIEU, ADIEU, HAMLET.
REMEMBER ME...

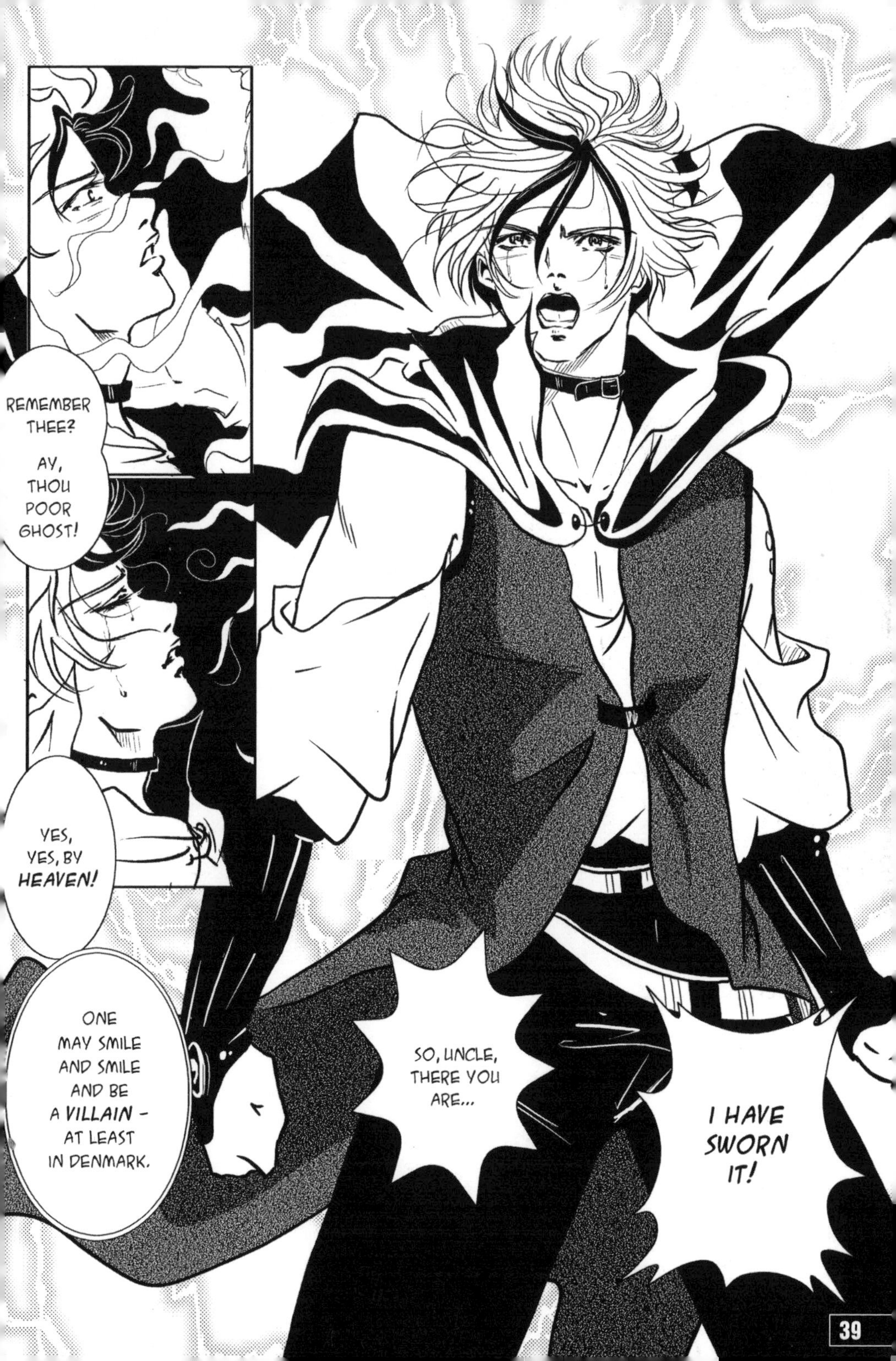
REMEMBER THEE?
AY, THOU POOR GHOST!
YES, YES, BY HEAVEN!
ONE MAY SMILE AND SMILE AND BE A VILLAIN - AT LEAST IN DENMARK.
SO, UNCLE, THERE YOU ARE...
I HAVE SWORN IT!

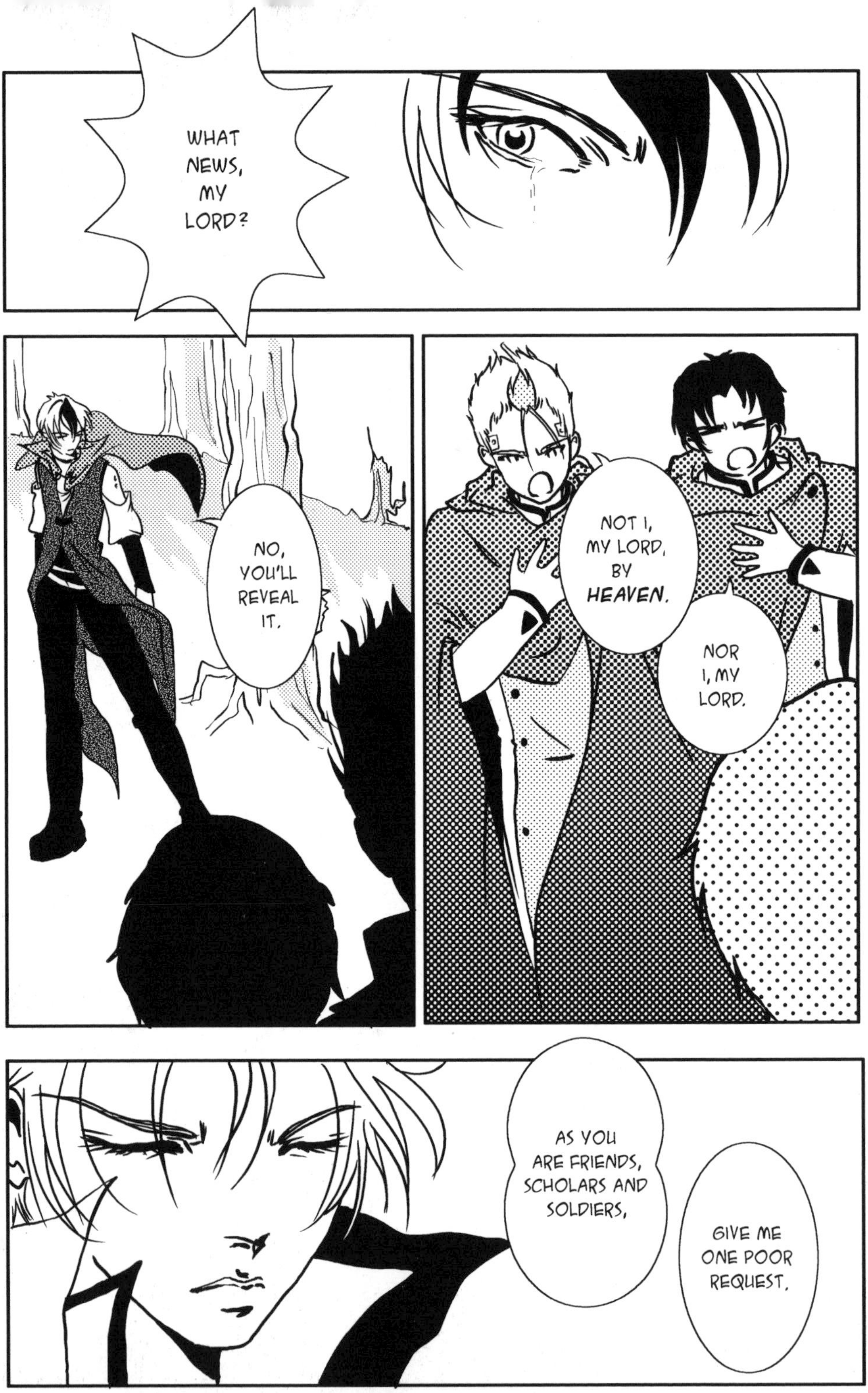
WHAT NEWS, MY LORD?
NO, YOU'LL REVEAL IT.
NOT I, MY LORD, BY **HEAVEN.**
NOR I, MY LORD.
AS YOU ARE FRIENDS, SCHOLARS AND SOLDIERS,
GIVE ME ONE POOR REQUEST.

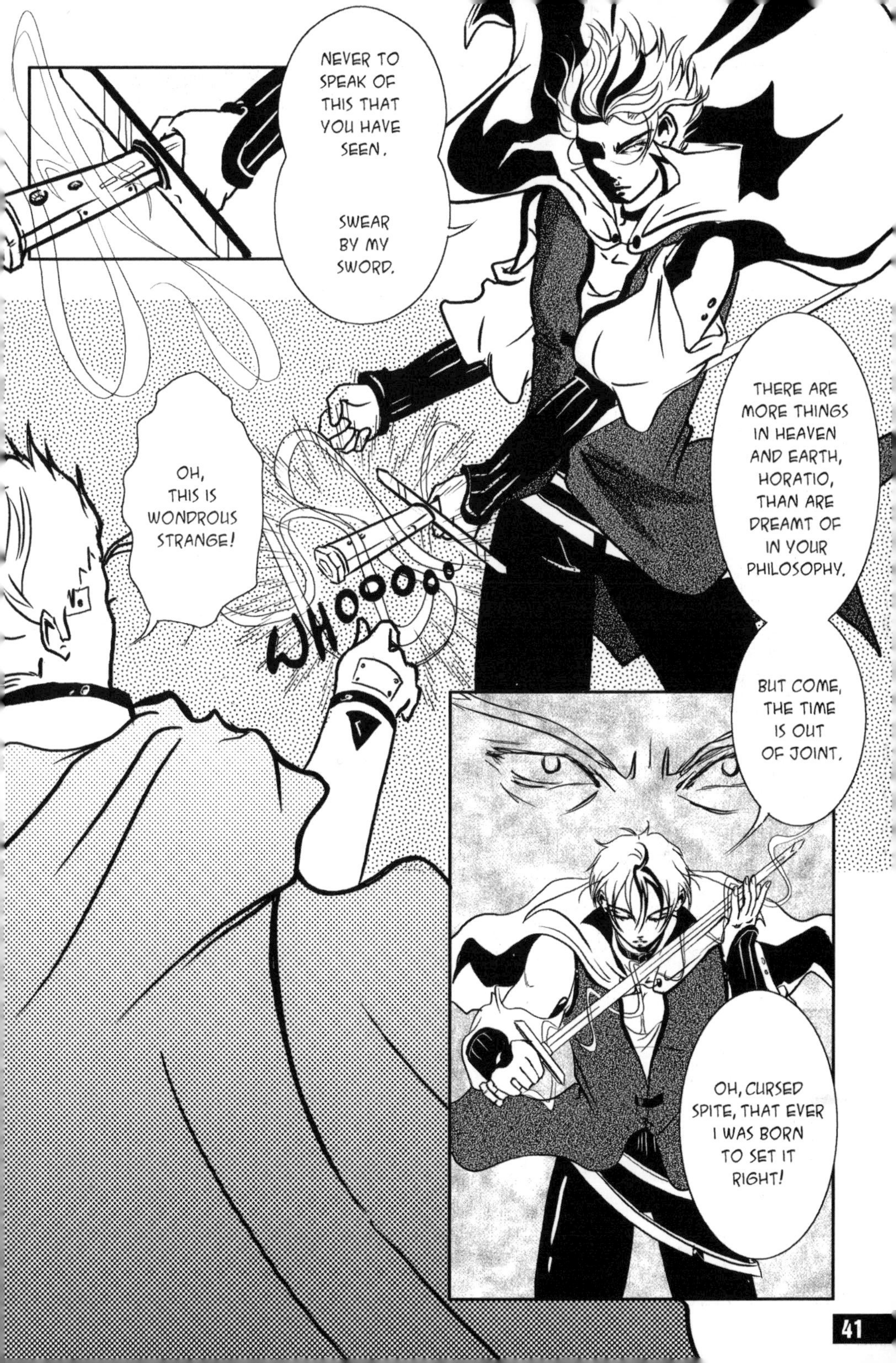
NEVER TO SPEAK OF THIS THAT YOU HAVE SEEN.
SWEAR BY MY SWORD.
OH, THIS IS WONDROUS STRANGE!
WHOOOOO
THERE ARE MORE THINGS IN HEAVEN AND EARTH, HORATIO, THAN ARE DREAMT OF IN YOUR PHILOSOPHY.
BUT COME, THE TIME IS OUT OF JOINT.
OH, CURSED SPITE, THAT EVER I WAS BORN TO SET IT RIGHT!

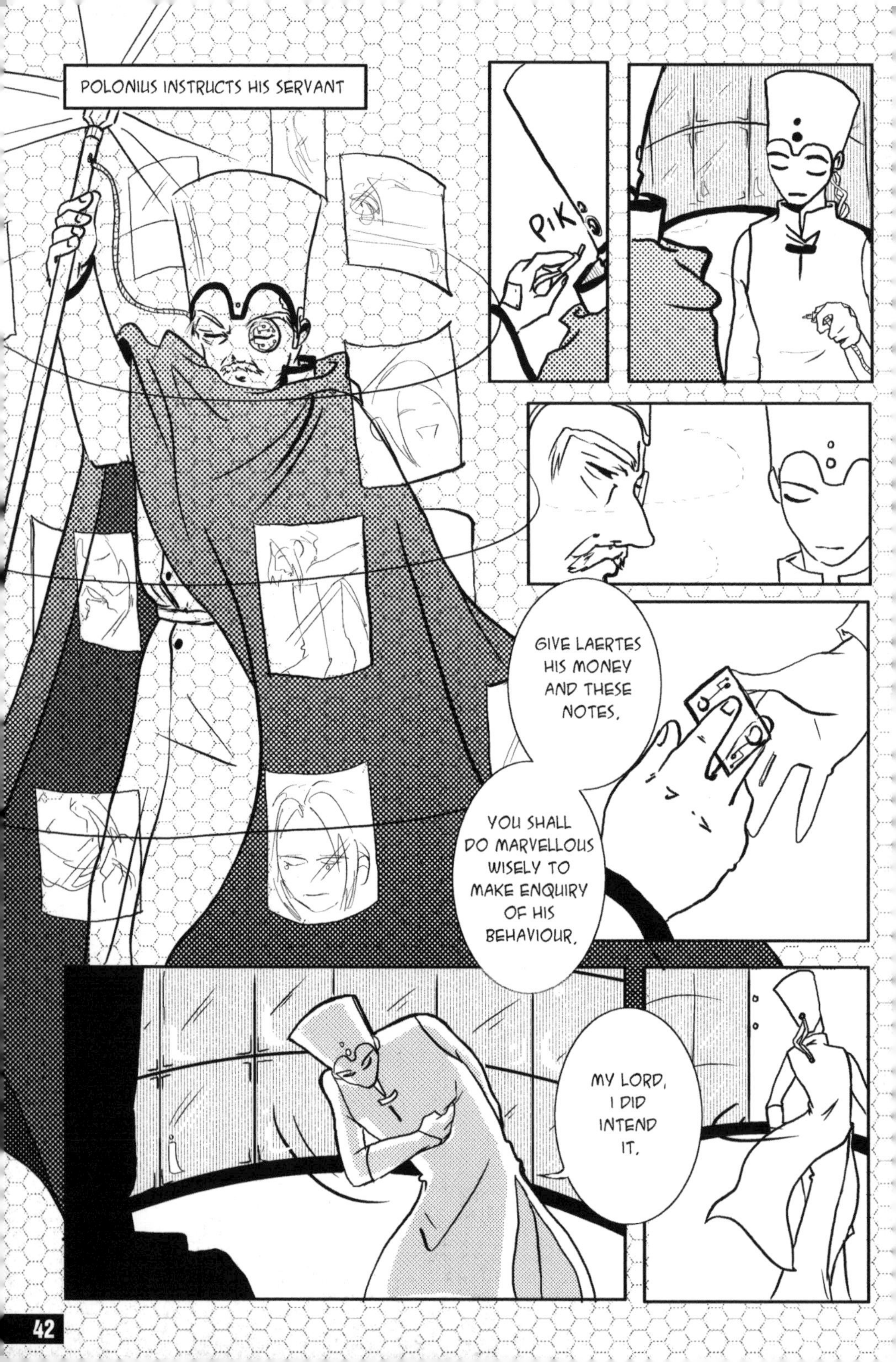
POLONIUS INSTRUCTS HIS SERVANT
PIK
GIVE LAERTES HIS MONEY AND THESE NOTES.
YOU SHALL DO MARVELLOUS WISELY TO MAKE ENQUIRY OF HIS BEHAVIOUR.
MY LORD, I DID INTEND IT.

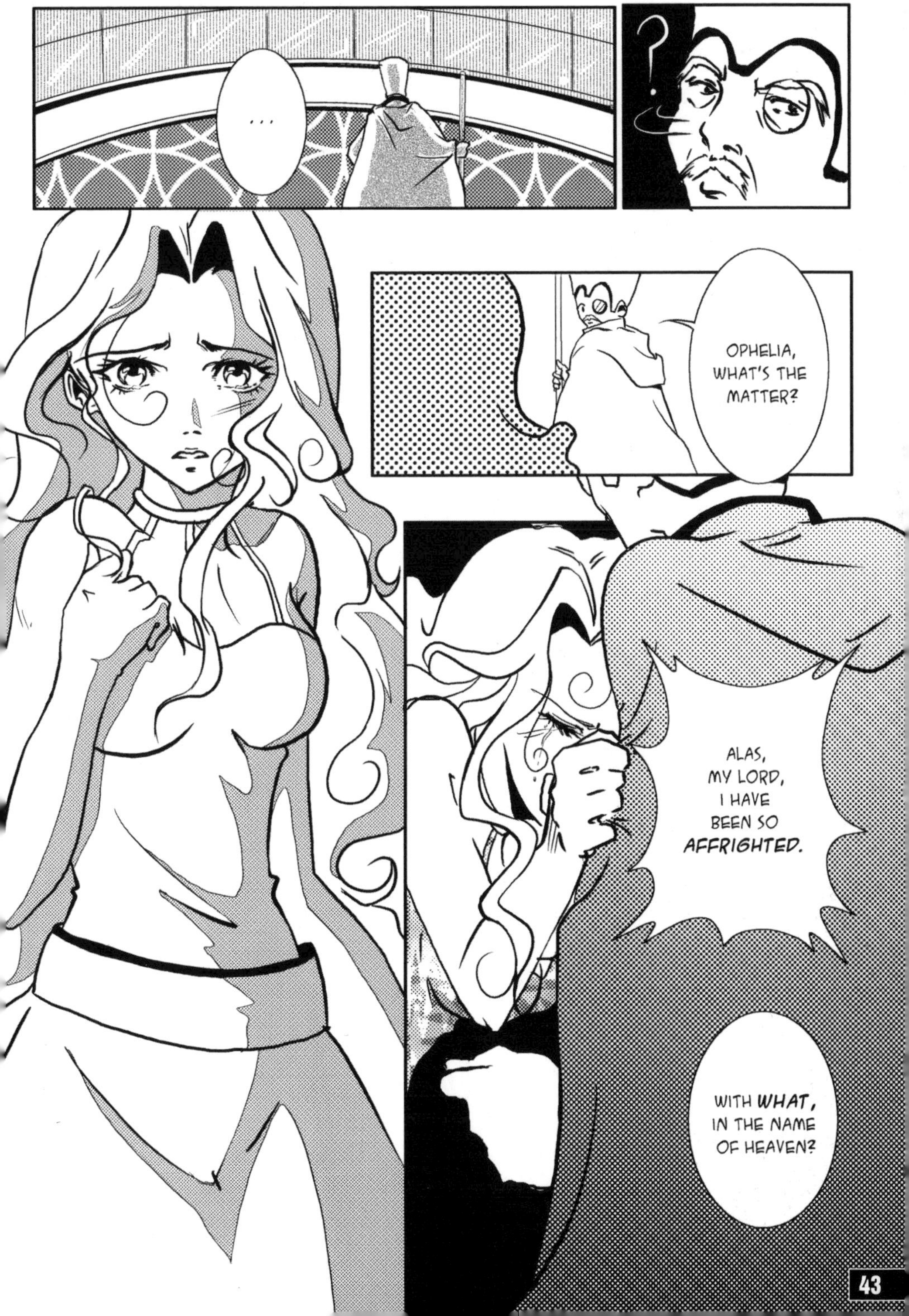
...
?
OPHELIA, WHAT'S THE MATTER?
ALAS, MY LORD, I HAVE BEEN SO **AFFRIGHTED.**
WITH **WHAT,** IN THE NAME OF HEAVEN?

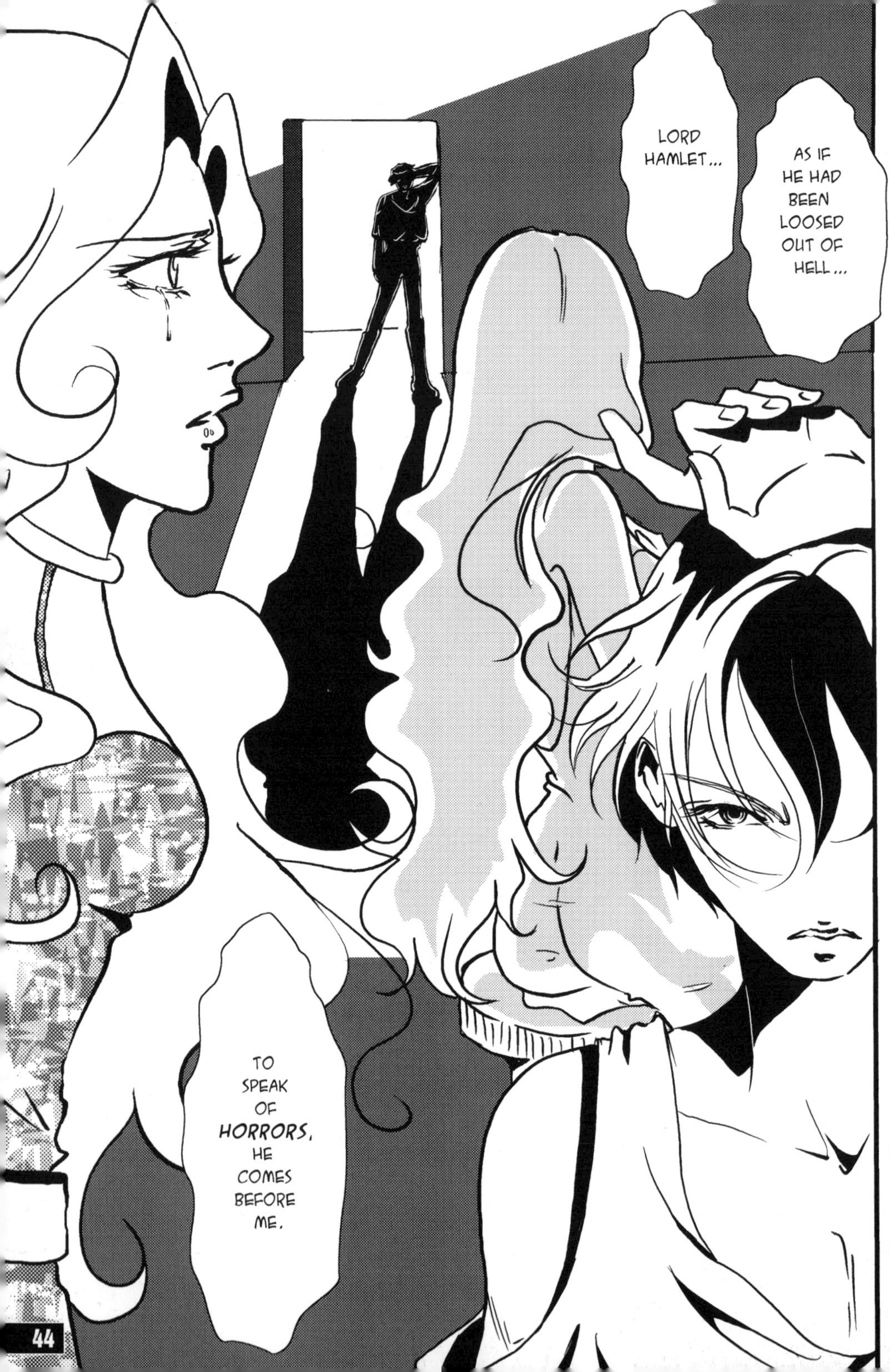
LORD HAMLET...
AS IF HE HAD BEEN LOOSED OUT OF HELL...
TO SPEAK OF HORRORS, HE COMES BEFORE ME.

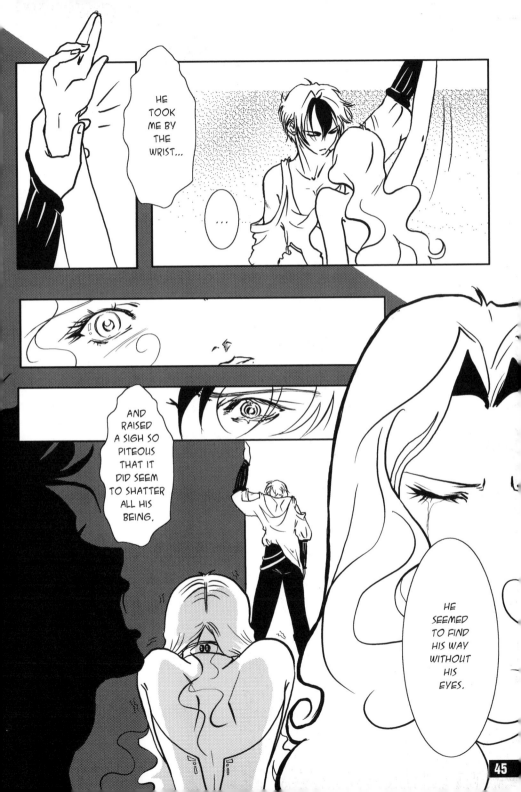

HE TOOK ME BY THE WRIST...

...

AND RAISED A SIGH SO PITEOUS THAT IT DID SEEM TO SHATTER ALL HIS BEING.

HE SEEMED TO FIND HIS WAY WITHOUT HIS EYES.

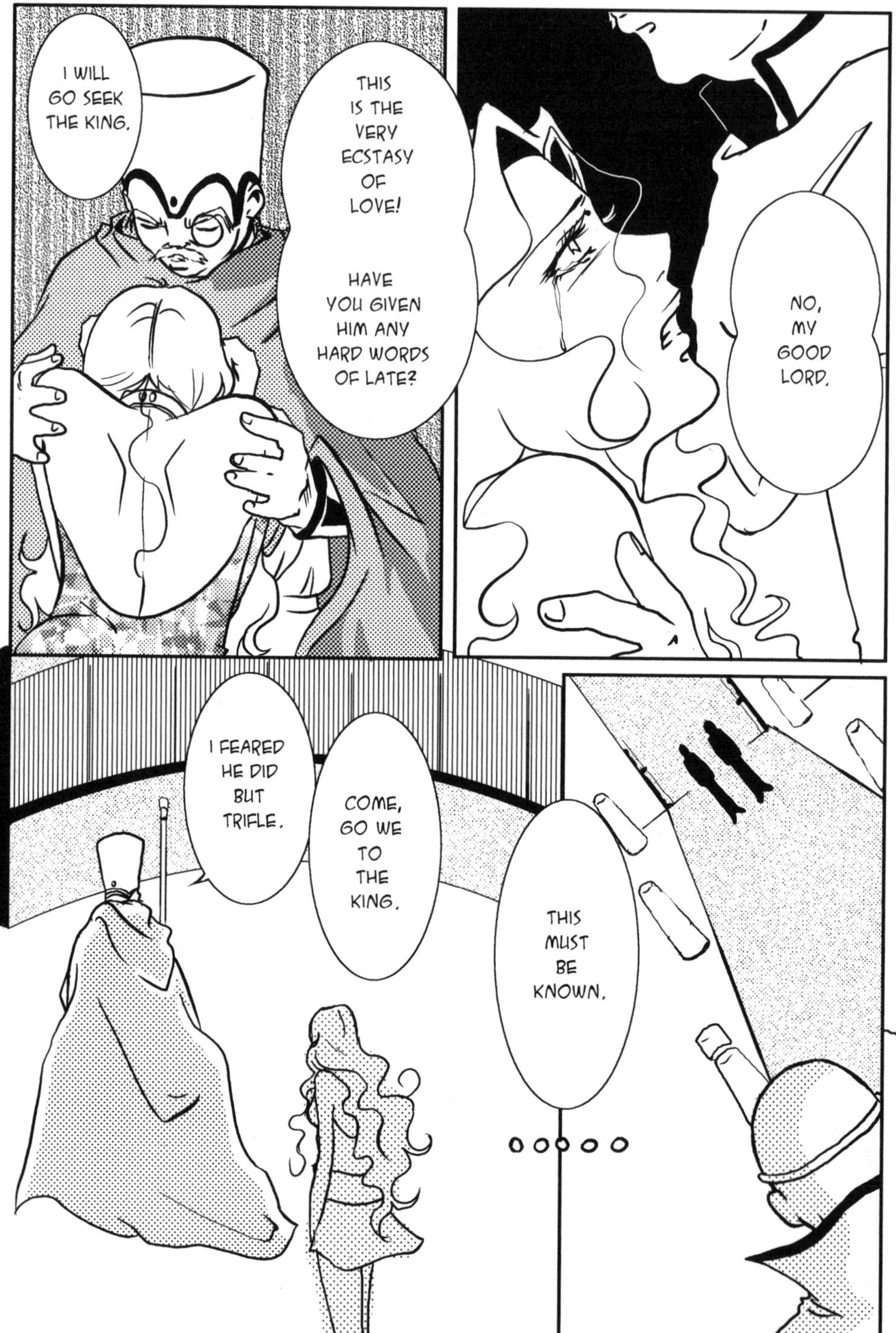
I WILL GO SEEK THE KING.
THIS IS THE VERY ECSTASY OF LOVE!
HAVE YOU GIVEN HIM ANY HARD WORDS OF LATE?
NO, MY GOOD LORD.
I FEARED HE DID BUT TRIFLE.
COME, GO WE TO THE KING.
THIS MUST BE KNOWN.
OOOOO

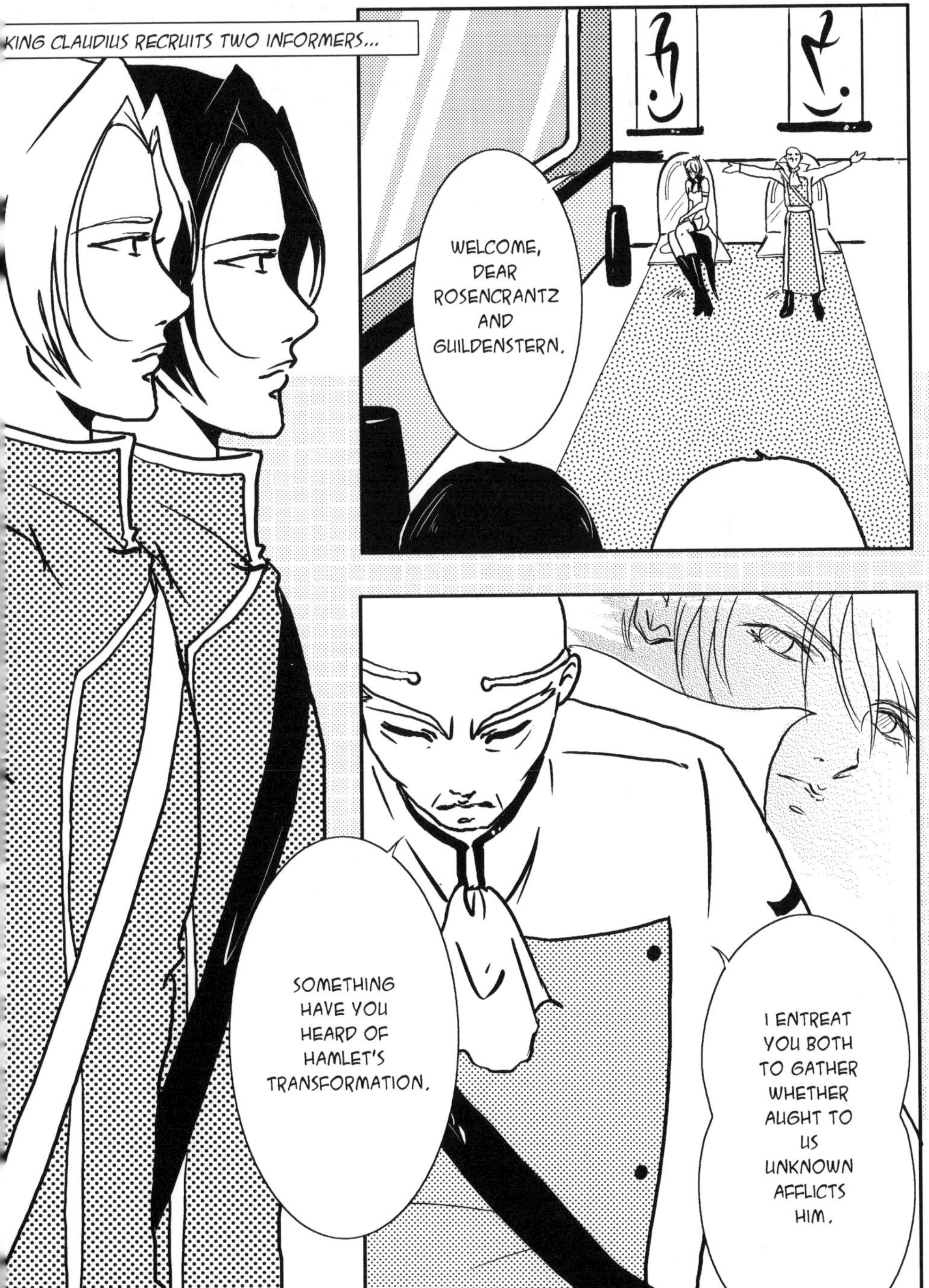
KING CLAUDIUS RECRUITS TWO INFORMERS...
WELCOME, DEAR ROSENCRANTZ AND GUILDENSTERN.
SOMETHING HAVE YOU HEARD OF HAMLET'S TRANSFORMATION.
I ENTREAT YOU BOTH TO GATHER WHETHER AUGHT TO US UNKNOWN AFFLICTS HIM.

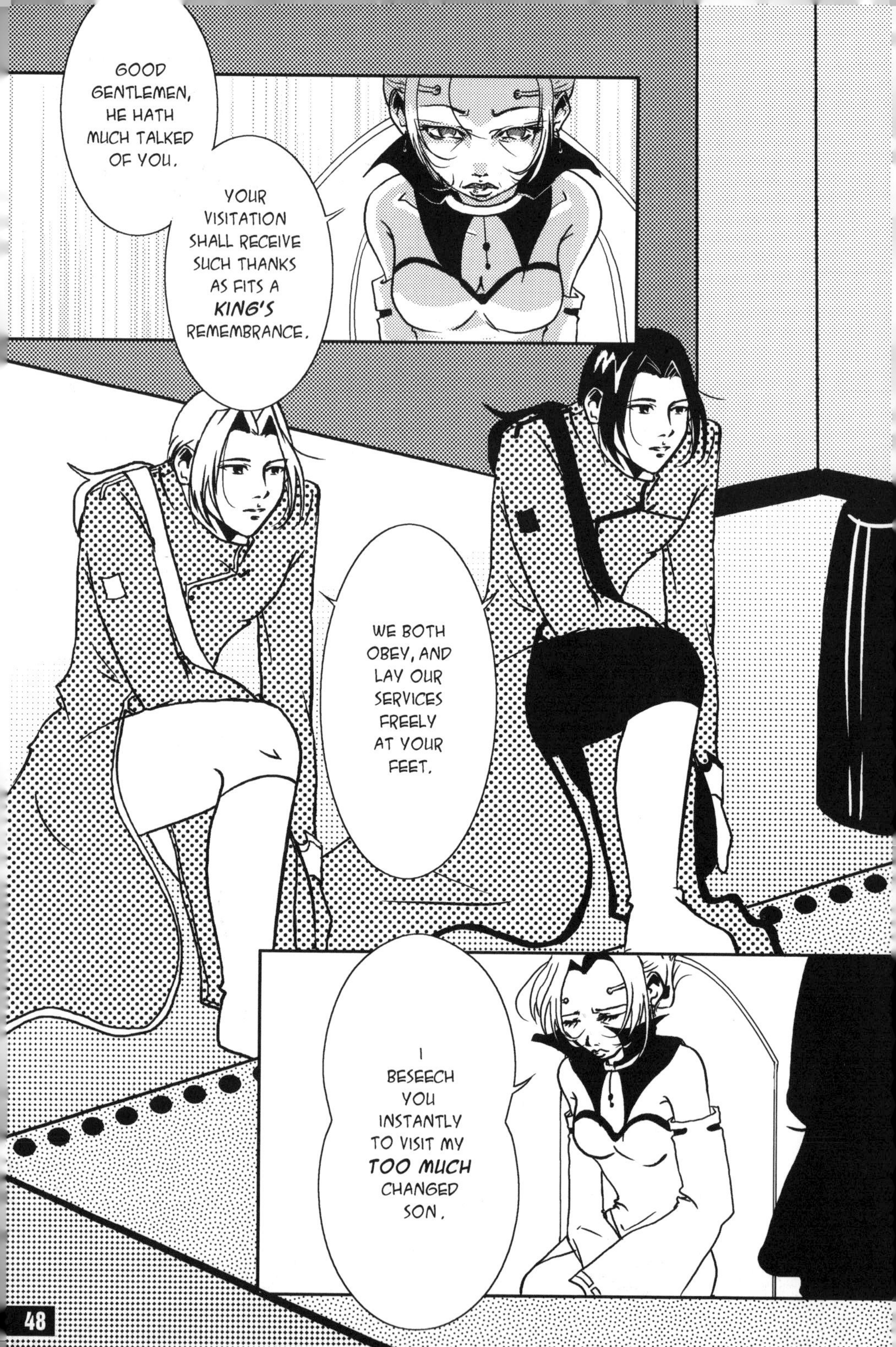
GOOD GENTLEMEN, HE HATH MUCH TALKED OF YOU.
YOUR VISITATION SHALL RECEIVE SUCH THANKS AS FITS A **KING'S** REMEMBRANCE.
WE BOTH OBEY, AND LAY OUR SERVICES FREELY AT YOUR FEET.
I BESEECH YOU INSTANTLY TO VISIT MY **TOO MUCH** CHANGED SON.

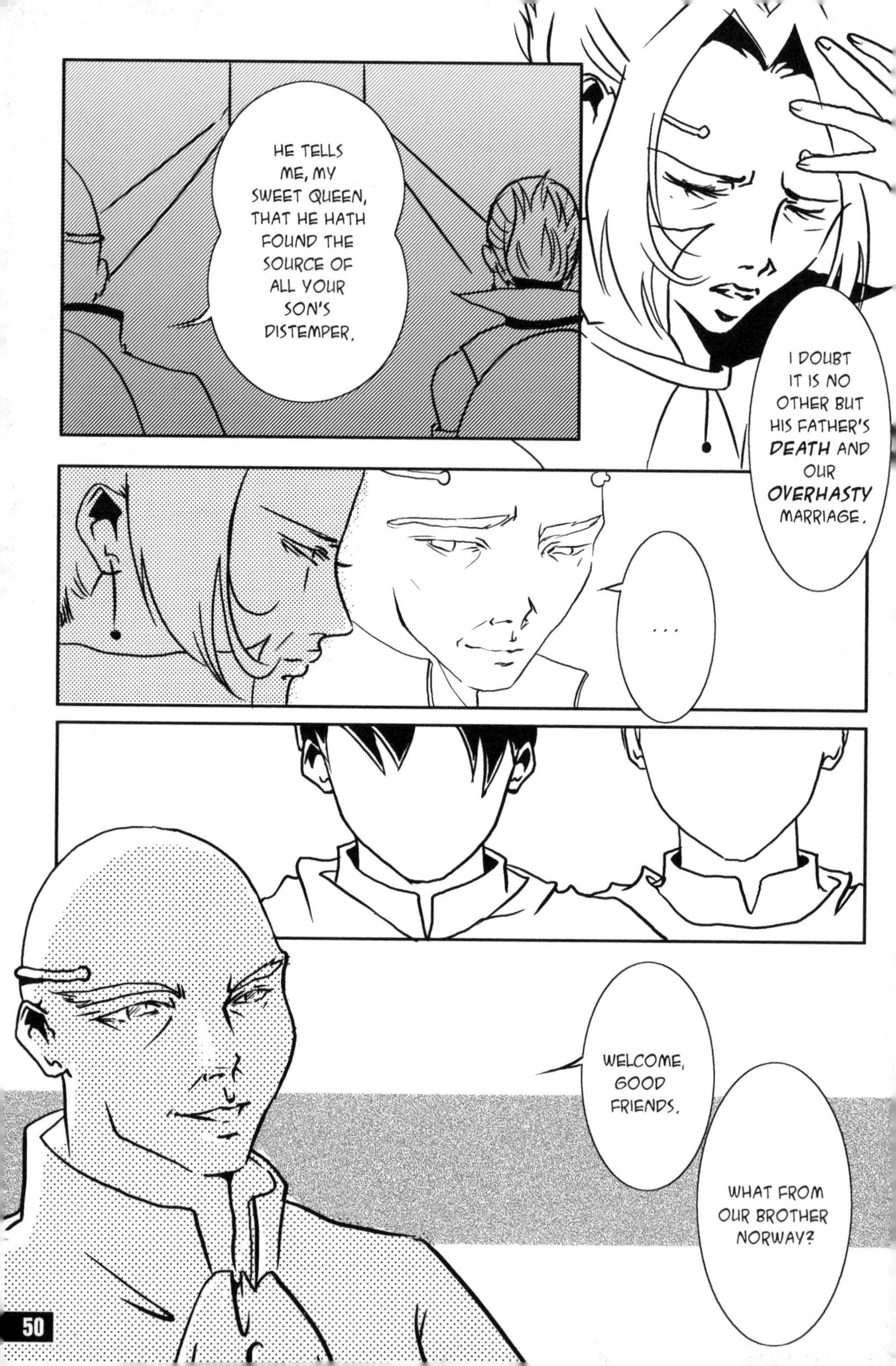
HE TELLS ME, MY SWEET QUEEN, THAT HE HATH FOUND THE SOURCE OF ALL YOUR SON'S DISTEMPER.
I DOUBT IT IS NO OTHER BUT HIS FATHER'S **DEATH** AND OUR **OVERHASTY** MARRIAGE.
. . .
WELCOME, GOOD FRIENDS.
WHAT FROM OUR BROTHER NORWAY?

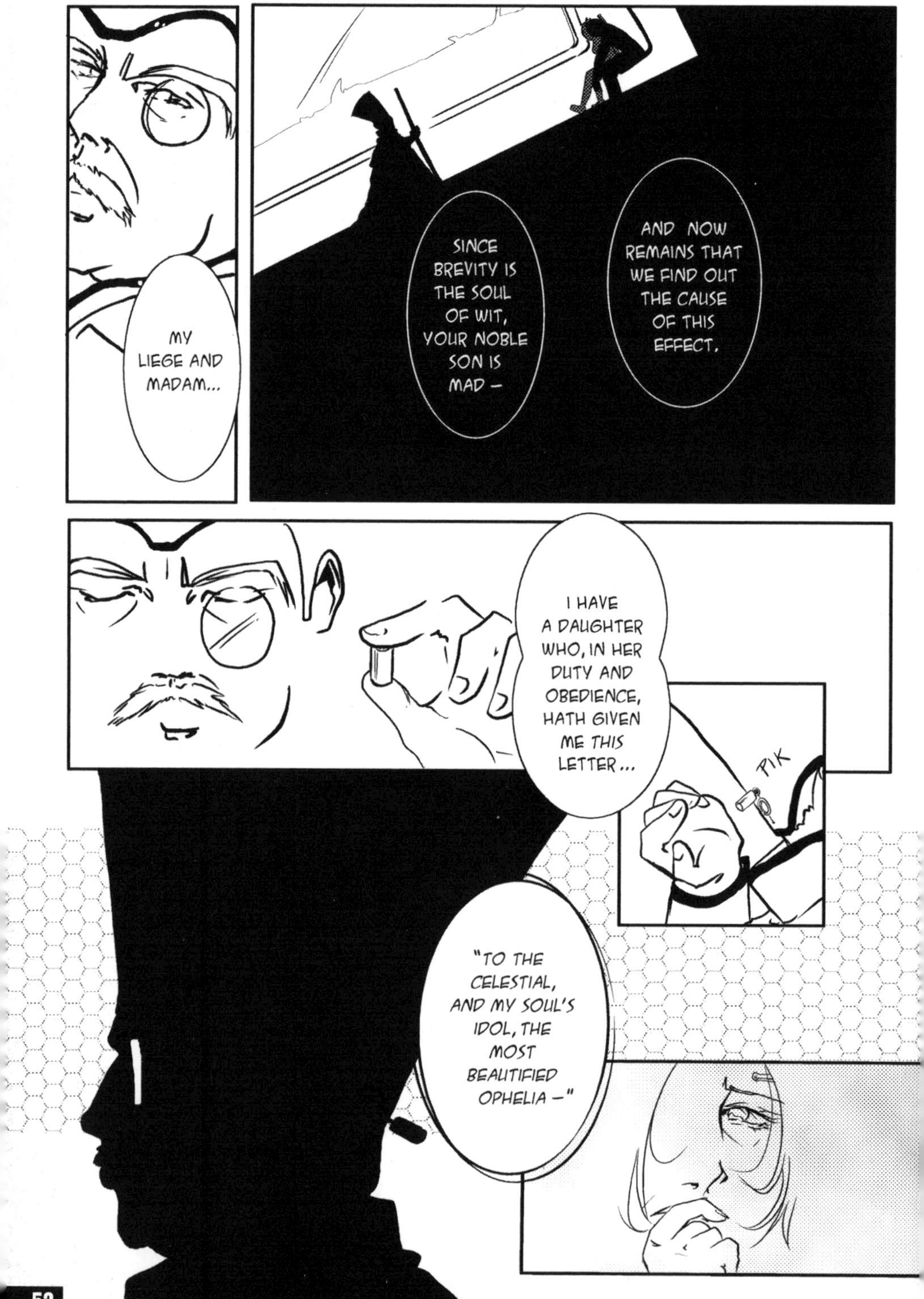
MY LIEGE AND MADAM...
SINCE BREVITY IS THE SOUL OF WIT, YOUR NOBLE SON IS MAD –
AND NOW REMAINS THAT WE FIND OUT THE CAUSE OF THIS EFFECT.
I HAVE A DAUGHTER WHO, IN HER DUTY AND OBEDIENCE, HATH GIVEN ME THIS LETTER...
PIK
"TO THE CELESTIAL, AND MY SOUL'S IDOL, THE MOST BEAUTIFIED OPHELIA –"

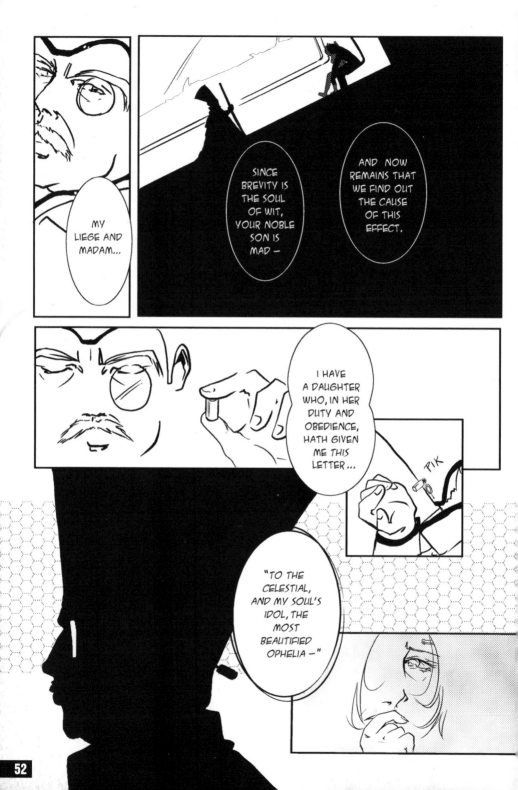

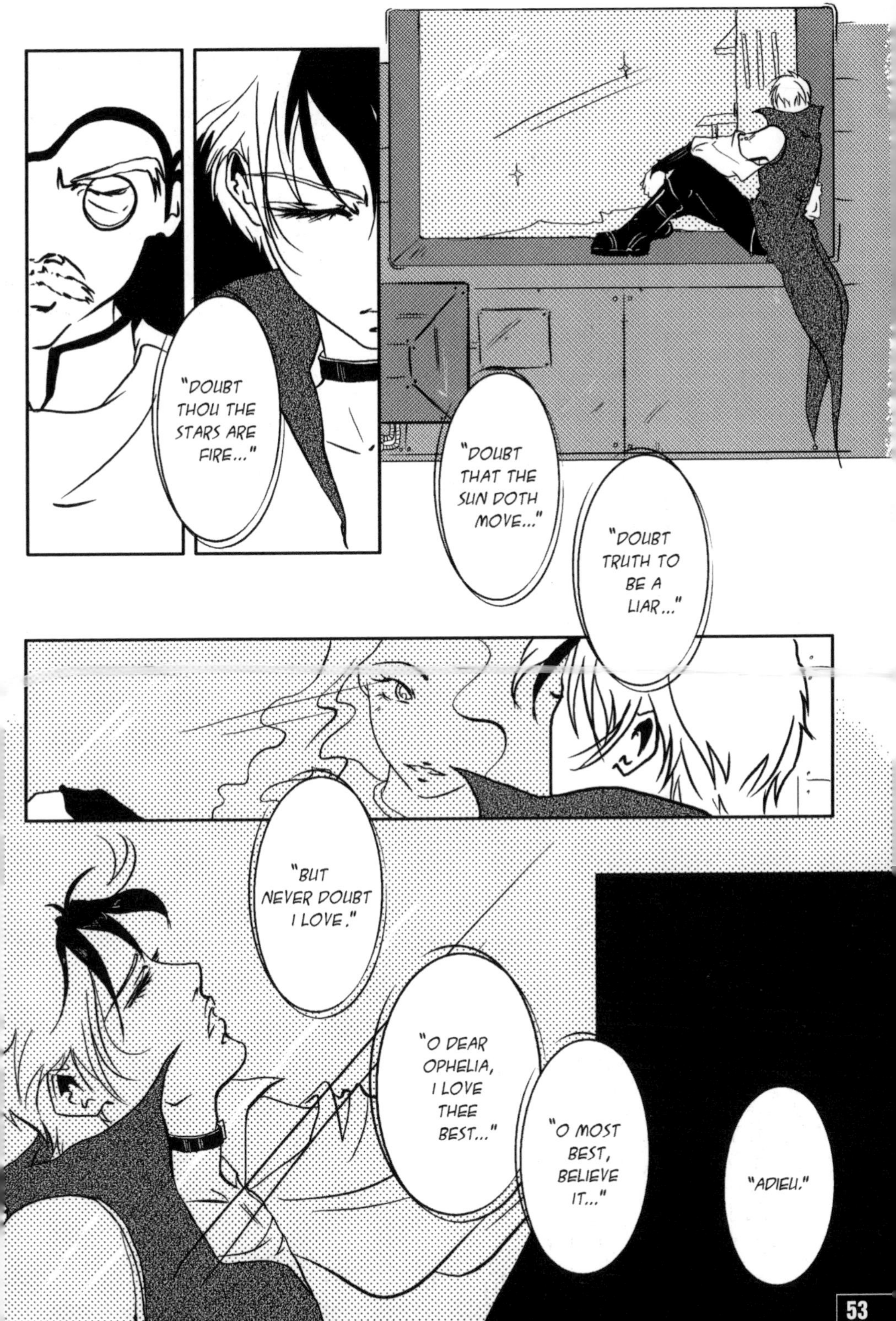
"DOUBT THOU THE STARS ARE FIRE..."
"DOUBT THAT THE SUN DOTH MOVE..."
"DOUBT TRUTH TO BE A LIAR..."
"BUT NEVER DOUBT I LOVE."
"O DEAR OPHELIA, I LOVE THEE BEST..."
"O MOST BEST, BELIEVE IT..."
"ADIEU."

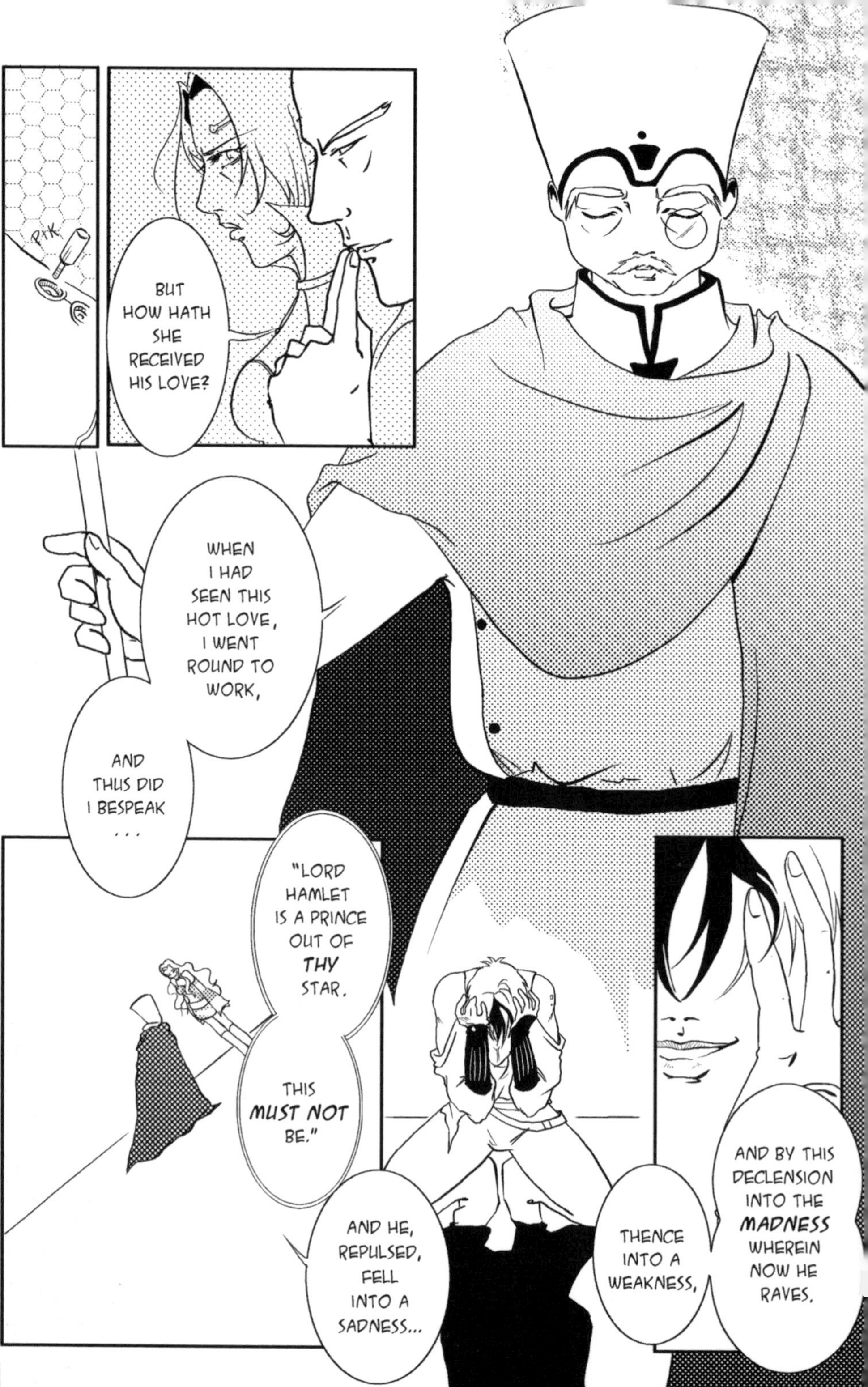
PtK
BUT HOW HATH SHE RECEIVED HIS LOVE?
WHEN I HAD SEEN THIS HOT LOVE, I WENT ROUND TO WORK,
AND THUS DID I BESPEAK . . .
"LORD HAMLET IS A PRINCE OUT OF THY STAR.
THIS MUST NOT BE."
AND HE, REPULSED, FELL INTO A SADNESS...
THENCE INTO A WEAKNESS,
AND BY THIS DECLENSION INTO THE MADNESS WHEREIN NOW HE RAVES.

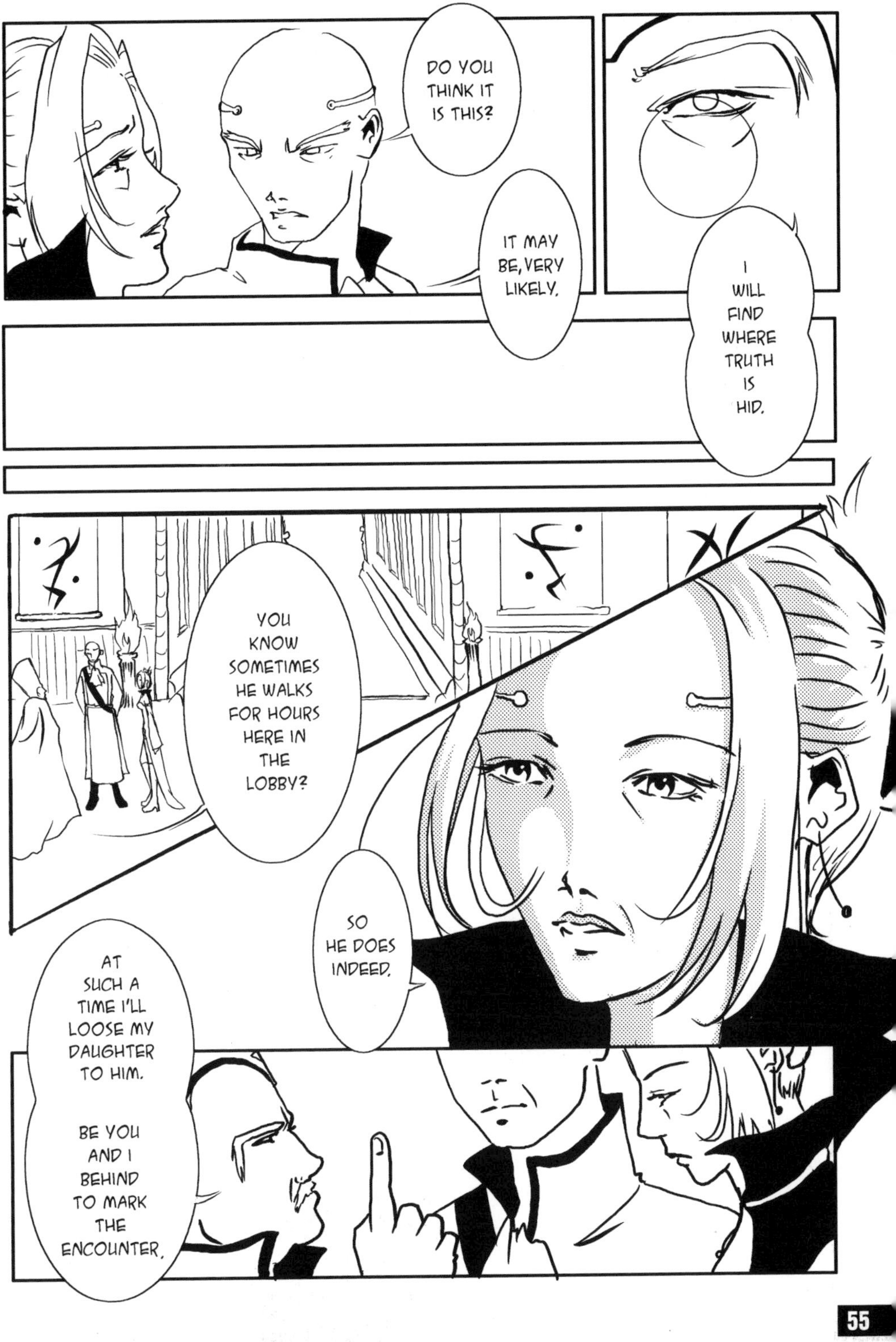
DO YOU THINK IT IS THIS?
IT MAY BE, VERY LIKELY.
I WILL FIND WHERE TRUTH IS HID.
YOU KNOW SOMETIMES HE WALKS FOR HOURS HERE IN THE LOBBY?
SO HE DOES INDEED.
AT SUCH A TIME I'LL LOOSE MY DAUGHTER TO HIM.
BE YOU AND I BEHIND TO MARK THE ENCOUNTER.

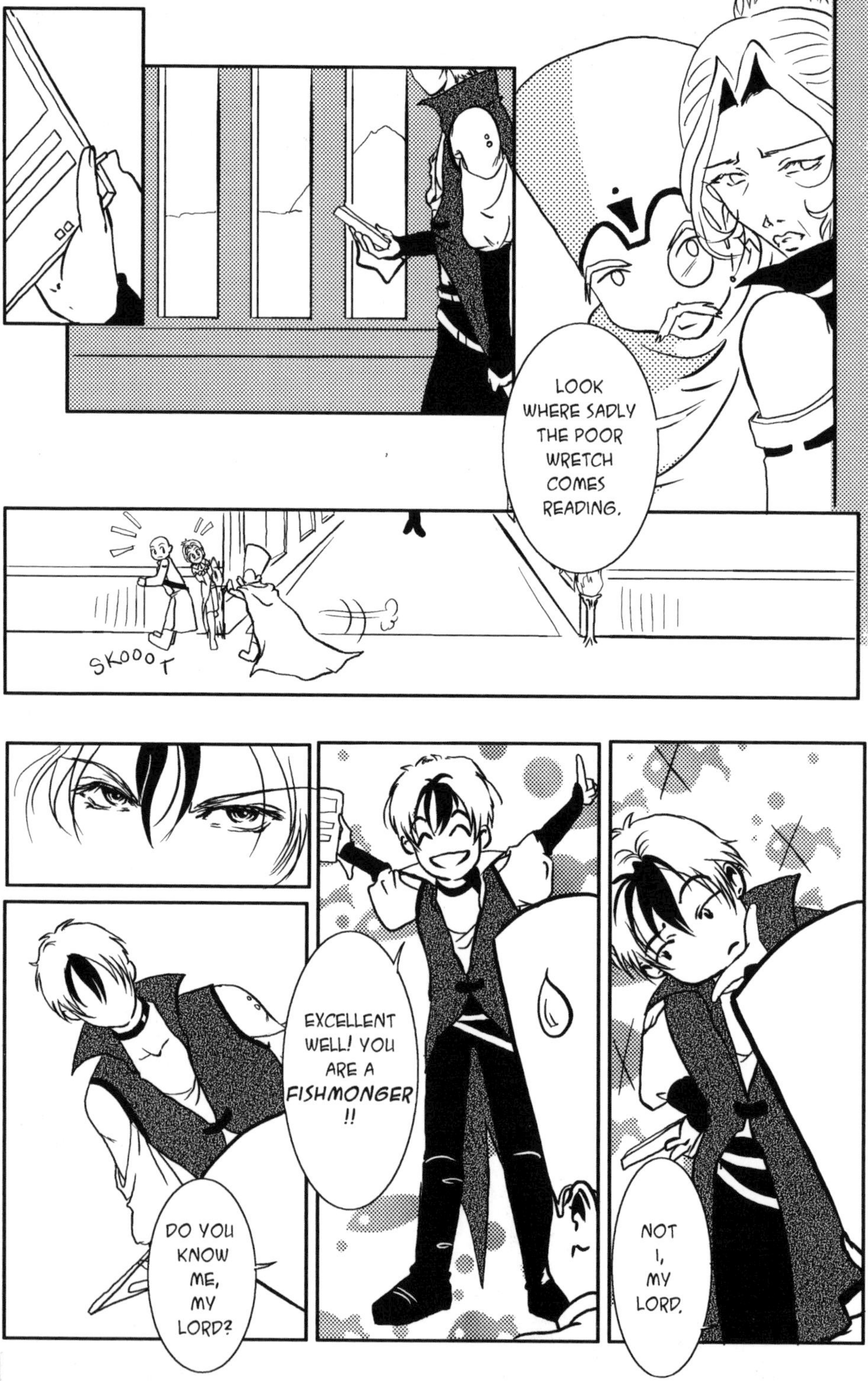
LOOK WHERE SADLY THE POOR WRETCH COMES READING.
SKOOOT
DO YOU KNOW ME, MY LORD?
EXCELLENT WELL! YOU ARE A FISHMONGER !!
NOT I, MY LORD.

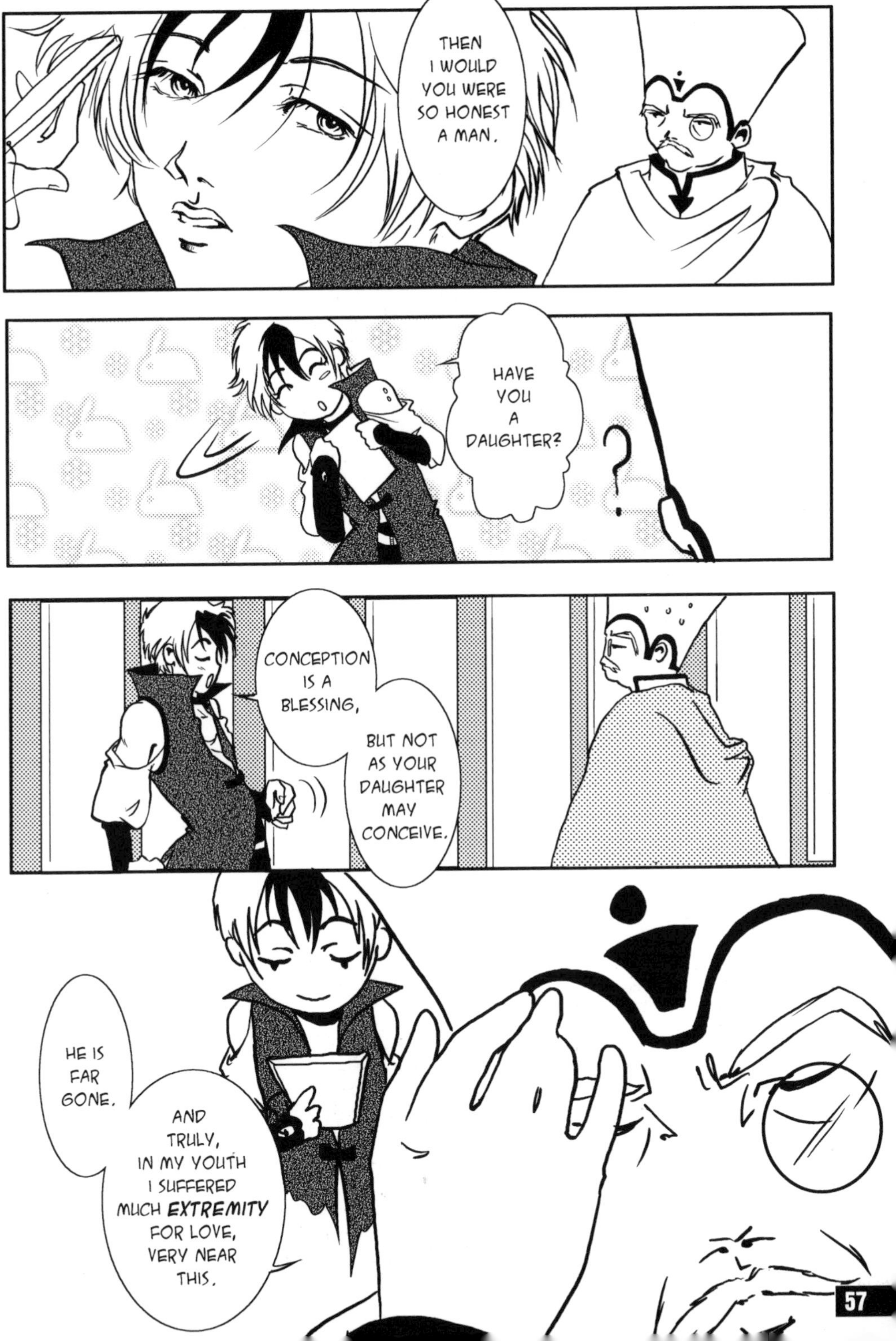

THEN I WOULD YOU WERE SO HONEST A MAN.
HAVE YOU A DAUGHTER?
?
CONCEPTION IS A BLESSING,
BUT NOT AS YOUR DAUGHTER MAY CONCEIVE.
HE IS FAR GONE.
AND TRULY, IN MY YOUTH I SUFFERED MUCH **EXTREMITY** FOR LOVE, VERY NEAR THIS.

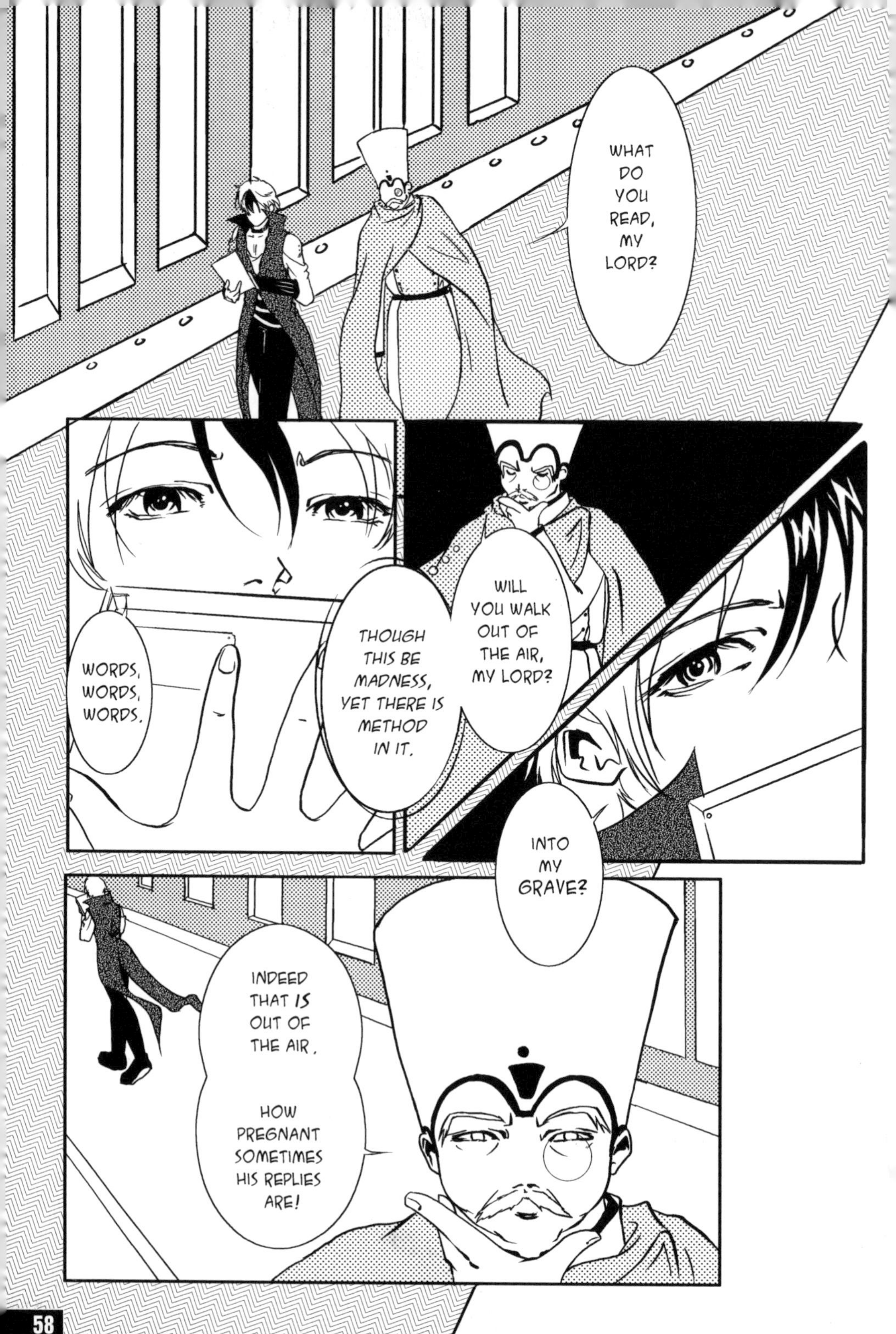
WHAT DO YOU READ, MY LORD?
WORDS, WORDS, WORDS.
THOUGH THIS BE MADNESS, YET THERE IS METHOD IN IT.
WILL YOU WALK OUT OF THE AIR, MY LORD?
INTO MY GRAVE?
INDEED THAT *IS* OUT OF THE AIR.
HOW PREGNANT SOMETIMES HIS REPLIES ARE!

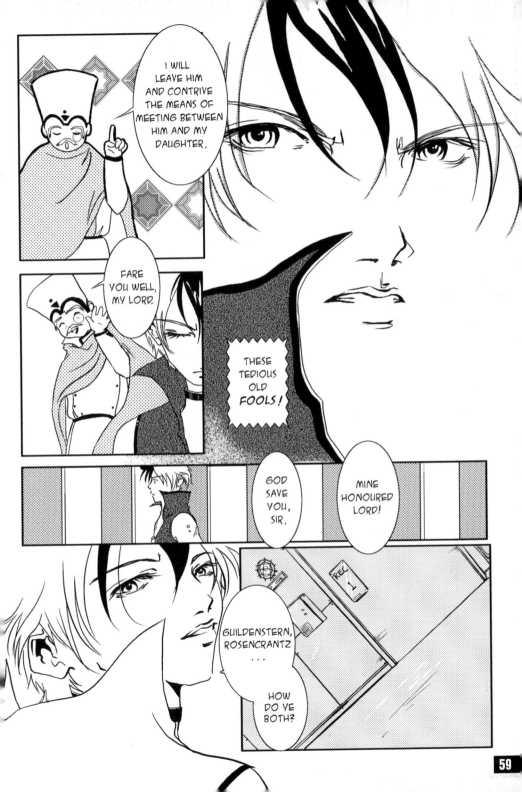

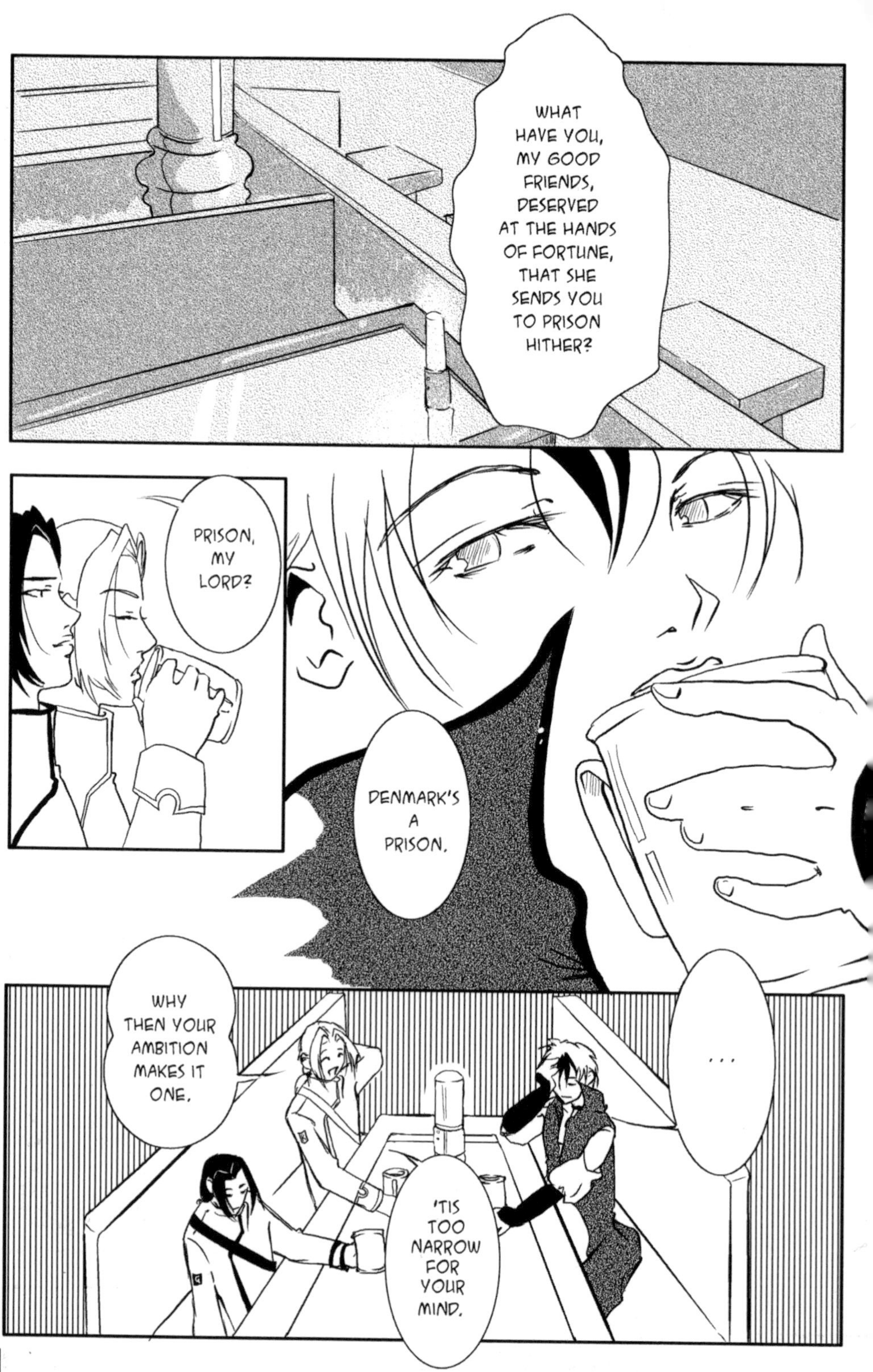
WHAT HAVE YOU, MY GOOD FRIENDS, DESERVED AT THE HANDS OF FORTUNE, THAT SHE SENDS YOU TO PRISON HITHER?
PRISON, MY LORD?
DENMARK'S A PRISON.
WHY THEN YOUR AMBITION MAKES IT ONE.
'TIS TOO NARROW FOR YOUR MIND.
...

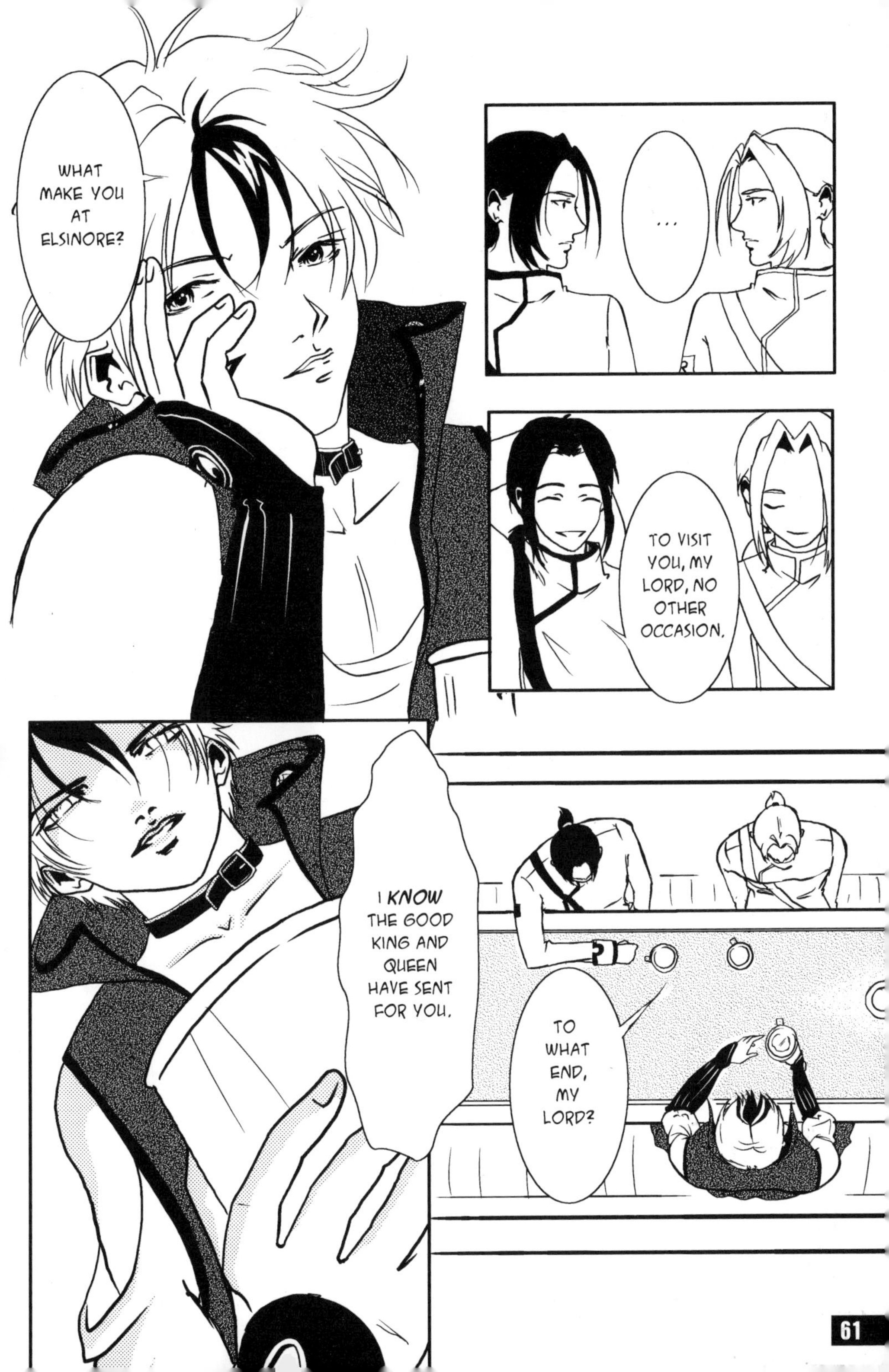
WHAT MAKE YOU AT ELSINORE?
...
TO VISIT YOU, MY LORD, NO OTHER OCCASION.
I *KNOW* THE GOOD KING AND QUEEN HAVE SENT FOR YOU.
TO WHAT END, MY LORD?

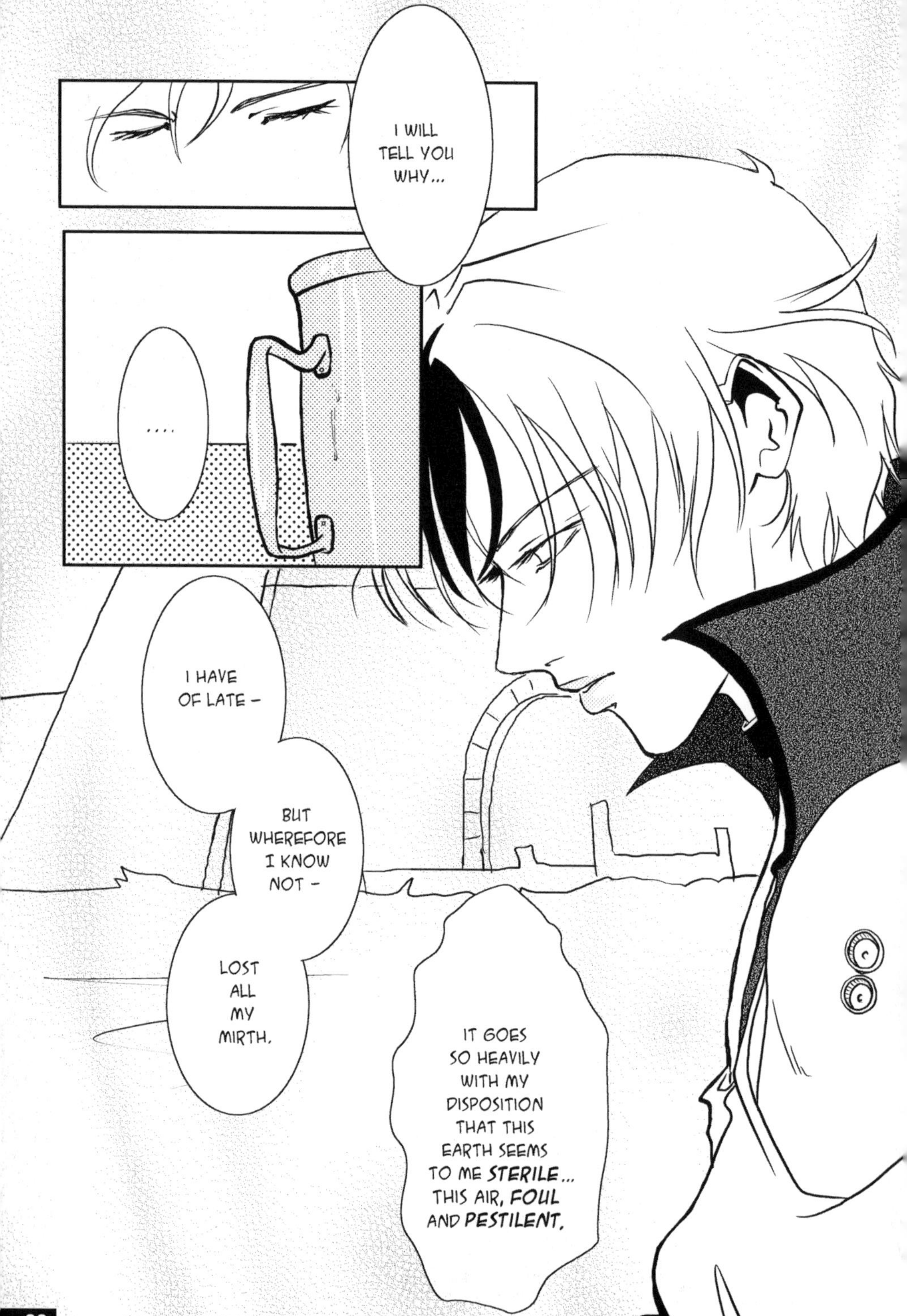
I WILL TELL YOU WHY...
....
I HAVE OF LATE –
BUT WHEREFORE I KNOW NOT –
LOST ALL MY MIRTH.
IT GOES SO HEAVILY WITH MY DISPOSITION THAT THIS EARTH SEEMS TO ME **STERILE**... THIS AIR, **FOUL** AND **PESTILENT**.

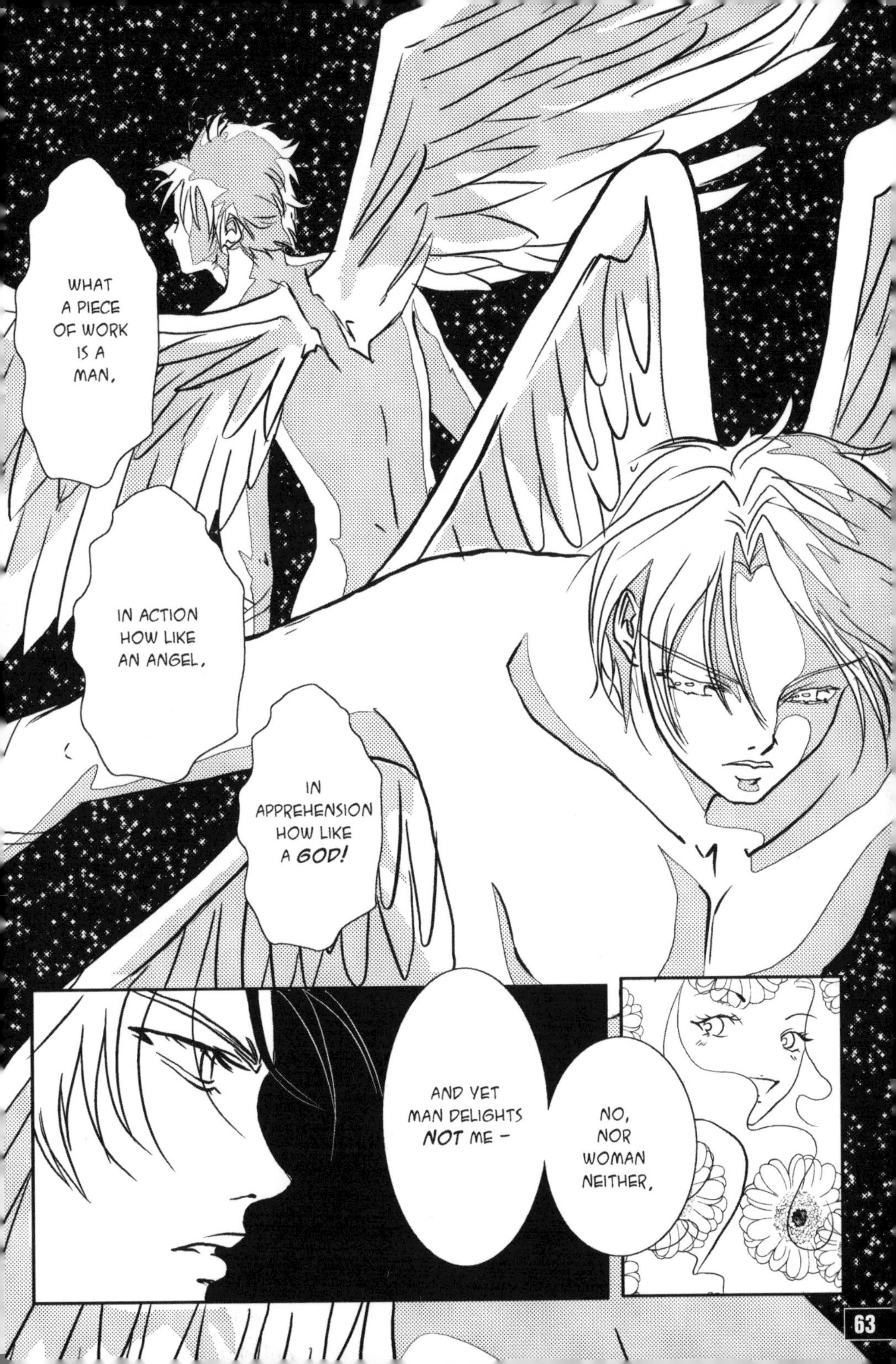
WHAT A PIECE OF WORK IS A MAN,
IN ACTION HOW LIKE AN ANGEL,
IN APPREHENSION HOW LIKE A *GOD!*
AND YET MAN DELIGHTS *NOT* ME –
NO, NOR WOMAN NEITHER,

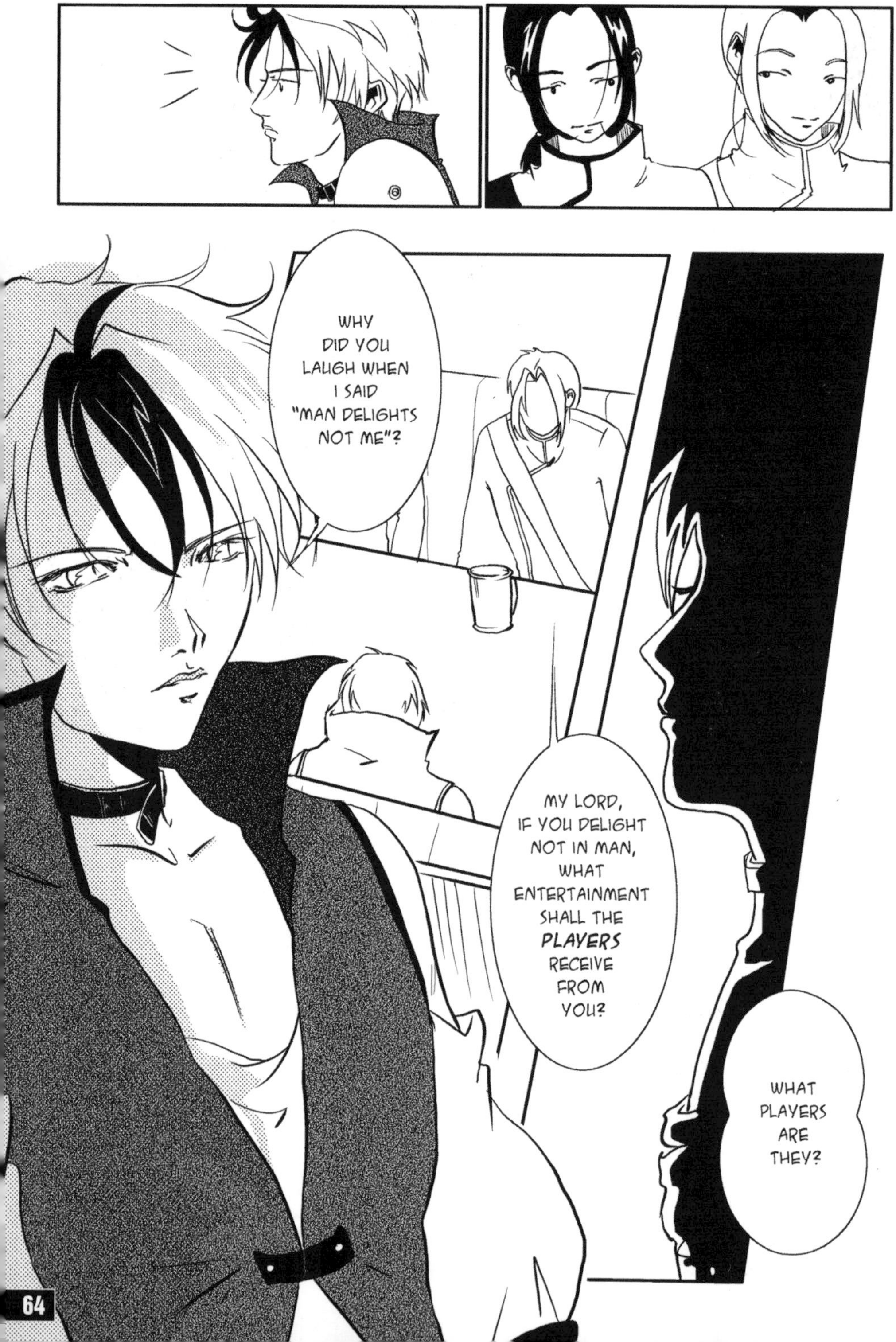
WHY DID YOU LAUGH WHEN I SAID "MAN DELIGHTS NOT ME"?
MY LORD, IF YOU DELIGHT NOT IN MAN, WHAT ENTERTAINMENT SHALL THE **PLAYERS** RECEIVE FROM YOU?
WHAT PLAYERS ARE THEY?

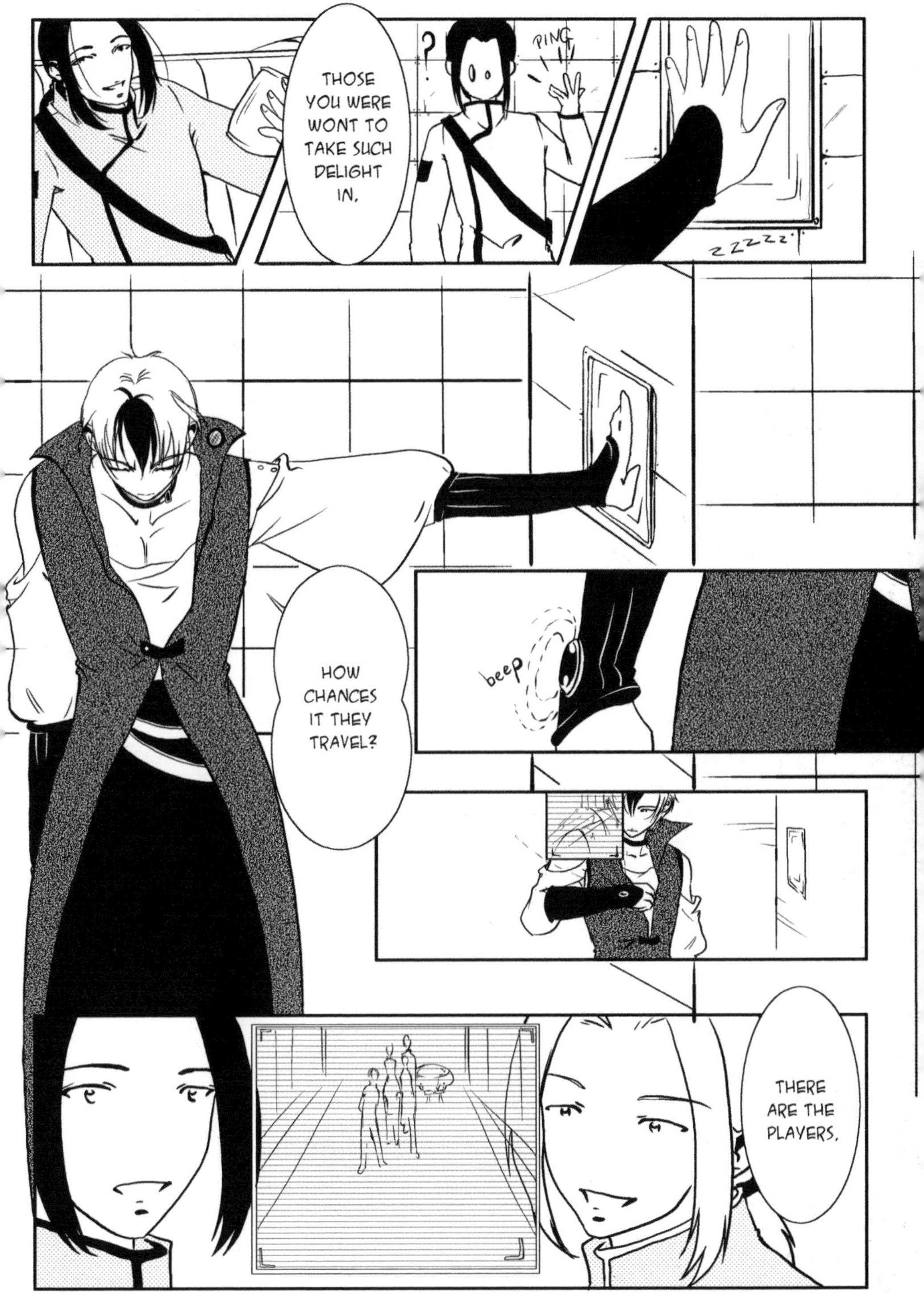
THOSE YOU WERE WONT TO TAKE SUCH DELIGHT IN.
?
PING
ZZZZZ
HOW CHANCES IT THEY TRAVEL?
beep
THERE ARE THE PLAYERS.

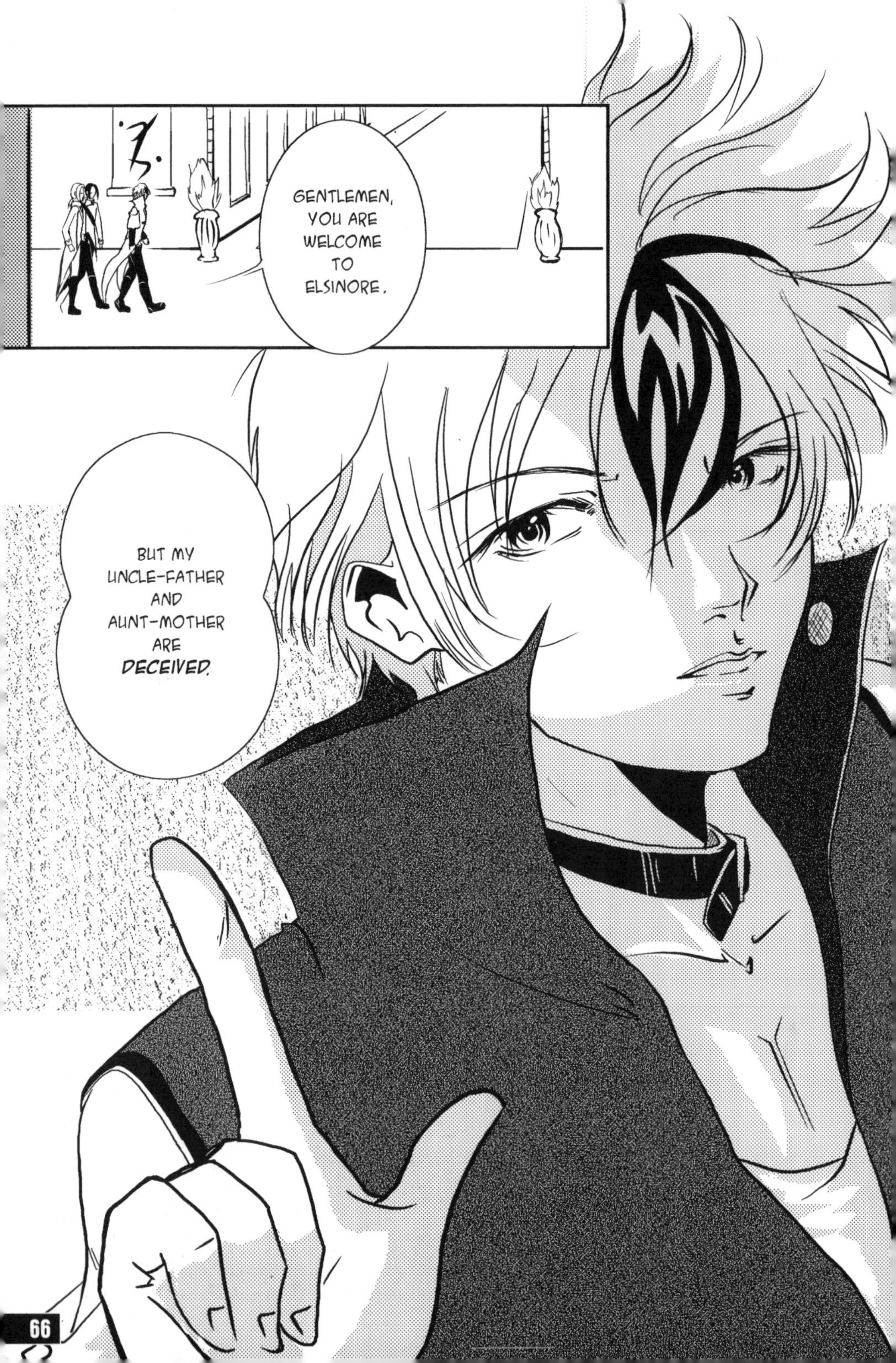

GENTLEMEN, YOU ARE WELCOME TO ELSINORE.
BUT MY UNCLE-FATHER AND AUNT-MOTHER ARE DECEIVED.

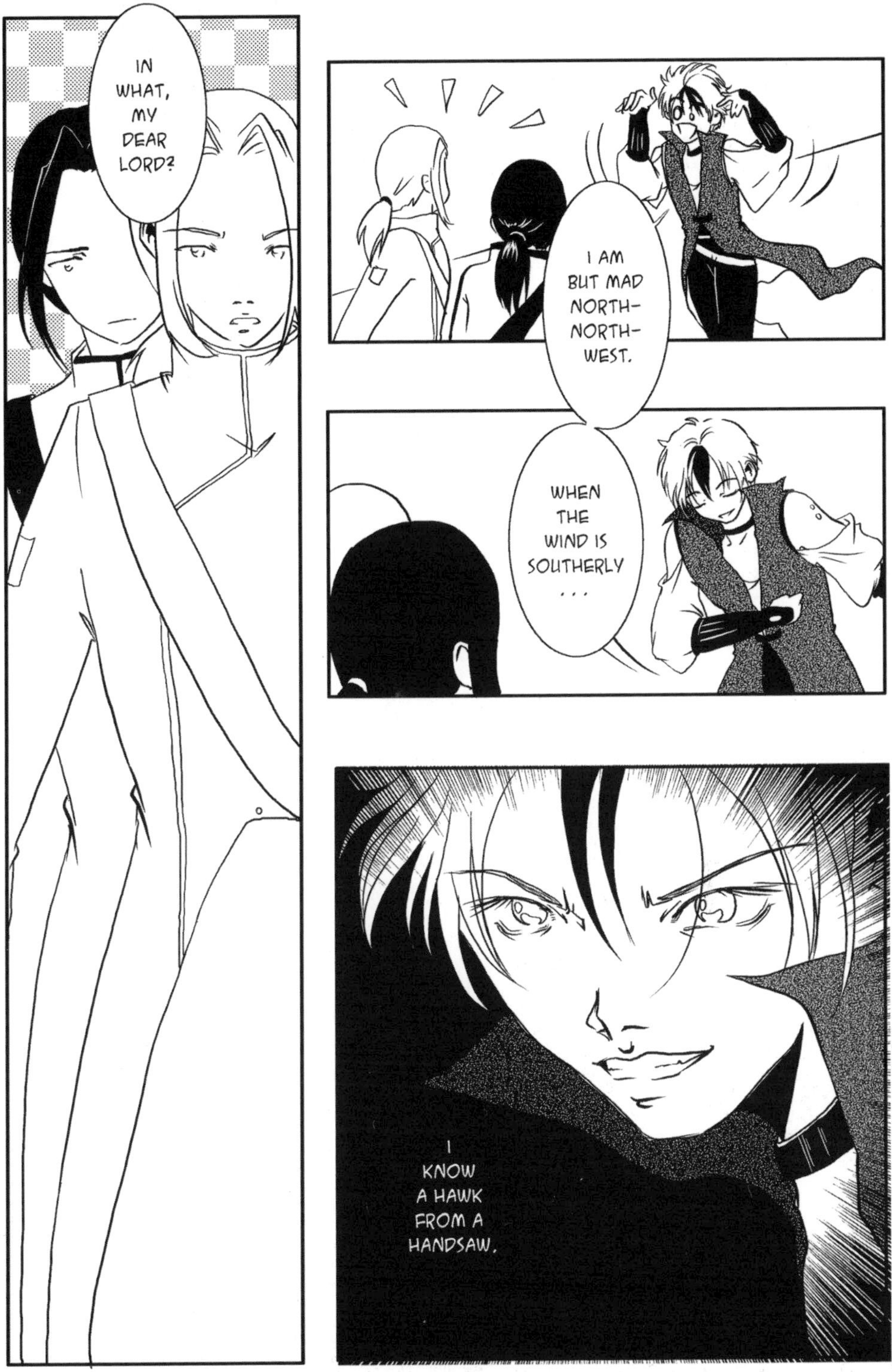
IN WHAT, MY DEAR LORD?
I AM BUT MAD NORTH-NORTH-WEST.
WHEN THE WIND IS SOUTHERLY . . .
I KNOW A HAWK FROM A HANDSAW.

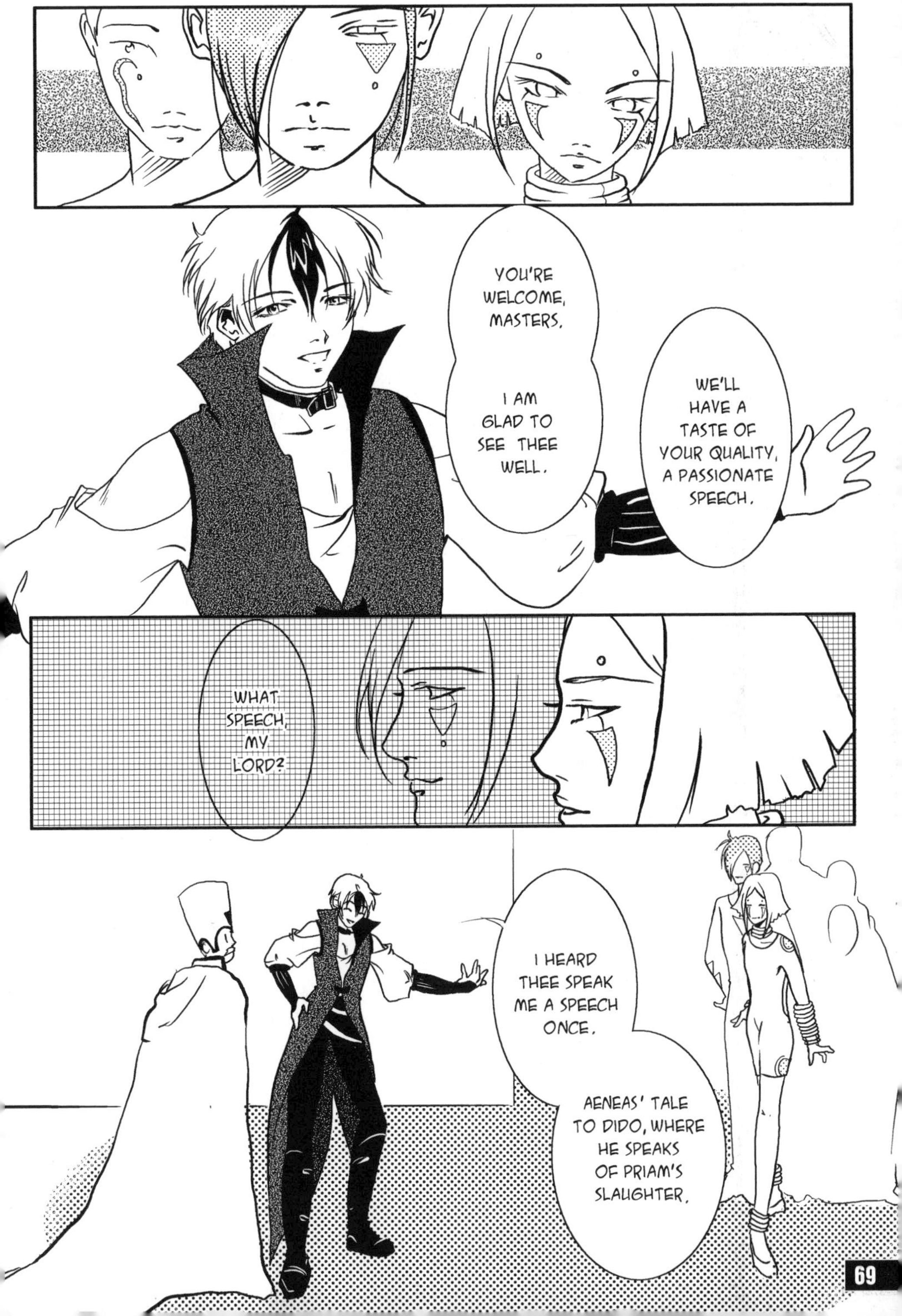
YOU'RE WELCOME, MASTERS.
I AM GLAD TO SEE THEE WELL.
WE'LL HAVE A TASTE OF YOUR QUALITY, A PASSIONATE SPEECH.
WHAT SPEECH, MY LORD?
I HEARD THEE SPEAK ME A SPEECH ONCE.
AENEAS' TALE TO DIDO, WHERE HE SPEAKS OF PRIAM'S SLAUGHTER.

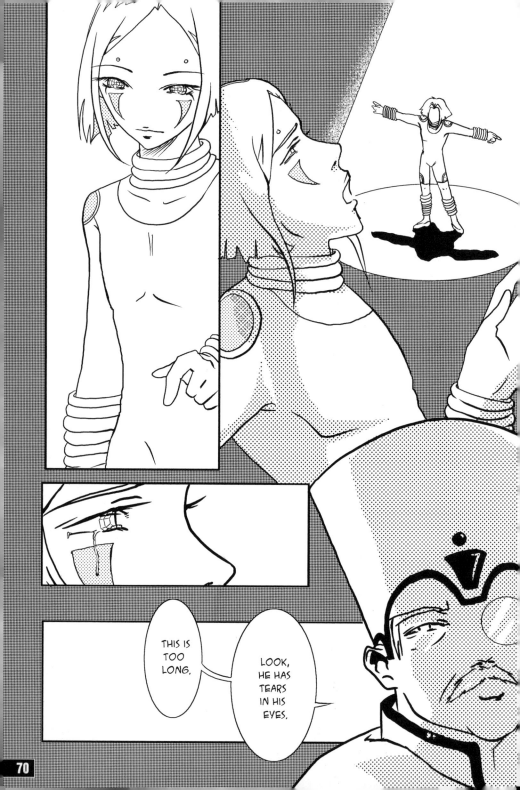

THIS IS TOO LONG.

LOOK, HE HAS TEARS IN HIS EYES.

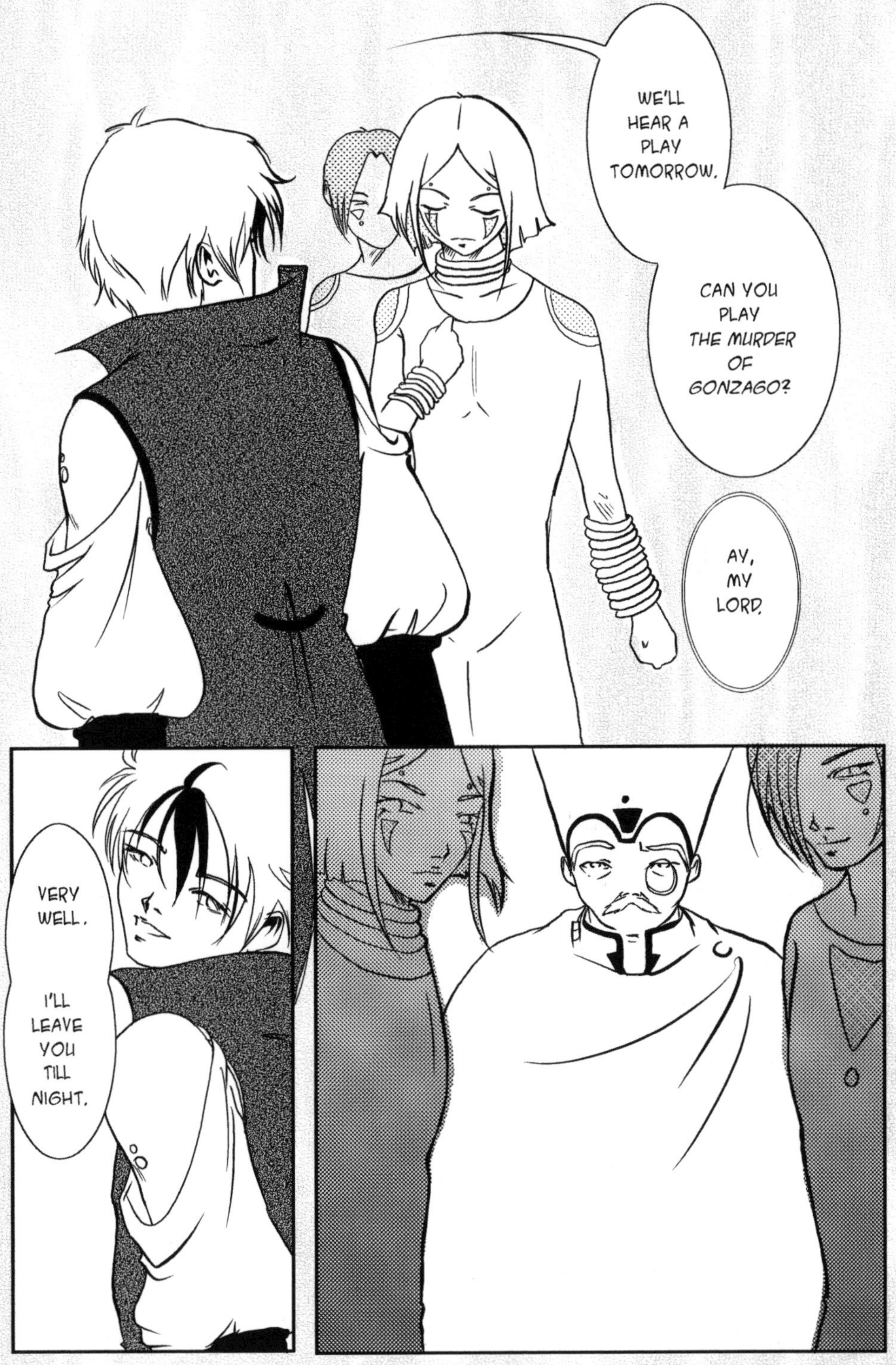
WE'LL HEAR A PLAY TOMORROW.
CAN YOU PLAY THE MURDER OF GONZAGO?
AY, MY LORD.
VERY WELL.
I'LL LEAVE YOU TILL NIGHT.

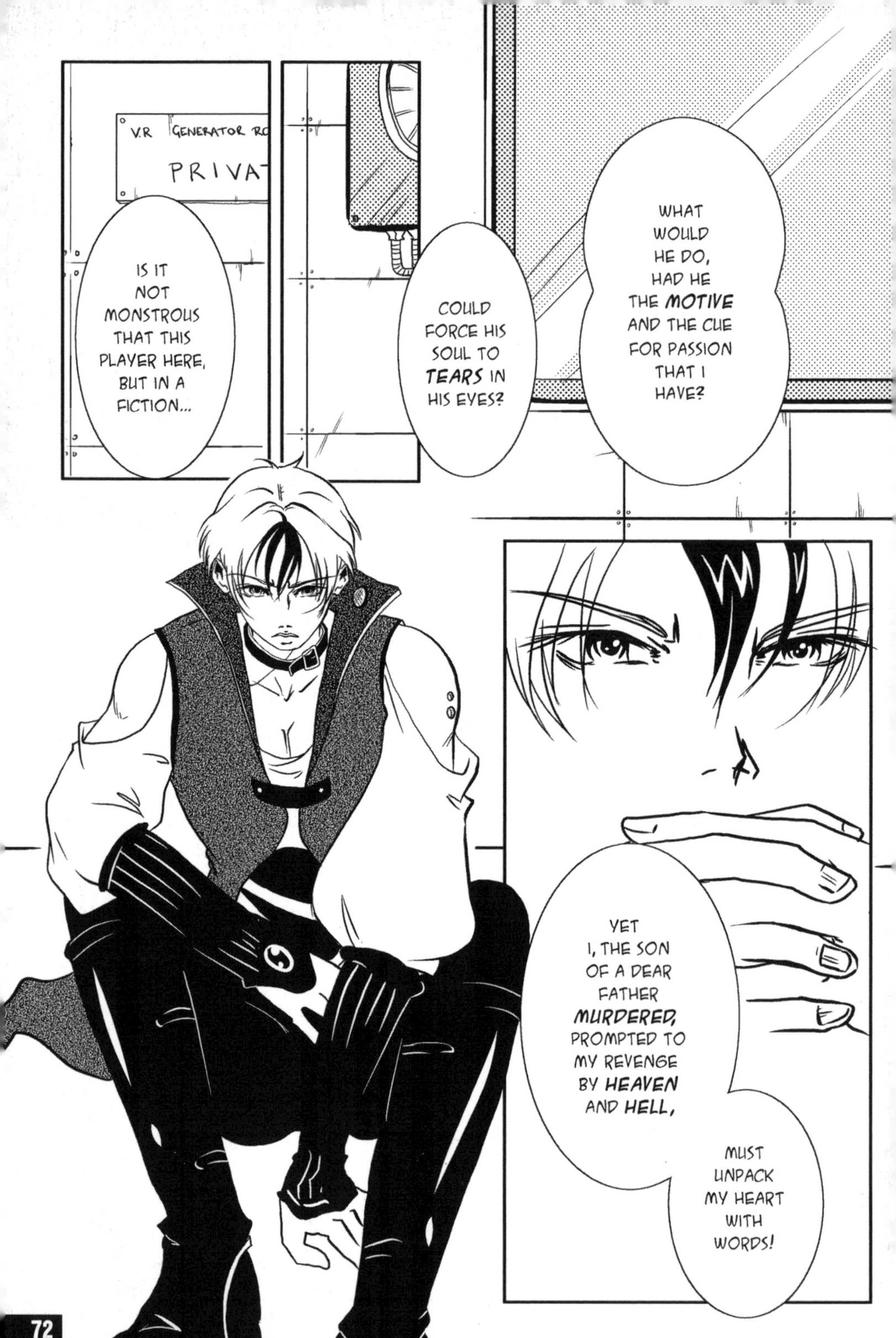
V.R GENERATOR RO
PRIVAT
IS IT NOT MONSTROUS THAT THIS PLAYER HERE, BUT IN A FICTION...
COULD FORCE HIS SOUL TO TEARS IN HIS EYES?
WHAT WOULD HE DO, HAD HE THE MOTIVE AND THE CUE FOR PASSION THAT I HAVE?
YET I, THE SON OF A DEAR FATHER MURDERED, PROMPTED TO MY REVENGE BY HEAVEN AND HELL,
MUST UNPACK MY HEART WITH WORDS!

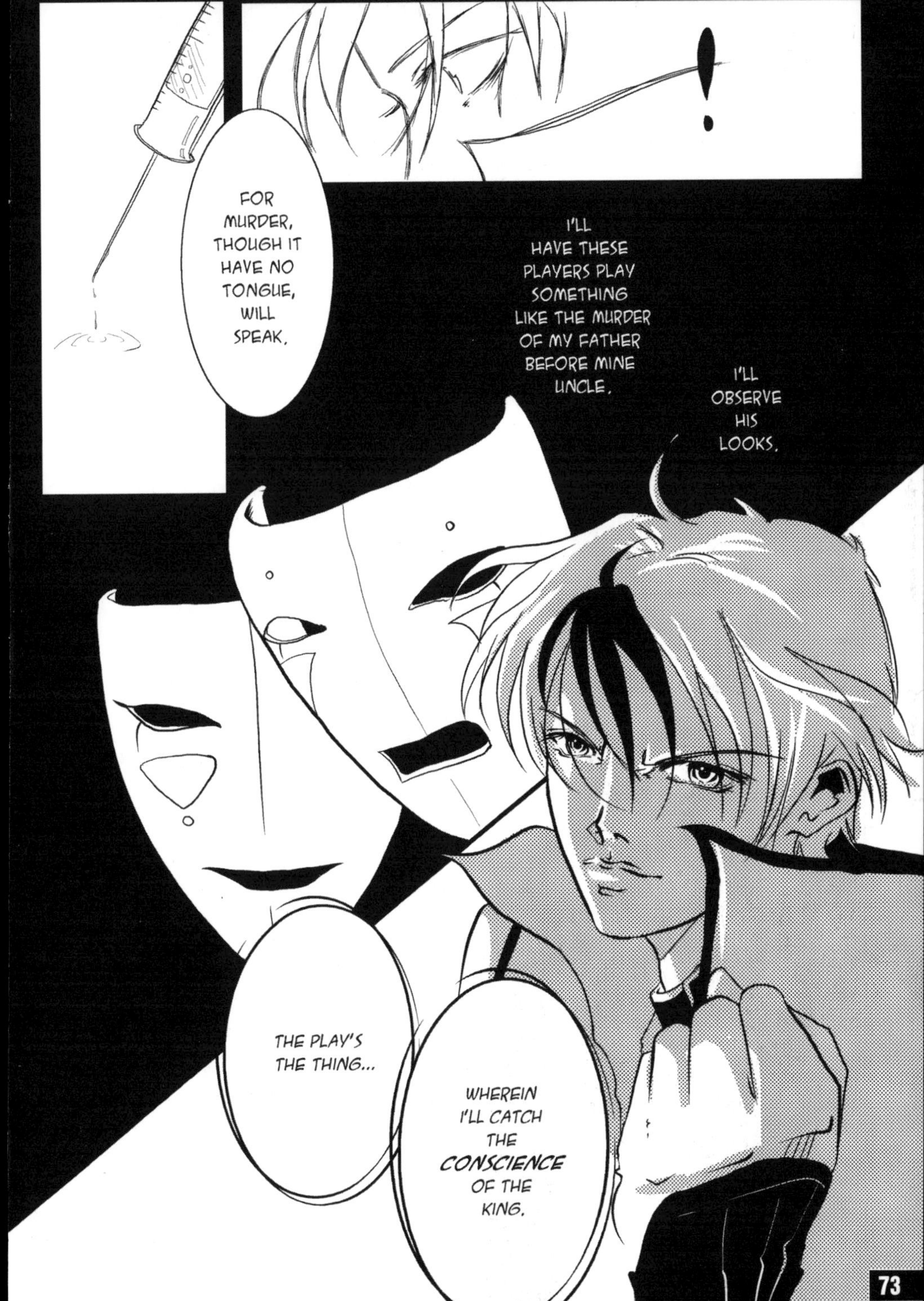
!
FOR MURDER, THOUGH IT HAVE NO TONGUE, WILL SPEAK.
I'LL HAVE THESE PLAYERS PLAY SOMETHING LIKE THE MURDER OF MY FATHER BEFORE MINE UNCLE.
I'LL OBSERVE HIS LOOKS.
THE PLAY'S THE THING...
WHEREIN I'LL CATCH THE CONSCIENCE OF THE KING.

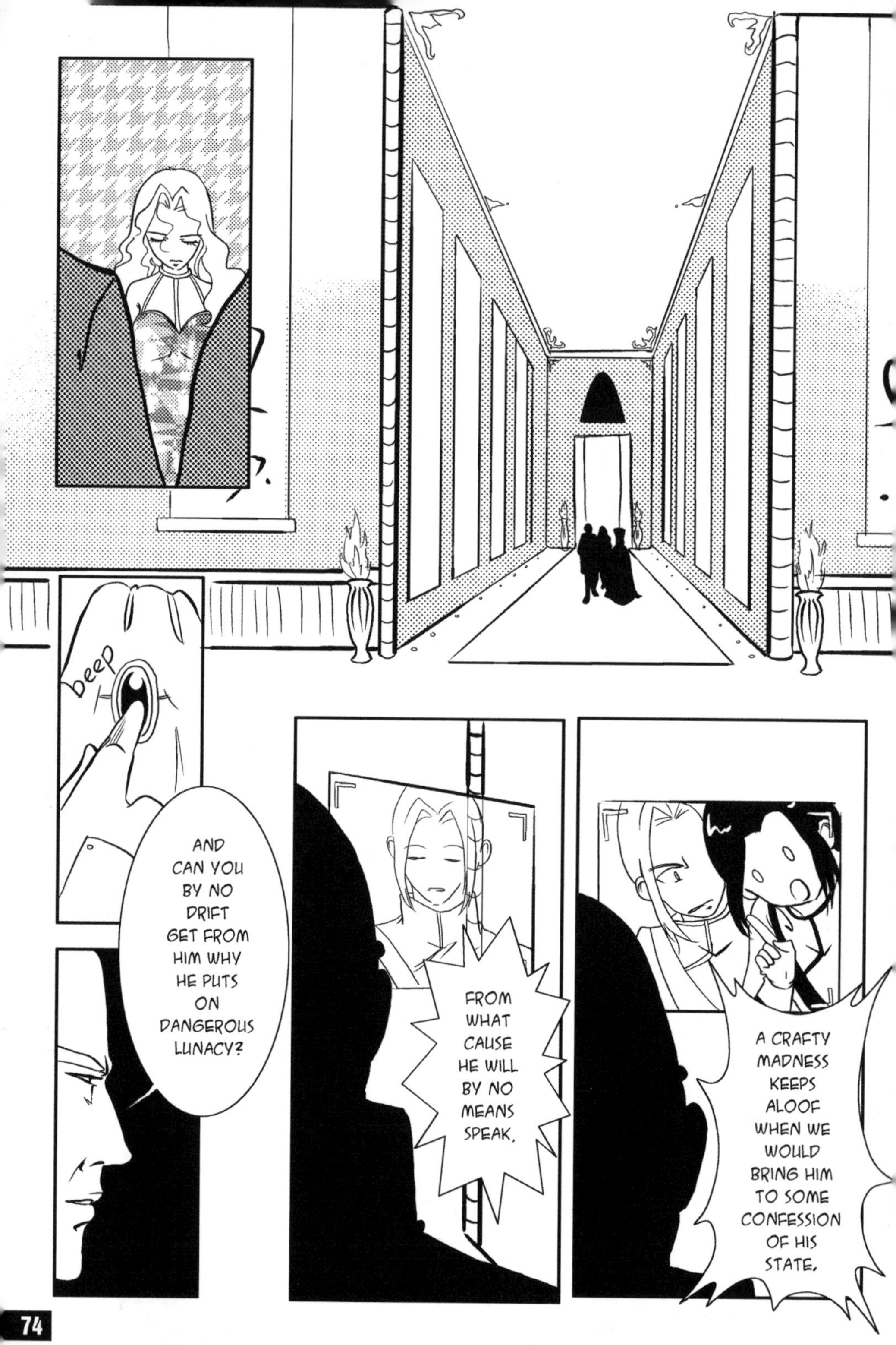
beep
AND CAN YOU BY NO DRIFT GET FROM HIM WHY HE PUTS ON DANGEROUS LUNACY?
FROM WHAT CAUSE HE WILL BY NO MEANS SPEAK.
A CRAFTY MADNESS KEEPS ALOOF WHEN WE WOULD BRING HIM TO SOME CONFESSION OF HIS STATE.

DID YOU ASSAY HIM TO ANY PASTIME?

shove

MADAM, CERTAIN **PLAYERS** ARE ABOUT THE COURT.

THEY HAVE ALREADY ORDER THIS NIGHT TO PLAY BEFORE HIM,

HE BESEECHED ME TO ENTREAT YOUR MAJESTIES TO HEAR AND SEE THE MATTER,

beep

GOOD GENTLEMEN,

DRIVE HIS PURPOSE ON TO THESE DELIGHTS,

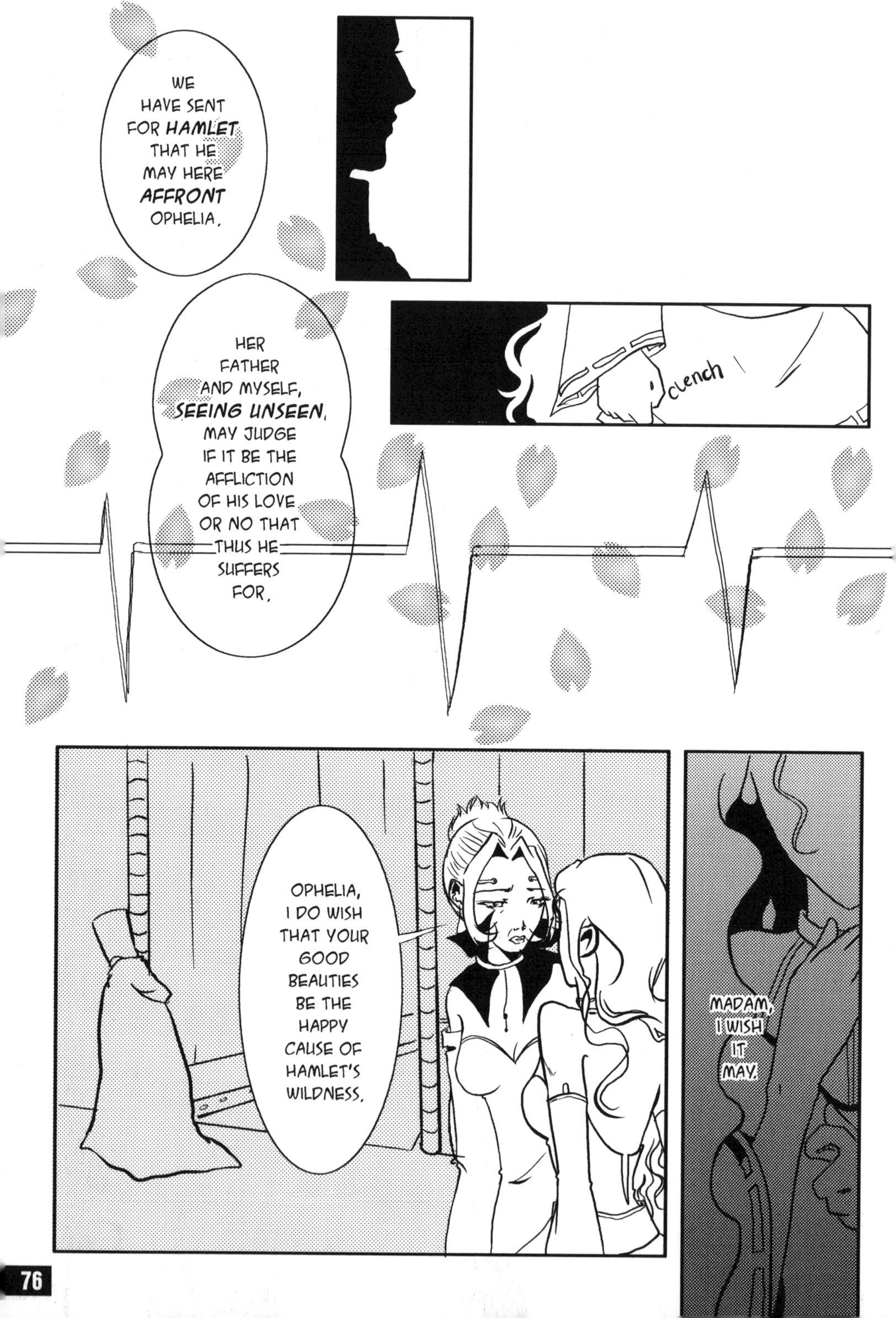
WE HAVE SENT FOR HAMLET THAT HE MAY HERE AFFRONT OPHELIA.
HER FATHER AND MYSELF, SEEING UNSEEN, MAY JUDGE IF IT BE THE AFFLICTION OF HIS LOVE OR NO THAT THUS HE SUFFERS FOR.
clench
OPHELIA, I DO WISH THAT YOUR GOOD BEAUTIES BE THE HAPPY CAUSE OF HAMLET'S WILDNESS.
MADAM, I WISH IT MAY.

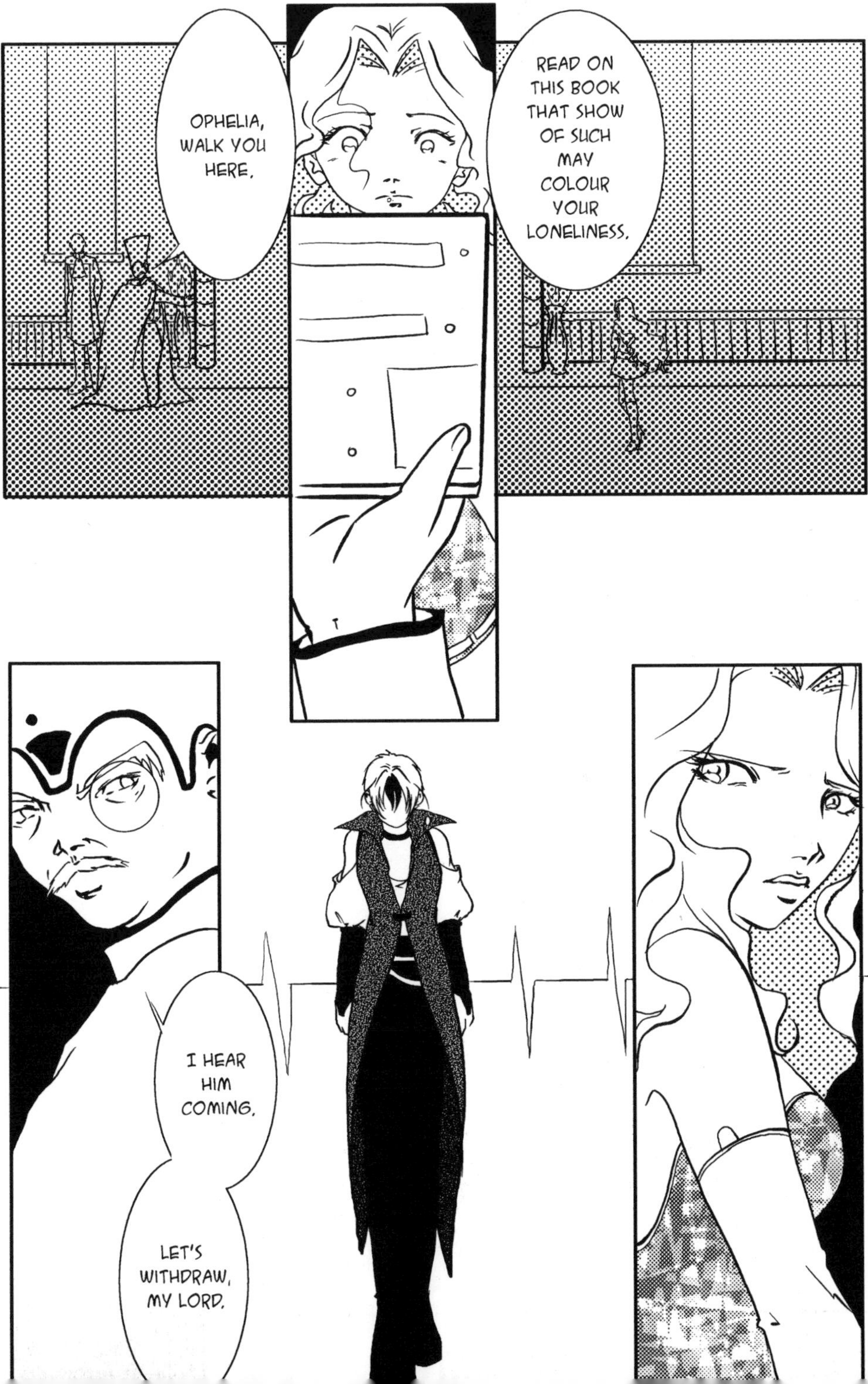
OPHELIA, WALK YOU HERE.
READ ON THIS BOOK THAT SHOW OF SUCH MAY COLOUR YOUR LONELINESS.
I HEAR HIM COMING.
LET'S WITHDRAW, MY LORD.

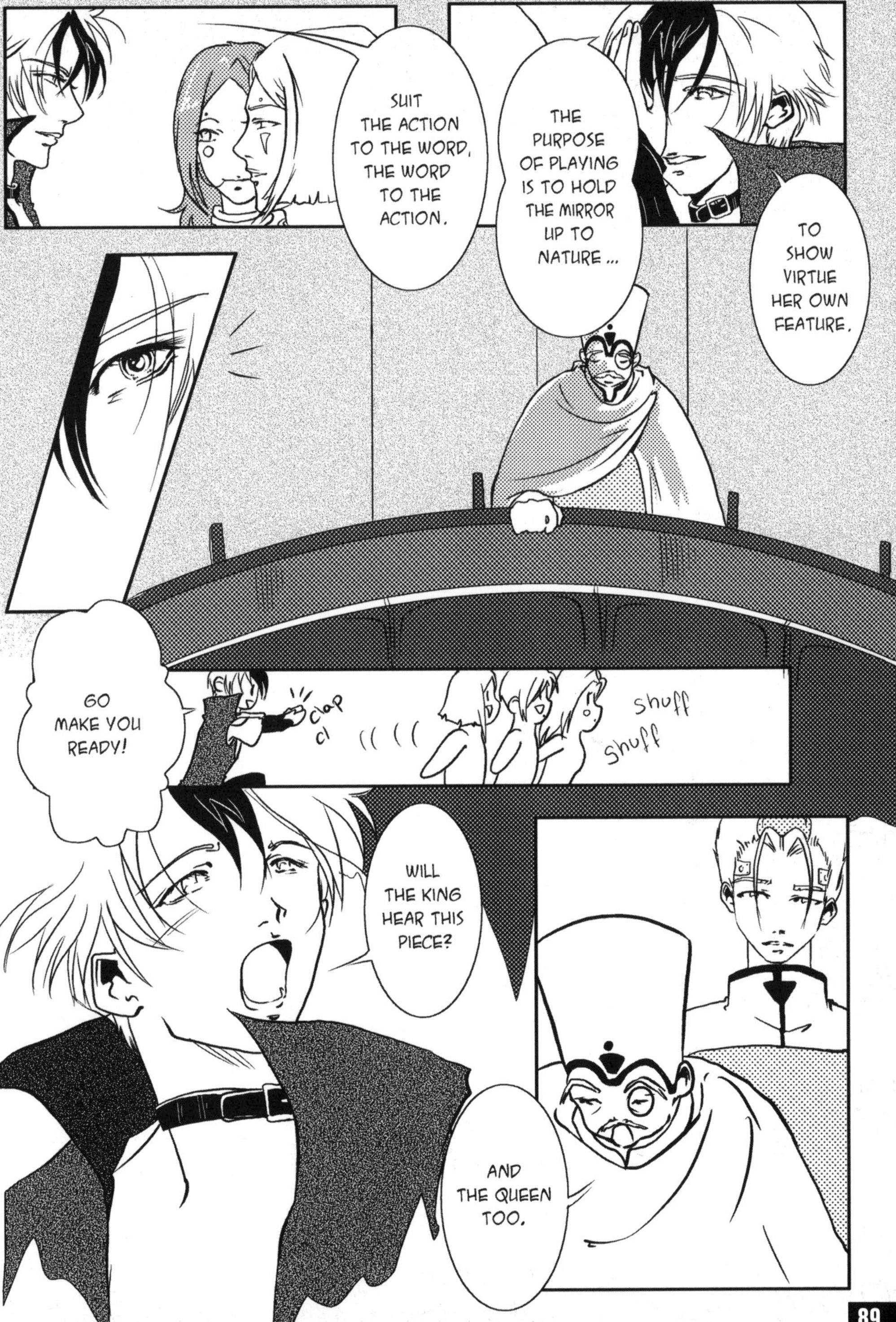
SUIT THE ACTION TO THE WORD, THE WORD TO THE ACTION.
THE PURPOSE OF PLAYING IS TO HOLD THE MIRROR UP TO NATURE ...
TO SHOW VIRTUE HER OWN FEATURE.
GO MAKE YOU READY!
clap
cl
shuff
shuff
WILL THE KING HEAR THIS PIECE?
AND THE QUEEN TOO.

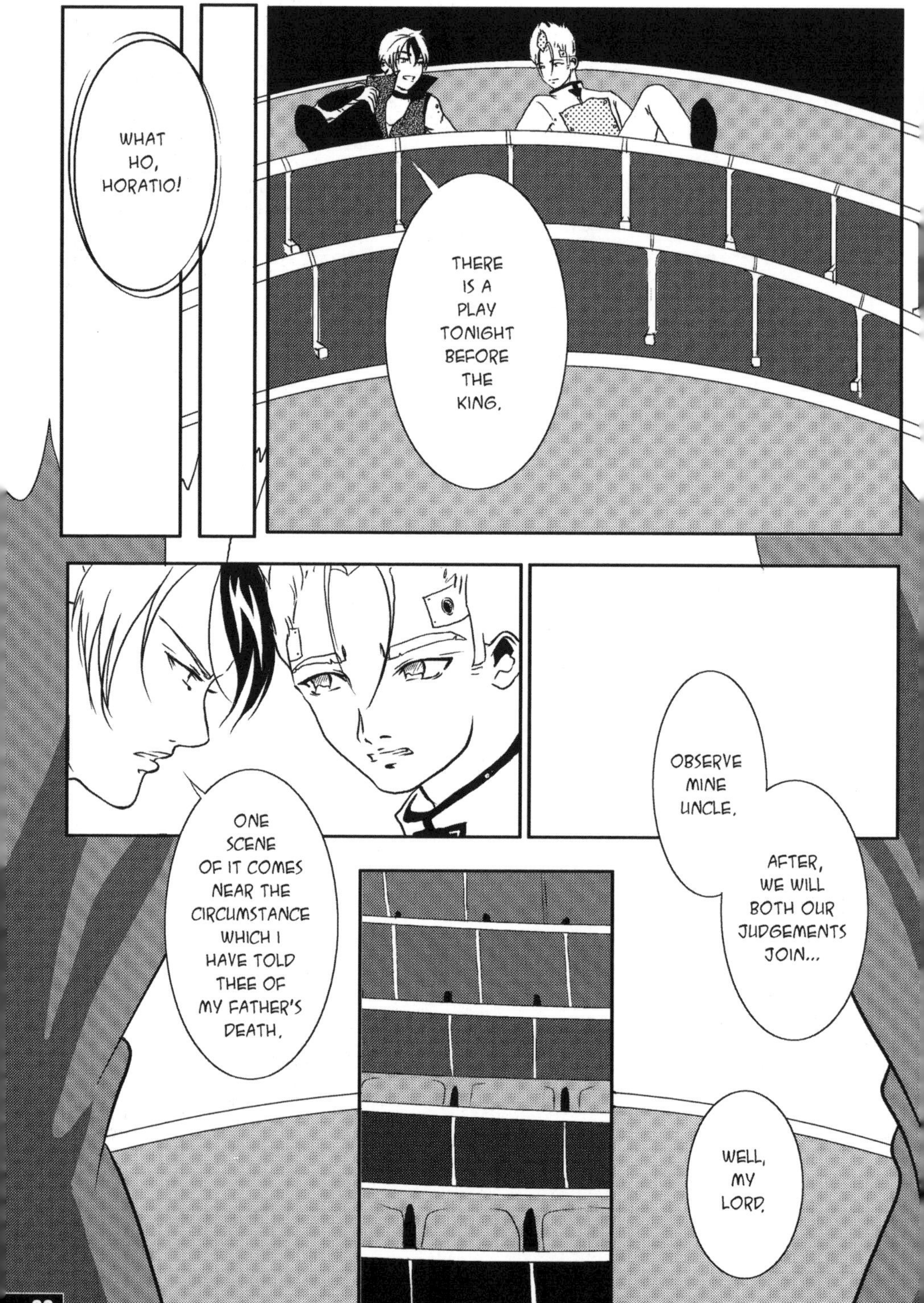
WHAT HO, HORATIO!
THERE IS A PLAY TONIGHT BEFORE THE KING.
ONE SCENE OF IT COMES NEAR THE CIRCUMSTANCE WHICH I HAVE TOLD THEE OF MY FATHER'S DEATH.
OBSERVE MINE UNCLE.
AFTER, WE WILL BOTH OUR JUDGEMENTS JOIN...
WELL, MY LORD.

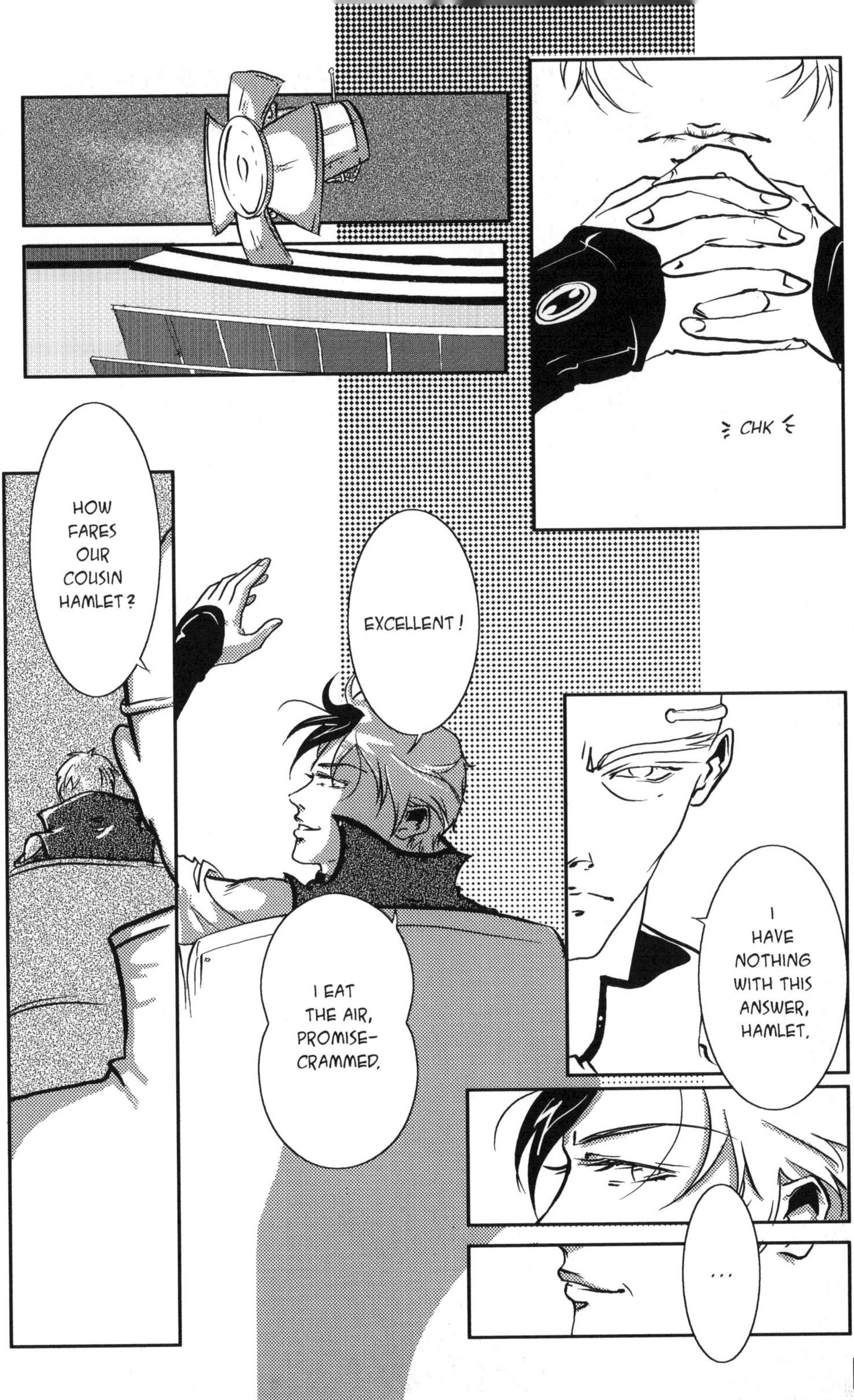
CHK
HOW FARES OUR COUSIN HAMLET?
EXCELLENT!
I EAT THE AIR, PROMISE-CRAMMED.
I HAVE NOTHING WITH THIS ANSWER, HAMLET.
...

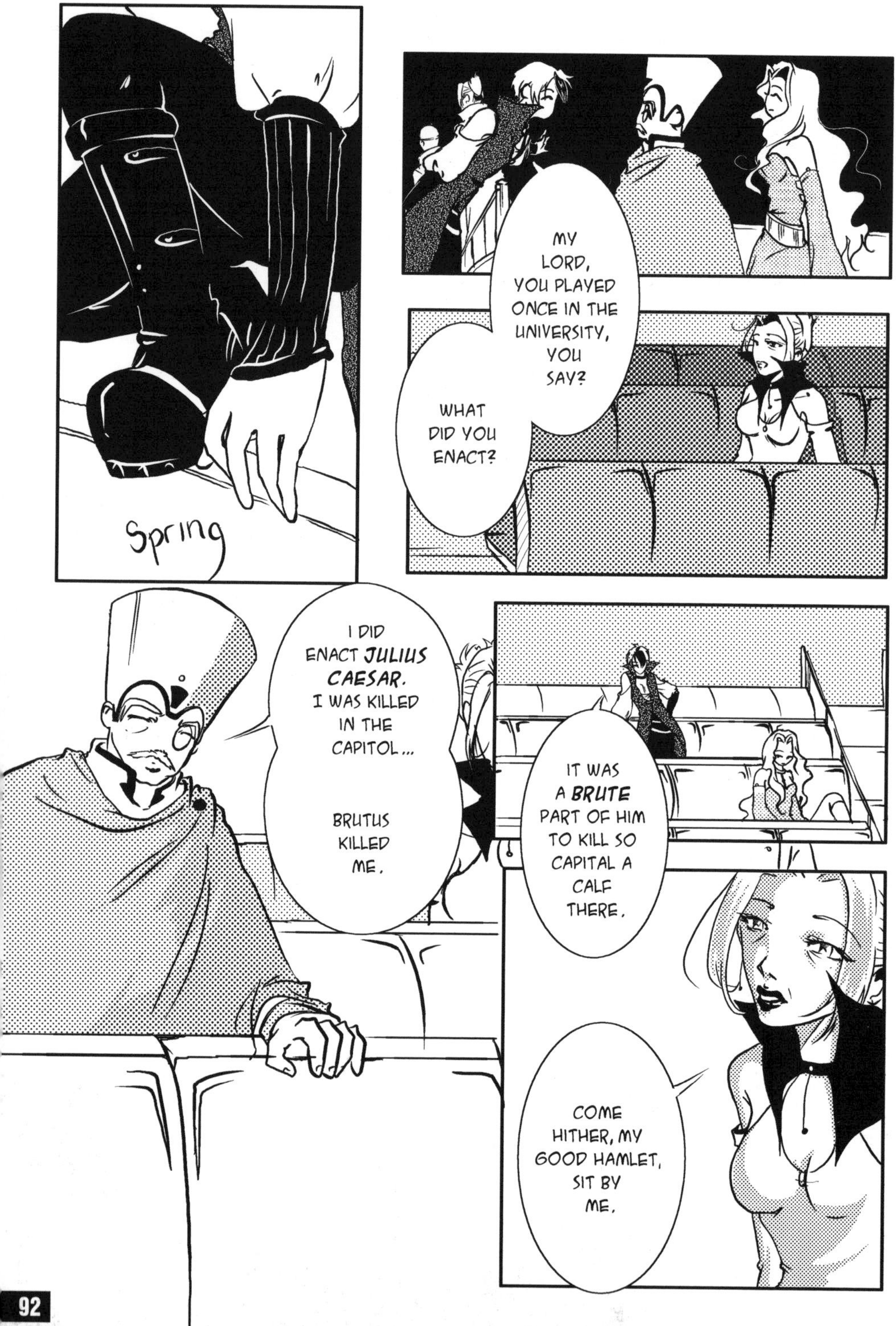
Spring
MY LORD, YOU PLAYED ONCE IN THE UNIVERSITY, YOU SAY?
WHAT DID YOU ENACT?
I DID ENACT **JULIUS CAESAR.** I WAS KILLED IN THE CAPITOL...
BRUTUS KILLED ME.
IT WAS A **BRUTE** PART OF HIM TO KILL SO CAPITAL A CALF THERE.
COME HITHER, MY GOOD HAMLET, SIT BY ME.

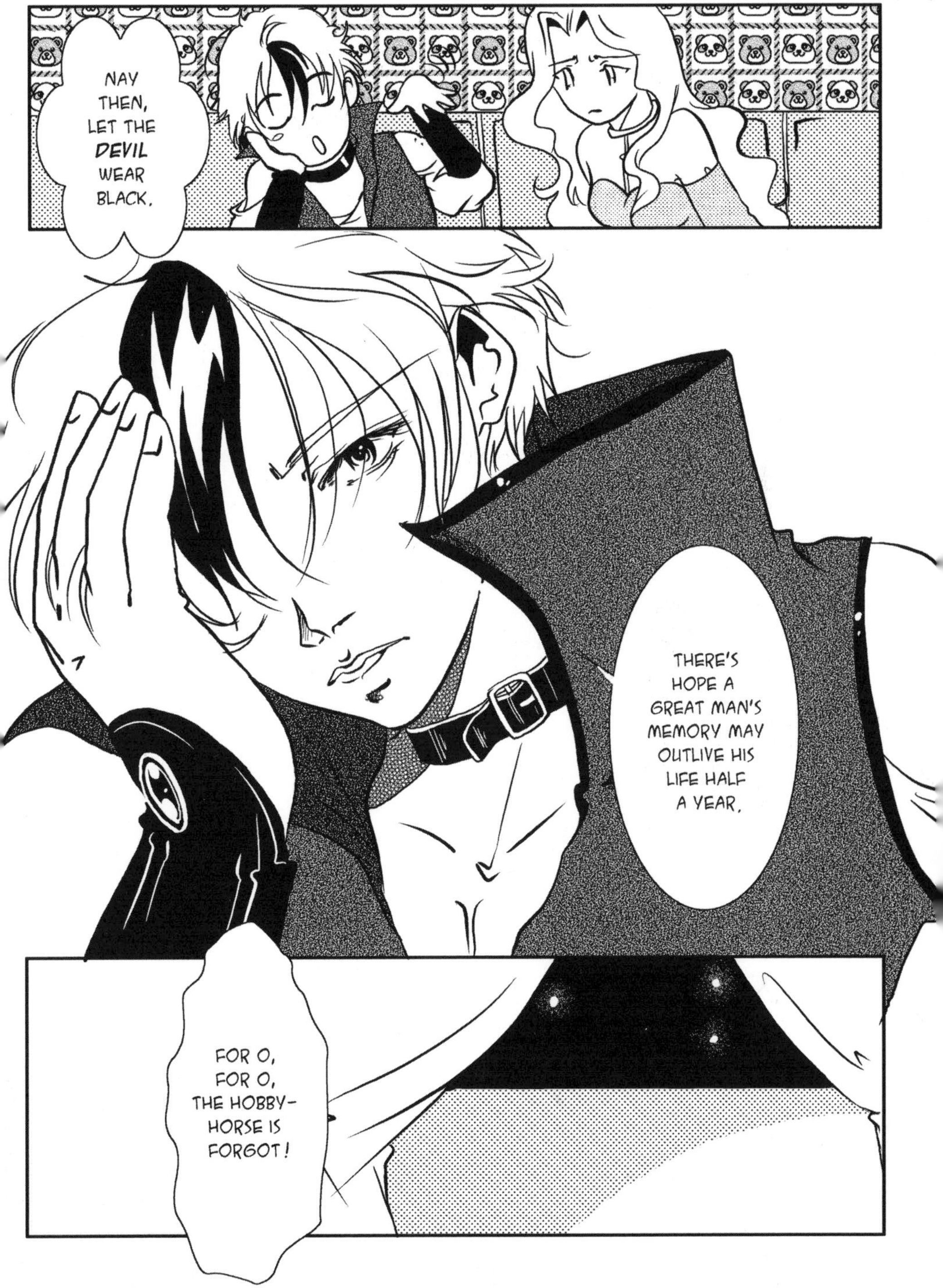
NAY THEN, LET THE DEVIL WEAR BLACK.
THERE'S HOPE A GREAT MAN'S MEMORY MAY OUTLIVE HIS LIFE HALF A YEAR.
FOR O, FOR O, THE HOBBY-HORSE IS FORGOT!

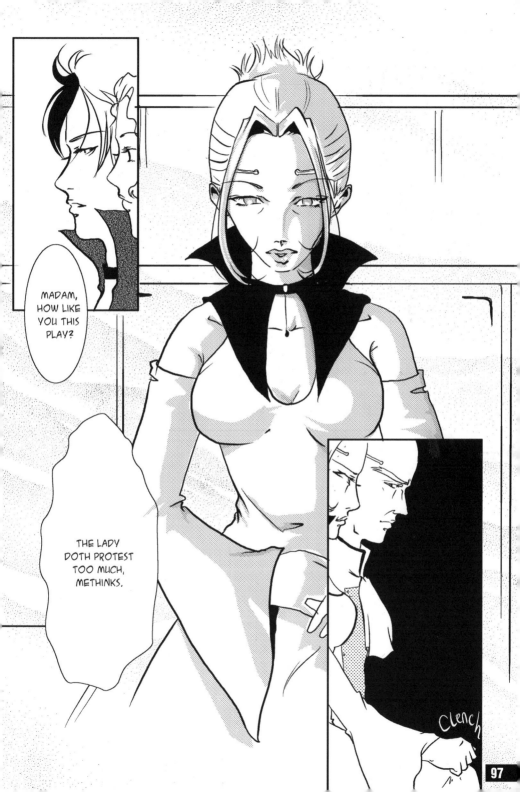

MADAM,
HOW LIKE
YOU THIS
PLAY?

THE LADY
DOTH PROTEST
TOO MUCH,
METHINKS.

Clench

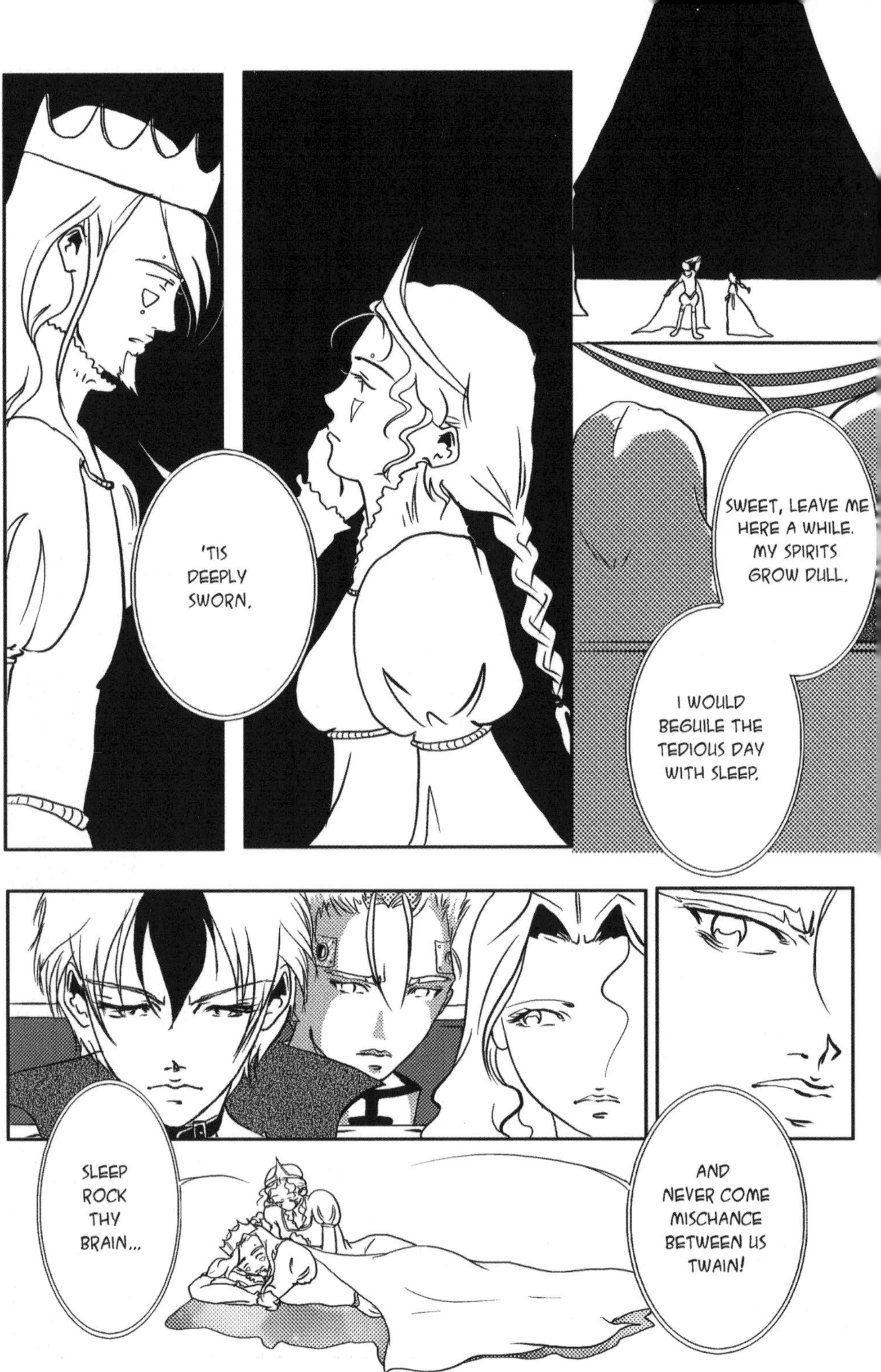
'TIS DEEPLY SWORN.
SWEET, LEAVE ME HERE A WHILE. MY SPIRITS GROW DULL.
I WOULD BEGUILE THE TEDIOUS DAY WITH SLEEP.
SLEEP ROCK THY BRAIN...
AND NEVER COME MISCHANCE BETWEEN US TWAIN!

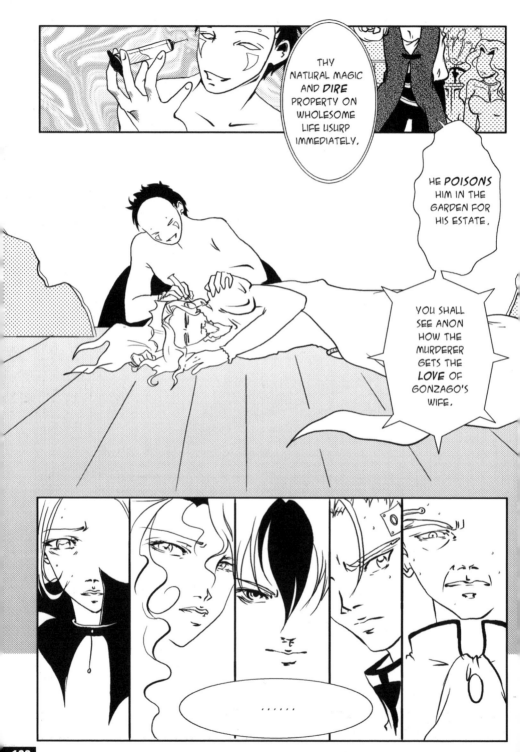

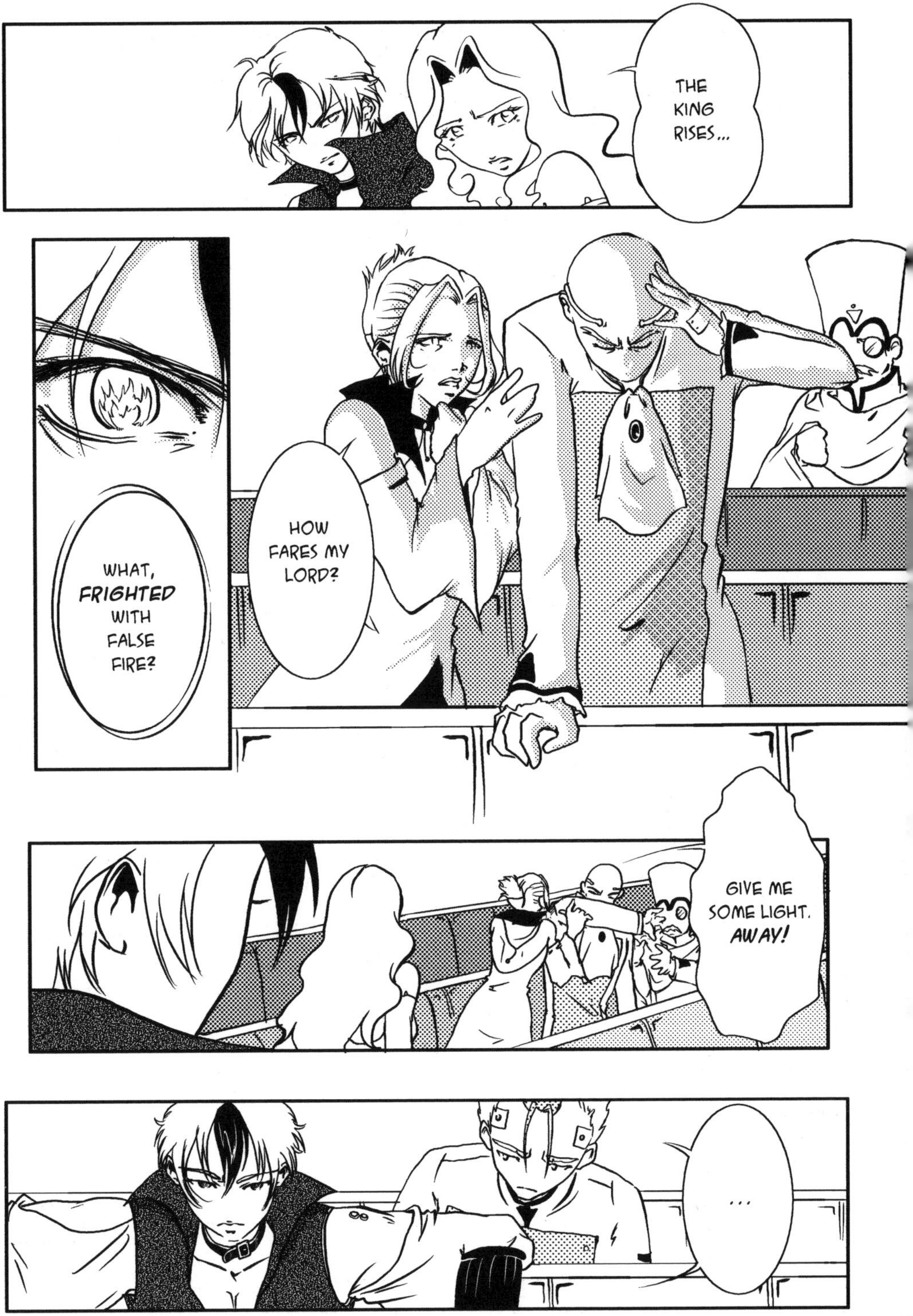
THE KING RISES...
WHAT, **FRIGHTED** WITH FALSE FIRE?
HOW FARES MY LORD?
GIVE ME SOME LIGHT. ***AWAY!***
...

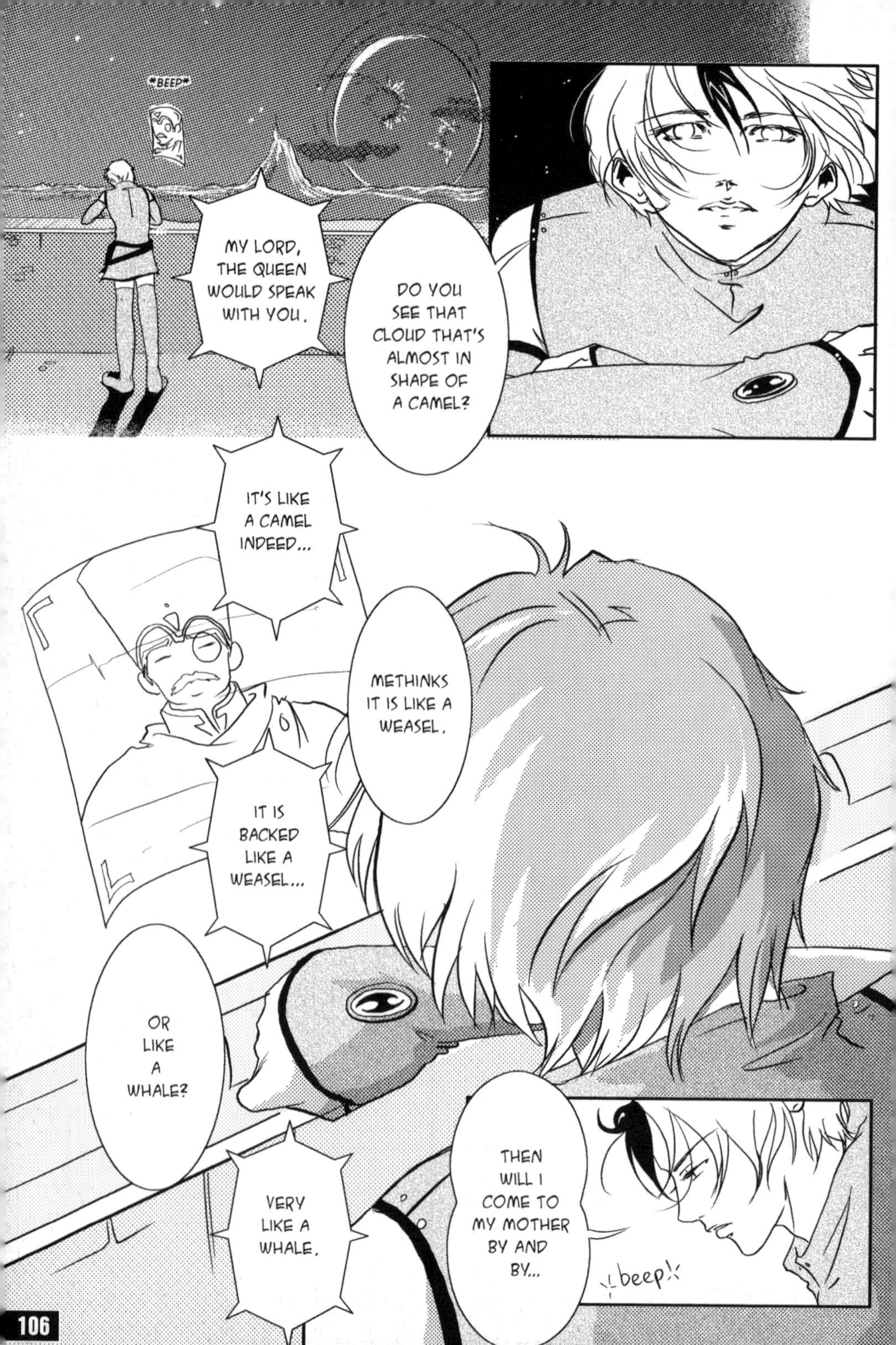
BEEP
MY LORD, THE QUEEN WOULD SPEAK WITH YOU.
DO YOU SEE THAT CLOUD THAT'S ALMOST IN SHAPE OF A CAMEL?
IT'S LIKE A CAMEL INDEED...
METHINKS IT IS LIKE A WEASEL.
IT IS BACKED LIKE A WEASEL...
OR LIKE A WHALE?
VERY LIKE A WHALE.
THEN WILL I COME TO MY MOTHER BY AND BY...
beep!

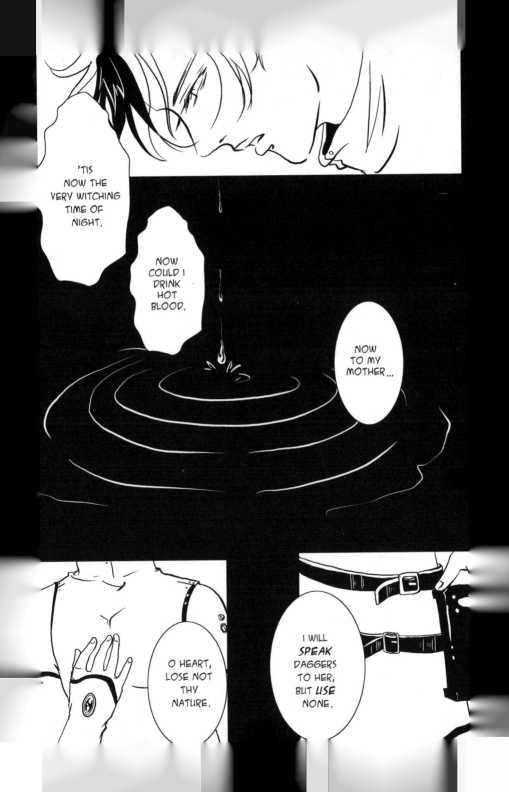

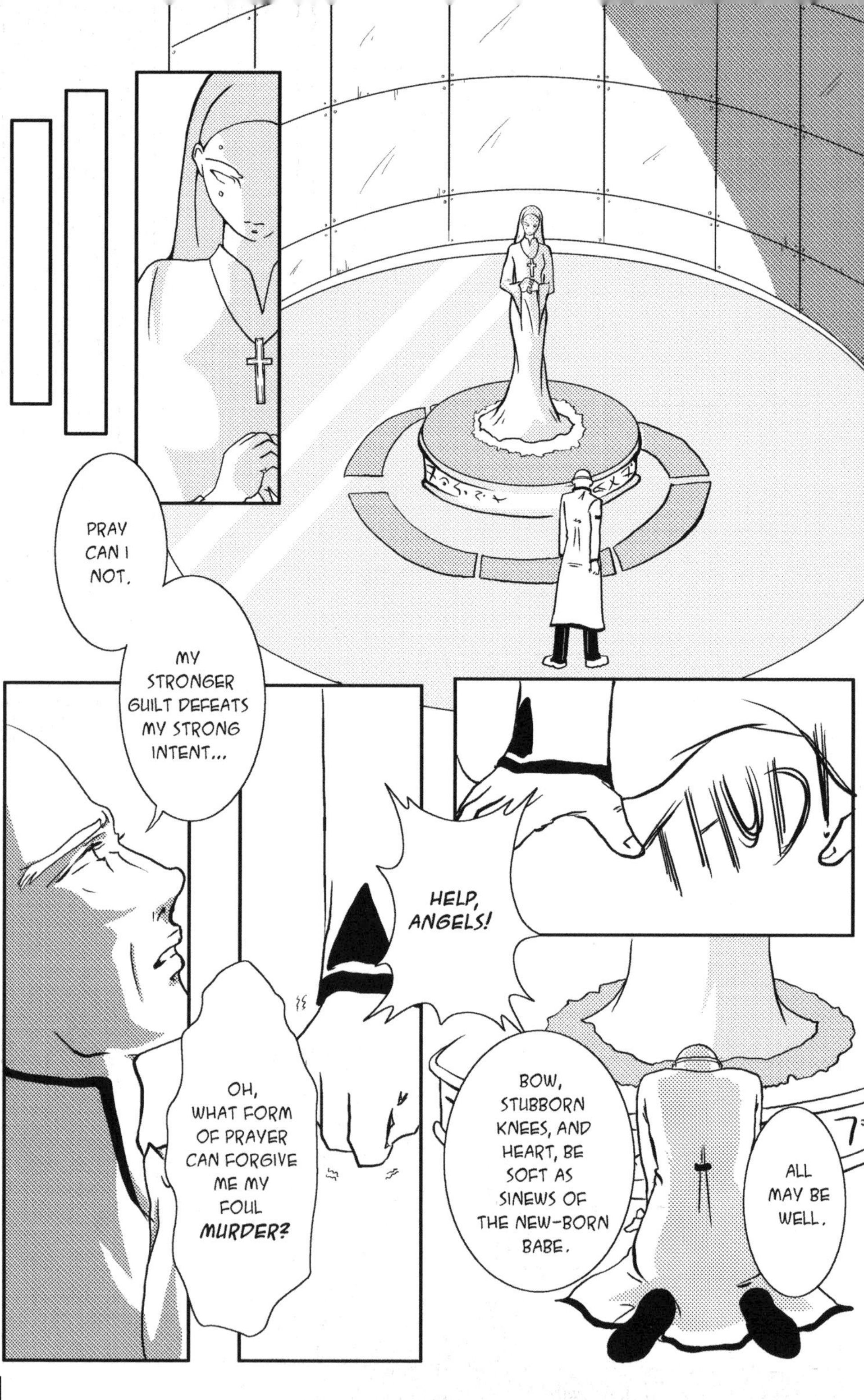
PRAY CAN I NOT.
MY STRONGER GUILT DEFEATS MY STRONG INTENT...
OH, WHAT FORM OF PRAYER CAN FORGIVE ME MY FOUL **MURDER?**
HELP, ANGELS!
THUD!
BOW, STUBBORN KNEES, AND HEART, BE SOFT AS SINEWS OF THE NEW-BORN BABE.
ALL MAY BE WELL.

NO...

WHEN HE IS DRUNK OR IN HIS RAGE...

OR IN TH' INCESTUOUS① PLEASURE OF HIS BED...

THEN *HIS* SOUL MAY BE DAMNED.

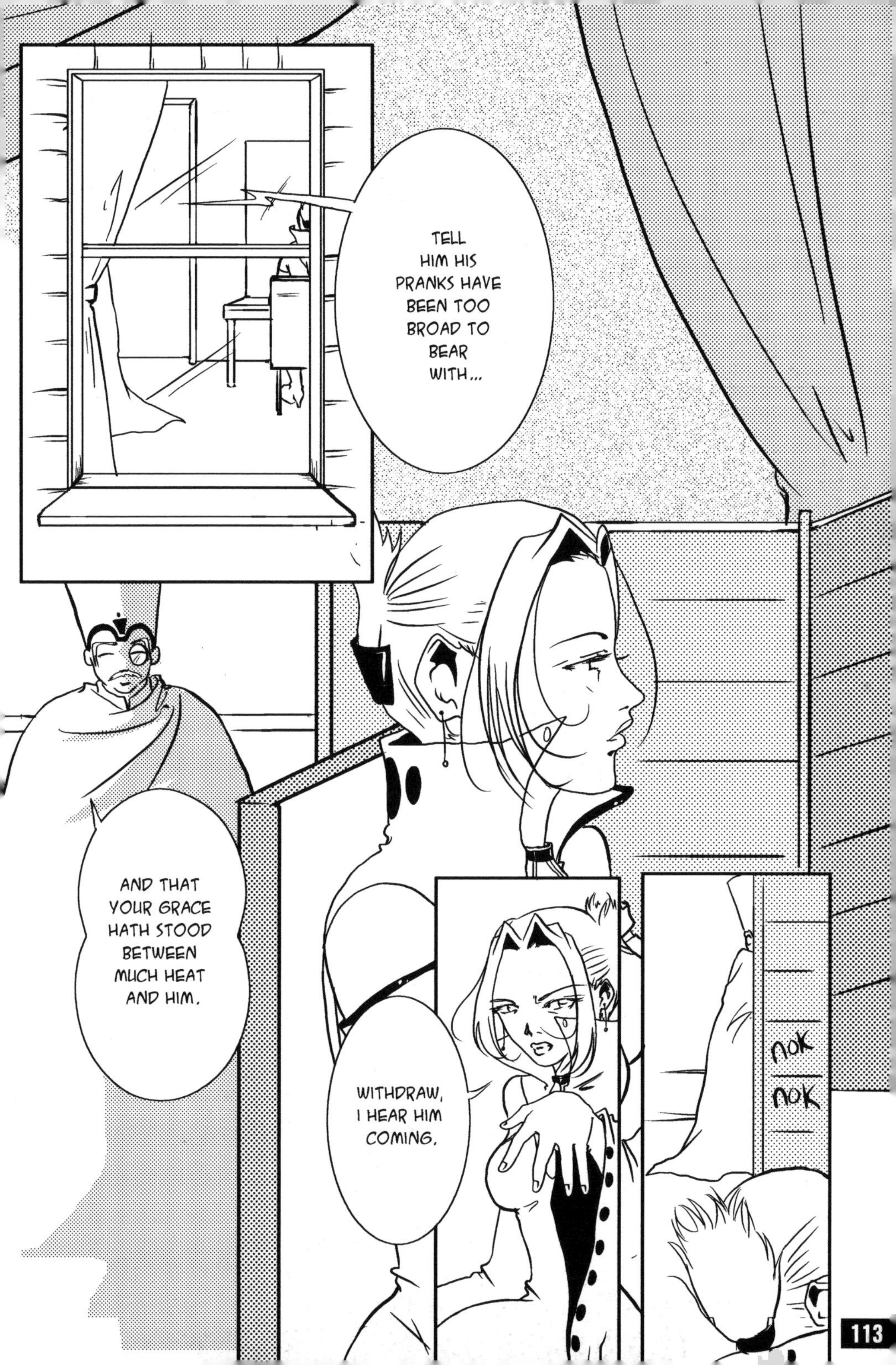
TELL HIM HIS PRANKS HAVE BEEN TOO BROAD TO BEAR WITH...
AND THAT YOUR GRACE HATH STOOD BETWEEN MUCH HEAT AND HIM.
WITHDRAW, I HEAR HIM COMING.
NOK
NOK

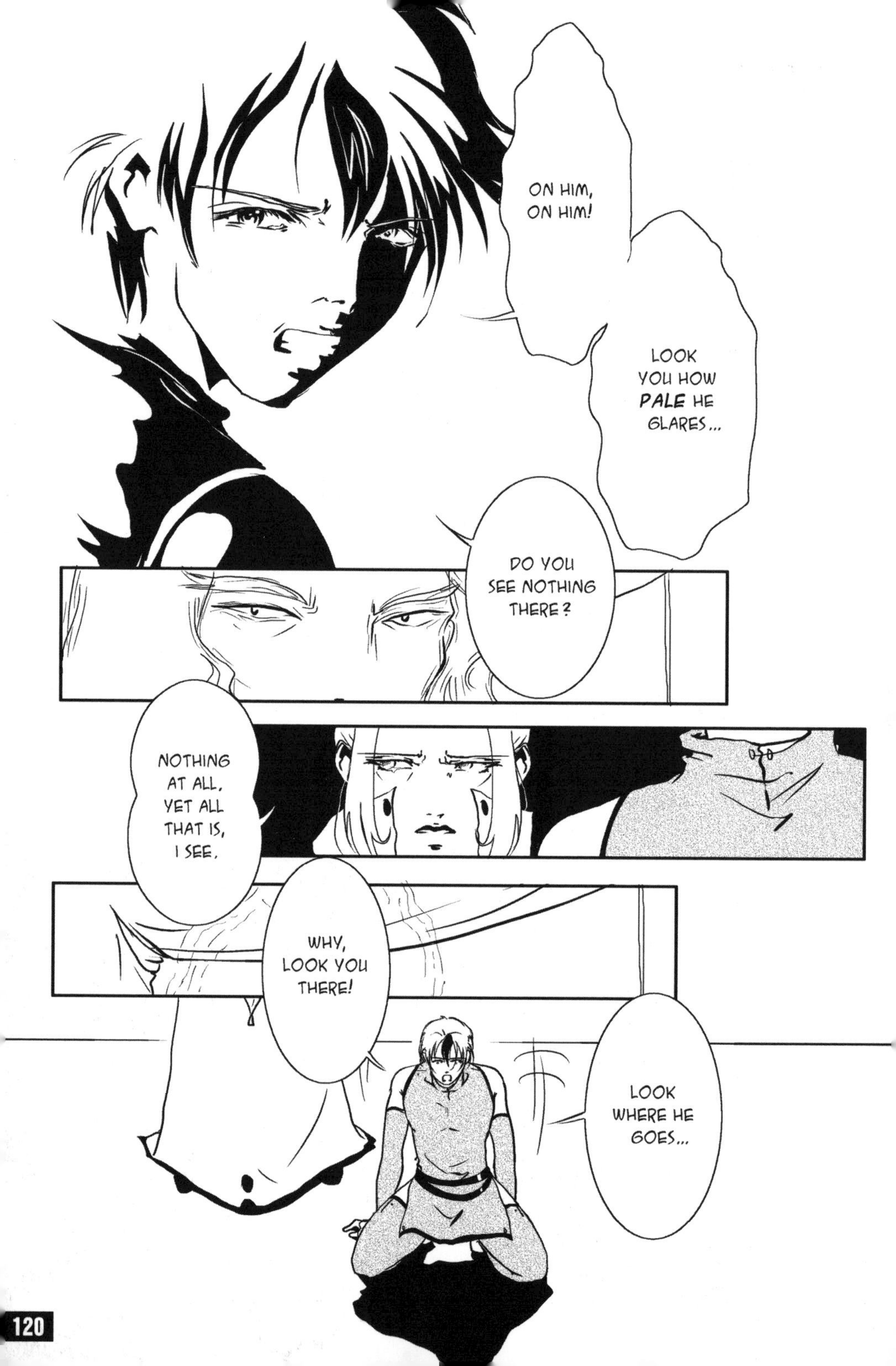
ON HIM, ON HIM!
LOOK YOU HOW PALE HE GLARES...
DO YOU SEE NOTHING THERE?
NOTHING AT ALL, YET ALL THAT IS, I SEE.
WHY, LOOK YOU THERE!
LOOK WHERE HE GOES...

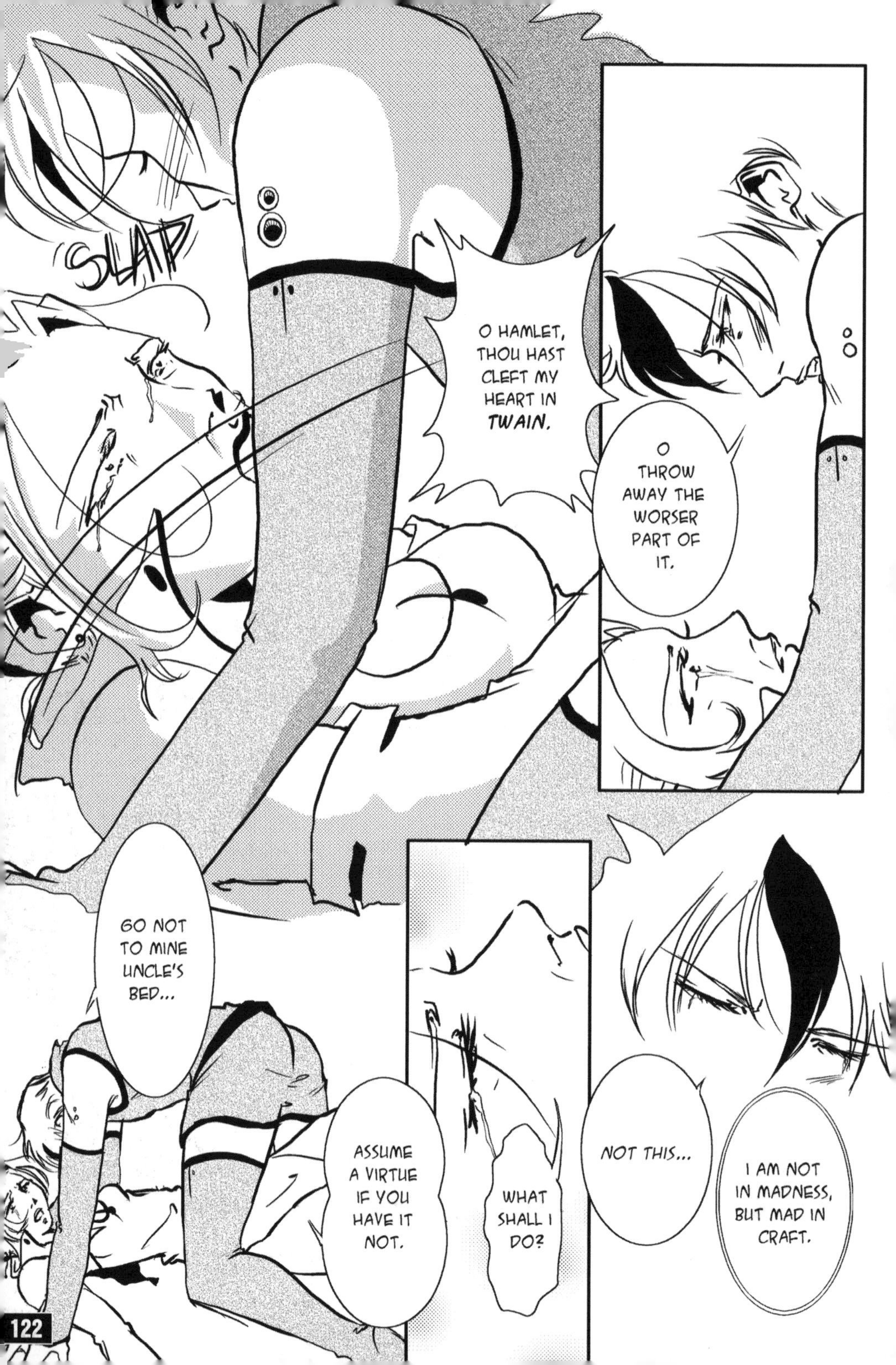
SLAP
O HAMLET, THOU HAST CLEFT MY HEART IN *TWAIN.*
O THROW AWAY THE WORSER PART OF IT.
GO NOT TO MINE UNCLE'S BED...
ASSUME A VIRTUE IF YOU HAVE IT NOT.
WHAT SHALL I DO?
NOT THIS...
I AM NOT IN MADNESS, BUT MAD IN CRAFT.

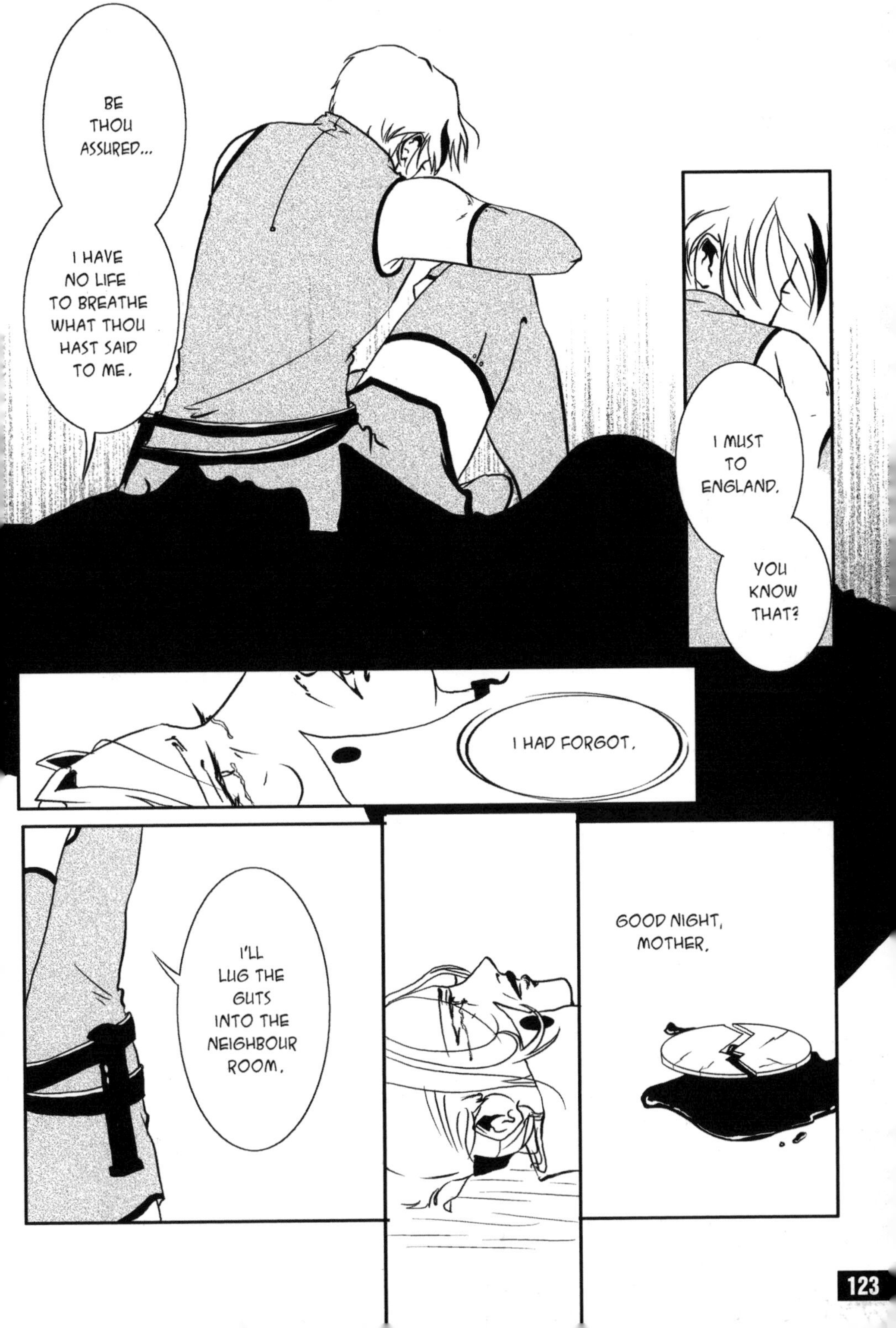
BE THOU ASSURED...
I HAVE NO LIFE TO BREATHE WHAT THOU HAST SAID TO ME.
I MUST TO ENGLAND.
YOU KNOW THAT?
I HAD FORGOT.
I'LL LUG THE GUTS INTO THE NEIGHBOUR ROOM.
GOOD NIGHT, MOTHER.

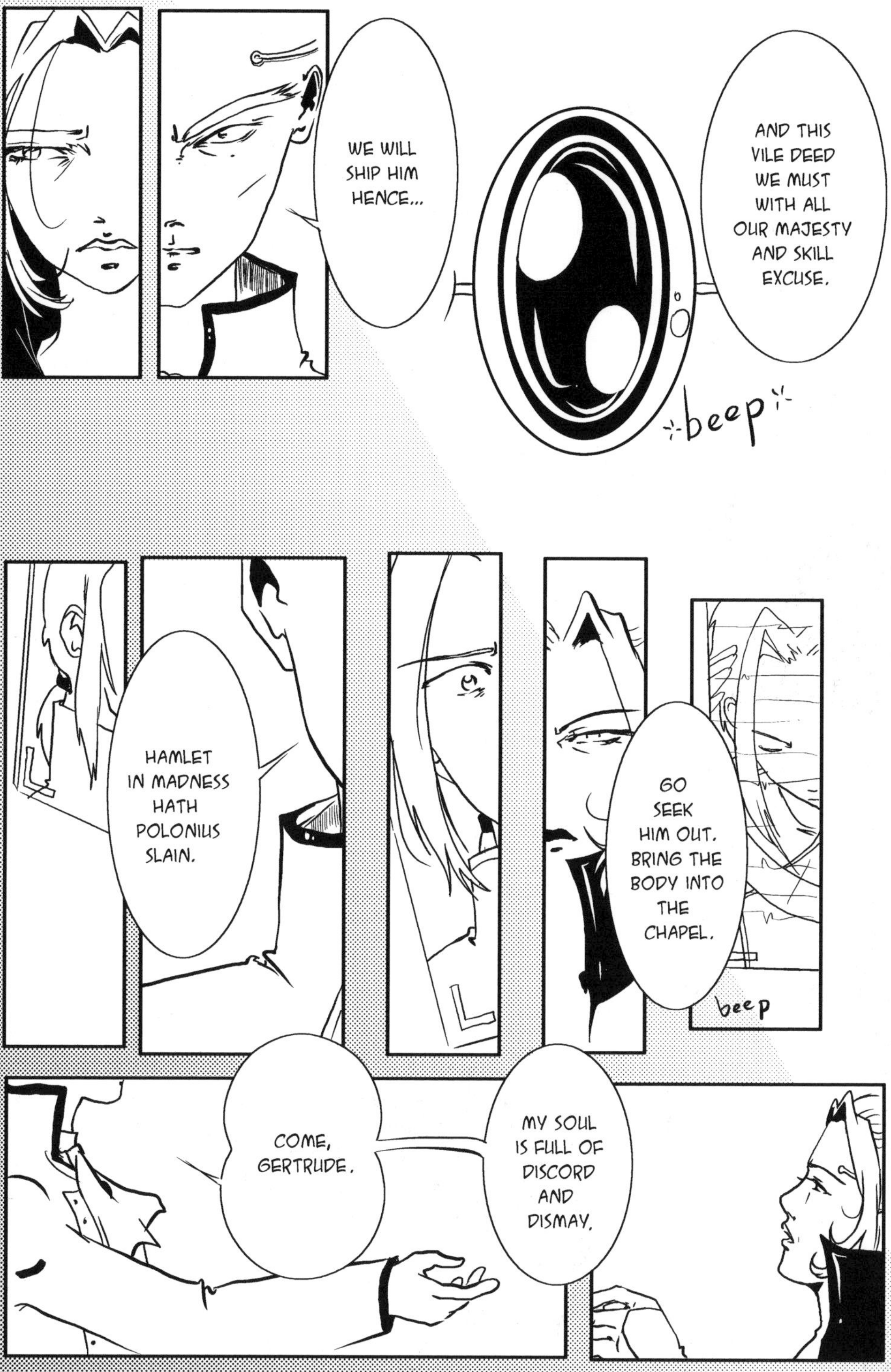

WE WILL SHIP HIM HENCE...
AND THIS VILE DEED WE MUST WITH ALL OUR MAJESTY AND SKILL EXCUSE.
beep
HAMLET IN MADNESS HATH POLONIUS SLAIN.
GO SEEK HIM OUT. BRING THE BODY INTO THE CHAPEL.
beep
COME, GERTRUDE.
MY SOUL IS FULL OF DISCORD AND DISMAY.

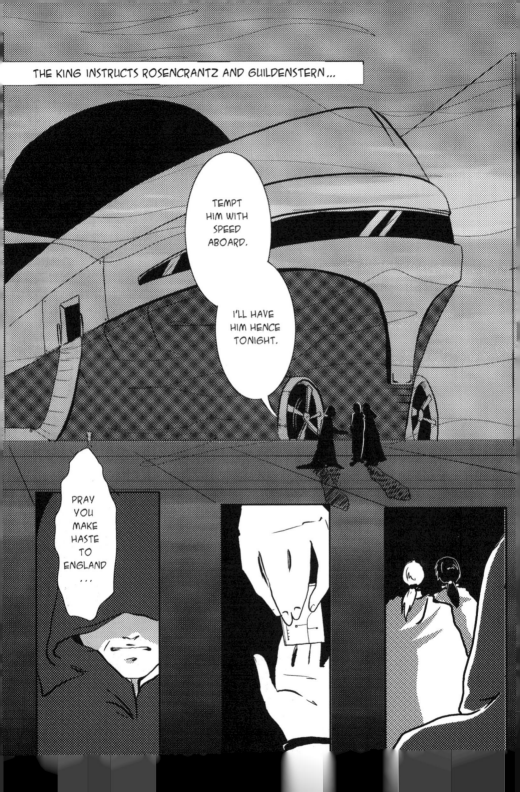

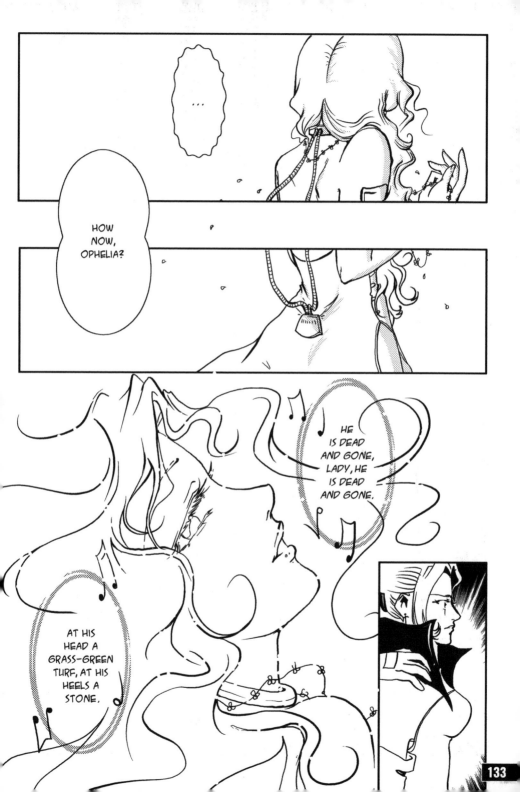

133

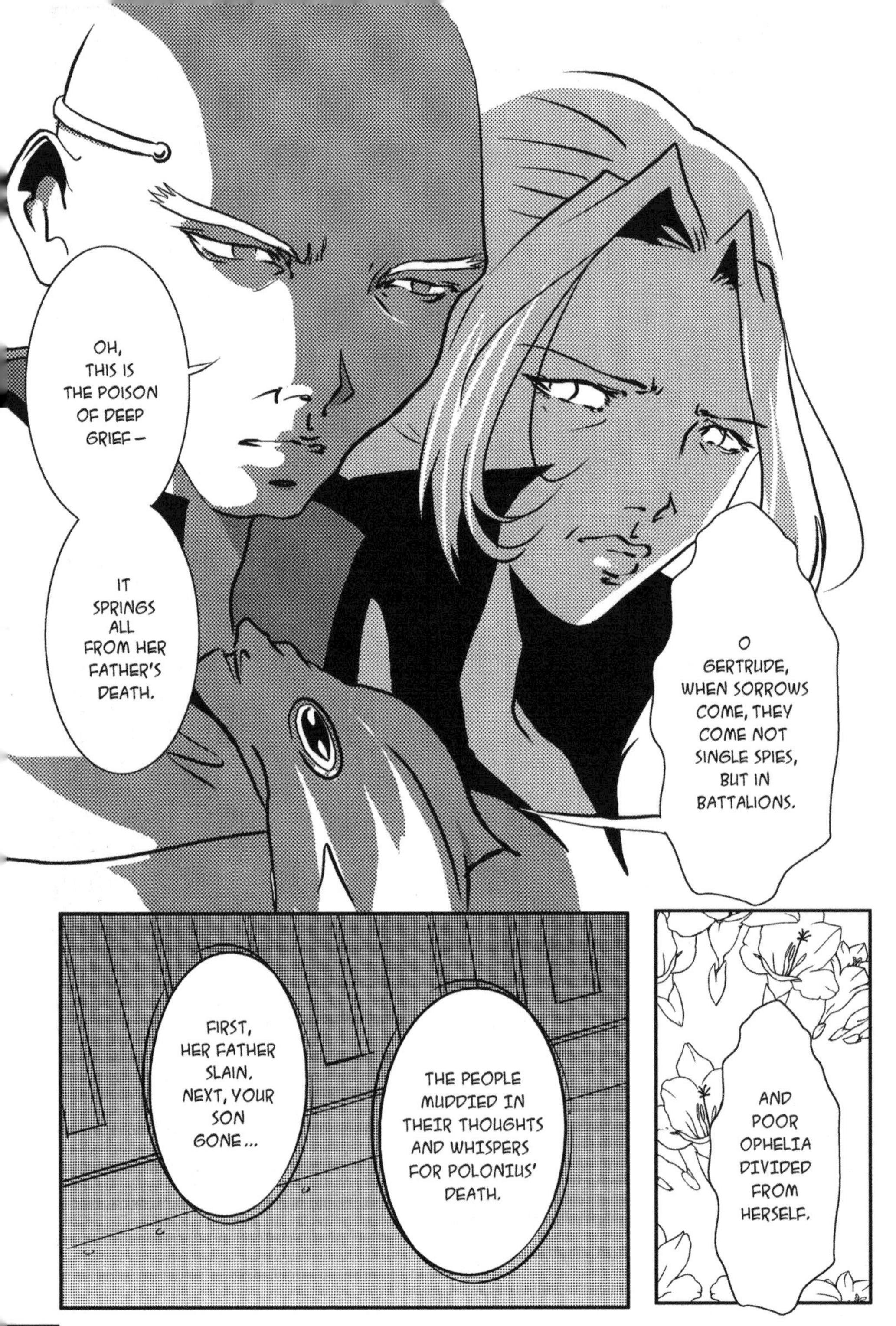
OH, THIS IS THE POISON OF DEEP GRIEF –
IT SPRINGS ALL FROM HER FATHER'S DEATH.
O GERTRUDE, WHEN SORROWS COME, THEY COME NOT SINGLE SPIES, BUT IN BATTALIONS.
FIRST, HER FATHER SLAIN. NEXT, YOUR SON GONE...
THE PEOPLE MUDDIED IN THEIR THOUGHTS AND WHISPERS FOR POLONIUS' DEATH.
AND POOR OPHELIA DIVIDED FROM HERSELF.

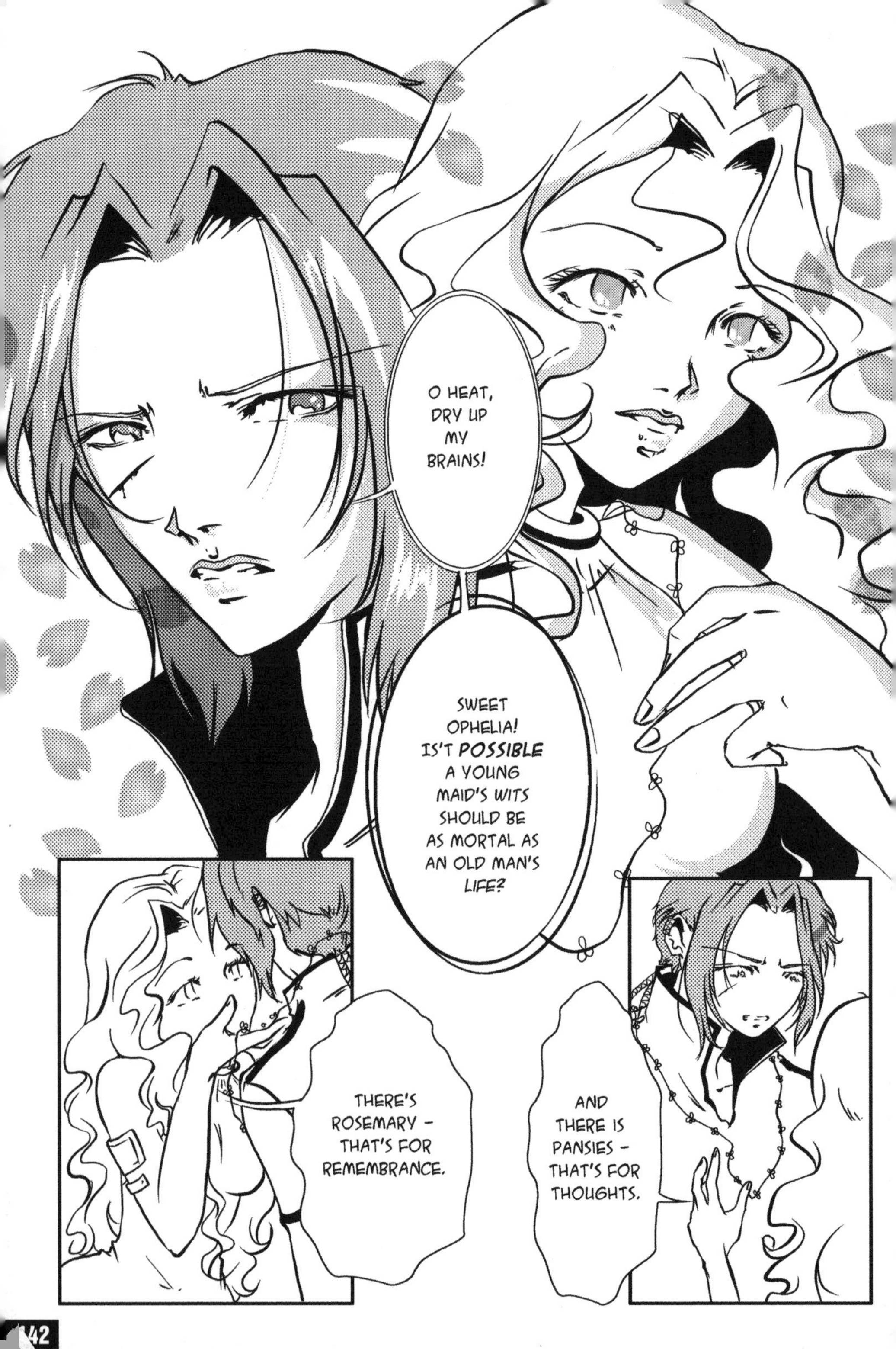
O HEAT, DRY UP MY BRAINS!
SWEET OPHELIA! IS'T **POSSIBLE** A YOUNG MAID'S WITS SHOULD BE AS MORTAL AS AN OLD MAN'S LIFE?
THERE'S ROSEMARY - THAT'S FOR REMEMBRANCE.
AND THERE IS PANSIES - THAT'S FOR THOUGHTS.

143

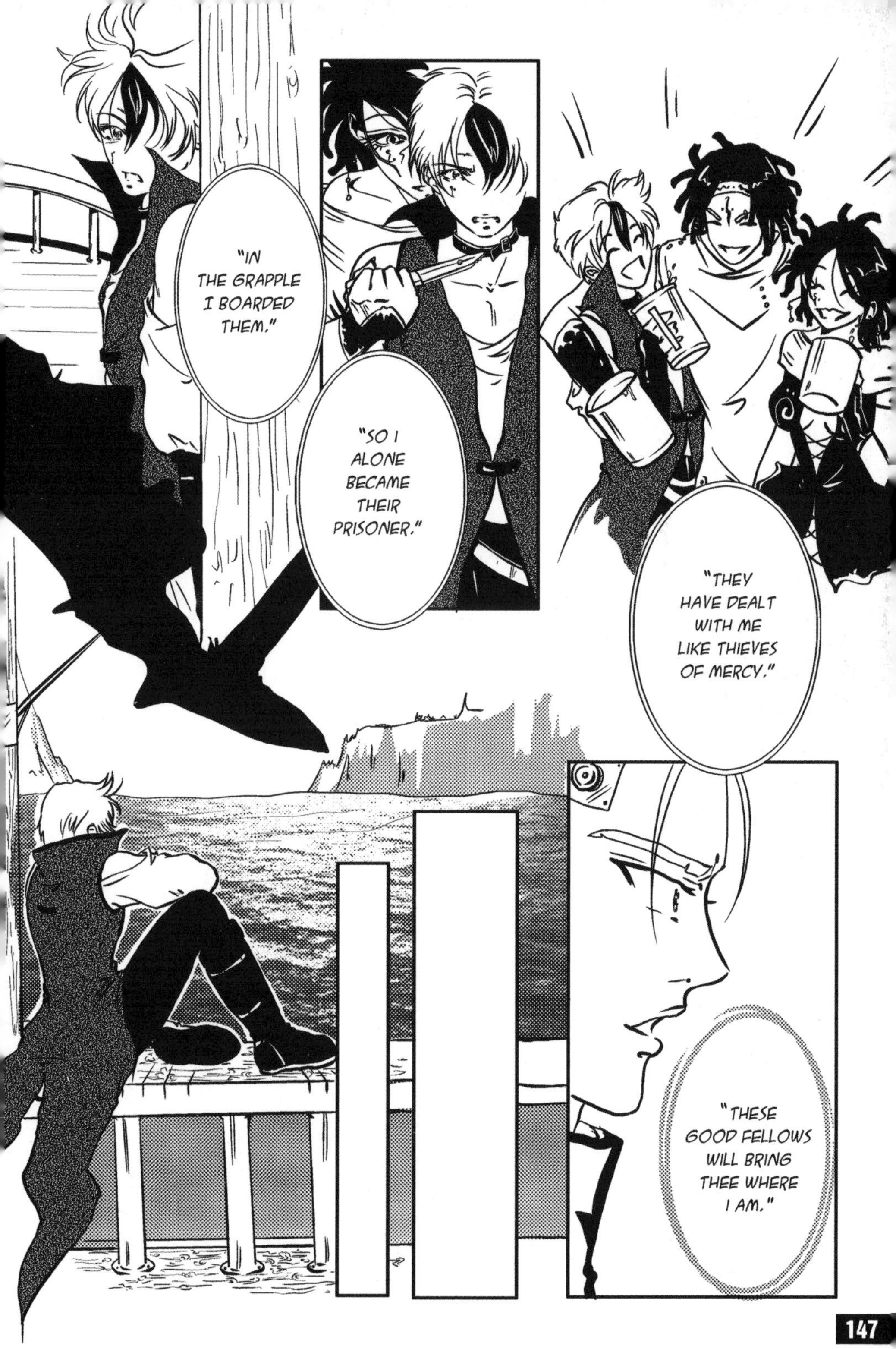
"IN THE GRAPPLE I BOARDED THEM."
"SO I ALONE BECAME THEIR PRISONER."
"THEY HAVE DEALT WITH ME LIKE THIEVES OF MERCY."
"THESE GOOD FELLOWS WILL BRING THEE WHERE I AM."

YOU MUST PUT ME IN YOUR HEART FOR FRIEND.

HE WHICH HATH YOUR NOBLE FATHER SLAIN PURSUED *MY* LIFE.

BUT TELL ME WHY YOU PROCEEDED NOT *AGAINST* THESE FEATS.

THE QUEEN HIS MOTHER LIVES ALMOST BY HIS LOOKS.

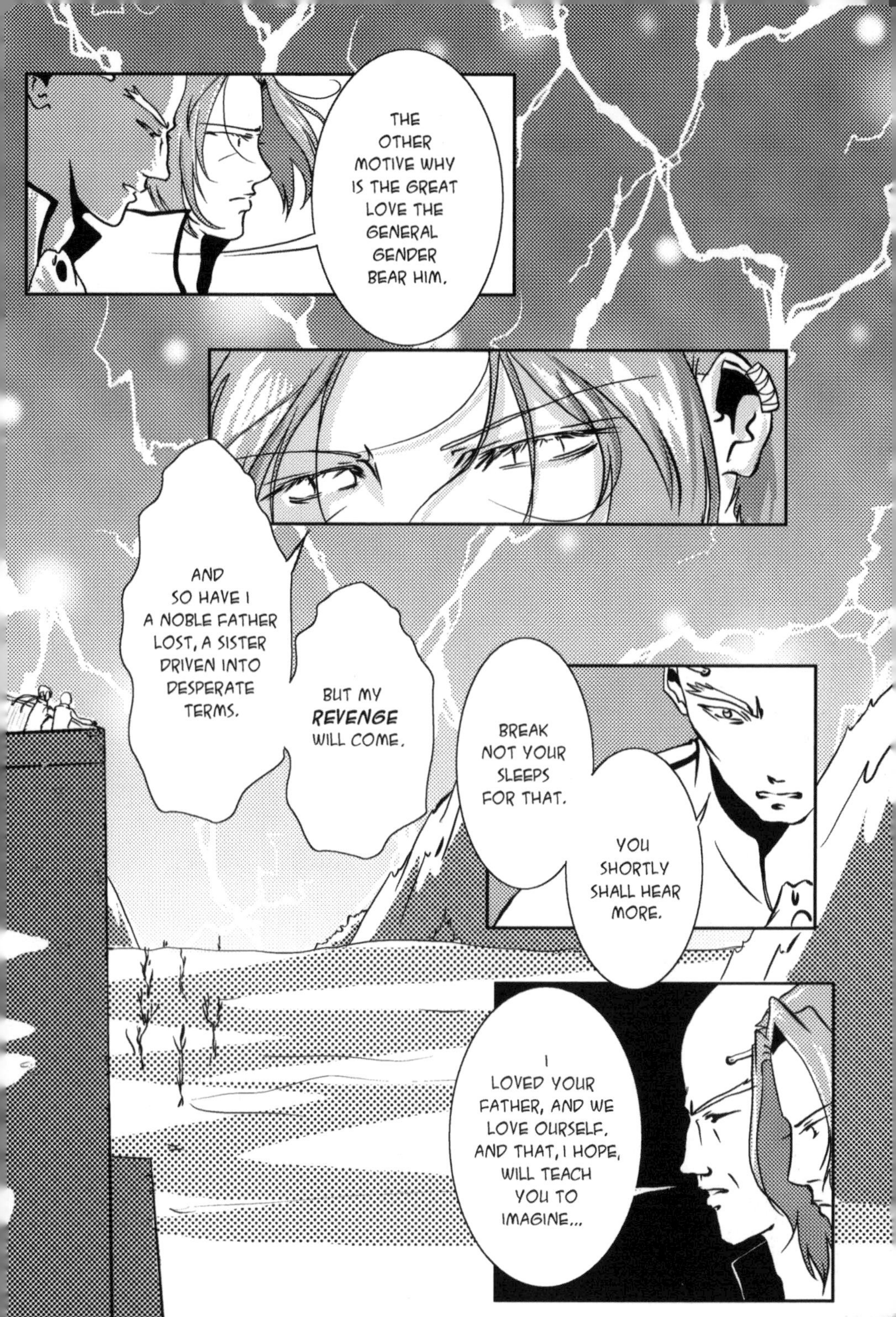
THE OTHER MOTIVE WHY IS THE GREAT LOVE THE GENERAL GENDER BEAR HIM.
AND SO HAVE I A NOBLE FATHER LOST, A SISTER DRIVEN INTO DESPERATE TERMS.
BUT MY **REVENGE** WILL COME.
BREAK NOT YOUR SLEEPS FOR THAT.
YOU SHORTLY SHALL HEAR MORE.
I LOVED YOUR FATHER, AND WE LOVE OURSELF. AND THAT, I HOPE, WILL TEACH YOU TO IMAGINE...

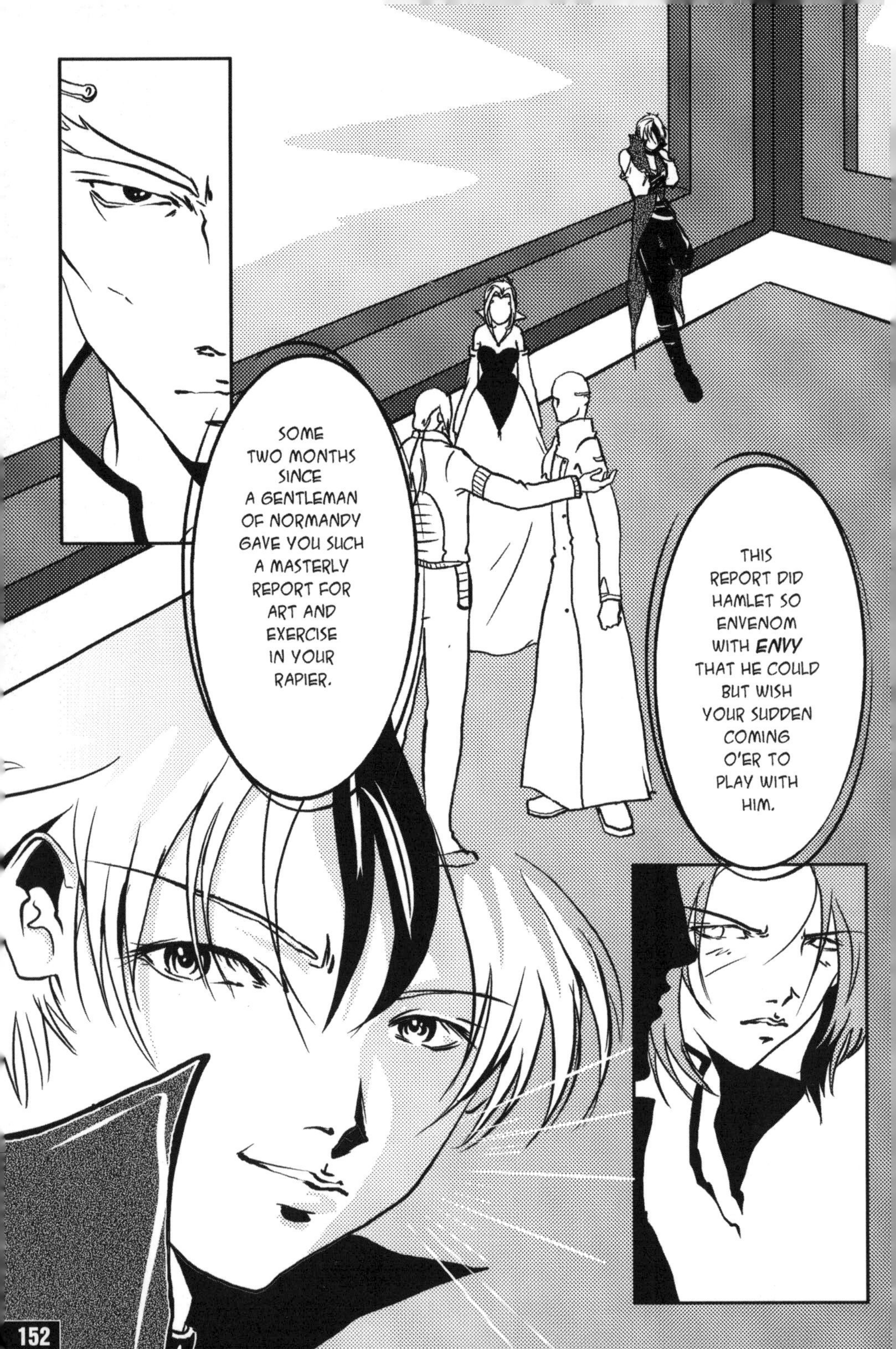
SOME TWO MONTHS SINCE A GENTLEMAN OF NORMANDY GAVE YOU SUCH A MASTERLY REPORT FOR ART AND EXERCISE IN YOUR RAPIER.
THIS REPORT DID HAMLET SO ENVENOM WITH ***ENVY*** THAT HE COULD BUT WISH YOUR SUDDEN COMING O'ER TO PLAY WITH HIM.

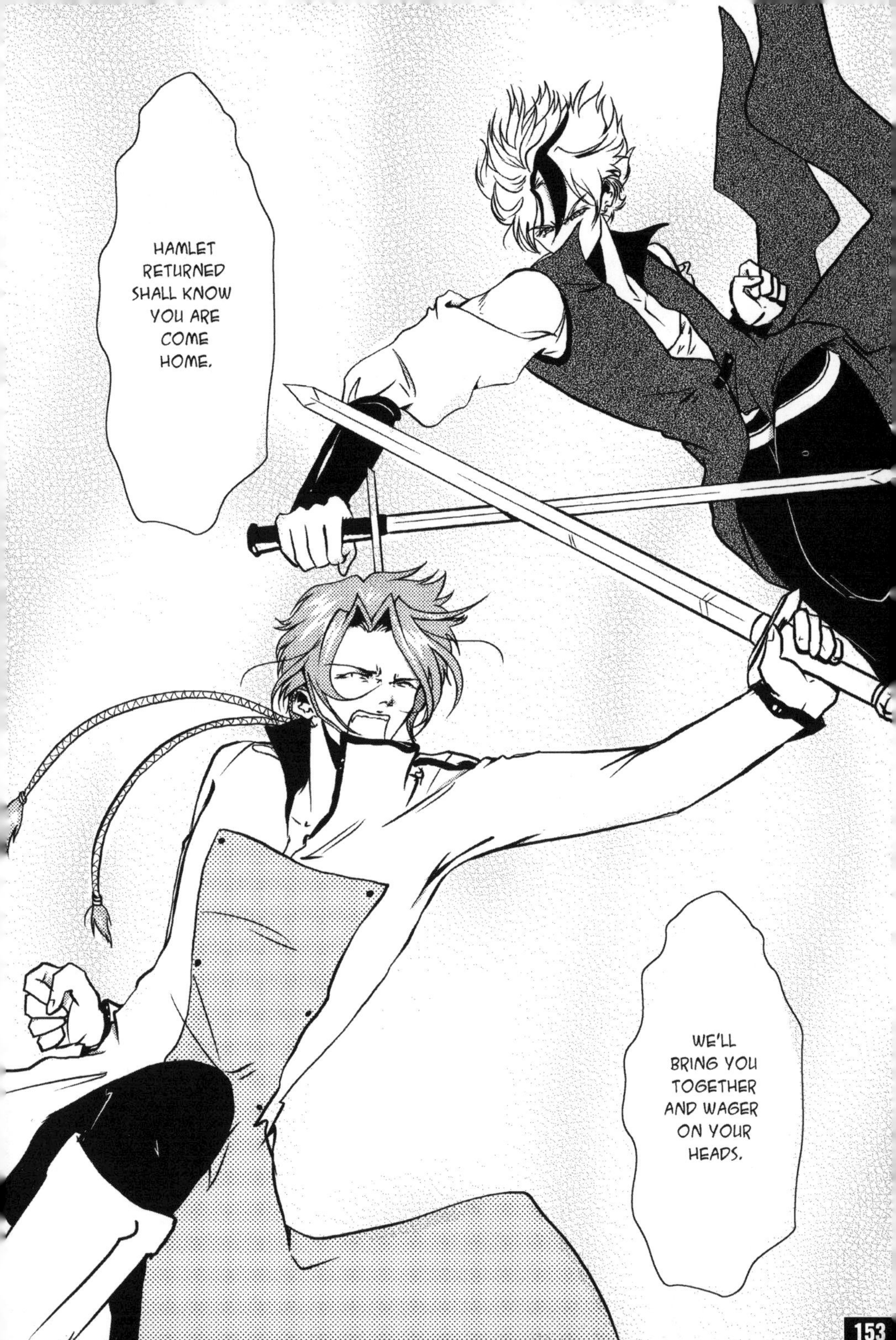
HAMLET RETURNED SHALL KNOW YOU ARE COME HOME.
WE'LL BRING YOU TOGETHER AND WAGER ON YOUR HEADS.

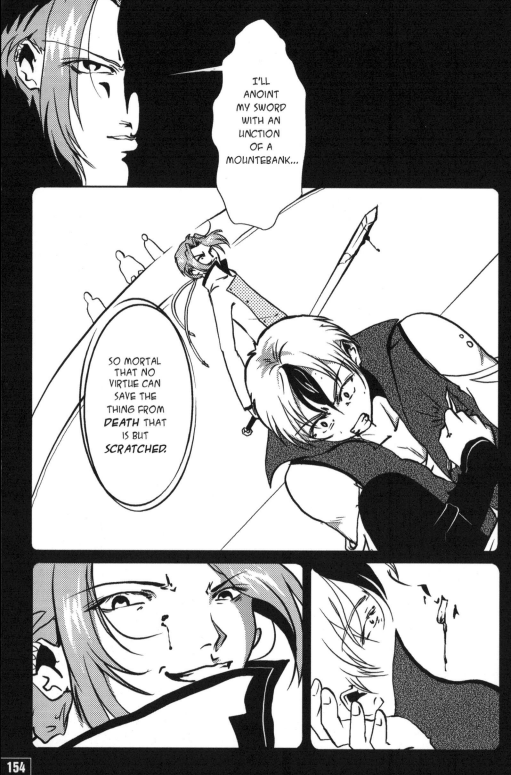

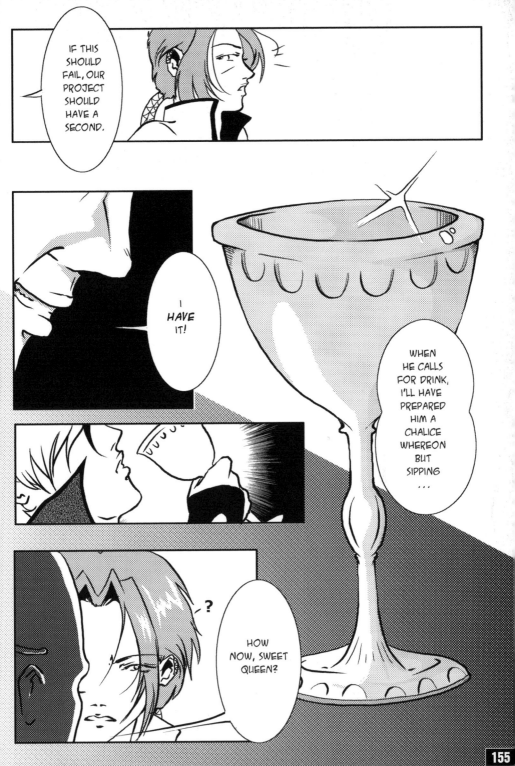

...

YOUR SISTER'S **DROWNED,** LAERTES.

A WILLOW GROWS ASLANT A BROOK...

DROWNED? WHERE?

WITH FANTASTIC GARLANDS DID SHE COME TO HANG, AND HERSELF FELL IN THE WEEPING BROOK.

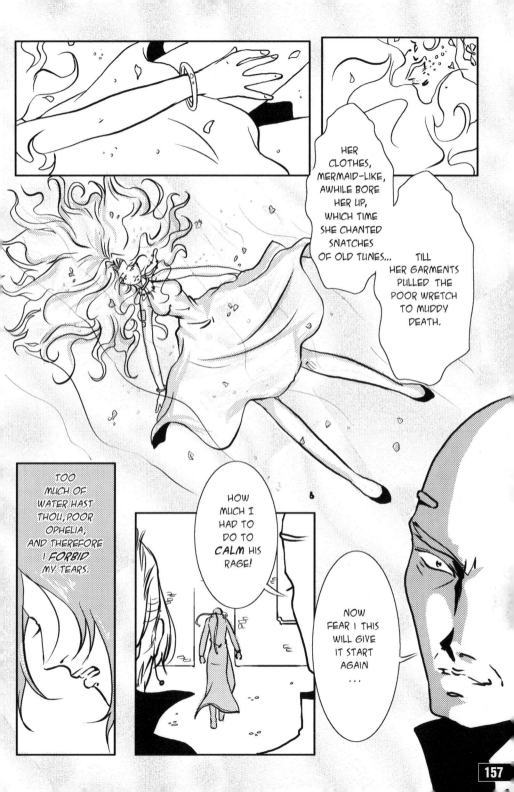

HER CLOTHES, MERMAID-LIKE, AWHILE BORE HER UP, WHICH TIME SHE CHANTED SNATCHES OF OLD TUNES...

TILL HER GARMENTS PULLED THE POOR WRETCH TO MUDDY DEATH.

TOO MUCH OF WATER HAST THOU, POOR OPHELIA, AND THEREFORE I *FORBID* MY TEARS.

HOW MUCH I HAD TO DO TO *CALM* HIS RAGE!

NOW FEAR I THIS WILL GIVE IT START AGAIN ...

HERE COMES THE KING, THE QUEEN ...

THE COURTIERS.

WHO IS THAT THEY FOLLOW?

HER DEATH WAS DOUBTFUL ...

SHE SHOULD IN GROUND UNSANCTIFIED HAVE LODGED TILL THE LAST TRUMPET.

FOR CHARITABLE PRAYERS, SHARDS, FLINTS AND PEBBLES SHOULD BE THROWN ON HER.

YET HERE SHE IS ALLOWED HER VIRGIN RITES.

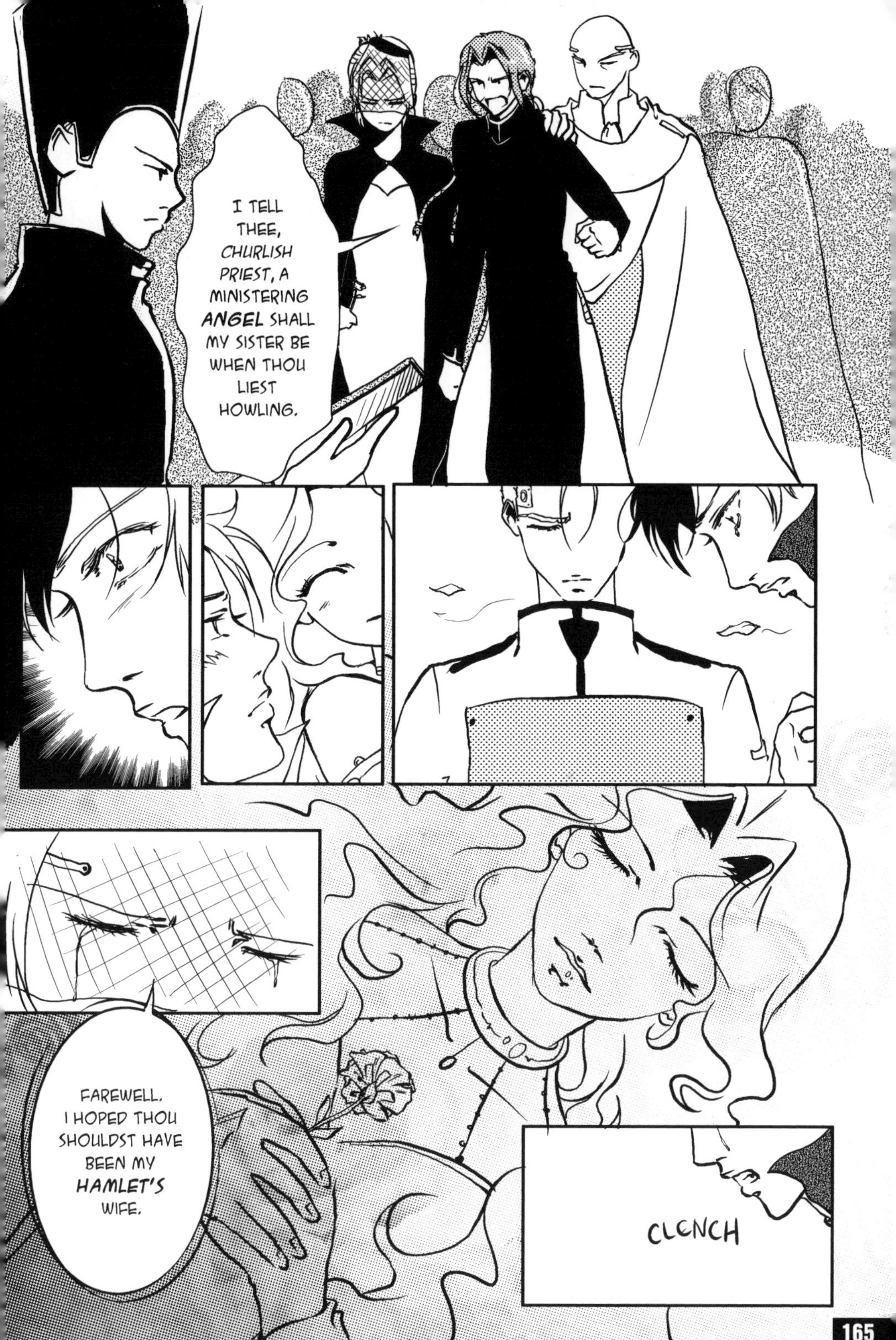
I TELL THEE, CHURLISH PRIEST, A MINISTERING ANGEL SHALL MY SISTER BE WHEN THOU LIEST HOWLING.
FAREWELL. I HOPED THOU SHOULDST HAVE BEEN MY HAMLET'S WIFE.
CLENCH

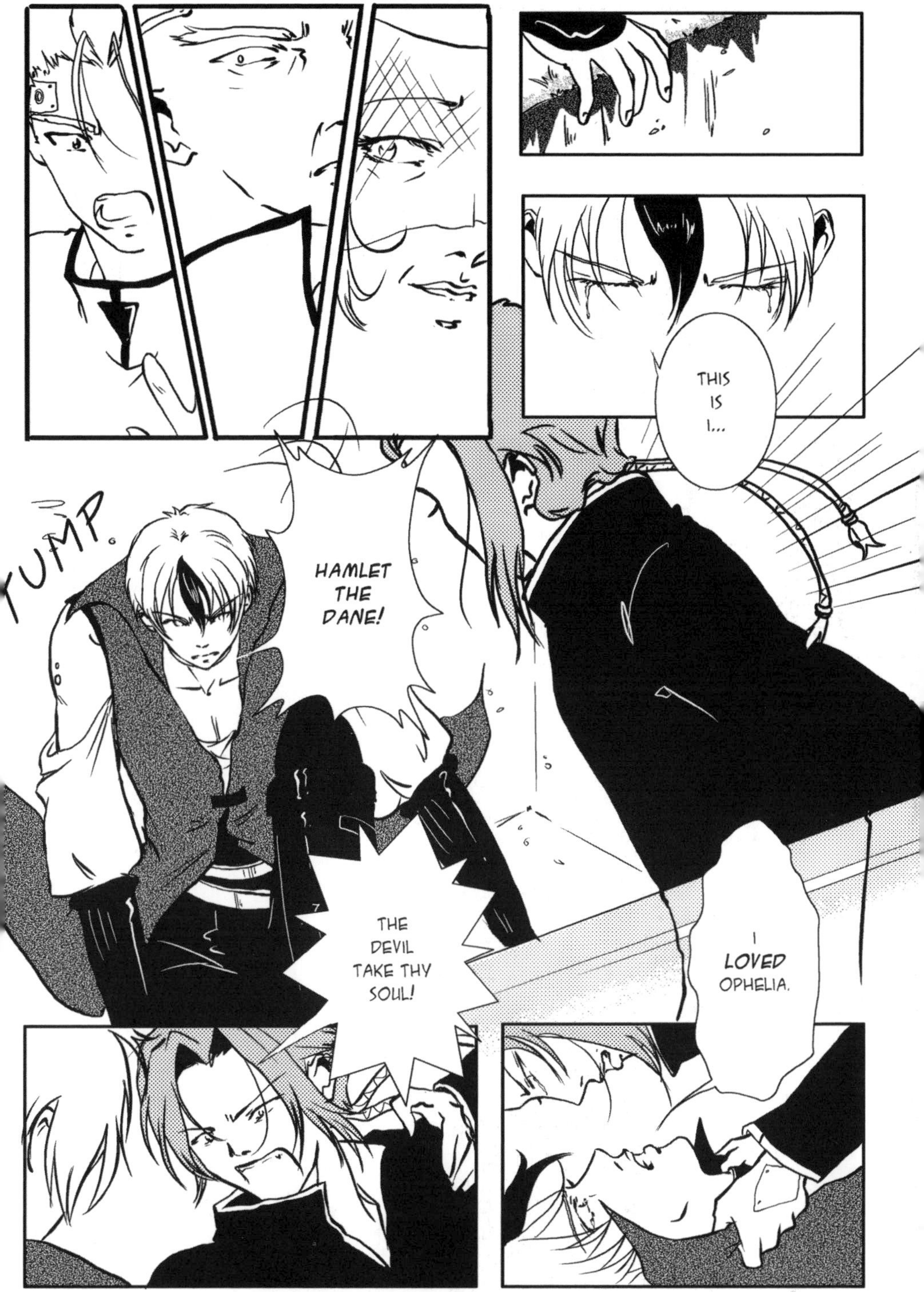
THIS IS I...
TUMP.
HAMLET THE DANE!
THE DEVIL TAKE THY SOUL!
I LOVED OPHELIA.

169

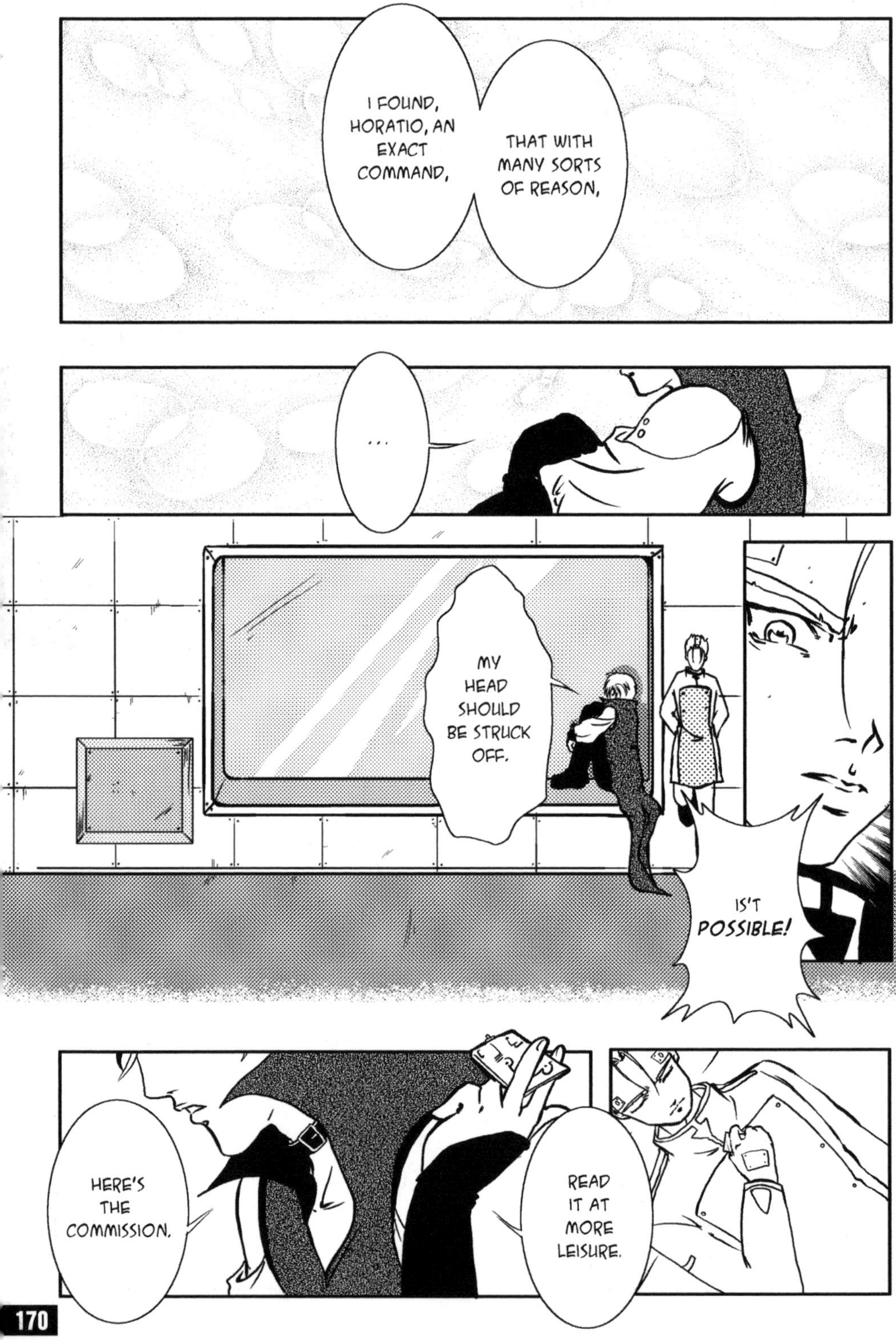

I FOUND, HORATIO, AN EXACT COMMAND,
THAT WITH MANY SORTS OF REASON,
...
MY HEAD SHOULD BE STRUCK OFF.
IS'T POSSIBLE!
HERE'S THE COMMISSION.
READ IT AT MORE LEISURE.

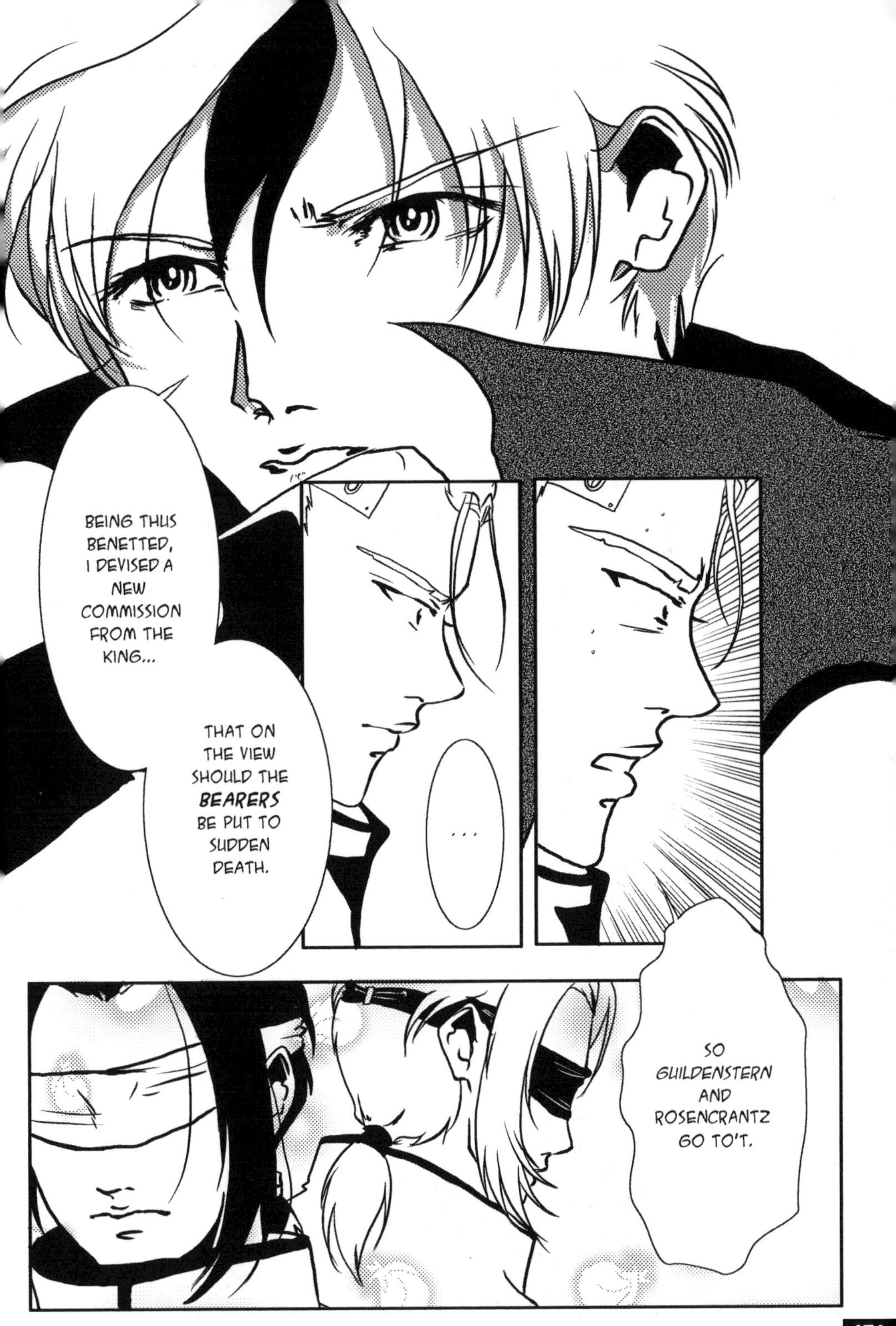
BEING THUS BENETTED, I DEVISED A NEW COMMISSION FROM THE KING...
THAT ON THE VIEW SHOULD THE BEARERS BE PUT TO SUDDEN DEATH.
...
SO GUILDENSTERN AND ROSENCRANTZ GO TO'T.

172

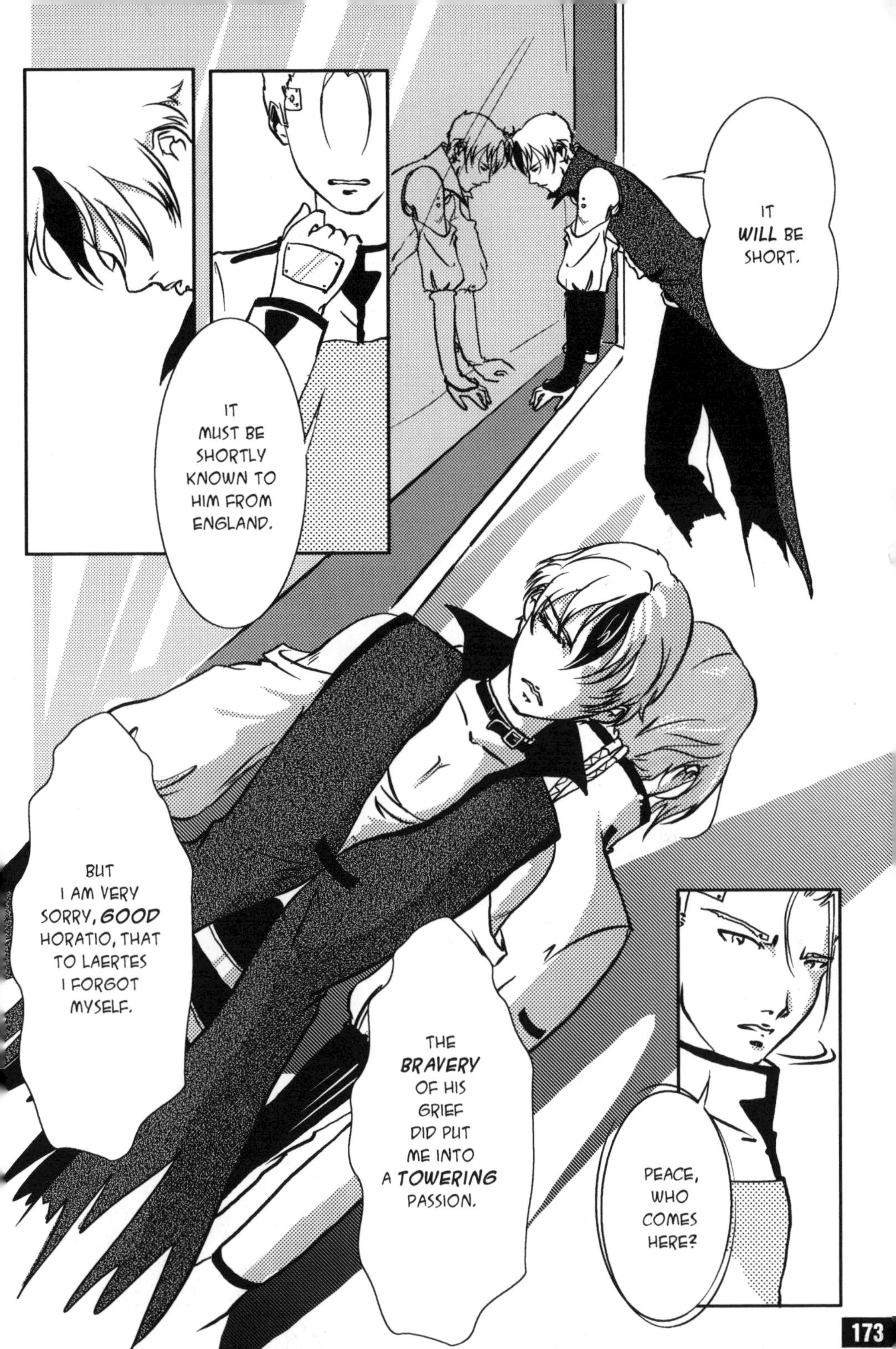
IT MUST BE SHORTLY KNOWN TO HIM FROM ENGLAND.
IT WILL BE SHORT.
BUT I AM VERY SORRY, GOOD HORATIO, THAT TO LAERTES I FORGOT MYSELF.
THE BRAVERY OF HIS GRIEF DID PUT ME INTO A TOWERING PASSION.
PEACE, WHO COMES HERE?

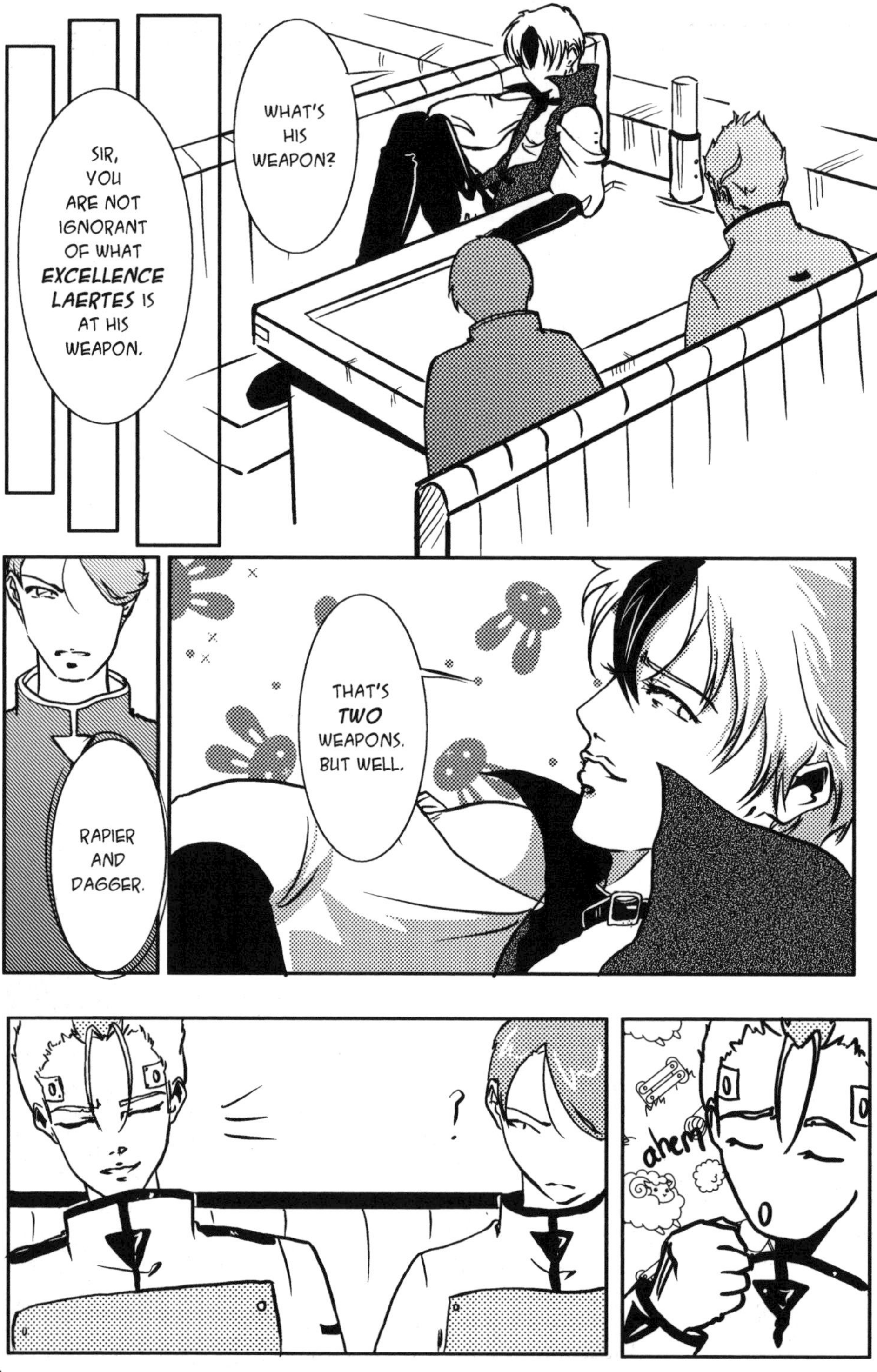
SIR, YOU ARE NOT IGNORANT OF WHAT **EXCELLENCE LAERTES** IS AT HIS WEAPON.
WHAT'S HIS WEAPON?
RAPIER AND DAGGER.
THAT'S ***TWO*** WEAPONS. BUT WELL.
?
ahem

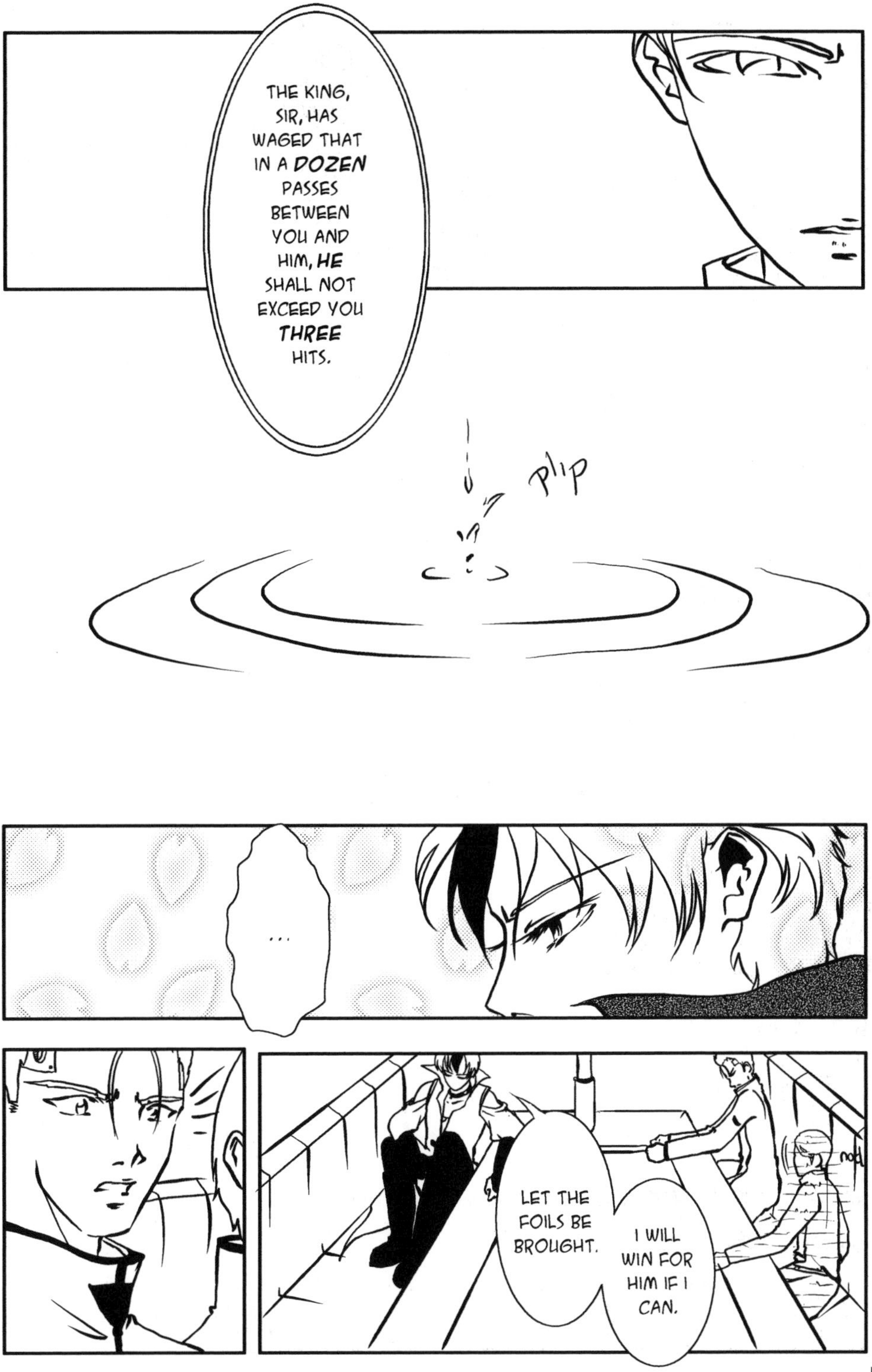
THE KING, SIR, HAS WAGED THAT IN A DOZEN PASSES BETWEEN YOU AND HIM, HE SHALL NOT EXCEED YOU THREE HITS.
plip
...
LET THE FOILS BE BROUGHT.
I WILL WIN FOR HIM IF I CAN.
nod

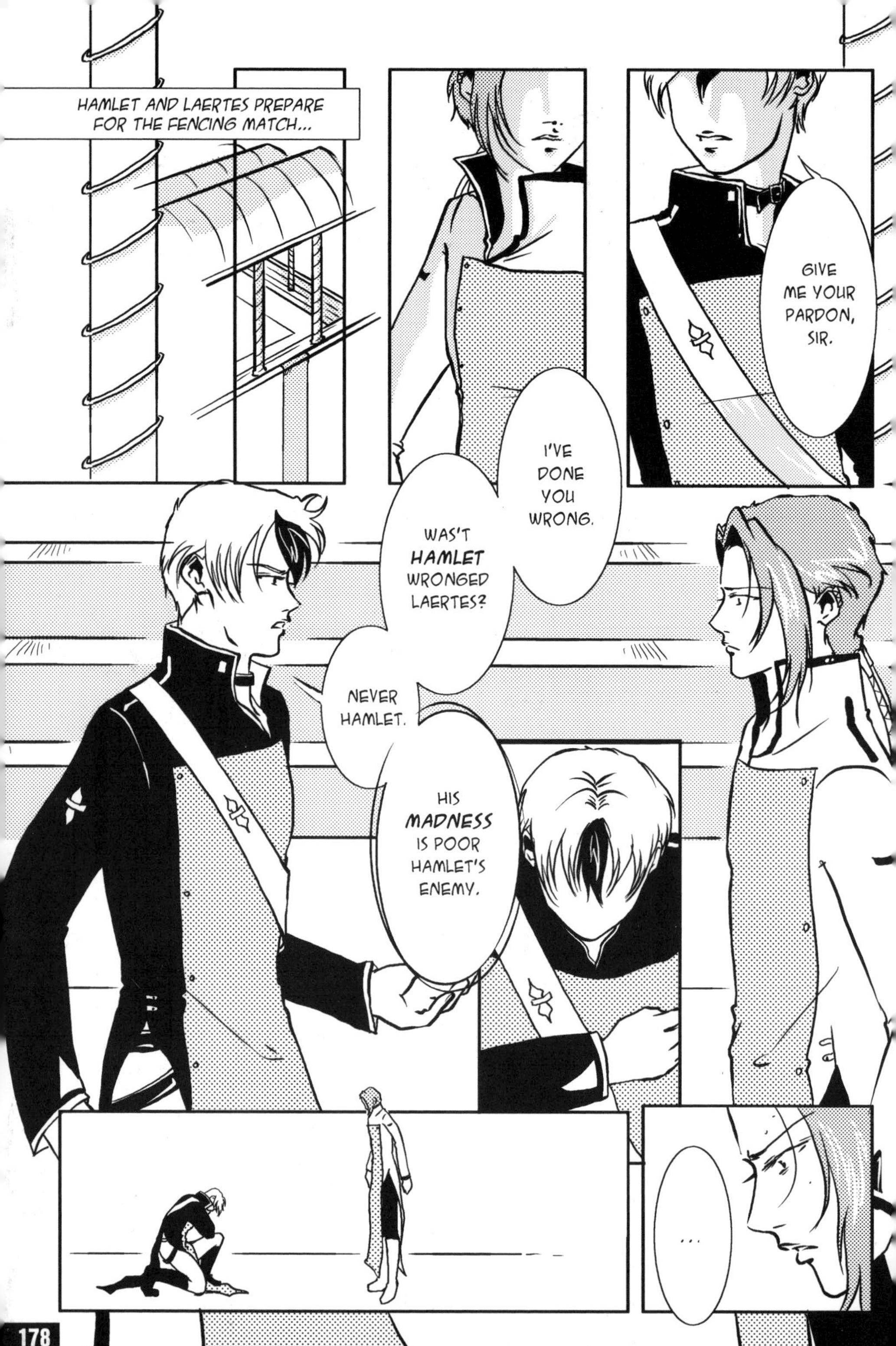
HAMLET AND LAERTES PREPARE FOR THE FENCING MATCH...
GIVE ME YOUR PARDON, SIR.
I'VE DONE YOU WRONG.
WAS'T **HAMLET** WRONGED LAERTES?
NEVER HAMLET.
HIS **MADNESS** IS POOR HAMLET'S ENEMY.
...

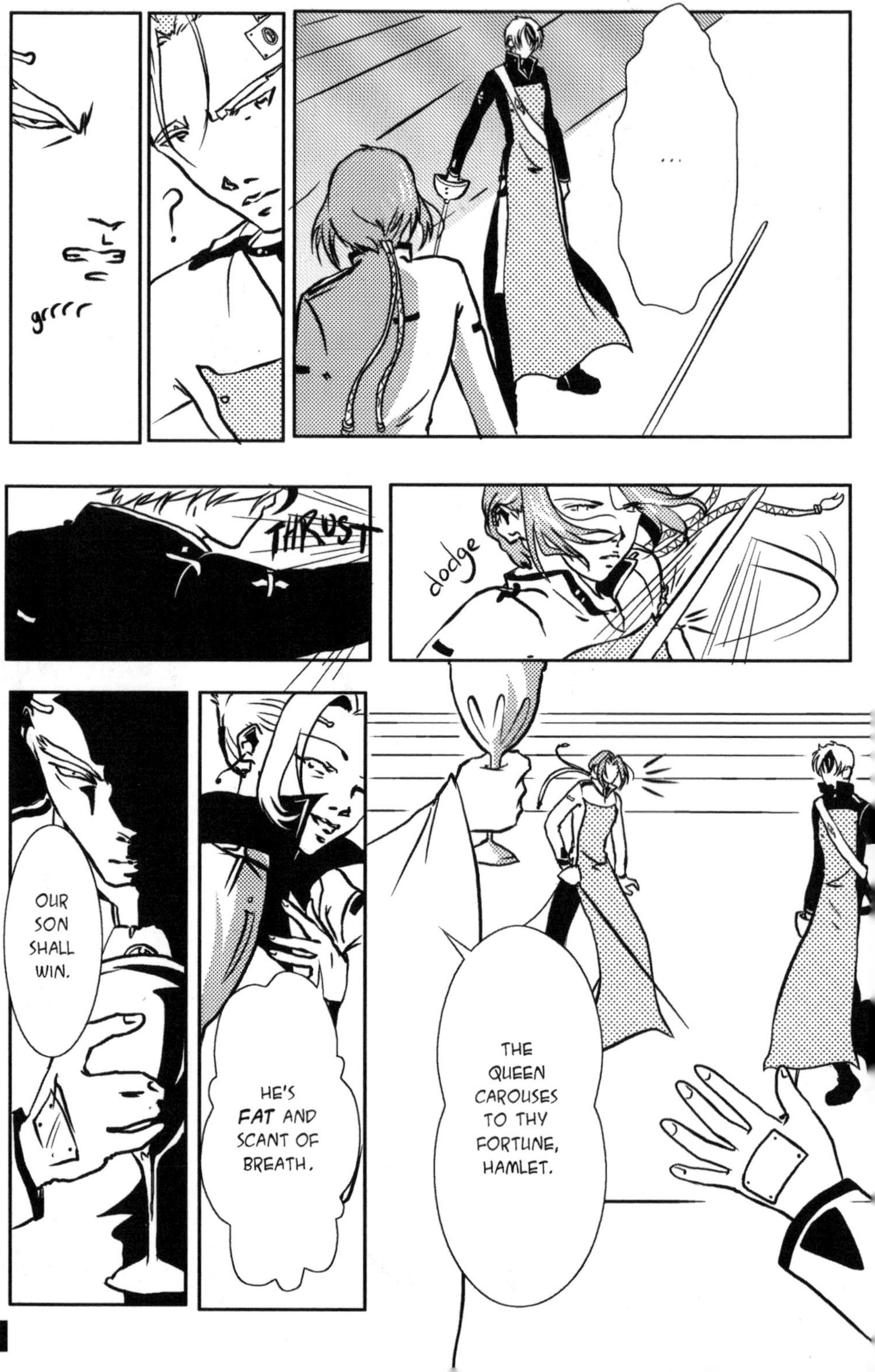
grrrr
?
...
THRUST
dodge
OUR SON SHALL WIN.
HE'S FAT AND SCANT OF BREATH.
THE QUEEN CAROUSES TO THY FORTUNE, HAMLET.

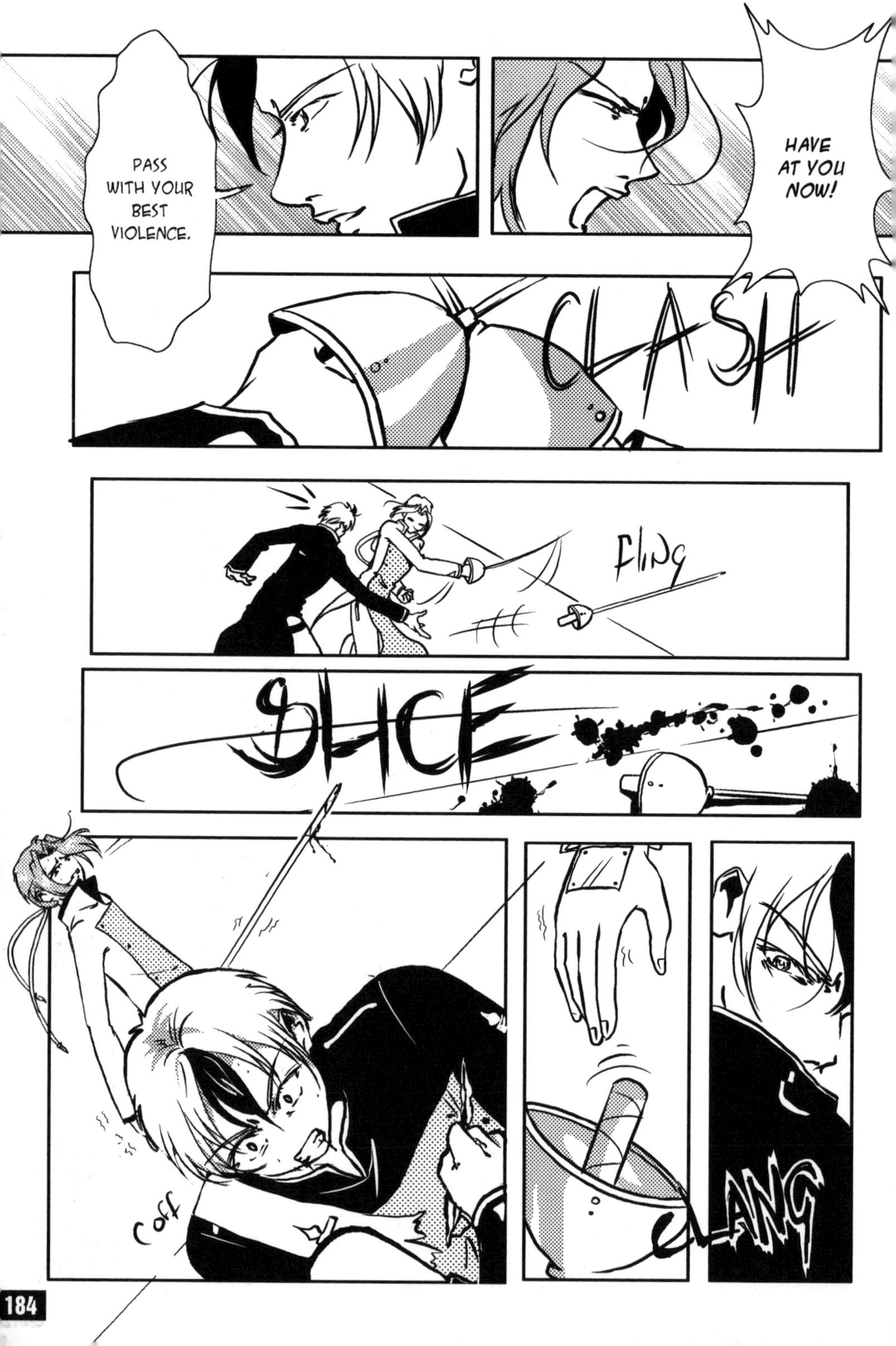
PASS WITH YOUR BEST VIOLENCE.
HAVE AT YOU NOW!
CLASH
FLING
SLICE
COFF
CLANG

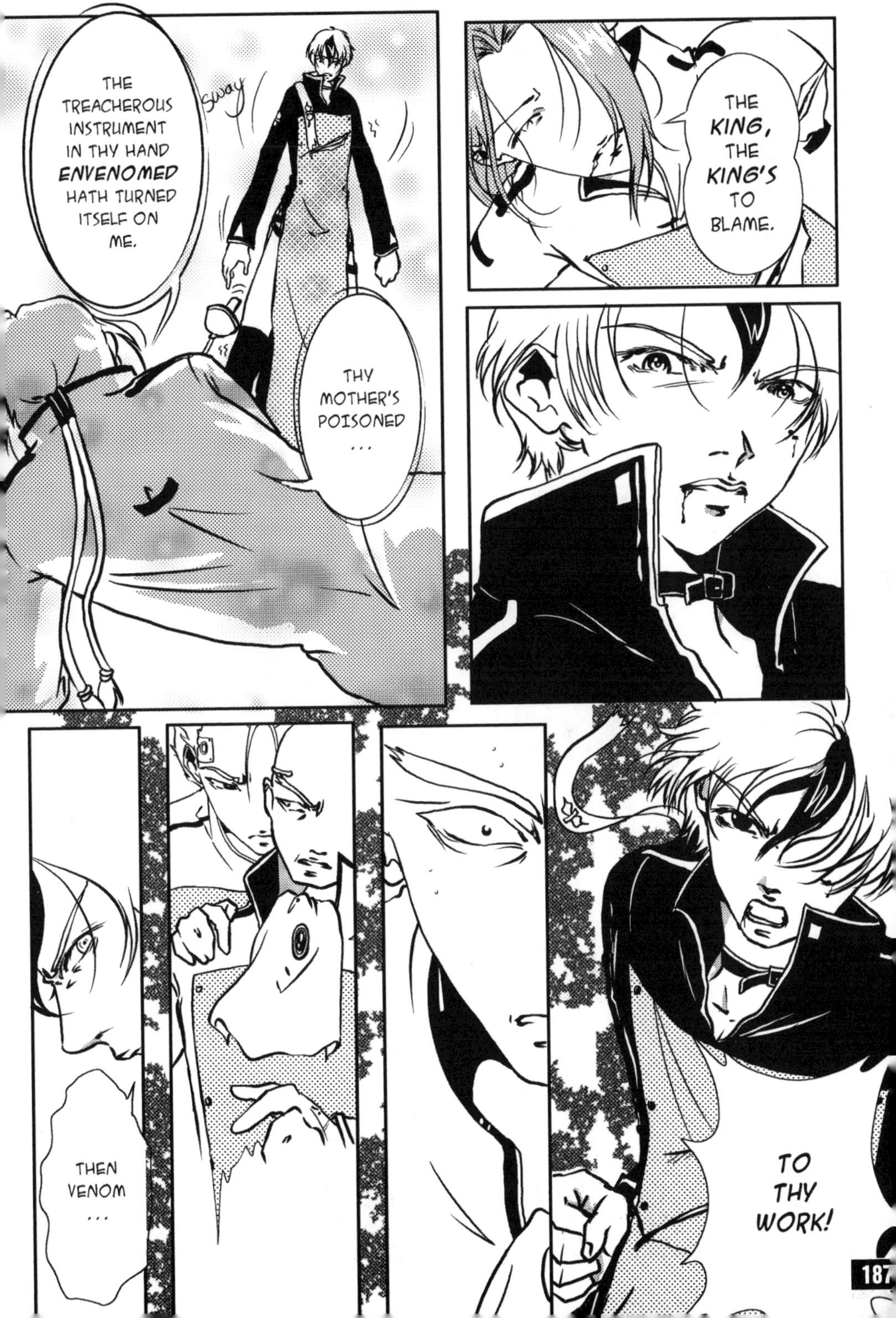
THE TREACHEROUS INSTRUMENT IN THY HAND ENVENOMED HATH TURNED ITSELF ON ME.
SWAY
THY MOTHER'S POISONED ...
THE KING, THE KING'S TO BLAME.
THEN VENOM ...
TO THY WORK!

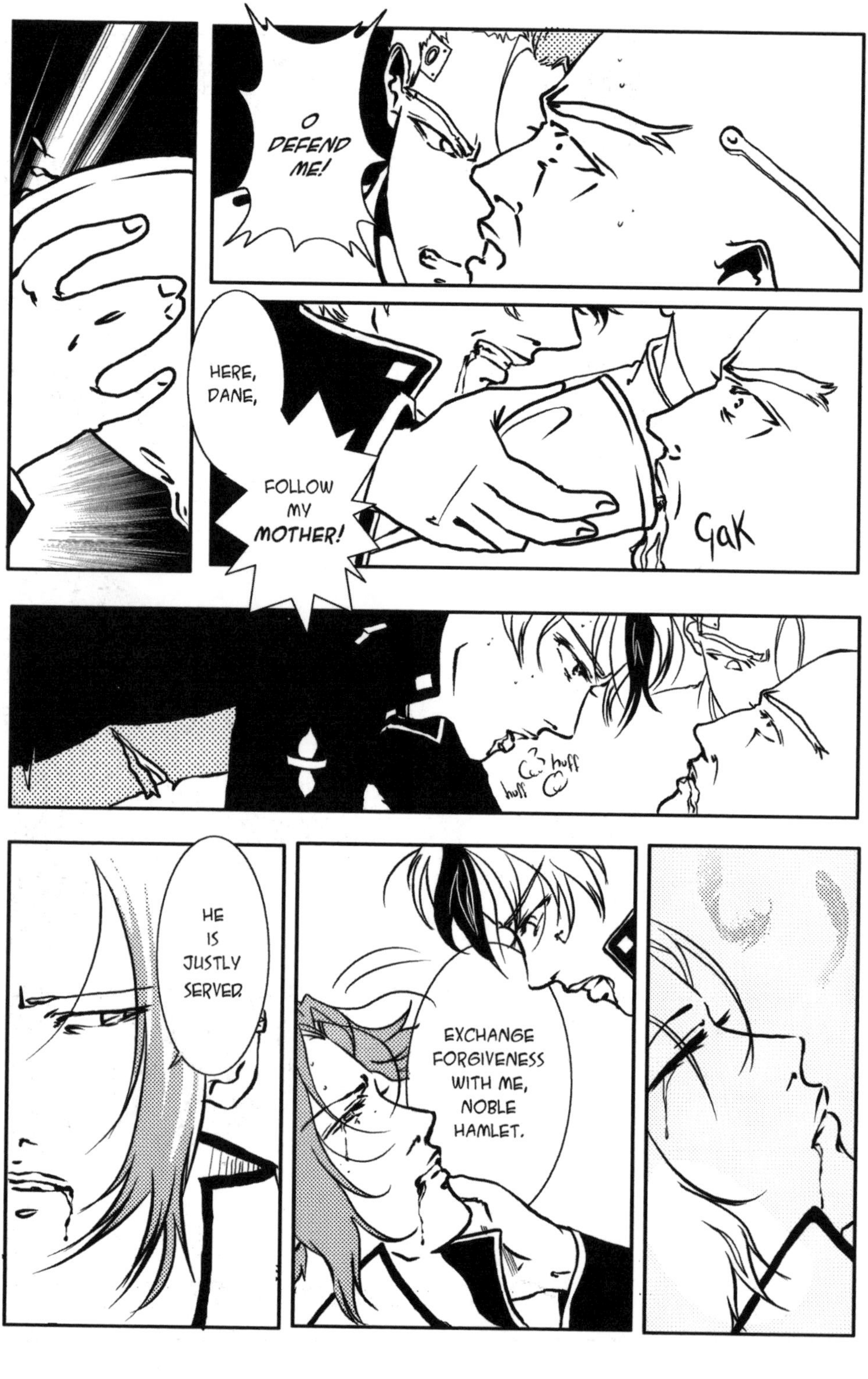
O DEFEND ME!
HERE, DANE,
FOLLOW MY MOTHER!
GaK
huff
huff
HE IS JUSTLY SERVED.
EXCHANGE FORGIVENESS WITH ME, NOBLE HAMLET.

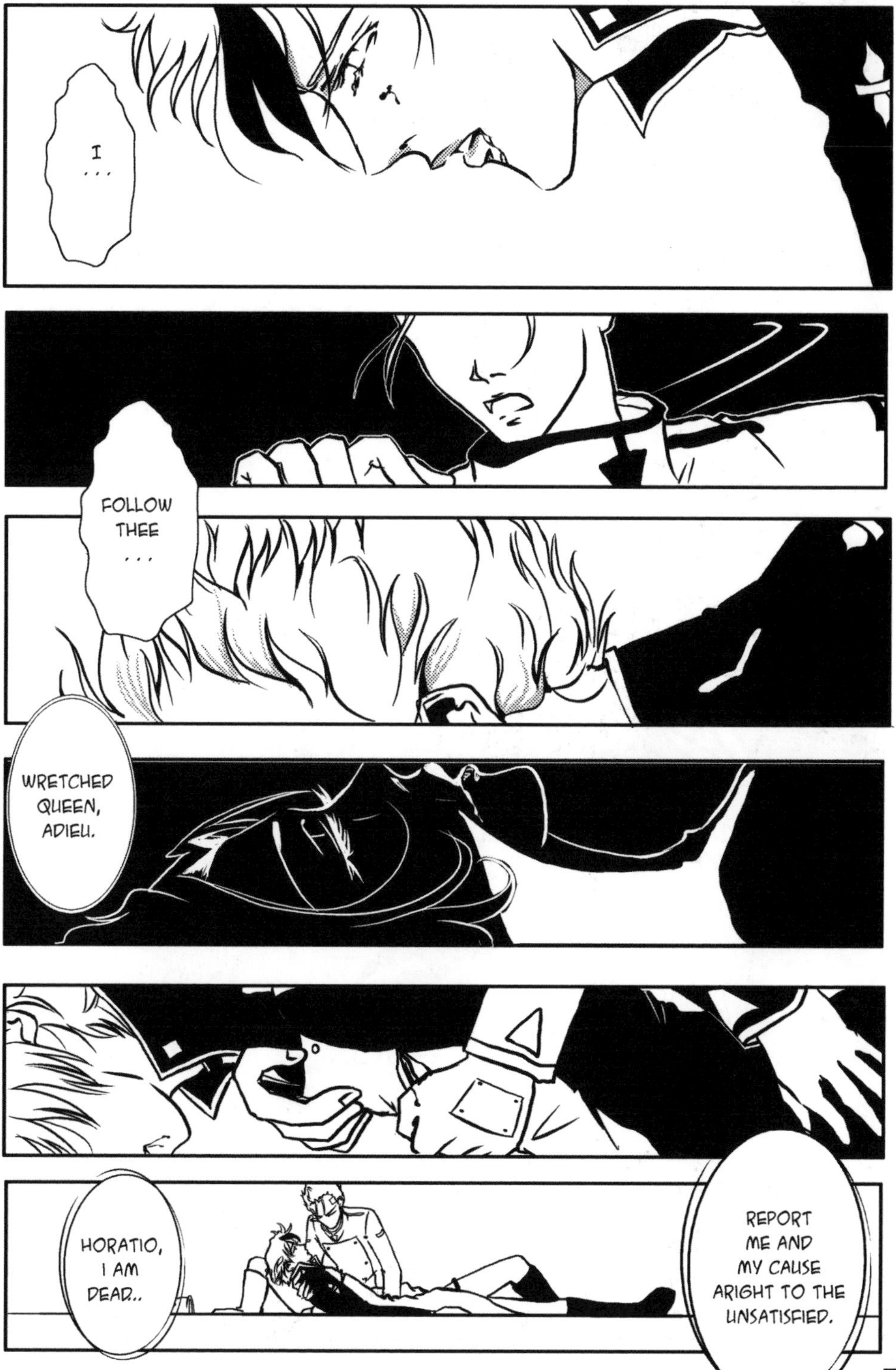
I . . .
FOLLOW THEE . . .
WRETCHED QUEEN, ADIEU.
HORATIO, I AM DEAD..
REPORT ME AND MY CAUSE ARIGHT TO THE UNSATISFIED.

TO
THE YET
UNKNOWING
WORLD HOW THESE
THINGS
CAME ABOUT
...

AND
LET **ME**
SPEAK
...

GIVE
ORDER THAT
THESE BODIES
BE PLACED
TO THE
VIEW,

BEAR
HAMLET
LIKE A
SOLDIER
...

AND
FOR HIS
PASSAGE,
THE SOLDIERS'
MUSIC AND
THE RITES OF
WAR SPEAK
LOUDLY
FOR HIM.

PLOT SUMMARY OF HAMLET

The ghost of Prince Hamlet's father appears to the guards of Elsinore Castle. Hamlet's trusted friend, Horatio, reports it to Hamlet.

Laertes, son of Polonius, is leaving for Paris. He warns his sister Ophelia against Hamlet's attentions. Polonius, the Court Chamberlain, also commands Ophelia to avoid contact with Hamlet.

Hamlet speaks to the ghost of his father. The dead king reveals that his brother Claudius murdered him to get the throne and marry Queen Gertrude, Hamlet's mother. Hamlet vows to avenge his father's murder. Hamlet pretends madness to disguise his plans from everyone loyal to King Claudius.

Claudius and Gertrude recruit two of Hamlet's friends, Rosencrantz and Guildenstern, to keep watch on his strange behaviour. Polonius believes that Hamlet is mad for love of Ophelia, and proposes that Claudius and he watch in hiding as Ophelia meets Hamlet.

A band of travelling actors arrive at Elsinore. Hamlet plans to use their staging of a play to expose the king's guilty conscience.

Claudius and Polonius spy on Ophelia's encounter with Hamlet. Claudius remains unconvinced that Hamlet has lost his reason over Ophelia. Hamlet presents his *Mousetrap* play, which includes a mimed performance of a king being poisoned. Claudius recognizes his murder of Hamlet's father and flees in dread.

Hamlet visits his mother's chamber. Polonius, spying behind a curtain, is stabbed to death by Hamlet. Gertrude now believes Hamlet is truly insane.

Claudius orders Hamlet's departure for England. Rosencrantz and Guildenstern bear the king's secret command for Hamlet's immediate execution upon arrival.

Meanwhile, Hamlet's murder of Ophelia's father has driven her into real madness, as Laertes discovers when he returns from France seeking revenge for his father's death. Hamlet sends Horatio a message that his voyage has been intercepted by pirates, and that he is returning to Elsinore with them. Claudius now devises a plot with Laertes to kill Hamlet in a fencing match. Gertrude enters with news of Ophelia's death by drowning. Hamlet confronts Laertes at Ophelia's burial. Hamlet protests his true love for Ophelia.

Hamlet explains to Horatio that he rewrote the king's order so that Rosencrantz and Guildenstern will suffer the execution meant for him in England.

Hamlet accepts the king's wager of a fencing match with Laertes. Laertes fences with a poisoned sword and Claudius has a poisoned drink ready for Hamlet. During the match swords are exchanged and both Laertes and Hamlet are fatally wounded. Gertrude drinks from the poisoned cup and dies. Laertes reveals the king's treachery and Hamlet kills Claudius before dying himself.

Prince Fortinbras of Norway enters and claims his right to the Danish throne.

A BRIEF LIFE OF WILLIAM SHAKESPEARE

Shakespeare's birthday is traditionally said to be the 23rd of April – St George's Day, patron saint of England. A good start for England's greatest writer. But that date and even his name are uncertain. He signed his own name in different ways. "Shakespeare" is now the accepted one out of dozens of different versions.

He was born at Stratford-upon-Avon in 1564, and baptized on 26th April. His mother, Mary Arden, was the daughter of a prosperous farmer. His father John Shakespeare, a glove-maker, was a respected civic figure – and probably also a Catholic. In 1570, just as Will began school, his father was accused of illegal dealings. The family fell into debt and disrepute.

Will attended a local school for eight years. He did not go to university. The next ten years are a blank filled by suppositions. Was he briefly a Latin teacher, a soldier, a sea-faring explorer? Was he prosecuted and whipped for poaching deer?

We do know that in 1582 he married Anne Hathaway, eight years his senior, and three months pregnant. Two more children – twins – were born three years later but, by around 1590, Will had left Stratford to pursue a theatre career in London. Shakespeare's apprenticeship began as an actor and "pen for hire".

He learned his craft the hard way. He soon won fame as a playwright with often-staged popular hits.

He and his colleagues formed a stage company, the Lord Chamberlain's Men, which built the famous Globe Theatre. It opened in 1599 but was destroyed by fire in 1613 during a performance of *Henry VIII* which used gunpowder special effects. It was rebuilt in brick the following year.

Shakespeare was a financially successful writer who invested his money wisely in property. In 1597, he bought an enormous house in Stratford, and in 1608 became a shareholder in London's Blackfriars Theatre. He also redeemed the family's honour by acquiring a personal coat of arms.

Shakespeare wrote over 40 works, including poems, "lost" plays and collaborations, in a career spanning nearly 25 years. He retired to Stratford in 1613, where he died on 23rd April 1616, aged 52, apparently of a fever after a "merry meeting" of drinks with friends. Shakespeare did in fact die on St George's Day! He was buried "full 17 foot deep" in Holy Trinity Church, Stratford, and left an epitaph cursing anyone who dared disturb his bones.

There have been preposterous theories disputing Shakespeare's authorship. Some claim that Sir Francis Bacon (1561–1626), philosopher and Lord Chancellor, was the real author of Shakespeare's plays. Others propose Edward de Vere, Earl of Oxford (1550–1604), or, even more weirdly, Queen Elizabeth I. The implication is that the "real" Shakespeare had to be a university graduate or an aristocrat. Nothing less would do for the world's greatest writer.

Shakespeare is mysteriously hidden behind his work. His life will not tell us what inspired his genius.